WHAT LOVE CAN BE

Shelby Falls Series

Katharine Hope Levy

Romance Without Borders Publishing

Content warnings include, but are not limited to:

Loss of a child
Parental loss
Pregnancy issues
Grief

*This book is dedicated to the open-hearted,
open-minded Fins of this world.*

Prologue

~ Mark ~

When I was seven, my parents were killed in a car accident. They were driving home one night, minding their own business, when along comes some idiot who drives up the exit ramp and kills them all. He just wasn't paying attention I guess. But in that split second, he destroyed four lives, including mine. Because from second grade on, I was orphaned and subjected to the nickname *Annie*—as in "little orphan Annie." Kids can be cruel in their never-ending quest to be funny. It wasn't funny though. Not even a little bit, even though I laughed every damn time some little twerp said it. Because I wasn't about to give them the satisfaction of thinking they got to me.

I wasn't placed in whatever the politically correct term for orphanage is these days. I was lucky enough to have an aunt and uncle who took me in and raised me as their own. As years went by, no one even knew they weren't my real parents and I even started calling them mom and dad. But on the inside I always knew I wasn't really theirs. I was their nephew, not their son. And I don't care what anyone says, there *is* a difference. Because as much as they love me and I love them, there's no substitute for the bond that is created with a parent. I'm sorry if that sounds ungrateful or harsh, but that's how I feel.

Sometimes when I lay in bed at night, I try to imagine what my ideal life would look like. Having material things? Sure, those things are nice, but that kind of happiness is fleeting. No, what I really want is very simple. I want to be part of a family that I can call my own, where I feel like I belong. *My* family. I want to fall in love with someone whom I love unconditionally and who loves me the same way, and I want us to have kids who I can spoil, and I want them to feel loved and accepted for who they are.

While I've been successful in most facets of my life, when it comes to my goal of having a family, I've failed miserably. I could say that I haven't met the right person yet, but that would just be an excuse. I think my biggest problem is that I tend to skip the friendship stage and immediately focus on the physical aspects of a relationship. As if clinching the physical will somehow lead to the emotional gratification I'm seeking. But there are no shortcuts where love is concerned. That's the easy way in. The much harder course is to actually get to know someone. But in order to do that, you have to be willing to open yourself up. And with that comes the possibility of loss, which is something I don't do well with. Sex is easy and there are no hurt feelings as long as you're both just looking for a good time. But the path to love, well, that's hard. The potential pain that comes with trusting another person and risking your heart paralyzes me at times.

What I do know is that I'm in a semi-catch 22. Because I know I'll never truly be happy if I don't take this risk, but there's no guarantee I'll be happy if I do. One path's outcome is certain, while the other's is unknown. If there *is* someone out there with whom I actually feel brave enough to trust my heart, I just hope I don't blow it. Because finding someone you really connect with is rare and, if I ever do find her, I need to find the courage within me to grab hold of her and give it my all.

* * *

I trust that you will read this story with open hearts and minds, understanding that no one is perfect and we all fail each other at times, but there is always room for compassion, forgiveness and, most of all, love.

I know this to be true, and that's all because of Fin.

Chapter One

~ *Mark* ~

Present Day
Sunday, May 28th

"The twists and turns of our lives don't always seem to make sense, until they do." ~Mark Jansen

They say that things can only get better. But in my case, things don't always get better. Sometimes they get worse—much, much worse. And today only serves to reinforce this belief because today I find myself standing in the middle of a parking lot wondering how the hell I could have made such a horrible mistake and been this much of an asshole to another person. But I was.

I'm not an asshole, at least I don't think I am. But my life has taken some unfortunate turns that have no doubt shaped who I am and how I relate to others. However, while this may help to explain who I am, it should never be used as an excuse for my actions. When I'm wrong, I'm the first to admit it, and today it looks like I am definitely in the wrong. But I won't know that for sure until I find out the truth, and for that, I need to find Sharon.

As my friend Matt Conroy speeds out of the parking lot of the Shelby Falls Diner in disgust, I look down at my hands which are noticeably trembling. I don't think I've ever trembled before. Trembling is a sign of fear and I'm really not afraid of much. Not since fate took my parents from me. Back then, I just cried a lot. Every morning I would wake up and realize what had happened to them, and then I would cry some more. Until one day, I just stopped crying. And I haven't cried since.

But fear is definitely what I'm feeling right now. Fear that there might be an innocent child out there who I didn't even know was mine until today. Maybe I'm not the person I thought I was. Because that person would never abandon a woman carrying his baby. Never. Not after everything I went through as a kid.

I take off in my Ford Ranger and head straight to the Tex-Mex restaurant where I'm hoping Sharon still works. That's the first and last place I ever saw her. Their website says they don't open until noon on Sundays and it's only eleven thirty. But lucky for me, there's a guy unlocking the side door of the restaurant just as I pull into the lot.

"Excuse me!" I call out while swiftly exiting my truck. "I'm trying to get in touch with someone who I think works here. Her name is Sharon."

I actually don't even know her last name. *Pitiful.*

The guy looks me over. He seems a little reluctant at first but then nods. "Yeah, she's my boss. What's this about?"

I try to hide my nerves and give him my most disarming smile. "I just need to speak with her. It's kind of important. Do you think maybe you could let me in?"

"We don't open for half an hour, but if you want, I'll let her know you're here. What's your name?"

"Mark Jansen." I pause, suddenly realizing my name may not be familiar to her. "Just tell her I'm a friend of Matt Conroy's."

The guy nods. "Sure, I know Matt. He's a good guy."

Yes, Matt is a very good guy. The best. He's my oldest friend and I've always considered him one of my best friends—that is up until this morning when he basically told me to fuck off. That's when I knew I'd really crossed the line. Because I've known Matt since middle school and even when I've been an absolute prick, he's always stuck by me. That's just how he was made—loyal to the core, kind, and very level-headed. But this time is different because last night at Matt's cousin's wedding, after doing one too many Tequila shots, I made some very offensive comments to Matt's wife, Jennifer, and then went on to share some less-than-flattering things about Matt. Jennifer is nine months' pregnant and Matt would lay his life down for her, so let's just say he was pissed. Matt doesn't get angry very often so when he does, it's kind of unsettling.

I need to find a way to make things right with them both, and I will. But you know what the most ironic thing about all of this is? It looks like what I told Jennifer about Matt did turn out to be true—just not about him. There I was telling Jennifer that Matt had gotten this hot redhead, Sharon, pregnant about two years ago when it turns out *I'm* probably the one who got her pregnant. And now *I'm* the one who might have a child out there who has never known his or her father.

As I wait for the guy to return, so many emotions are swirling around in my head and my heart is pounding out of my chest.

Why is it taking him so long to return and what if Sharon refuses to speak to me?

My worries are soon interrupted by the reappearing guy.

"Okay, so she says she doesn't know who you are and that she's getting ready for the lunch crowd. Sorry man, I tried." He turns to leave.

But I quickly grab the door before it slams shut.

"Wait—please," I plead. "I don't mean to bring you into this but I really need to speak to her. How about you just go on ahead? I won't tell her it was you who let me in—I swear."

The guy exhales impatiently but seems to sympathize with my plight and just turns and heads inside without saying a word, leaving me still holding the open door.

After waiting a minute or so, I go inside. The sound of clanking pots emanates from the kitchen but there is no one in sight, so I wait by the hostess station for someone to appear. That's when I happen to notice a note taped to the inside of the podium that says "Sharon's cell." I quickly save the number to my contacts. Still no sign of anyone, however, and the frantic pounding in my chest is getting louder.

And then I see her.

Wow.

It's been two years but she looks exactly the same: striking, beautiful. Her copper red hair and green eyes were very memorable. The eyes especially. She's jotting something down on a notepad as she walks in my direction, counting to herself, and when I clear my throat to get her attention, her eyes quickly dart upwards.

"Can I help you?" she asks before I see recognition in her eyes, immediately followed by anger.

My mouth is suddenly bone dry. "Hi Sharon, I...I

don't know if you remember me but—"

"I know who you are," she snaps. "What can I do for you?"

"Nothing. I mean, not nothing. I just want to talk to you if you have a minute? If now isn't a good time, maybe I could meet you after your shift?"

A fire seems to ignite in her piercing eyes. "I'm the manager so I don't work a *shift* anymore. And no, I'm not interested in speaking with you—ever. You can leave now. You're very good at that as I recall."

Her eyes are as fiery as her hair and it feels like a hot flame has just blown me backwards.

"I deserve that, I know I do," I say. "But please—I found out something today and I think we should talk."

Her defiance now turns to confusion. I watch her as she studies my face. She must be able to sense my determination because she eventually lets out a frustrated sigh and slams her notepad down on the podium. "You've got five minutes."

I obediently follow her as she turns heel to walk towards the back of the restaurant. As on edge as I am, that's somehow not stopping me from noticing just how sexy she is or what a perfect ass she has in her black pencil skirt, accompanied by killer heels. Despite her petite stature, she exudes a fearlessness as she ushers me down the hall, her heels echoing with each step. Once we reach an office, she brusquely turns to allow me to enter first and, as I gingerly walk past her, the pen in her hand catches my eye. For a split second, the crazy thought of her wielding it at me flashes through my mind. She looks that angry. But I also notice something else. She's not wearing a wedding ring.

We both take a seat, her behind the desk and me on

the other side. She sits upright, arms crossed, and just stares at me—or should I say glares—as she waits for me to speak.

I need to find a way to do this without upsetting her more, but there's just no good way to embark on this topic. So I just need to take the plunge. "I saw Matt Conroy today and he told me some things I hadn't realized until today."

Her eyebrows narrow slightly and she now looks a little unsettled, which makes me even more nervous.

"I...I don't know quite how to say this," I finally say, "but first I just want you to know that I completely misread the situation with us and I'm very sorry."

Her jaw clenches and, despite my nerves, I still can't help but notice again just how pretty she is. She's so damn pretty. This is making it even harder. I stall some more, desperately trying to find the right words.

She finally loses her patience. "You're going to have to be more specific, Mark. I'm not a mind reader." She accentuates the "k" in my name, as if trying to injure me with her diction.

I finally just blurt it out. "I know about the baby." I scan her face for her reaction.

She turns beet red and I can't tell if she's about to unload on me or cry. But she remains ominously silent so I continue.

"And I'm wondering if I'm—or—I'm not sure—Matt just said you were pregnant, that's all."

She looks stunned and swallows hard. I feel my whole body tense up in anticipation of hearing the truth.

"Yes, I was pregnant...two years ago." Her voice sounds different now—a little defeated—but still cold as ice. "But I already told you that—two years ago—so why are you here?"

"Because I didn't know until today that I could be the father."

She lets out a spontaneous laugh. "You didn't know, or you didn't **want** to know?! I **told** you, you just didn't believe me!" Tears now begin gathering in her eyes, causing the green in them to resemble stained glass. But her tears are soon chased away by her fury. "Oh, that's right, because you think I'm a liar and a scammer—oh, and apparently a slut too! So why don't you tell me why you're really here, Mark."

There's that "*k*" dagger again.

I inhale a deep breath. "I'm here because...I don't know how to ask this, but did you...have the baby?" My heart is racing wildly because the answer to this question will change my entire life.

But she doesn't answer. Instead, she abruptly stands up. "Get out—NOW." She points to the door.

"Wait, I'm sorry, the last thing I wanted to do was upset you. But Matt didn't tell me anything more than that you were pregnant and he helped you out. He didn't say anything beyond that."

I now see a pain in her eyes that wasn't there before. But her eyes quickly harden again, robotic in her response. "I lost the baby—our baby."

When I hear the words, a chill comes over me like I've never felt before.

"Sharon...I—"

"So now that you have what you came for, I would appreciate it if you would leave."

I don't think I will ever be able to forget the look she's giving me. She looks furious, yet just beneath the surface there is an intense pain and vulnerability in her eyes.

This is all my fault.

It feels like all of the air is being sucked out of me and I suddenly feel like I can't breathe. I don't know what I was expecting her to say, but it wasn't this. I must look like a wreck because she's now staring at me with what looks like actual concern and she offers me the final piece of information I came for.

"I'd planned to have the baby on my own but"—she looks down—"I lost the baby during my first trimester." Her voice trails off as if distracted by an intense memory.

I feel ill.

"My G-d, Sharon, I'm so sorry. I should have been there for you. I don't know what to say except that I'm so sorry."

She looks at me with a combination of sorrow and bewilderment. I'm confusing her, I know I am.

My grief quickly turns to anger. Anger for not believing her when she first told me she was pregnant with our child, and anger for not being there to support her through the hell she undoubtedly went through. Maybe if I'd been there, she wouldn't have miscarried. No, I know that wouldn't have made a difference. Maybe it's better I wasn't there. My presence probably would have just made things worse.

My thoughts are interrupted by Sharon's voice. "I'm sorry but I have to work."

She actually looks genuinely concerned about me when I don't deserve her understanding at all. I deserve her condemnation.

"I'm sorry for coming to your workplace like this," I

say. "I didn't know how else to find you. Thank you for speaking with me. You've been much kinder than I deserved." I open the office door for her, but before we exit, a persistent question gnaws at me, the answer to which I almost don't want to know. "Can I ask you one last question?"

She reluctantly nods.

"Did you know the baby's gender?"

She seems startled by the question but quickly shakes her head, and then tears begin to well up in her eyes. My eyes meet hers, both of us speechless, and all I can do is nod and leave, my heart slowly shattering into little shards.

As I get into my truck and turn to back out, I catch sight of the back seat and the memories of my night with Sharon come rushing back to me.

Chapter Two

~ *Sharon* ~

Two Years Earlier

I do a little bit of everything at the restaurant, but my favorite thing by far is bartending. Ever since I can remember, I've been told that I'm very easy to talk to, so tending bar comes naturally and the regulars all know me. In our quiet little New England town of Shelby Falls, most places close by about nine, so our Tex-Mex restaurant, whose last call isn't until around midnight, usually has a steady influx of patrons and I've managed to make enough money in tips to put myself through college and now graduate school.

Tonight's been a little slow for a Friday night, but it's Memorial Day weekend, so people may be out of town. After serving a cosmo to a woman who has spent the last half hour shamelessly flirting with the other bartender, Jim, I turn my attention to the man sitting in front of me, Matt Conroy. His classic good looks are undeniable, but more than that, he's a genuinely nice guy and it's so good to see him out for a change. Since his wife tragically passed away from cancer about a year ago, I don't think he socializes very much. I usually just see him at the restaurant for his graphic design firm's work lunches. But tonight he's actually out with a friend and it warms my heart.

"Hey there, Matt! I see you're not flying solo tonight." My eyes migrate over to his cute friend as I mix a drink.

"Oh, sorry, I should have introduced you. This is my friend, Mark," Matt says, giving Mark a pat on the back. "He's the reason I'm here tonight. He insisted I get out, and I have to admit, he was right for a change."

"What are you talking about? I'm always right. Going all the way back to middle school." Mark grins as he glances my way.

Matt smirks. "You're delusional but I still love you, man."

"I think we need to cut him off," Mark says to me with a light laugh. "He's not usually this nice to me."

My smile widens. Mark is cute—very cute.

"Do you want another round?" Matt asks Mark.

"No, I think we're good." Mark captures my eyes with his, holding my gaze a little longer than he should.

And that's when I notice his eyes. They're blue—very, very blue. He gives me a grin and I smile right back. His body language reflects a confidence and openness as he rests his forearms comfortably on the bar. I do love a man with confidence and his dirty blonde waves and natural tan are sending off a relaxed, sexy vibe. I spot a chain peeking out from underneath his pale blue golf shirt, which he fills out nicely.

Yup, he's definitely my type.

As I turn my attention back to mixing drinks, I can feel Mark's eyes drift to what I'm wearing. It's a black barmaid's outfit that I usually wear when I tend bar. The upper portion is form-fitting and the skirt is short and slightly flared at the waist, accentuating my waistline and legs. My manager prefers that I wear it because, let's face it, it's good for business. But for the fact that it sometimes leads guys to become overly flirtatious, I actually enjoy wearing it once in a while. I somehow feel a little different from my usual self when I wear it. A little sexier, flirtier, freer.

I sense Mark's eyes still on me but I'm careful not to look up. Plus, I feel a blush coming on from the attention he's showing me. He's not being creepy; he just seems friendly and perhaps a little flirtatious. I'm glad I'm wearing this outfit tonight because he seems particularly enamored with it.

"So what name goes with those beautiful green eyes of yours?" Mark eventually asks me.

I raise my eyes to meet his, which I can now confirm are a very deep blue, like the color I imagine the ocean to be off of the Florida Keys. I've never been there, but I want to go one day.

"I'm Sharon. So are you Mark with a '*k*' or a '*c*'?"

He chuckles. "A '*k*.' Are you Sharon with an '*n*' or a silent '*h*'?"

"Huh?" I start to giggle. "That doesn't even make sense!"

"Exactly. Making sense is overrated." He wiggles his brows, causing me to giggle again.

"You're a funny one," I say. "If you're really nice, I might even tell you my first name. Sharon's my middle name."

His brow arches. "I'll get it out of you eventually. Persistence is one of my most annoying traits."

"I can definitely vouch for that," Matt interjects as he finishes off the last of his beer.

I can't help but smile at Mark. He's funny and definitely a flirt, but my gut tells me there's more to him than his charm and good looks.

"If you won't tell me your first name," he says, "will you at least tell me what your favorite flower is?"

"Oh, that's easy. Orange ranunculus."

He raises his eyebrows again. "Really?"

I grin. "Yes, why do you ask?

"Just wanted to know. I think the flower you choose says a lot about a person."

"So what does it say about me?"

"That you're independent and don't conform."

"You can tell that just from my flower choice?"

"Absolutely. Not only did you pick a flower that a lot of people have probably never heard of, but you chose orange. Orange isn't as popular a color as, say, pink, which means you gravitate to unique things and aren't afraid to go against the grain."

"Hmm, that's really interesting. So then what's your favorite flower?" I ask.

He doesn't hesitate to answer. "Orange ranunculus."

I giggle. "No, really, what's your favorite?"

"I *am* being serious. That's my favorite flower—as of about thirty seconds ago." He gives a wide grin.

"You are a shameless flirt, Mark with a '*k*.'"

He responds with a quick wink, causing me to sigh internally. *Absolutely adorable.*

As I take away Matt's empty glass, I notice that he's looking a little pale so I immediately bring him a glass of ice water. I don't think Matt's a heavy drinker so he may have overdone it, but I certainly don't want to embarrass him by calling attention to it.

"You're welcome to lay down in the back office," I say discreetly into his ear. "There's a couch and a private bathroom in there that you can use."

Matt nods appreciatively. "I'll be back in a few minutes," Matt tells Mark as he gets up.

"You okay?" Mark asks.

"Yeah, I'm fine. Be right back."

"Jim, can you handle things out here for a few minutes?" I ask my co-worker as my eyes signal in Matt's direction. We encounter this kind of thing once in a while and Jim nods.

As I lead Matt away, I briefly glance back and find Mark's watchful eyes on us. He looks concerned, but there's also something else in his expression—an anxiousness.

Chapter Three

~ Sharon ~

Present Day
Sunday, May 28th

As I watch Mark leave the restaurant after his unexpected visit today, I feel an almost unbearable weight descend upon me. Revisiting what happened between us two years ago—even for a moment—was extremely upsetting.

Why did he really come here after all this time?

A tear dares to escape from my eye but I quickly wipe it away. I can't fall apart. I have a full work day ahead, so I grit my teeth and force a fake smile.

I can do this.

It's several hours later before I come up for air. This turned out to be the day from hell. After Mark's unwelcome visit and all the joy that that brought me, we had a deluge of lunch customers and we were understaffed, which of course was my responsibility as manager. So I've spent the last few hours waiting tables along with managing the restaurant and my feet now feel like they're going to fall off. I should **not** have worn these heels today and I can't wait to get home, take a hot shower, and climb into bed.

As I drive home, my mind creates a playlist consisting of only one selection which is set on repeat: my conversation with Mark.

Does he seriously expect me to believe that he didn't know he was our baby's father until today? And why does he suddenly believe me when he didn't originally?

None of this makes any sense. And yet the shock in his eyes tells me he's being honest.

Even though he was an insensitive asshole when I originally told him I was pregnant two years ago, I still can't help but empathize with what he must be feeling right now. He's a human being after all and the loss of a child is a kind of pain I wouldn't wish on anyone—not even Mark Jansen. I always try to put myself in others' shoes and I can't imagine what he must have felt like today when he realized he might have a child. Maybe he was upset, or scared, or even happy. I don't pretend to understand him, but what I do know is that finding out about the loss of our baby within just a few hours of realizing you might be that baby's father must have been emotionally devastating. Maybe I shouldn't have kicked him out like I did, but I just couldn't handle being around him in that moment. It's been two years but the wounds are still not fully healed.

I make my way up the outer stairs to my apartment. It's at times like these that I wish I had a ground floor unit. But when I first rented the apartment, I thought it would be more private being on the second level. Plus, having lived in many apartments over the years, I know how annoying it is to have a neighbor above you who likes to jump rope at the crack of dawn (true story).

Just as I drop my things down on the kitchen counter, my phone signals an incoming text. My mom always texts me on work nights to make sure I've gotten home safely, so I quickly respond with a thumbs up and a blowing kiss emoji. All I want to do right now is get these damn shoes off my feet and take a shower. It's only a little after nine o'clock but I can barely keep my eyes open at this point.

Showers are one of my favorite things on this earth. Just give me a powerful shower head and I instantly unwind. But Mark Jansen is even ruining my shower tonight. As the water cascades over me, I just can't seem to shake these thoughts of him. He really did look distraught when he left the restaurant. *Why do I even care?* For all I know he's out picking up some random woman right now, just like he did with me. Matt told me that he's a womanizer, which is why I ultimately decided not to push him about the pregnancy in the first place. I didn't need another asshole in my life or the baby's.

I towel dry my hair, climb into bed, and begin my nightly ritual of checking my texts and emails.

And there it is.

A text from an unknown number from half an hour ago.

> Mark: **Hi Sharon. It's Mark Jansen. I'm sorry to disturb you again but I couldn't let the day end without thanking you for speaking with me today. You have every right to hate me yet you still gave me the chance to tell you how sorry I am. And I am - about everything. I'm so sorry for how I treated you and I'm deeply sorry for your loss. I feel it now too - the loss. I should have been there. I realize my sorries are not helpful to you now and there's absolutely no excuse for how I treated you. NONE. I'm concerned that my stopping by may have caused**

you even more pain. That's the last thing I wanted to do. So if I can just ask one more thing of you, can you please just let me know you're ok? Again, I'm very sorry.

His words rush right past my mind and directly into my heart, and I'm very shaken. I should be angry with him, I know I should. But I'm really not. *Why not? Am I really this much of a pushover? He apologizes and that's all it takes to gain my forgiveness?*

I do feel angry, but the anger and resentment I'm feeling right now is more over the fact that things might have turned out differently—so differently—if he had just believed me in the first place. My anger is soon replaced by an aching sadness.

I know I mustn't indulge in thoughts of what might have been. It's all in the past now, where it belongs. But I don't know what to do with this—with him. *Should I respond? And who gave him my number?*

Despite my better instincts, my heart is pleading with me to answer him. I can't help it; he sounds sincere and he seems upset. Not responding to him would be cruel and I'm not interested in exacting revenge. *No, I just need to make sure he's okay.*

Me: Hi Mark. Thanks for checking in on me. I'm doing fine. Over time I've been able to accept the loss and move forward.
I hope you're ok too. It will just take time. Take care

I hope I don't sound too cold or dismissive. I don't mean to, but I don't need his pity.

I now see dots. *Wait, he's responding? I thought my*

"take care" was pretty clear.

> Mark: **Thanks for letting me know you're ok. I was worried.**
> **And thank you for the advice. My state of mind isn't great at the moment, but you don't need me revisiting all of this with you. It means a lot just to have been able to apologize to you. I'm glad you're ok, but that shouldn't surprise me. You're a very strong person. I could see that from the moment we met. Ok, well, take care of yourself Sharon.**

Gulp. I now have a huge lump in my throat. He's getting to me. I can feel it. Damnit, this is the same feeling I had when we first met. This connection we have. He was so sweet that night, and he made me smile. But what really got to me was a vulnerability that I saw in his eyes when we were together. When we were intimate, I caught a glimpse of it. He was confident, yet cautious—even perhaps a little insecure. And there was a yearning in him that I wanted so badly to satisfy. I wanted to know him—very much—and I thought he wanted to know me too. *So why did he have to turn out to be such an asshole?*

I stare at my phone, wishing I could text him back but knowing what a risk that would be. He hurt me terribly and I need to protect my heart. So then why is my heart fighting me on this?

I don't mean to sound crude but my heart can go fuck itself. I'm going to sleep.

Chapter Four

~ *Mark* ~

Two Years Earlier

It's been almost twenty minutes since Matt and the cute bartender, Sharon, disappeared into the back of the restaurant and I'm starting to get worried—actually, more like jealous. What could they be doing back there for so long? Is it possible they're planning the menu for one of Matt's firm's lunches? That seems like a stretch. So naturally my next thought is that they're fooling around. I didn't sense any flirtation between them, but then again Matt never lets on when he likes a woman. But Sharon didn't seem overly flirtatious with him either, except when she whispered something in his ear which resulted in them leaving. I groan inwardly at the thought of them "together."

I'm usually a pretty good judge of a woman's interest in me and Sharon seemed into me—and I'm definitely into her. I can't put my finger on exactly what it is about her, but when our eyes met, I felt a pull, and not just a physical one. She's beautiful, but it was more than that. She's the first woman in a long time whom I found myself wanting to get to know beyond the superficial. I don't know, maybe I misread her signals, but I really thought I felt something between us.

Thankfully, just as I finish off the scotch I've been nursing, Matt and Sharon reappear from the back. She's smiling and I feel myself deflate just a little. I'm not sure what happened back there and I don't think I want to know.

Matt rejoins me at the bar. "Sorry about that," he says. "I wasn't feeling great. I probably just had a few too many. Mind if we call it night?"

"Sure." I feel somewhat reassured by his explanation.

"Are you okay to drive?" he asks.

"Yeah, I'm fine. Why don't you go on ahead and I'll take care of the bill."

He tries to hand me his credit card but I refuse.

"Thanks, man," he says. "And thanks for dragging me out tonight. It was just what I needed."

As soon as Matt walks away, I decide to approach Sharon who is back behind the bar. When my eyes meet hers, I swear she blushes for a second before giving me an inviting smile. Did I mention that she has a fantastic smile? Well she does.

"Will you still be here in about a half an hour?" I ask her, careful not to come on too strong.

"I should be. I'm working 'til midnight."

"Well don't go anywhere. I have to take Matt home, but maybe we can hang out after your shift? That is, if you're free?"

The corners of her mouth curve up slightly. "Oh, sure. I'd like that."

My heart beats a little faster. "Good, then I'll see you in a few."

I give her a wink as I leave and she responds with a cute salute goodbye.

On the drive back to Matt's house, he isn't offering up any information about what, if anything, happened between him and Sharon, and I don't ask. He wouldn't tell me even if I did ask; he's always been very private when it comes to women. But Sharon's response to my invitation has already put my mind at ease. I doubt she'd want to hang out with me if she and Matt just hooked up. I'm going to take this as a good sign.

By the time I drop Matt off and return to the restaurant, it's eleven o'clock, so I go directly to the bar to find Sharon. But she isn't there.

That's odd.

I know we just met but I was really looking forward to hanging out with her. Given how disappointed I'm now feeling, I'm positive this isn't just a sexual attraction on my end. I've had my share of one nighters with women who are similarly just interested in a good time, and this feels different—because Sharon is different.

"Boo," a voice says from behind, startling me.

I turn around to find Sharon smiling up at me and still wearing that sexy barmaid outfit. She looks so pretty, and very hot, and all my worries scatter at the sight of her bright smile.

"I thought maybe you darted off," I say.

"Darted off?" A small giggle escapes her gorgeous pink lips. "Does anyone actually say that in this century?"

She's so damn cute.

I shake my head in embarrassment. "You're making me nervous, and when I get nervous I start using nonsensical phrases."

"Yeah, I can see that." Her green eyes study me with curious amusement. "Anyway, if you're still up for hanging out, my manager says it's quiet so I can leave early."

"Great. So then where shall we mosey off to?" I give a knowing grin.

"Geez, I don't know. Maybe to parts unknown?" There's a flirty playfulness in her eyes.

"Well, we're intelligent people. We should be able to figure this out."

She gathers her purse and we walk out to the parking lot. But she stops before we get into my truck.

"Wait a minute," she says. "I just realized I can't go anywhere in this outfit. I look ridiculous."

I slowly take in her outfit again, which is showcasing her perky breasts, slim waistline, and gorgeous legs, and I feel a sudden and intense urge to kiss her.

"You don't look ridiculous at all." I dare to inch closer to her. "You look beautiful, and sexy as hell."

Even though it's dark and the only thing illuminating our faces are the restaurant's exterior lights, she's definitely blushing.

"Well, regardless, I can't wear this out in public," she declares. "Can we just stop at my place so I can change into a pair of jeans?"

"As long as I can watch."

She rolls her eyes at me. "Are you always this forward with women?"

"Does it bother you?"

"Nope," she declares, hopping into my truck.

She has now captured my full and undivided attention and I feel myself hardening at just the thought of her undressing. I don't start the ignition just yet.

"Sharon, you do know that if it were up to me, we'd be undressing one another right now and exploring every inch of each other."

Her brows raise. "Here?"

"Absolutely."

She looks a little taken aback but then glances at the back seat, as if actually considering my proposal.

And that's all it takes. I'm now fully aroused. This is honestly not how I saw the evening going, but I don't think I can resist her. If she's up for this, I know I am.

"So...I grabbed a few IPA's from the bar," she says. "Are you familiar with the cliff?"

"Of course."

Chapter Five

~ Mark ~

Present Day

No sooner do I wake up this morning than my mind returns to yesterday—and Sharon—and the baby. The knot in my stomach that untwisted overnight has retwisted itself. After seeing Sharon, I spent the entire drive back to Boston replaying our conversation over and over again in my mind. I couldn't shake the feeling that my visit had really upset her. So I eventually broke down and texted her last night just to make sure she's okay. She responded but clearly wants nothing to do with me and I can't say that I blame her. I wouldn't want anything to do with me either. I'm just relieved that she seems okay.

The problem is, I'm not okay at all. I can't help but hold myself at least partially responsible for her miscarriage. She was undoubtedly under a lot of stress when I left her to figure things out all by herself. *If only I had believed her.* It's killing me that I didn't give her the chance to explain, and the stress I caused her couldn't have been good for the pregnancy.

Even though I only knew about the baby for a few hours, I still feel a heavy sadness and grief. I'm thirty-nine, have never been married, and although the idea of being a father scares me a little, I know I would have loved our baby with all my heart. Because having a family I can call my own is something I've wanted my entire life.

As I button the cuffs of my dress shirt and put on my tie, I try my best to pull myself together. I have a meeting with the CEO of a Boston tech company today and I can't allow myself to become derailed like this.

I manage to make it in to the office by nine a.m. but the only thing I can focus on is the acute loss and guilt I'm feeling. All I want to do is reach out to Sharon again because she's the only one who would understand how I'm feeling. But contacting her again would be incredibly selfish of me. I've already hurt her enough.

I try to concentrate on my work, but there's no point. Even my paralegal, Jessica, is noticing my lack of productivity and even offered to run out and pick me up a coffee, which she rarely does. She's usually grumpy on Monday mornings.

*I need to get a grip. **Seriously.***

But ten minutes later, I cave like a sand castle.

> Me: **Hi Sharon. I know I'm probably the last person you want to hear from. So if you don't want me to contact you, just say the word and I promise you'll never hear from me again.**

I send it and stare at my phone like a fucking idiot. Unbelievably, I soon see dots…and then words.

> Sharon: **It's ok, I understand. Are you ok?**

Am I okay? I'm speechless. This woman, whom I so clearly wronged, actually cares how **I'm** doing? Fucking incredible.

> Me: **I'm not sure how to answer that. Honestly, I'm shocked that you answered. Thank you.**

I'm just trying to figure out how to cope with everything you told me. I'm a wreck and I know I have no right to be. I'm sorry - I hope this isn't upsetting you. I feel selfish texting you again so please just tell me if you want me to stop and I will. I don't want to upset you.

Sharon: It's ok. And you absolutely DO have a right to feel any way that you're feeling. I understand how hard this is. I was a total mess after what happened. Are you in Shelby Falls?

Me: No, I had to drive back to Boston last night for work today

Sharon: You're an attorney right?

Me: Yep. But try not to hold that against me

Sharon: Oh there are plenty of other things I could hold against you, don't worry

Me: Very very true

I pause to see if there's more, but there isn't. Something inside me won't let this—or her—go.

Me: Are you working today?

Sharon: No, I have the day off

Me: Cool. What are your plans?

Sharon: Studying for my social work exam

Me: Oh, so you finished your Master's?

Sharon: Yes, graduated a few weeks ago so I just need to pass this exam and then hopefully

I can get a full time position

Me: **That's great! Really happy for you. I remember you said you hoped to work at a school one day**

Sharon: **Wow, you have a good memory. Yes that's true. What kind of law do you practice?**

Me: **Mergers and acquisitions. Fun stuff**

Sharon: **Are you at work?**

Me: **Yeah and I should probably go and do some actual work. haha**

Sharon: **Yeah and I should study**

Me: **Ok you go ahead. And thank you - you really helped get my mind off of things**

Sharon: **You're welcome**

I don't think I can stop myself from what I'm about to ask next.

Me: **I don't know how you'd feel about this but would it be ok if I texted you again some time?**

No more dots. She's thinking. Not a good sign, but I completely understand. She was just being polite. But just as I begin to text her to save her from having to decline, she texts me back.

Sharon: **Sure**

I can feel the blood sprinting to my cheeks. I think I'm blushing—fucking blushing.

Me: **Ok cool. Back to work. Study hard**

She responds with a thumbs up.

A spontaneous smile spreads across my face. She's incredible, mind-blowingly incredible. I know damn well I don't deserve her kindness, but by some miracle, she must believe that I do. I put my phone down and can't get this silly smile off my face.

And it's all because of her.

Chapter Six

~ Sharon ~

Present Day

As I close out Mark's text, I feel myself grinning...*Grinning!*

What's the matter with you? Have you learned absolutely nothing?
And now I'm talking to myself.

I know, I know, allowing him to text me again is probably a huge mistake. I should be clear that this can't continue. But he may never text me again so there's no point in following up just yet, right?

I now push all thoughts of Mark out of my head because I really do need to focus on my exam today. I've worked too hard to let anything—or anyone—distract me.

After making myself a cup of coffee, I settle in on the couch for a day of studying.

I sit bolt upright at the sound of an incoming text and look down at my phone. 5:04 p.m. *Shit! How long have I been asleep*?! I spot a new text from Mark.

> Mark: **Hi. Did you get a lot of studying done today?**

A huge yawn escapes from my mouth.

Me: **Umm...not exactly...**

Mark: **Why, what happened?**

Me: **Sleep happened...I think your text actually woke me up**

Mark: **Oh - sorry about that!**

Me: **No, it's a good thing. I need to study**

Mark: **Ok I'll let you go then**

Me: **That's ok. I just meant I have to study in general, not this second. Were you able to get any work done today?**

Mark: **Yes and I have you to thank for that. Texting with you really helped**

Me: **It'll get easier in time**

Mark: **It will if you'll keep being my guardian angel**

Me: **Haha. I'm no angel**

Mark: **Well I beg to differ**

Me: **Are you still at work?**

Mark: **No, on the T going home**

Me: **Where do you live?**

Mark: **Newton**

Me: **Gotcha. Apartment or house?**

Mark: **House**

Me: **That's awesome that you have your own**

house. I've never lived in a house

Mark: **Never?**

Me: **Nope, I've always lived in apartments or condos**

Mark: **Sounds kind of cool actually**

Me: **Maybe it could be but our buildings were always older and the hallways used to smell like dinner all day long :)**

Mark: **If it was a steak dinner, maybe not such a bad thing**

Me: **It'll make me appreciate a house if I ever save enough for a down payment**

Mark: **You'll get there**

Me: **Hope so. What style of house do you have?**

Mark: **A cape. I love it and the neighborhood. The only problem is that it smells like my lousy cooking**

Me: **Lol. I love to cook**

Mark: **What do you like to cook?**

Me: **Everything. What's your favorite food?**

Mark: **My mom makes this amazing lemon chicken. She always makes it for me when I'm home**

Me: **Sounds good. Would love the recipe**

Mark: **I'll get it for you if you promise to let me taste yours one day**

I stop texting. *Was that meant to be sexual?*

Mark: **Sorry, didn't mean for that to sound inappropriate. I'm talking about the chicken, I swear!**

I giggle to myself.

Me: **Darn. jk :) Maybe I'll make the chicken for you one day as long as you aren't too much of an asshole**

Omg. Was that really necessary? Yes, I believe it was.

Mark: **Ugh. I deserved that. I'll try my best. You do seem to be having a good effect on me. I'm not as "assholish"**

Me: **I was just kidding - well, sort of. Anyway, I really do need to study. Have a good night Mark**

Mark: **You too**

I let out a resigned sigh. Not assholish at all...

Chapter Seven

~ Mark ~

Two Years Earlier

There's a cliff in Shelby Falls that's located at the end of a quiet dirt road. It overlooks the town below and is the ideal spot for stargazing...and other things. Surprisingly, it's not that well known, but in high school I took a date or two here and sometimes I'd just come here to think. I've stood atop this cliff many times, and when you're standing here all by yourself, there's an almost mystical quality in the air. All you can hear is the shallow sound of your own breathing and the hum of the universe.

I'm glad Sharon suggested coming here. When we arrive, I'm happy to see that we're the only ones here. It's a privilege to have the view all to ourselves, not to mention the privacy factor. Once we're parked, Sharon offers me a beer.

"So, what do you do when you're not bartending?" I ask, taking a swig.

"Wait tables," she says with this sweet little giggle that makes my heart leap. Yes, that's right, I said leap.

"And when you're not waiting tables?" I ask.

"I'm getting my Master's in Social Work."

"Oh, that's great. Do you know what you'd like to do ultimately?"

"Maybe work with kids. I worked as an aide at a high school during college and I absolutely loved it."

I nod. "Sounds like a good plan. Do you go to school full time?"

"No, I'm part-time. I'm putting myself through school since my mom really can't afford it." She takes a swig of her beer. "So what do you do?"

"I'm an attorney in Boston."

She looks genuinely surprised. "Oh! Wow! Do you enjoy it?"

"I do actually."

"I wouldn't have pegged you for a lawyer. Plus, the lawyers I've met always seem to drive BMWs. A pickup truck doesn't really fit the profile."

I chuckle. "That's probably true. But I've never really cared about what other people think. I like what I like, and I happen to like a bigger vehicle. It's more comfortable and also safer in my opinion."

She nods. "So where did you go to school?"

I hesitate because I know this can sometimes be off-putting. "Harvard undergrad and BU law."

Her eyes widen. "Really?! Your parents must be so proud of you."

I pause at the reference to my parents. "I think they are."

"Of course they are! And you should feel proud too. I hear the bar exam is a killer." She smiles warmly and I swear my heart is now singing. Off tune, but yeah, it's singing.

I notice her wiggle her feet out of her heels.

"You've been on your feet all night," I say. "Here, why don't you stretch your legs out." I motion to my lap.

She gives me a surprised yet grateful look. "Oh, well...okay...are you sure?"

I nod and she lifts her legs and places her feet on my

lap.

"If you want, I can give you a foot massage," I offer.

Her eyes widen. "Really? Are you sure?"

I smile. "I wouldn't offer if I wasn't sure." I begin to massage her feet which have some kind of sparkly blue nail polish on them. Not sure I've ever thought of toes as being "cute," but hers are—along with everything else about her.

"Thank you," she says with a small sigh. "That feels amazing. I don't think I've ever had a foot massage before."

My brows lift in disbelief. "Huh? What kind of guys have you been dating?"

"Apparently not the right ones!"

While I massage her feet, we talk about everything from music to sports to history. Somehow I manage to successfully suppress my urge to revert to mindless flirting because I'm really enjoying our conversation. There's something so inviting in her demeanor and even though we just met, it feels like we've known each other a lot longer than just a few hours. I don't think I fully realized what a facade I put on in my quest to attract a woman until just now. But with Sharon, there are no pretenses. It feels completely natural.

My fingers eventually migrate to her calves but she continues to talk without any acknowledgment of this. But I can tell she's enjoying the massage because mid-sentence, she stops and lets out a satisfied "Oh." She doesn't say it in a sexual way, she's just enjoying it. But man, the way she says it really gets to me.

I soon feel the very subtle movement of her feet on my lap and I could swear she's trying to arouse me. Her foot movements soon grow more purposeful as she gently explores my crotch. When she finds my now very pronounced erection, she meets my eyes and I swear there's a victorious look in them.

This woman...

Nevertheless, neither of us acknowledge what's taking place on my lap—or in my boxers. She continues nonchalantly asking me about myself and I continue answering her questions as coherently as I can under the circumstances. But my cock is now expressing its own wishes loudly and clearly and I'm afraid I won't be able to curb my arousal much longer.

I finally capitulate. "How about we move to the back seat and I can give you a back massage?" I offer, sounding much more eager than I intended.

She gives me a knowing look. "You're really pulling out all the stops tonight, aren't you."

I grin. "Nothing wrong with a little pampering once in a while, is there?"

She gives me a daring look before effortlessly climbing over and into the leather back seat. I really wasn't expecting that response but I of course oblige and hop out of the truck and get in back with her.

"Why don't you lean back and this time I'll give *you* a massage," she says with a flicker in her eyes

I'm not sure what she has in mind but I lean back in my seat and await her next move. She slowly lifts up my shirt and I help pull it over my head. The only thing remaining is my chain with the horseshoe charm my mother was wearing the day she died. Sharon notices it but thankfully doesn't ask about it.

"Now unzip your pants," she instructs me.

I'm stunned but do as I'm told.

Then she begins to slowly and sensually run her palms over my chest. I can feel my heart starting to pound out of my chest and there's no hiding the straining bulge in my boxers that is screaming for her touch. But instead of touching me there, she straddles me and continues to stroke my chest and shoulders. With my eyes closed, I focus on the feel of her soft hands on my skin. Her hands feel incredible. I want to open my eyes to look at her but I feel like if I do, my walls will start to come down completely for her and I'm not sure I'm prepared for that. But something inside me is demanding that I open my eyes, and when I do, I'm met with the most magnificent green eyes I've ever seen. They're light green surrounded by a darker green rim, and they're warm and nurturing.

I don't know why, but she suddenly shifts off of me.

Is she stopping?

Thank G-d the answer to that question is *No*. Instead, her hands slowly migrate downwards from my pecs towards my bulge which is desperately trying to break free from my boxer briefs. She gently touches me over my briefs, cupping me, stroking me, slowly at first, then faster, and then slower again. I'm experiencing the most intense pleasure and my body is aching for her. I seriously don't know how much more of this I can take before I give in to the pleasure and erupt.

I finally have to lift her hands off of me. "I need you to stop or I'm going to come."

Her lips curve upwards ever so slightly in triumph.

This woman has to be my soulmate. There's no other explanation.

I force myself to sit up and face her, trying to regain

some semblance of control over my crumbling body. "Now it's your turn," I say. "And, as I recall, you promised to let me watch you undress."

She gives a teasing smile. "I made no such promise."

"Well, will you? Undress?"

She glances out the window. It's now nearly one a.m. and we are still the only car at the cliff. Satisfied that we have privacy, she slowly unbuttons the form-fitting bodice of her outfit, revealing a black demi-cup bra which masterfully pushes her breasts up to form the most beautiful, milky white cleavage. The top of her outfit drops down to her waist and her glistening copper red hair flawlessly drapes over her shoulders.

She's absolutely beautiful.

She slowly takes off her outfit and then kneels before me in nothing but her bra and cotton bikini briefs. They're not the typical satin panties women often wear, which actually makes them a whole lot sexier in my opinion. Sharon is natural and confident and unaffected. To say that she's sexy is an understatement. I am so consumed with desire for her that I can't focus on anything except the idea of being inside her.

That's when she begins tugging at my pants which I gratefully remove. Soon all that remains on our bodies is her bra and underwear and my briefs. I unclasp her bra and watch it as it drops to the seat, revealing the most gorgeous, tantalizing breasts I've ever seen. They're perfect—yes, perfect—and her nipples are a fresh pink and look like little taut buds. I'm almost afraid to touch her.

She must sense my nervousness because she takes my hand and brings it to her bare chest. I exhale as I touch her breasts for the first time, and she responds with a sweet sigh and soft smile. I gently play with her nipples and quickly learn how she likes to be touched. She feels like velvet and smells so good, like some kind of rare tropical fruit. I lean in and press my lips to her breast and then take my time exploring her chest with my lips. As I run my tongue across her peaks, something seems to ignite inside her. She arches her back while kneeling before me, her auburn hair dangling down her back. I steady her by her waist and plant soft kisses all over her stomach and downwards. As I take in her sweet scent, I slowly pull down her underwear to her knees, salivating at the prospect of tasting her sweetness. She's groomed but natural and her hair is soft and auburn and I just want to bury my face in her. She smells like arousal and I spread her wet folds apart and begin gently sucking on her delicate, sweet center. I think she's moaning, or maybe it's me moaning; all of my senses are blending together. When I hear her gasping, my entire body reacts.

She tugs at my briefs and I pull them off, her eyes immediately dropping down to my cock. She's staring at my cock and I don't think I've ever been this turned on in my entire life.

"You're huge," she says softly, the edges of her lips curving upwards.

THAT IS IT.

I gently lower her down onto the seat and hover over her, my throbbing shaft hanging down and straining to touch her silky skin. I begin gently rubbing myself back and forth against her stomach for some relief. She feels so fucking good. I'm usually pretty controlled in these situations, but G-d damnit if I'm not moaning like a virgin. When my tip accidentally catches the inside of her naval, we both stop and smile with anticipation.

"What next?" I ask quietly, now at her total mercy.

She looks at me with lust-filled eyes and reaches for my ass, pulling me down to her as she widens her legs. Her assertiveness is such a turn on and I desperately want to be inside her—if that's what she wants.

I press up against her, her soft curls lightly teasing my balls as I slide back and forth through her moist folds. She begins to softly moan under her breath. *Holy fuck, she's so damn hot.* She wastes no time guiding me inside her.

I enter her slowly at first, to be sure I don't hurt her. She's so tight and wet and my size makes it even tighter. While my finger teases her sensitive area, I ride her very slowly. She lets me dictate the speed and rhythm of our movements and I alternate between slower and faster thrusts depending upon her body's response. She's giving me these beautiful moans and I open my eyes so that I can witness them fully. Her eyes are closed and she's absolutely breathtaking. Her breasts move with each thrust into her and I can feel her walls gripping me tighter. Now I'm the one moaning.

We're so close and then it occurs to me that I don't have a condom.

"Why are you stopping?" she says breathlessly.

When I explain, she reassures me that she's on birth control, so I immediately resume and my thrusts soon grow more forceful and determined as I simultaneously pleasure her with the pad of my middle finger. She's getting louder and the intensity of our mutual pleasure causes me to stop for a moment to slow our arousal.

But as soon as I resume, her body tenses up and she climaxes, her walls gripping me hard, over and over again. I swear it's the best sex I've ever had and I can't bring myself to pull out. She feels so damn good. When I can't hold out a second longer, I begin to withdraw, but not before my body succumbs to the pleasure. Just as I'm pulling out, I start to come and end up releasing all over her stomach, even reaching the valley between her breasts. It's an intensely pleasurable climax and I'm feeling light-headed and have to lay back. We both lay still, destroyed.

Once I'm finally able to see straight, I turn to her. "Sorry I cut it so close but you felt so damned good." I bring her hand to my lips. "That was amazing."

"It really was." She gives a drowsy smile. "And like I said, I'm on the pill so you really didn't need to pull out."

"I know that but I have a friend who got pregnant even on the pill so I just like to play it safe. I'm used to it. But I'm really sorry it got so messy."

I take my T-shirt and carefully clean her off. Some women don't like it when it gets messy but it doesn't seem to bother her at all.

The moonlight is just bright enough for me to be able to admire the beautiful curves of her body. "I can't decide which I like better. You *in* that sexy outfit or you out of it." I grin as I watch her begin to get dressed.

"I knew you liked it." Sparkles fill her eyes. "I could feel your eyes on me all night."

"When I admire something or someone, I'm not particularly subtle about it. I hope I didn't offend you."

"No, not at all. I like that about you. You're very straightforward about what you want and it's refreshing. I like it...and you."

I'm once again in awe of this woman. I can't believe she actually likes the very thing that I've always considered a flaw in my personality. The fact that I can be completely myself around her is so liberating. I need to hug her, and do. This all just feels so right. As we pull back, our eyes lock and it hits me right between the eyes just how rare she is. Like no one I've ever met before.

I don't want this to end.

"Would you maybe like to get together tomorrow?" I try my damnedest not to sound too eager.

"Yes," she immediately responds with a smile. "I'm working until four but I'm free after that."

I can breathe again. "Perfect. I'm going golfing in the morning so I'll come by the restaurant around four then."

"Great!"

As we drive back to the restaurant, we speak very little but it doesn't feel awkward, just comfortable. However, once we reach her car, a strange nervousness comes over me. I'm not sure why since we certainly weren't embarrassed about an hour ago in my back seat.

I walk her to her car. "So then I'll see you tomorrow," I say.

She nods. "Yes."

My heart is now beating vigorously against my chest, urging me to speak. We just stand there staring at each other while I try to come up with something—anything—to say, but my mind has gone completely blank.

"Okay, well, good night then," I say lamely.

"Good night." She gives a cute little wave as she turns to unlock her car, but this feels completely wrong.

"Wait," I say anxiously.

She turns to look at me and I immediately take her in my arms. "I want to kiss you good night," I say. "I'm just nervous as hell for some reason."

She smiles reassuringly and wraps her arms around my neck, pressing her body to mine. "There's nothing to be nervous about. I like you."

I lean in and kiss her on her cheek, then the other, and then my lips finally meet hers for the very first time. They're soft and sweet like her, and her kisses are full of warmth and affection. I eagerly return her kisses, holding her close, and my tongue soon finds hers, connecting us in a deep, lingering kiss. She feels so good and I'm certain I've never felt this kind of emotional rush before. It's as if time is standing still, but it's two thirty in the morning and we're in the middle of a deserted parking lot.

"Good night, Mark with a 'k,'" she finally whispers.

"Good night, Sharon."

Chapter Eight

~ Mark ~

Present Day

Every morning this week I've woken up in the best mood. Not that I'm not usually in a good mood, but this feels different. And it's all because of Sharon. We've texted every day since I saw her on Sunday. There's just something about her that makes me feel so happy and relaxed. I don't feel like I need to try to impress her and I've been more myself with her than with anybody else I can think of, other than my parents. She's not even bothered by my flirtatiousness, and if I didn't know any better, I'd say she might even enjoy it.

It's hard to believe, but she doesn't appear to be holding a grudge against me either. She's the kind of woman who would be honest if she was. She speaks her mind and I know where I stand with her. I knew she was special when we met two years ago and now I know I wasn't wrong. She's amazing.

After finishing up a bowl of cereal, I check my texts one last time before leaving for work, hoping that maybe she's texted this morning. So far I'm always the one to text first, but once I do, she's quick to respond. I'll text her once I'm on the T. I want to ask her something.

Me: **Morning, are you up?**

Sharon: **Yes, studying before work**

Me: **Are you working late today?**

Sharon: **Just til 5**

Me: **That's good. So I have a question for you**

Sharon: **ok**

Me: **I was thinking of coming home tonight for the weekend. Would you maybe like to get together tomorrow?**

I hold my breath as a long pause ensues, and then....

Sharon: **What did you have in mind?**

Fuck. I didn't want to be presumptuous and assume that she would say *Yes,* and now my mind is a complete blank.

Me: **Anything you want. Lady's choice**

I halt my texting. *"Lady's choice"? Where the hell did that come from? Well, now I'm stuck with it.*

Sharon: **I don't think I'm old enough to be a Lady yet. I'm only 29 and the only Lady I know is Lady Grantham**

Me: **Who's that?**

Sharon: **From Downton Abbey**

Me: **Never watched that show. The only Lady I've ever heard of is Lady Elaine Fairchilde and I'm sure I just dated myself with that one**

Sharon: **Who's Lady Elaine Fairchilde?**

Me: **Exactly.**
Anyway, how about Princess' choice? Is that

better?

Sharon: :) Much better. I'll need to use my given name of course and I'll also need a diamond tiara just to make it official

Me: I'm on it. I forgot that Sharon isn't your real name

Sharon: It's my middle name

Me: So what's your first name?

Sharon: If I told you, what would be the fun in that?

Me: Just give me a clue

Sharon: I'll think about it

Me: I'll wear you down eventually. My stop is next so think about what you want to do tomorrow and text me

Sharon: I didn't say yes yet

Me: You're killing me you know

Sharon: Well I wouldn't want to kill you just yet. It's kind of fun taunting you

Me: Thanks - I think

Sharon: I'll think of something fun to do but I should warn you, giving the power of the purse to a princess may not have been your wisest move

Me: No worries. I'll be sure to stop at the ATM

and take out a LOT of money

Sharon: **And I'll try not to take advantage of you...too much**

Me: **If you're trying to turn me on, you've succeeded...Gotta go**

Sharon: **;) byeee**

Chapter Nine

~ Sharon ~

Present Day

This morning I woke up with the most ridiculous, and frankly embarrassing, smile on my face. And it's all because of Mark.

It's only been a week and I've already completely forgotten all of the reasons why I should NOT become involved with Mark Jansen. I realize his past behavior towards me was very insensitive and hurtful, but I really do believe he's sorry and I don't think he intentionally tried to hurt me. I refuse to be one of those people who is so arrogant and narrow-minded as to think that people can't change and grow, or to limit myself to those who have never (allegedly) made a single mistake. Everyone, and I mean everyone—myself most certainly included —has made mistakes. No one would be speaking if we never forgave one another and I am not going to withhold forgiveness for principle's sake. I just don't function that way. Mark has fallen on the sword multiple times this week (I'm surprised he's not dead at this point) and his apology has actually brought peace to that part of my life. If someone is genuinely sorry and shows themself to be a kind person, then I'm willing to give them another chance. Some may regard this as naive or foolish, but I'm not willing to forego a chance at real happiness based solely on past actions. Happiness is simply too rare, and I think Mark is worth the risk.

I relax back into my sheets, waiting for Mark's morning text. We agreed to get together today and I'm really looking forward to it. I can't wait to see his reaction when he finds out what I have planned.

My phone vibrates right on schedule.

> Mark: **Good morning Princess no name. What did you decide on for today?**
>
> Me: **It's a surprise**
>
> Mark: **I hate surprises**
>
> Me: **Even better. Wanna pick me up at 10?**
>
> Mark: **Ok I just need your address**

I text him my address and then take a shower with that ridiculous smile still plastered all over my face. By the time I'm done, however, I can feel myself starting to get a little nervous. *Is this a date?* It feels like it is, and my instincts tell me he wants more than friendship. *But what do I want?* I don't know yet.

It's a little cool out this morning, so I throw on a pair of jeans and a lightweight sweatshirt. Nothing too flirty or revealing that might be misinterpreted. The first time we met I was wearing that skimpy barmaid's outfit and we know where that led.

I take a few minutes to straighten up before Mark gets here so that he doesn't think I'm a complete slob. I suppose you could say that my apartment has that "lived in" look. I'm usually tired when I get home from work or school and tend to just crash. But otherwise it's a cute apartment and it more than suits my needs. I do wish I could afford some new furniture though. My current furnishings consist of a combination of hand-me-downs and Christmas Tree Shop finds and, let's face it, there's only so much one can do with throw pillows. Still, while I'm sure my place doesn't compare to Mark's house, it's very comfortable and it's my home.

After rearranging the couch pillows for far too long, I wait nervously for ten o'clock to roll around. Finally, at five minutes to ten, I hear someone walking up the outside stairs of my building, followed by a knock on my door. I like that he's early. It shows that he's just as eager as me.

When I open the door, I find him standing before me holding a small plant. An orange ranunculus to be exact.

"Hi! Wow, thank you!" I'm stunned that he actually remembered my favorite flower. He even got the color right.

"I hope you still like ranunculuses—or is it ranunculi?—because I had one hell of a time finding this one."

"Actually, I've become very environmentally conscious and my favorite flowers are now dandelions. So you could have just stopped at the side of the road and picked some. And then I could've used them to make dandelion stew for us."

He now looks very confused. "Stew?"

I giggle. "I wish you could see the look on your face. Are you always this gullible?"

He gives a chuckle as he shakes his head with embarrassment. "Not usually." He seems a little nervous. It's very endearing.

"Seriously though, thank you so much," I say. "And yes, they're still my favorite." I give him a smile as I take the plant. "Come on in."

He steps into my apartment a little tentatively, as if concerned about doing something wrong. He then takes in the room.

"I like your place," he says. "Do you have a roommate?"

"A roommate?" I repeat, amused. "No, I like being on my own."

"Me too. I like my own space."

"Exactly. I want to be able to take long showers, and if I want to leave dishes in the sink, then I will."

"Absolutely." He grins.

I'm immediately drawn to his sweet, unassuming smile and his blue eyes. I was so angry at him the other day that I really wasn't able to appreciate just how handsome he is. His dirty blonde waves and that little bit of stubble on his face are very sexy and the Henley shirt and dark grey jeans he's wearing highlight his trim, fit body. In a word, he's hot.

I watch him scan the room as if he's looking for something. His eyes land on some framed photos and he walks over and picks up a family picture. "Is this your family?"

"Yes, that's my mom and my brother, Dan."

He smiles. "You look just like your mom."

"Yeah, everybody says that. Actually, sometimes people think we're sisters!"

"I can see why. And your dad?"

I hesitate briefly because this isn't something I would share with just anyone. But my gut is telling me Mark won't judge me or my family and, although we don't know each other well, I somehow feel very comfortable with him.

"My parents are divorced and my father isn't a part of our lives," I reveal.

"Oh, I'm sorry."

"It's okay. He was in the military and got deployed overseas when I was a baby, and then when he returned, he got into trouble with the law and landed himself in prison. I haven't seen him since I was very young so I really don't remember him." I examine Mark's face for any hint of judgment but see only warmth in his eyes. My instincts were definitely correct about him.

He's quiet as he contemplates his next question. "Has it been hard for you not having your dad in your life?"

"I've never really known any differently so it's not like I had something and lost it. My brother was older when all of this happened so I think it was harder on him. But my mom raised us and she's a wonderful mother."

"Sounds like you're very lucky to have her and your brother." Mark carefully returns the picture to its spot on the table.

"Yes, I do feel lucky. Do you have any siblings?"

He shakes his head. "No, it's just me." His eyes immediately shift away from mine and I sense that he doesn't want to talk about his family, and I certainly don't want to pry.

"So, we should probably get going," I say. "I don't want to be late."

"Sure, can I just use the bathroom first?"

Shit—I forgot to clean the bathroom.

"Just one sec," I say, scurrying down the hallway as he watches me with confusion. Luckily the bathroom is in good shape and I return, much less flustered. "I just wanted to be sure you had a clean hand towel."

"Okay, thanks. Be right back," he says with amusement.

As he walks away, my eyes shamelessly gravitate to his firm ass. It's nice. *Very* nice. I remember him telling me he likes to golf and he definitely has the body of a fit golfer, with his defined arms and not an ounce of fat on him. I'm not ashamed to admit that I'm still very attracted to him.

My deteriorating thoughts are soon interrupted by his return.

"So where are we going exactly?" he asks.

"You'll see..." My eyes flicker playfully at him.

As we make our way to Mark's truck, he swiftly runs ahead to open the door for me. It's very chivalrous and sweet.

Once inside, he turns to me, his expression now more serious. "Before we go, I just wanted to thank you."

"Thank me? For what?" I ask.

"For agreeing to see me today when you could have just as easily refused. I don't want to presume, but maybe you'll even find a way to forgive me one day."

I don't know quite how to respond and I really don't feel like discussing this right now. "Maybe we can talk more about this another time, but not today. Today is our 'fun' day, okay?"

He nods. "Okay, of course."

"But Mark?"

"Yes?"

"Thank you, too."

"Me? Why?"

"Because, oddly enough, your apology turned out to be just what I needed to finally gain closure. I didn't realize just how unfinished it all was until you showed up."

He nods, then looks at me, clearly wanting to say something more.

"What is it?" I ask.

"Nothing, I just"—he pauses—"I just wanted to say that you look very pretty today. I didn't get a chance to tell you earlier. But you do...look pretty I mean."

"Oh, thank you." I feel butterflies begin to flutter inside me. He's being awfully serious and is clearly holding back, and I need to intervene. "So, I'm just curious," I say, "what did you do with the real Mark? I kinda liked that guy. Did you throw him off a bridge or something?"

His whole face relaxes and he even laughs. "What do you mean?"

"You're so serious. How about if you just relax and be yourself. That's the guy I want to spend the day with."

"I just want to make sure I'm being respectful towards you. I don't want you to regret agreeing to go out with me today," he jokes.

I smile, appreciative that he's being so considerate, but it's not necessary. "I see...Well then let me put your mind at ease. But please, don't let this go to your head, okay?"

He looks over at me curiously.

"When we first met, one of the things I really liked about you was that you weren't afraid to say exactly what you were thinking," I explain. "Not everyone has the self-awareness and confidence to do that and I really like that about you. It's not disrespectful—at least I don't see it that way. You're just honest. I'll take honest any day."

His whole demeanor shifts and I can see any stress he was carrying begin to fall away.

He rotates his entire body to face me. "Well, then in

that case, I'd like to say what I've wanted to say from the moment I saw you last Sunday. You aren't just pretty, you're beautiful. I forgot how beautiful you were until I saw you again. Took my breath away, honestly."

My breath hitches and I feel myself starting to blush, and when I blush, there's no hiding it. Even my neck gets red and then freckles miraculously appear all over the bridge of my nose and cheeks—kind of like what happens when you use one of those invisible pens to uncover a hidden image. I've always disliked my freckles.

Mark is concentrating on me, as if he's trying to interpret my expression, which is making me even more self-conscious. Then, as if he's arrived at a conclusion, he leans in and kisses me on the cheek. When he pulls back, his eyes seek direction from me. But I don't speak. I can't. I'm a blushing mess.

His eyes are twinkling at me with amusement. "There was a freckle on your cheek that looked a little lonely so I thought maybe it needed a kiss."

"What?" I say, giggling, as I feel a second round of blushing coming on. "Mark Jansen, I think you're losing it."

"Maybe so."

He begins driving and when I glance over at him, I notice his lips are curved up slightly into a tiny smile. And his lips, well, they're fabulous too.

Chapter Ten

~ Mark ~

Two Years Earlier

As I putter around the golf pro shop waiting for the rest of my foursome to arrive, my mind invariably wanders to thoughts of Sharon. Ever since I left her last night, I haven't been able to think about anything but her and our night together at the cliff. It's going to be a very long day until four o'clock rolls around. That's when her shift at the restaurant ends and I can see her again.

Last night was incredible on every level. And the sex...well...it was phenomenal. Usually I feel pressured to be the one to initiate sex with a woman, but with her, it felt like a very mutual pursuit. She was right there with me the entire time and then she took charge in a way I've never experienced before. When she told me to lean back and unzip my pants, it was fucking hot as hell. If she wasn't working today, I probably would have been at her doorstep at the crack of dawn blasting some '90s tune on a boombox. *Pitiful, I know.*

Somehow I manage to redirect my brain long enough to play nine holes with some friends from high school, but I feel like all I'm doing is counting the minutes until I can see Sharon again.

"Nice shot, Jansen," my friend Sam says with a fist bump.

I'm definitely having a great golf day. I wonder if Sharon golfs. If she doesn't, I'd love to teach her. Something tells me she'd be a quick study and is probably a fierce competitor.

"Mark, are you even listening?" Sam asks, interrupting my Sharon trance.

"Sorry, I just have work on my mind," I lie.

After effortlessly making my next putt, my mind naturally drifts to that incredibly sexy outfit Sharon was wearing last night. Her body is stunning.

By the ninth hole, I am desperate to get off the course and beg off rather than stay for drinks like I usually do. I just want to get back so I can shower and get ready to meet Sharon at the restaurant.

I'm not usually insecure with women but there's something about Sharon that has me nervous. Is it because I think I might want more from her than just a casual fling? Maybe. But is that what she wants?

I put on a new shirt and my favorite pair of shorts and head over to the restaurant. I'm a little early, so I take a seat in the lobby and wait for four o'clock to roll around. Every time someone walks by I look up from my phone, but it's always a false alarm. She must be in the back bartending.

At about ten of, a guy saunters in and asks the hostess if Sharon is in, which obviously catches my immediate attention. He says he's there to surprise her. The guy looks to be about my age, he's in great shape, very confident, and something about this isn't sitting well with me at all. But before I can draw any firm conclusions, Sharon comes out and the second she sees the guy, a huge smile spreads across her face and she rushes into his arms.

All I can hear is their laughter, nothing else.

Fuck.

Why am I even surprised? Of course she has a boyfriend. Women as beautiful and sweet as her always do and this looks like the serious kind. She looks so damn happy too. A wave of disappointment floods me and all I know is that I need to get out of here before she sees me. As soon as her back is to me, I quickly exit.

Once outside, I feel myself seizing up with emotion. It feels like I've had the wind knocked out of me. I liked her a lot. I really did.

I get into my truck and then I just sit there, in shock, trying to understand what the fuck just happened. I feel like such a fool for thinking this was more than it was. I should have known better than to get my hopes up this time. She's gorgeous and sweet and sexy and any guy would kill to have her in his life. She's that special.

I've had my share of meaningless flings and I know the difference between lust and emotional intimacy. I definitely felt the latter with her last night. And I thought she did too. But even if she did, she clearly has serious feelings for another guy and I can't—and won't —compete with that. I'm just the guy she cheated with, nothing more.

I try like hell to will the sadness and disappointment from my heart. I know we just met, but somehow it felt like we'd known each other a lot longer than that. It felt different with her. At least I thought it did.

The only way that I know of eradicating this kind of pain is to drive all thoughts of this woman completely out of me. She can't live in my mind or I won't be able to get past this.

And this is exactly why I don't let people get too close to me. Because of this unbearable sadness that feels like it's burying me alive.

Chapter Eleven

~ *Sharon* ~

Present Day

"At some point, you're going to have to tell me where we're going," Mark says.

"You'll see..." I confess I'm enjoying withholding information from him just a little.

When we finally reach the end of a narrow, bumpy dirt road, my phone app announces that we've arrived at our destination. Mark looks thoroughly confused, which is to be expected.

"Where are we?" he asks as he helps me out of the truck.

"A goat farm!"

"There's such a thing as a goat farm?"

"Of course there is. Where do you think you get goat milk?"

"*I* don't get goat milk anywhere and I'd like to keep it that way."

"Well you've had goat cheese, haven't you?"

He nods. "So we're going to watch how goat cheese is made on our first date?"

A thrill runs through me at his reference to this being a "date."

"It's much more exciting than that," I say as we walk towards a red barn with several outdoor pens.

As we enter the barn, a woman greets us enthusiastically from behind a small desk. "Well hello, folks! How can we help you today?"

"Hi! I called yesterday and made a reservation for the baby goat party," I say.

Mark shoots me a look like he thinks I'm nuts.

"Oh, yes, McAdams, is it?" The woman looks to Mark for confirmation but he just looks dumbfounded.

"Yes, that's us," I cheerfully confirm.

"Great! Let me go get you some feed and then I can show you to the doelings and bucklings!"

Once the woman leaves, Mark turns to me. "Feed?"

I grin. "For the doelings and—"

"—bucklings, I got it."

I grin.

He shakes his head with amusement. "If this goat party is anything like Coachella, I'm out."

I giggle. "Oh come on, it'll be fun. I've always wanted to do this."

The woman soon reappears with two buckets of feed. "Okay, here you go." She hands us each a bucket. "Just head over to the big oak by the barn and I'll go let them out."

"Wait, they don't stay in their spot—I mean pen—if that's what it's called?" Mark asks her.

"No, they roam freely and you can feed them and play with them. They're a lot of fun. You'll see."

The woman shoots me an amused look after seeing Mark's discomfort. I take his hand in mine and lead him to an area under the tree where we sit and wait.

"Maybe I should have gotten to know you a little bit better before giving you decision making authority over our first, and maybe last, date," he jokes.

"Have a little faith in me!"

He leans back against the tree, studying me quietly.

"You're very complicated," he finally says with a curious fascination in his eyes. "I've clearly underestimated you."

I give a devilish grin. "You definitely have."

He now turns his attention to what I'm wearing. "You know, if it was just the two of us here, I'd have that sweatshirt off of you faster than you can say *goat-tastic*."

I muffle a laugh. "Hmmm..."

"Yes, exactly...hmmm..." He raises and lowers his eyebrows flirtatiously and we both start to laugh.

Just then, the woman returns, followed by several romping baby goats. Before we're even prepared for what's to follow, the goats rush us and we're suddenly flat on our backs with goats all over us. They're everywhere! I can't get up no matter how hard I try and I can't remember the last time I've laughed this hard. Mark finally manages to sit up just as a goat tries to climb up his back like it's a ramp.

"Hey, dude! I'm not a jungle gym!" he playfully scolds the goat as he lifts him or her off of him.

Meanwhile, a goat is now attempting to sit on my head.

"Listen, bud, if anybody's going to be doing that kind of thing, it's going to be me," Mark kids, gently nudging the goat off of me.

I try to sit up, but these goats are tenacious.

"Elmer, get off this nice lady," the woman intervenes. The goat promptly gets off of me and I finally sit up, my hair in complete disarray.

As Mark meets my eyes, we both burst out laughing.

"I think these goats are very intelligent," he says. "Look at that one over there trying to tip over the bucket of feed!"

"Juno, where are your manners?" The woman promptly redirects Juno elsewhere.

I take a smaller goat in my arms and it soon calms down and closes its eyes. "Awww...he's so adorable!" I say.

Meanwhile, Mark is now hand feeding several goats who have surrounded him. I can tell he's enjoying this, which is exactly what I wanted: an opportunity to clear our minds and have fun.

After spending about a half an hour with the goats, they're led back into the barn. We soon head back to the parking lot and I notice a definite pep in Mark's step.

"Those goats are crazy. I think they would benefit from some CBD," he quips.

"Oh you loved them, I can tell."

He shakes his head but is grinning the entire time. "Actually, I did like the *goat-tivity* scene next to the barn. But I'm not sure my pastor would find it nearly as amusing."

I stifle a laugh. "My personal favorite was the *goat-el* with the goats in the hotel lobby drinking coffee."

"Goats and caffeine should never mix," he jokes. "That should be a law if it's not already."

I notice that he still has some hay in those dirty blonde waves of his and watch him as he rakes his fingers through his hair, trying to remove the loose straws. My mind instantly recalls how soft those waves felt the night we were together and I inwardly sigh.

Once we get back into Mark's truck, he looks over at me and begins to chuckle.

"What is it?" I ask.

"There's some hay in your hair and it's sticking

straight up," he says. "Here, let me get it out for you."

As he leans in, I feel an unmistakable rush of attraction for him. My face is dangerously close to his neck as he carefully pulls a few straws of hay from my hair. The gentleness with which he performs this task is actually very sensual and the closer he is to me, the harder it is for me to remain still. He smells so good and it brings me right back to the night we were together.

"One last piece," he says before locking eyes with mine. "All set."

Oh, I'm definitely not all set. I want him—very badly —and I'm having trouble looking away from his eyes which seem to change color in different light. Right now they resemble a deep blue sky.

Our faces remain within inches of each other and neither of us is pulling away. It's a veritable standoff. This is so unlike the Mark I knew. He's so restrained. I find myself licking my lips nervously and he looks at them, and then me, with curiosity. He swallows hard but just as I think he's going to try something, he doesn't.

"Are you okay?" he finally asks.

I'm at a complete loss for words and blurt out my last thought. "You have very long eyelashes."

He smiles. "Really? No one's ever told me that before."

"Oh." I'm now feeling very embarrassed and quickly change the subject. "This was so much fun today."

"Yeah, I had a great time. Thanks for planning it."

"I've always wanted to do this but could never find anyone willing to come with me."

"Well, any time you get the urge to play with goats— or any farm animals really—you just give me a call." He gives me a wink and I feel myself weakening. This is the Mark I fell for.

"Can I ask you something?" I say.

"You can ask me as many things as you like."

I brace myself because his answer may sting. "There's something that's never made sense to me."

"Okay..."

"Why didn't you come back to meet me at the restaurant the day after we...you know...were together, like we'd planned?"

He looks at me hesitantly.

"I just need to understand why," I add. "Did you change your mind or something?"

He immediately shakes his head. "No, absolutely not." He hesitates and then reluctantly adds, "I did come back."

"You did?"

He takes a deep breath before continuing. "Yes. I got there a little early so I waited in the lobby for your shift to be over. But then—" He stops himself and looks at me hesitantly again.

"What?"

"While I was waiting, this guy came in asking for you. He said he wanted to surprise you and when you came out, you looked really happy to see him. So I figured it must have been serious between the two of you and I left."

My mouth drops open. *What guy?* I haven't had a steady boyfriend since college and I have no idea who he's talking about. As I try to remember that day, I can see that Mark is perplexed by my lack of a response.

And then I remember something. "Wait a minute, was that Memorial Day weekend?"

He nods. "Yeah, actually it was. I was in town for the long weekend. Why?"

I grin with relief. "Because that was the weekend my brother, Dan, came to visit! He's in the military and that was the weekend he surprised my mom and me. The guy you saw me with wasn't my boyfriend, it was my brother!"

Mark's eyes widen. "Seriously? That was your brother?!"

"Yes! That was my pain-in-the-ass brother! And all this time I thought you stood me up!"

"No, I never would have stood you up," he insists. "I really liked you and I was looking forward to seeing you again. The whole thing really bummed me out actually." He shakes his head, still in disbelief at our misfortune.

"Ugh. I'm so sorry," I say regretfully. "I liked you a lot too. That's why I could never understand why you didn't show up that day."

He runs his hands through his hair with frustration. "Wow, I really messed things up, didn't I. I'm such an idiot."

"No, you're not an idiot at all. I bet I was jumping up and down like a crazy person when I saw my brother, too, because I hadn't seen him in almost a year. I would have reached the same conclusion if I'd been in your shoes. I'm so sorry."

"Please don't apologize. You didn't do anything wrong. It's my fault."

I can see he's upset and I instinctively lean in to hug him. His arms remain stiff at first but he eventually reciprocates and my head finds a home on his chest. I gently caress his back.

"Mark," I say softly into his warm chest, "knowing

you came back for me makes me feel so much better."

He swallows hard. "Of course I came back for you." There is a quiet gentleness in his voice as he lightly strokes the back of my head.

Suddenly all of the hurt and rejection I'd felt back then rises to the surface, followed by immense relief. I squeeze him tighter and we embrace in silence. When we finally separate, I meet his eyes which are warm but still remorseful.

"I think I understand now why you reacted the way that you did when I told you I was pregnant."

His eyebrows raise. "You do? I'm glad one of us does."

"Yes, here we'd had this amazing night together and then the very next day you see me running into the arms of another guy. How could you ever trust me after that? And we barely knew each other so of course you would have been suspicious when I called you about the pregnancy. It makes perfect sense."

"I appreciate you trying to make me feel better," he says, "but don't. There's no excuse for what I did. Regardless of whether I was upset or not, that didn't justify how I acted. If I didn't believe you, for whatever reason, I still should have heard you out. But instead I acted like a complete asshole and wouldn't listen to a thing you had to say, and I'm sure I made you feel horrible, and very alone. I will never forgive myself for doing that to you."

I won't let him beat himself up this way.

"Okay, look, could you have handled things better? Yes. But you're human and you did the best you could. I know that now."

"No, I could have done a whole lot better."

"Would it make you feel better if I said you were an

asshole?"

"Don't joke about this," he says in protest. "I'm trying to take responsibility for my actions."

Alarm bells suddenly go off inside me. "Wait a minute, is that why you're here? Because you feel GUILTY? Because I certainly don't need you viewing me as your pity case. If that's what this is, then please just take me home now." I can feel the heat and resentment rising in me as my protective walls go up.

His eyes widen. "***What?*** No, that's not it at all! Yes, I do feel terrible for what I did to you—I do—okay? But that's not why I'm here. I'm here because I like you. You aren't anyone's pity case and I know you don't need anything from me. It's actually the opposite. I need *you*."

There is an angst in his voice that makes me believe him. All of my emotions are suddenly going haywire, and then, without any warning at all, I start to cry.

"I'm so sorry," he says, frantically looking for tissues in the car. "I didn't mean to upset you, I—"

But I swiftly interrupt him. "No, you didn't do anything wrong," I say in between my tears. "What you said was really really sweet. Thank you." I lean in and wrap my arms tightly around his middle so that there's no mistaking my affection for him. He instantly reciprocates, securing me in his caring arms.

After a minute or two, I feel him exhale and he finally seems to relax a little, his lips lingering on the top of my head. My face remains pressed to the front of his shirt, now damp from my tears, but I don't want to leave his arms. They're so warm and comforting.

"Are you okay?" he finally asks as he pulls back, gently brushing away my remaining tears with his thumb.

I stare into his eyes and nod. "Sorry about your shirt." I use a tissue and give a light laugh. "I guess I just needed to cry. It's a lot to process, you know?"

He nods and I notice that his eyes look like they're misting, but he quickly sniffles away any forming tears, like he's an expert at such things. But my eyes don't let go of his and that's when I see a deeper anxiety in them. This isn't just about his guilt over how he treated me, or even about the pregnancy. All I know is that I care about him and if there's something I can do to help him, I'm going to do it.

I touch his cheek for a moment but then he abruptly withdraws from me. I don't know him well enough to understand what he might be feeling but I know how I'm feeling.

So I reach for his hands. "Mark, I want you to know something."

His eyes are fixed on mine and I see renewed worry in them.

"I want you to know that I forgive you—for everything," I say.

He starts to protest but I press my fingers to his lips to stop him.

"No, just listen. Bad things happen sometimes and no one is perfect. But you weren't trying to hurt me and I wasn't trying to hurt you. We know that now. So I forgive you. And when I forgive someone, I really do forgive and forget. It's a blessing actually."

He nods tentatively.

"I also want you to know how sorry I am that we never got the chance to get to know each other because I felt like there was something really good happening between us."

"Me too," he quickly interjects.

I smile at the immediacy of his response. "And I also need you to know that what we did the night we were together wasn't something I've ever done before. I've never slept with someone I barely knew. I'm not like that."

"Understood."

"I was just extremely drawn to you that night, and for some reason I didn't fight it. Something felt very different with you. Different good, not different bad."

His eyes are fixed on mine and I suddenly get this oddly familiar feeling, like he's someone I've known for a very long time.

"Definitely different good," he says with a shy grin, his confidence starting to peek through. His fingers form a delicate trail up my arm, causing my insides to rejoice and I think he senses it.

"So is it my turn yet?" he asks.

My mouth curves upwards. "Yes."

"Okay, well I'm not very good at this so you'll have to just bear with me." He pauses. "Like you said, something felt very different between us that night. I felt a connection with you almost from the second we met. I remember your smile—and your eyes. You smile with your eyes, you know."

I give a tiny smile and this causes him to smile too.

"One of the things I really admired about you was how comfortable you were, and still are, in your own skin," he continues. "You're always so unapologetically yourself. It's so refreshing. Anyway, I guess what I'm trying to say is that I like you and if you'd be willing to give me another chance, I'd really like to see you again —like date you I mean." He gauges my reaction before continuing. "But I don't have the best track record when it comes to dating, so you'd have to be our navigator."

His sweet, hopeful eyes are melting my heart.

"Everyone does say I have an excellent sense of direction," I joke. "I won't let you down, I promise."

He breathes out with relief. "So then that's a *Yes*? You'll go out with me again?"

"Yes, I will go out with you again."

We smile eagerly at one another and then, without warning, our lips spontaneously take over. He wraps me up in his arms as we consume one another. It's hard to describe but it kind of feels like I'm on a free-fall in some kind of heavenly abyss. Pleasure is swirling around in my head and his kisses are making me weak. We gasp for air, not wanting to part our lips for even a second. It's the most intense kissing I've ever experienced.

"Your lips," I say incoherently, "I love your lips."

He smiles, but not for long, because we're too absorbed in kissing. He finally pulls back, but only to ask if we can go back to my place.

I pause to focus. "I don't think that's a good idea right now. You understand, right?"

"I'm not sure."

I touch the side of his face reassuringly. "It's not that I don't want to, but I think we should wait. Let's not rush this, okay?"

He looks uncertain but accepting. "Okay, I want you to be comfortable, and I'm sorry, I'm just so attracted to everything about you. But you're right. I can take you home."

"Don't apologize for wanting more. I want more too in case you couldn't tell." My eyes lock with his and I smile. "Don't worry."

His eyes are all I can see in this moment. They're trusting and hopeful. He slowly leans in for an embrace and I sense his need for me, but it doesn't feel sexual, it feels emotional. I wish we could make love, but I know that giving in to our desires right now would be a huge mistake. We need to give our hearts and minds time to catch up.

We finally release our hold on one another and begin the drive home.

He glances over at me with a shy twinkle in his eyes. "You have no idea how glad I am that the guy I saw you with was your brother and not your boyfriend."

"Nope, it was just Dan, whose ass I will be kicking the next time I see him. He has the absolute worst fucking timing in the universe."

I roll my eyes and we both laugh.

As we drive, his hand finds mine and I feel myself smiling from ear to ear. I glance Mark's way and he's smiling too.

Everything is going to be just fine.

Chapter Twelve

~ Mark ~

Present Day

I woke up at the crack of dawn, and ever since then, I've just been laying in bed replaying yesterday's date with Sharon, hoping—praying—that she felt the same emotional connection that I felt. This is exactly how I felt after we spent the night together two years ago. It's this overpowering, almost desperate, yearning for her, like nothing I've ever felt for anyone before. Just her.

I think she felt it. I hope she did.

We made breakfast plans for today and it's finally 7:30 a.m., so hopefully it's not too early to text her.

Me: **Good morning**

No response. She did say she likes to sleep in. I'm just so eager to see her again and am clearly having difficulty exerting any self-restraint whatsoever where she's concerned. I still know so little about her and I want to know all of her.

At about eight o'clock, she finally texts back.

Sharon: **Good morning :) Sorry, I just woke up**

Me: **I bet you look gorgeous in the morning**

Sharon: **Haha. I doubt that**

Me: **What do you sleep in?**

Sharon: **A bed**

Me: **Very funny. I mean what do you wear to bed?**

Sharon: **Usually a T-shirt**

Me: **I like it...Underwear?**

Sharon: **Depends**

Me: **As in undergarments? :)**

Sharon: **No!**

Me: **So are you wearing any underwear now?**

Sharon: **Let me check.
Nope**

Me: **Fuck, can I please come over?**

Sharon: **Not a good idea**

She's right, I know she is. But damnit, I want her, and it only took two seconds for the image of her in bed without any underwear on to make me hard as a rock.

Me: **Ok I'll stop.
So when can you be ready for breakfast?**

Sharon: **In about an hour?**

Me: **Ok I'll pick you up then.
Going to take an ice cold shower now...**

Sharon: **Going to take a long hot shower now...
with lots of shower gel**

Me: **That was just mean**

Sharon: **:) See you in a few**

I know I'm coming on a little strong, but I want her to know I'm serious about her. And she seems completely unfazed by my directness. I just need to not blow this up like every other quasi-relationship I've been in. That's the old me.

I take an uncharacteristically quick but highly productive shower and am dressed and out the door within half an hour. Knowing how much she loves showers, I stop to buy her some shower gel on my way to her place. Maybe someday we'll put it to good use, if I'm lucky.

After climbing the exterior flight of stairs to her apartment, I'm mid-knock when the door swings open and there's a guy standing before me.

Who the fuck is this?

"Hi! You must be Mark," the guy says with a smug grin.

I need to calm down. I'm speechless and all that comes out of my mouth is "Yup."

"Your guest has arrived," the guy sings out while never taking his eyes off of me. "And he comes bearing gifts!"

I hear Sharon's voice coming towards us and she soon appears at the front door, smiling brightly when she sees me and looking nothing short of enchanting in a sleeveless floral sun dress. I try not to stare but I'm so attracted to everything about her and can't take my eyes off of her. Her hair is cascading down her bare shoulders and I immediately and vividly recall the last time I saw those shoulders two years ago. Her voice snaps me out of my flashback.

"So I see you've met my brother, Dan," she says, attempting to convey an apology with her eyes.

I knew I recognized his face. Yup, this is the same guy who came to the restaurant two years ago and unknowingly fucked up my life. I can't say I'm a big fan at this point.

"It's nice to meet you," I eke out as pleasantly as I can, extending my hand out to him. "Sharon's told me a lot about you."

"Oh she has, has she." Dan smirks and raises an eyebrow at his sister.

"Come on in," Sharon hurriedly interrupts, as if trying to save me from her brother. As she ushers me into her apartment, she whispers, "Sorry, he just stopped by."

"I heard that!" Dan bellows from behind us.

Sharon turns and shoots him an admonishing look and then we all take a seat in the living room.

"So Mark, how did you two meet exactly?" Dan asks, but then immediately holds his hand up to stop me. "Wait, let me guess, the restaurant, right?"

I'm already sick of this guy.

"That's right." I meet his eyes and don't look away.

"And how long have you been dating?"

Sharon interrupts. "What's with all the questions, Dan? Cool it."

This seems to be sufficient rebuff for now and Dan leans back in his chair, eyeing me closely.

"So what are we having for breakfast, sis?"

"Well, **we** were planning on going out," she says, motioning to me.

"What? And pass up your incredible omelets?" Dan now turns to me with an amused gleam in his eye. "You know, she makes the most amazing omelets. Have you had them yet?"

"Can't say that I have. But I do love omelets...a lot, and I'm sure hers are the best." I meet her eyes and notice her face begin to flush with embarrassment. *So fucking cute.*

"Well that just won't do," Dan says. "You need to try them. Why don't we just eat here?"

Sharon looks over at me for direction.

"Whatever you want is fine with me," I assure her.

"Well, okay then," she says a little tentatively at first. But then I see an unmistakable excitement in her expression as she hops up to go to the kitchen.

The moment she leaves, Dan is back at it again, but that's okay. This overprotective brother thing is to be expected. If I had a sister, I'd be ten times worse.

Dan studies me for a moment. "So what's your story?"

"Story?"

"You know, everyone has a story."

"Do you want the unabridged edition or the Cliff Notes version?"

He shrugs. "You decide."

"Let's see, I grew up here in Shelby Falls, then I went to college and law school in Boston, and now I practice law there."

"Those are just facts, that's not your story. But that's okay, I get the gist. How did you and Fin meet?"

"Fin?"

Dan's eyes suddenly widen with alarm. "Fuck," he says. "She's gonna kill me."

"Who is?"

"My sister," he says, gesturing to the kitchen. "Fin."

Sharon pops her head out. "Yes?"

Now I'm totally confused. Until it clicks.

Her eyes quickly dart to mine as she now realizes her mistake.

"Hello Fin." I grin.

She groans. "Well thanks a lot, Dan. You spoiled all my fun!"

"Well you answered me!" Dan replies as she gives him the finger and returns to the kitchen, shaking her head with annoyance.

I smile at Dan. "Fin, huh? Never would have guessed that name."

"Yeah, well Finola actually. But we call her Fin for short...or Phineas if I really want to annoy her."

"Sharon's her middle name though, right?" I want to confirm that at least that part was true.

"Yeah, she doesn't like to use her real name at the restaurant. Some guys can be real hound dogs if you know what I mean."

I nod. Makes sense. Smart.

"So how long have you been dating my sister? She's never mentioned you before."

"Technically only about twenty-four hours."

"Seriously?"

"Well, we met about two years ago, but yeah, yesterday was our first real date."

"So you guys have known each other for two years?"

"Well, not exactly. Maybe I'll let Sharon—I mean Fin —explain."

At that moment, Fin returns with two plates and asks us to come to the table. She peaks inside one of the omelets and places it in front of me, then places the other one in front of Dan.

"Bon appetit!" She gives me a wink and returns to the kitchen.

"She likes to surprise us with the fillings," Dan says. He lifts his up cautiously, trying to see what's inside. "One time she filled mine with peanut butter. It was terrible."

"That's because I didn't use the smooth kind!" she yells from the kitchen. "I only had crunchy!"

"She also has freakishly good hearing," Dan whispers.

"I heard that!" She peeks her head out from the kitchen. "Wait for me before you dive in. My omelet is almost done. I want to see your reactions."

Dan mouths, "Just say you like it. It's easier that way."

She returns with her omelet and takes a seat, looking at me expectantly. "Go ahead, try it."

I take a tentative bite and my taste buds applaud. "This is delicious! What's in it?"

"Cream cheese and salsa," she declares proudly.

I stop chewing. This woman is either a mind reader or my soulmate. "How did you know I like that combination?"

"I didn't. I made it up. So you like it?"

"No...I *love* it." Definitely my soulmate.

As her face flushes with pride, the only conclusion that I can draw is that she is the cutest human being I've ever laid eyes on.

She starts to eat, happily humming the theme song to *Phineas and Ferb*. And yes, as if there was any doubt, I loved that show.

Breakfast with Dan ends up going really well. He's in the military and is stationed in San Diego, but he's in town for the next few weeks, and we end up having a great conversation about his cybersecurity work for the military. I'm very relieved that he seems to be warming up to me. I'm also relieved that he doesn't seem to know who I am.

When we're finished with breakfast, I help Fin with the dishes and Dan leaves soon after. The moment the door closes behind him, Fin launches into an apology.

"I'm so sorry my brother crashed our date like that. That's kind of his thing, as you know from personal experience unfortunately." She takes a seat next to me on the couch.

"It's okay, I'm glad I got to meet him. He's a nice guy and I like his sarcastic sense of humor."

"He's a great brother. A little overprotective at times, but he really is my best friend. He liked meeting you, too."

"So I take it he doesn't know I'm the guy who stood you up at the restaurant?"

"No—and he doesn't know about the pregnancy either—so please don't ever let that slip." A hint of worry comes over her face.

I nod and can feel the heat rising in my face. Any discussion of the pregnancy is clearly still very triggering—for both of us—and I quickly pivot away.

"So do you have time to hang out a little longer today, or do you have to study? Your exam is this week, isn't it?"

"Yes, but if I'm not ready by now, I'll never be. I'll do a little more studying later, but we can still hang out for a little while longer if you'd like. What would you like to do?"

I smile. "I have thoughts, but they wouldn't meet with your approval. Well, actually, maybe they would meet with Sharon's approval, but not with Finola's. Speaking of which, I'm not sure what to call you. I'm kind of confused at this point."

She giggles. "You can call me whatever you'd like."

"I like *Fin*. It suits you. But maybe I'll still call you *Sharon* when we're in bed together." I grin.

"Don't you mean *if* we're in bed together?"

"Oh, it's happening."

"Well, you're awfully sure of yourself, aren't you. We shall just have to see." She taps me playfully on my nose. "But anyway, back to what we should do today. You have me very curious. What are these thoughts of yours that you think I won't approve of?"

I shake my head, actually feeling a little embarrassed. "Nope, those thoughts are private. Today I just want to spend more time with you."

She nods and then there's that smile of hers. Gets me every time. Without thinking about my next move, I instinctively put my arm around her. She seems to welcome it and subtly moves in a little closer to me. I am now acutely aware that my hand is touching her bare shoulder and it takes every bit of willpower not to run my fingers along her baby soft skin. But I need to honor her wishes and take things slowly, as much as it's going to kill me. Plus, I really do want to get to know her better.

"So, how long have you lived in Shelby Falls?" I ask.

"Since I was about five. My mom moved here for work. How about you?"

"I moved to Shelby Falls when I was seven." I now

feel myself starting to panic because I know where this conversation could lead, if I allow it to.

"So you've lived here a long time. Why did your parents move here?"

My heart starts to race. "I...well, my coming here wasn't planned. There was...an accident, and I had to come here to live with my aunt and uncle."

Fin immediately sits up, her concerned eyes now squarely meeting mine. "I had no idea. I'm very sorry. We don't have to talk about this if you don't want to."

But there's something in her eyes that's so warm and genuine that I want to share more with her. I trust her.

"It's okay. It's just not something I talk about a lot. Well, really at all. It happened a very long time ago." I pause, trying to figure out how to even say it. It's very hard.

She waits quietly for me to continue, resting her hand on my chest—on my heart actually.

"When I was seven, my parents were killed in a car accident. Some guy drove up the exit ramp on the highway and they all died instantly. I don't remember them very well. I mean, I have some vague memories, but that's all. My aunt and uncle took me in and raised me."

Fin tries to mask the devastation on her face as best as she can. "I'm so sorry."

"I don't really remember that period very well but my...aunt and uncle—I call them mom and dad now—they said it took me a long time to get over the loss and that in the beginning, I used to cry a lot, especially at night in my bedroom. They were wonderful to me, but as much as they loved me, and I of course love them too, it's not the same as having your own parents."

"You're right, it's not the same thing."

I feel the hair on the back of my neck stand up. "It's not, but wow, thank you for saying that. I think you're the only person who has ever actually validated my feelings about that. The therapists I went to as a kid always used to focus on the fact that my aunt and uncle loved me. They never really acknowledged how alone I was feeling without my parents. I'm sure they just didn't want me to dwell on what happened too much."

She nods. "I'm sure. But you suffered a terrible loss and it must have been overwhelming for you, especially given your age. Losing a parent is extremely traumatic at any age, but especially at that age. It's unthinkable. I know it happened a long time ago, but that kind of trauma stays with you always."

"It's always with me, yes."

Her caring eyes rest softly on mine and she reaches for my hand. She seems to really understand, maybe because her father wasn't a part of her life. Without saying a word, she leans in and wraps her arms around me and I hold her and close my eyes for a moment. It actually feels like her strength and energy are transferring to me, as though a void is being filled.

I haven't cried in decades but I think I'm about to now. Heated tears quietly fill my eyes and I know Fin knows. As I swallow hard, she holds me even tighter, never leaving my chest or looking up. I try not to make a sound as a few strong tears eventually fall. They feel cleansing and a feeling of tranquility soon follows. It reminds me of the quiet calm that follows a rain storm, just as the clouds are receding to make way for the sun.

I think Fin is my sun.

I pull back to look at her and when she lifts her eyes to meet mine, I see that tears have collected in her eyes too. I know those tears are for me and my heart swells for her.

"Thank you," I say. "Sorry I got so emotional. I never cry like that."

"Shhh…it's okay. Crying can be very cathartic."

"It felt good actually."

"Good."

As she gazes warmly up at me, I am completely overcome and can't help what I'm about to say.

"You are the most extraordinary person I've ever met, Fin."

"I'm not. You just don't know me that well."

"Oh, but you are. Trust me on this. It's strange, but I feel like I've known you my entire life. Maybe that's what it feels like when you have a strong connection with someone, I don't know. All I know is that I've been thinking about you all week."

Her soft gaze penetrates my eyes, and then my heart. "I've thought about you too." Her voice is the sweetest whisper.

I run my fingertips along her lips and she takes them and kisses each one. It's sensual and loving and her eyes never leave mine. Our faces inch towards each other and we share a passionate yet very gentle kiss. Her lips are soft and sweet, and my heart is booming. I just want to inhale her, merge my body with hers. But I pull back before I lose all ability to stop. This needs to be her choice. She's the navigator here.

"I'm sorry if I'm overwhelming you—I know this isn't how you saw today going and I can stop if you want me to."

"No, don't stop," she says softly.

I return to her lips and kiss her like I've never kissed

anyone before. Eagerly, desperately, urgently. And lovingly.

She pauses, her eyes conveying her desire. "Let's go to my bedroom."

I scoop her up in my arms and carry her to her bedroom. As I place her on her bed, she pulls me down on top of her and I can feel my pulse firing rapidly as we kiss. I've never felt this intensely about anyone and my emotions feel out of control. She soon moves on top of me—her body feeling like it was made just for me—and our mouths widen as our kisses grow even more needy.

I help lift off her shirt along with my own. My chain with my mom's horseshoe charm catches her attention briefly before she leans down and places her lips to my chest. My attraction for her is now full throttle and I feel like my heart is going to explode. We frantically remove the rest of our clothes and I watch her as she crawls back on top of me. She's so damn sexy and it feels so good having her nude body pressed against mine. I need her under me and roll on top, her soft purrs filling my ears as I kiss her neck. When I pause, I find her emerald green eyes smoldering with heat. Her legs widen and her eyes invite me inside.

I reach for my pants to retrieve a condom from my wallet.

"Let me," she offers.

I love her assertiveness and hand her the condom, rolling onto my back and watching her with weighty anticipation. But after several failed attempts at opening the condom wrapper, she finally gives up and rips it open with her teeth. "Finally!" she says.

I laugh at her exasperation. She's adorable and sexy...and mine.

Chapter Thirteen

~ *Fin* ~

Present Day

Just as I'm about to put the condom on Mark, he stops me.

"What's wrong?" I ask.

"Nothing." He carefully brushes a few loose strands of hair away from my face—a soft, contemplative look on his own. "You're very beautiful and I'm just enjoying the privilege of being able to look at you." His lust-filled eyes travel down to my breasts, then back up to my eyes. "You know, you're blushing," he says, drawing me down on top of him.

"You have that effect on me."

"Good. I like it when you blush. It means you like me."

"I do like you." My lips travel up his neck and to his ear and I whisper, "So are we going to do this or what?"

He laughs. "Yes, but you're making me nervous."

"Nervous? Why?"

"I don't know."

"We don't have to do this," I say, starting to roll off of him, but he immediately pulls me back.

"No, I want to. But I want you to know something first."

He definitely seems nervous and now it's making me nervous.

"I just want you to know that this isn't just sex for

me," he says. "I want our first time—well, our second time—but it kind of feels like our first time—to be special for us." He tucks a loose tendril of my hair behind my ear.

I study his expression. "Are you saying you think we should wait?"

He groans. "I don't know...maybe. I wish I wasn't right about this because, believe me, I want you in the worst way. But I'm willing to put my desire for you on hold until we're emotionally ready for this. What do you think?"

I lay back in bed to think for a moment.

He's right.

He watches me intently. "This is because I like you, Fin. That's why I think we should wait. Because Lord knows I want you." He glances down, then back up at me. "Exhibit A."

My eyes shift down to his still massive erection and when our eyes meet, I can't help but giggle just a little. "Well we can't have that, now can we?"

He chuckles. "I'll be fine."

"Are you sure? We can...do other things..."

"No, it's fine. How about if we just hang out and talk, if that's okay with you?"

"Okay."

I gather my bra and underwear and inadvertently let out a disappointed sigh as his gorgeous abs are once again covered by his shirt.

"You don't want to talk?" he says with a knowing grin as he pulls on his boxers.

"I do, I just, well, you know..."

He gives a commiserating smile and takes me in his arms, kissing me so sweetly. "We can wait. We're doing this for us."

"Us," I repeat as my heart fills with hope...and life.

The rest of the afternoon is absolutely glorious. We talk for hours in bed without a single lull. Every piece of information we learn about each other is fueling our attraction even more. But when I learn he's in a band, I regress to what I think is my thirteen year old self at a Backstreet Boys concert.

"So hold on, you're a drummer?!"

He grins at my reaction. "Yeah, I've played since high school. It's always been a great outlet for me."

"What kind of music do you play?!"

"Mostly rock."

"And what's the band's name?"

"In Transition."

"Cool name! I like it."

While he's trying to remain humble, the small smile on his face tells me he's very flattered and he happily continues. "We just play for fun in a few local bars in the Boston area. One of my bandmates has a few connections. It's really not a big deal."

"It *is* a big deal! It's a *very* big deal! When do you play next?"

"I'm not sure. I'll ask Josh. He's our bass guitarist and he schedules our gigs."

"Well I'm definitely coming to see you the next time you play. I'm so excited!"

He laughs. "I can see that, but once you hear us play, you're going to be very underwhelmed. Like I said, we just do it for fun."

"I bet you're amazing." I lightly run my fingers along his arm. "As I recall, you have an innate sense of rhythm and timing." As my eyes dive into his, my hinting smile gives away my indecent thoughts.

He grins and pulls me tight against his body. "You're very cute, you know that? And you certainly know how to boost my ego. I think I'd like to keep you around if you don't mind."

"Okay, I'll stick around, but only because you're easy on the eyes...and..."

He raises his brows. "And what?"

"Never mind."

"Oh, no, no, no, you can't just dangle an 'and' like that and then not tell me."

"I absolutely can, and I just did." I grin.

"You are such a tease." With a flirty gleam in his eyes, he starts tickling me, soon learning just how insanely ticklish I am. I discover that his chest is his most ticklish spot and I don't let up on him. He lets me pin him down a few times and we play-wrestle until we're both worn out, flat on our backs, out of breath. When he turns to look at me, he begins to laugh.

"What?" I say with a giggle.

"Your hair...it's, well, how do I describe it..."

I jump up to look in the mirror and am truly horrified. "Yikes! Well that's a look. I imagine this is what it would look like if I stuck my finger in an electrical socket."

He laughs and pulls me back down on the bed with him. "You look gorgeous, wild hair and all." He gives me a slow, sensual kiss and final moan before beginning to get up.

"Where are you going?" I frown, tugging at his arm.

"Don't you need to study?"

"Yes." I sigh, slowly sitting up in defeat. "Stupid

exam…"

He smiles and pulls me up to stand. We dress and be-grudgingly make our way to the front door, in no rush to say goodbye.

He takes me by the waist and draws me to him. "This is probably going to sound crazy but I'm really going to miss you this week."

I look up at him more seriously. "Me too."

"But it's probably better I'm not here. You don't need me distracting you right before your exam."

"I suppose. It's just that now that I've had a concen-trated dose of you, this is going to really, really suck."

He smiles. "If I could stay, believe me I would. But I have an early morning meeting and I also need to take care of something before I leave town."

"Oh?"

"Just something I need to do. I'll tell you about it an-other time."

I get on my tiptoes to reach his beautiful lips and we share a lingering kiss goodbye.

He speaks in a low, sexy voice into my mouth. "You know you're driving me wild."

"I sure hope so," I whisper, brushing my lips against his.

He gives me one final delicious kiss.

"Text me when you get home, okay?" I say. "Just so I know you made it back safely."

"Sure thing—and Fin?"

"Yes?"

"Thank you. I promise I won't let you down this time." He brings my hand to his lips before our hands unwillingly part.

As I watch him return to his truck and drive away, I

find myself humming happily to myself. Studying will just have to wait. I need a shower—badly.

Chapter Fourteen

~ Mark ~

Present Day

It's about four o'clock when I pull up to a classic crafts-man style home located in a quiet neighborhood in Shelby Falls. The lawn is lush and the brick walkway is adorned with yellow rose bushes that are in full bloom. It's Matt Conroy's house—actually, it's Matt and Jenni-fer's house now that they're married.

I opted not to call first because I'm definitely not winning any popularity contests in the Conroy house-hold these days after the shit I pulled at Matt's cousin's wedding last weekend. After one too many Tequila shots, I made some very offensive comments to Jenni-fer, and then when she rightfully chastised me, I told her Matt got Fin pregnant. *I still can't believe what a fuck-ing jerk I was.* I don't know if they'll ever forgive me, but I need to try to make things right between us.

As soon as I ring the doorbell, Matt's dog Barnaby, a Wheaton Terrier, appears at the window and begins barking. I hear footsteps and then the front door flies open. When Matt sees me, there is immediate annoy-ance in his eyes. That's okay, at least it's not rage.

"Before you say anything, can we please just talk for a minute?" I implore.

Matt has every right to be pissed at me but I'm hop-ing he's calmed down by now. He usually does and he's generally a pretty reasonable guy.

But he still looks very irritated with me, and he also looks exhausted.

"Mark, now isn't a good time. Jennifer's trying to get the baby down."

"Wait, she had the baby already?" I had no idea.

"Your parents didn't tell you? Yeah, she went into labor last Sunday. Actually it was the same day that you and I talked at the diner."

"Wow, congratulations, man! I'm really happy for you! Is it a boy or a girl?"

Matt can't conceal his proud smile. "A girl. Olivia. We named her after Oliver." His expression immediately softens at the mention of his brother who passed away from cancer when Matt was young. Matt meets my eyes and I can see that he wants to share more but he's holding back.

"That's beautiful, Matt. I'm really happy for you."

"Thanks." Matt's demeanor hardens again. "Anyway, now isn't a good time to talk."

"I understand. Can we talk another time when it's more convenient?"

I hear Jennifer's voice approaching. "Who's at the door?" she asks. But before Matt has a chance to answer, she appears in the doorway and sees me. "Oh," she says flatly, her eyes immediately darting to Matt's.

As uncomfortable as this is, I need to push through and try to fix my mess.

"Hi Jenn. Congratulations. I'm really happy for the two of you."

"Thank you." Her tone remains cold.

They're not inviting me in, but they're also not slamming the door in my face, so I'm going to take that as a positive sign for the time being.

"Is Olivia napping?" Matt asks Jennifer.

"Yes, she just fell asleep. I think I need to close my eyes too, so maybe you could take Barnaby for a walk? I'm afraid he's going to start barking again and wake her."

"Sure, I think I left the leash in the kitchen," Matt says. "I'll go grab it."

Jennifer remains in the doorway with a blank look on her face. I break the silence.

"Jenn, I came by to apologize to you and Matt for my behavior last weekend. There's no excuse but I'd like to try to explain."

But before I can say anything more, our eyes dart to Barnaby who begins yelping when he spots Matt holding his leash. Jennifer quickly ushers all of us outside for fear the dog will wake up Olivia.

"Mark, can we do this another time?" Matt says curtly. "Jenn's exhausted."

"It's okay," Jennifer interjects. "I'd like to hear what he has to say."

I pause to collect my thoughts. By the skeptical look on their faces, I know I'm going to need to proceed with extreme caution.

"When I bumped into you that night, Jenn, I was in a really foul mood," I begin. "I tend to get bummed out at weddings even on a good day, but that night I was feeling particularly sorry for myself. And then I had way too much to drink on top of it. Not a good combination for me."

Jennifer is listening but doesn't respond, so I continue.

"This is probably going to sound pitiful but right before I saw you, I ran into a woman I dated a few years ago and found out she recently got married. We weren't even serious but something about it just really got to me. I don't know, sometimes it just feels like everyone is able to find 'the one 'except me. And then I saw you, and you were pregnant, and it all just kind of hit me between the eyes, and the alcohol certainly didn't help."

Jennifer's demeanor begins to soften slightly. "I used to feel that way too at weddings," she says, "like the whole world was getting married and having a family except me. But then last August, Matt contacted me from out of the blue and from that day on everything changed." She glances adoringly at Matt. "It'll change for you too, Mark, you'll see."

I've known Jennifer since our college years but hadn't seen her in several years, until last weekend at the wedding. She was always very easy to talk to and extremely kind to me. I recall having some great conversations with her about life in general, and my love life specifically, and she always knew just what to say to cheer me up. I'm grateful that she's still that same sweet person.

"I'm really happy for you guys," I say with a smile. "I always thought you two belonged together."

While Jennifer appears to be thawing, Matt remains guarded.

"I know I said some really inappropriate things to you, Jenn, which I can't even repeat, and I hope you know I wasn't serious about any of it. I'm so sorry."

"The thing is," Jennifer says, "I could chalk all of this up to you just being in a bad mood, or the alcohol, or you just being you, but—"

"That's the thing, Jenn—I'm sorry, I don't mean to interrupt you—but I'm really not that guy anymore."

"Mark, inappropriate comments are one thing, but what you said about Matt really crossed the line."

I nod. "You're absolutely right. There's no excuse for what I said about him. *None whatsoever.*"

"How could you **possibly** think Matt would **ever** get someone pregnant and then not do right by her?" Jennifer scolds.

Matt tries to short circuit the conversation but Jenn shakes her head. "No, I want to hear his response."

I cautiously proceed. "There are some things you don't know, things that led me to jump to the wrong conclusions. I knew none of it sounded at all like Matt— you need to know that—but my mind just leapt to these ridiculous conclusions. It's a long story, but basically, I was a complete idiot."

Jennifer scrutinizes my face. "Well, I do appreciate that you're owning up to your mistakes and trying to make things right."

"I want you both to know that once Matt told me what really happened with—" I stop myself because I can feel my emotions stirring. "I'm sorry, this is hard for me to say." I take a deep breath before continuing. "Once Matt told me the truth about Sharon's pregnancy, I immediately went to find her and I now realize I misunderstood some things that happened between the two of us. I made a huge mistake." My voice is starting to shake and I need to stop to let my emotions settle.

Jennifer and Matt's eyes meet and they seem to arrive at some kind of unspoken understanding.

"How about the two of you go take Barnaby for a walk," Jennifer suggests. "I really need to close my eyes." She gives a weary smile and says something into Matt's ear, to which he nods.

Matt then motions to follow him out the door with Barnaby.

"Thank you for hearing me out," I say as we reach the road and begin walking. "I'm not sure how to make this right, but I promise you I will."

"Don't thank me, thank Jennifer. She's the one who wants us to work things out. I think she knows that despite all of this, it would be kind of a shame to let one bad night tank our whole friendship."

Thank G-d for Jennifer.

"I couldn't agree more," I say. "I think we first met back in eighth grade in Mr. Klondike's chemistry class, didn't we?"

Matt chuckles to himself. "Yeah, I think so. Remember how we used to call him Klondike Kenny? He was a lousy teacher but we had a blast in that class."

"We really did. He had that greasy comb-over thing too," I say with a laugh. "Remember when we did that experiment with the soda and the bottle shot up to the ceiling and exploded all over his desk? He was so pissed at us!"

"Remember when we convinced him we were half brothers?"

We both laugh.

"Classic," I say.

As we reminisce, the weight of guilt I've been feeling all week begins to slowly lift. Matt finally seems to be lightening up a little.

"So anyway, you and Sharon talked?" Matt asks.

He isn't using her real name and I don't want to betray her confidence, so she'll be Sharon for now.

"Yes, we talked, and she told me how you helped pay for her doctor's appointments. That should have been me and I really can't express to you how much I appreciate everything you did. I'm so ashamed of how I treated her and I'm just so thankful you were there for her."

He nods. "So she told you everything?"

"Yes."

Matt and I exchange a stern look. He clearly knows about the miscarriage and I absolutely don't want to discuss it.

"The most amazing thing is that even after everything I did, she says she forgives me," I continue. "But that doesn't matter because I'll never be able to forgive myself. Never." I start to get choked up just thinking about what an incredibly generous and forgiving person Fin is.

"Well, I'm glad you guys worked things out," Matt says.

"She's incredible, Matt. Believe it or not, we actually went out on a date yesterday."

"Really?"

"Yeah, there's definitely something between us. Even when we met two years ago, I could feel it. And the more I get to know her, the more I like her. We spent this whole weekend together and had an amazing time just talking. When I'm with her, I feel like I can just be myself. It's scaring the shit out of me, but I really want this to work."

Matt looks a little taken aback but nonetheless happy for me. "Well you definitely sound very serious about her."

"I am."

"Well, try not to overthink it too much," Matt says. "Just be yourself. It seems to be working for you so far." He gives me an encouraging smile.

I exhale with relief. "Thanks, man."

"So, I take it Sharon told you her first name then?" Matt says, grinning.

"Oh, good, so you know. I didn't want to betray her confidence."

"She told me around the time that she was pregnant."

Renewed guilt stirs in me. "Right. Well, anyway, I really appreciate you hearing me out and I'm so sorry if I caused you and Jenn any stress. I promise you that I will never disrespect you or Jenn like that ever again."

He looks at me with cautious optimism. "As long as you don't pull anything like this again, I'd say we're good."

I'm so relieved and spontaneously pull him in for a hug. Tears begin to well up in my eyes—for the second time today. He really is like a brother to me and, just as brothers do, Matt and I always manage to come through for each other.

As we reach Matt's house, Barnaby begins pulling Matt up the driveway and we stop in front of my truck.

"I'm sorry we've been so out of touch this past year," I say. "I've been so wrapped up at work, but I'm determined to change that going forward."

"I'm sorry, too," Matt says. "I've also been preoccupied but that's no excuse. Let's definitely make an effort to get back on track."

I nod. "So are you guys going to the gala at the country club this weekend?"

"Oh, right, I forgot all about that. I doubt it because we don't want to leave Olivia with a sitter just yet."

"Right, well maybe I'll stop by over the weekend so I can meet the newest member of the Conroy clan."

"Sure, she can meet her new uncle." Matt's eyes shine with joy at just the mention of Olivia. "But I've got to warn you, she may be little but she's very feisty!"

I smile at both the thought of Matt as a father and the fact that I'm going to be an uncle.

Chapter Fifteen

~ *Fin* ~

Present Day

Just as I place my sushi down on the counter, my cell rings. I'm sure it's Mark because I just texted him to let him know I'm home from my exam.

"So how'd it go?" he asks eagerly.

"I think it went pretty well. Fingers and toes crossed."

"I'm sure you aced it. You studied your ass off."

"That's for sure. I should have the results by next week, so that's good. I hate waiting."

"Well, I'm really proud of you and I want to take you out to celebrate. Are you working this weekend?"

"No, not until Monday luckily."

"Good, then you have plans with me Saturday night. There's a fundraising gala at the country club and my mom is the chair of the planning committee. So will you be my date?"

I hesitate. "I'm not sure I'd fit in with that crowd. I don't even have an appropriate dress to wear."

"It's not that fancy. Just wear a dress and it'll be fine. It's a fun event. I go every year and I'll see to it that you have a good time. Plus they always have sushi as one of the hors d'oeuvres. That's your favorite, right?"

"Unlimited sushi?! Okay, you convinced me. And besides, it does sound like fun."

"Okay, great." I can hear him smiling through the

phone.

"So how was *your* day?" I ask.

"Good except for the fact that I really miss you. You do realize that you've turned me into a lovestruck suitor."

"Well just warn me if you decide to show up outside my window to serenade me with your drums."

He laughs. "Don't tempt me. I just might do it."

I giggle. "So when will you be back in town?"

"Not until Saturday afternoon unfortunately. I've got a meeting with a client that morning so I'll pick you up at about five-thirty on Saturday, okay?"

"Sure," I say, suppressing a yawn. "You know what, I'm pretty tired. I think I better eat and go to sleep."

"Okay, you go ahead. I'm glad the exam went well and I'll speak to you tomorrow."

"Okay, g'night."

"Good night, Fin."

* * *

Mark is picking me up for the gala in a few hours and I still haven't decided what dress to wear. I've never been to the Shelby Falls Country Club before but I'm assuming it's fairly conservative. I could wear a simple black dress but that's so boring. I have a shorter, strapless dress, but I think it's too short for this crowd. Then I remember that I have another dress that I've never worn before. It's a halter style in a burnt orange and falls just above the knee. I hope the color isn't too bold, but I really have nothing else dressy so the orange dress will just have to do.

After taking a relaxing shower, I shave my legs and break out the curling iron, creating soft loose waves. I take special care with my makeup, even using mascara and eye shadow which I rarely wear. After putting on the perfect lipstick shade to compliment my dress, I take a final look in the mirror. I must admit, I look very nice.

It's a little after five o'clock when I receive a text from Mark letting me know he's running late, which isn't like him. When he finally does arrive, his sports jacket is off, his sleeves are rolled up, and he looks aggravated. I don't even think he sees me as he walks through the door.

"What's wrong? Are you okay?" I ask as I usher him inside.

"I got a flat tire about a mile from here, so I had to call for a tow. But they're backed up, so I decided to leave the truck there and walk the rest of the way here."

"You should have called me!" I scold. "I could have picked you up."

I immediately get him a glass of water which he downs.

"It's really not that far," he insists. "It's just hot as hell out there today."

"Sit down," I say, getting him more water. "Why don't you take off your shirt and I'll iron it for you."

He glances down at his shirt, now realizing it's all creased. "It's okay, I can do it."

"No, you just relax. I'll take care of it."

He looks a little surprised by my offer as he removes his shirt, revealing a plain white undershirt. There's nothing particularly sexy about it—and yet it is. And that's because he's in it.

"I think I need to wash up before we go," he says. "I wasn't dressed for that kind of heat."

"Of course! Let me get you a face towel."

I go to the linen closet in the hallway and when I turn around, he's standing directly in front of me.

"I'm sorry," he says. "I got so distracted by the flat tire that I didn't even tell you how beautiful you look. That color is stunning on you."

I can feel a blush coming on. *Not again.*

"And I also forgot to kiss you hello," he adds, gently pressing his lips to mine.

"Hello," I whisper into his mouth, smiling.

"I missed you, Finny—a lot."

"I missed you, too, Mark with a 'k.'"

Our bodies align and it feels so good to be in his arms again. Sighs of satisfaction escape from our mouths.

"I'm really looking forward to tonight with you," he says. "Let me just go wash up so we're not late."

"Sure, and I'll get the iron."

I iron his shirt with more care than I've ever ironed anything in my life. It's silly but I feel like the shirt is a part of him. I take a whiff of the fabric and can smell his woodsy deodorant, which then leads to indecent thoughts.

My thoughts are soon interrupted by the man himself.

"Thanks for ironing my shirt," he says, putting it back on along with his tie. He looks so lawyerly and I don't think I'm hiding my lust very well.

As if reading my thoughts, he smiles at me. "I think we'd better get going because in a minute I'm not going to want to go anywhere except your bedroom."

My heart instantly soars like a strummed harp. I try to mask my smile and quickly gather my purse to leave.

Unfortunately, we have to take my car because Mark's truck still isn't ready.

"It's not fancy, but it runs—well, most of the time anyway," I joke.

"No worries. I'll drive if you want," he offers.

"I want." I playfully tap him on the nose and drop my keys into his palm.

The Shelby Falls Country Club is a very exclusive golf club in town. I've never been to an affair there and have always wondered what it looked like inside the main building which was originally the early twentieth century home of the Cartwright family, a wealthy Shelby Falls family. The mansion sits atop a hill overlooking an 18-hole golf course and the view is nothing short of spectacular. As we make our way up the long, winding driveway to the mansion, I admire the lush green grounds and stunning views. Mark says it's the perfect spot to watch the sun rise and that he'll take me one morning.

We pull up to a circular driveway where valets in white uniforms are waiting. I cringe because I'm sure my car is the junkiest they've seen all night, but Mark doesn't appear embarrassed in the slightest. He takes the valet ticket and holds my hand securely in his as we enter the foyer which contains a large crystal chandelier fit for Cinderella's ball.

Almost immediately, Mark spots his mother and we weave through the room of mingling guests until we reach her.

"I'm so glad you could make it, sweetheart!" She gives Mark a big hug and kiss. "I was worried when I didn't see you. You're usually so punctual. Was there traffic?"

"No, it's a long story. Not important." He places his

hand on the small of my back and smiles. "So let me introduce you. Mom, this is Fin McAdams."

"Well hello, Fin!" She extends her hand out warmly to me. "Please, call me Leslie."

"It's very nice to meet you," I say.

"I'm sure everyone asks you this but is Fin short for something?"

"Yes, Finola."

"Oh! What a lovely name." She glances at Mark approvingly. "I was so glad when Mark told me you were joining us tonight. He's never brought a date to the gala before and I'm so thrilled you were able to come!"

Mark's face flushes ever so slightly and I can't help but be flattered that I'm the first woman to ever accompany him to this event.

"Thank you so much for including me," I say to Leslie. "Mark was just telling me how hard you work every year planning the event. It must be a huge undertaking."

"Yes, it's a lot of work, but it truly is a labor of love. Speaking of which, I need to let the kitchen know about a guest's dietary restrictions, so you'll have to excuse me. But why don't the two of you help yourselves to some wine and hors d'oeuvres."

"Sure, we'll see you inside," Mark says.

But once his mother leaves, he takes me by the hand and whisks me away in the opposite direction.

"Where are we going?" I laugh.

"I want to show you something." At the end of a deserted corridor, we reach a set of glass cabinets containing several trophies and group photos. He points to one golf trophy in particular. "See this one?"

I examine it and my eyes widen when I discover his

name engraved on it. "You won this?"

He grins. "Yeah, I was actually pretty decent in high school. It was for a junior golf tournament and I won that year."

I smile with pride. "Is there anything you *can't* do? I've never golfed before but it seems very difficult."

"I'd love to take you to the driving range some time. I bet you're a natural."

"Well, I am good at mini-golf, so…"

"That's good because I'm awful at mini-golf," he jokes.

"Well in that case, I challenge you to a mini-golf match. Winner take all."

"You're on." He gives me a cute wink. "Anyway, I just wanted to show you the trophy. We can head back into the party now."

His excitement over wanting to show me the trophy is so endearing and I just can't resist him a second longer. Seeing as the hall is empty and not well lit, I take the opportunity to plant a kiss on his perfect lips. I don't think he was expecting it but he immediately reciprocates, eagerly running his hands down my back to my behind. His hand palms my ass and lingers there.

"Your ass is perfect," he says between kisses.

"So is yours."

He chuckles. "You've been checking out my ass?"

I nod. "Of course."

He laughs. "I've never met anyone like you, Fin. You're so real."

We continue kissing as he slowly caresses my behind. It's very sensual and I can feel myself heating up with arousal.

"We better stop," I say, "or I'm going to want to take

you to the putting green and have my way with you."

"That sounds hot. My putter is definitely ready and I even have a few balls on hand."

Now I'm the one laughing.

"You don't believe me?" he says, taking my hand. "Check my pant pocket."

Our eyes lock as I slowly reach inside his pocket and easily find his rigid shaft.

"Nice putter," I say, my eyes fastened to his. "I bet you have a very nice stroke, too."

"The best." His voice is low and sexy as hell.

"You'll have to show me one of these days."

"Soon, very soon."

Never leaving his eyes, I stroke his shaft through his pocket until his breathing quickens. He's very hard and I want him—very badly.

"Okay, you win," he finally says, removing my hand from his pocket. "I'm going to need a minute."

We stare at each other and I'm seriously contemplating telling him we should go back to my place this very instant.

"Fin…" I can hear the longing in his voice.

"Yes?"

"I think we should go to the party for a little while or my mom is going to wonder where we are. And then maybe later we can finish what we started here."

"Excellent idea."

He takes my hand and we return to the party which is now well underway. As we make our way to the bar and hors d'oeuvres, a woman who looks to be about my age approaches Mark. She's very friendly towards him and he immediately introduces us. Her name is Samantha and she proceeds to chat Mark up as if I don't exist.

I sip my lemon drop patiently as Mark politely engages in small talk, but the second there's a break in the conversation, he excuses us, claiming there's someone he needs to introduce me to.

"Sorry about that," he immediately apologizes. "I haven't seen her since last year's gala, and she's a talker."

"It's fine, Mark, really. We're here to socialize."

"Well, I'd much rather be dancing with you."

He sets aside my drink and leads me to the dance floor. I haven't been out dancing in ages and Mark is a really good dancer—not that I'm surprised—he's a drummer after all. The music is mostly light rock, which isn't the greatest dance music, but it really doesn't matter; we're still having a great time together.

And then "I Feel The Earth Move" by Carole King comes on.

"Oh my gosh, I love this song! It's one of my favorites!" I tell him.

His brows raise. "*This* is one of your favorite songs?"

"Yes, why?"

"Oh nothing," he says, amused. As the song plays on, he just can't help himself and starts making fun of the line about the sky "tumblin' down," pretending things are falling from the sky and hitting him on the head. He has me laughing so hard that people are beginning to stare. I don't think I'll ever be able to take this song seriously again. Soon, even he starts cracking up and the two of us can't contain our laughter. I honestly can't remember having this good a time on a date...*ever.*

Our smiles endure long after the song is over.

A slower song comes on and he draws me to him, pressing his cheek to my head. "So are you having a good time?" he asks.

I beam up at him. "I'm having a *great* time. Because I'm with the sexiest guy in the room."

He blushes slightly, holding me closer. "G-d, Fin, I'm so crazy about you," he says softly in my ear.

We spend the next few dances stealing kisses and smiling way too much. Being with him feels so easy, so unbelievably good, and neither of us are focused on anything or anyone but each other. When we talk, it's as if every part of him is tuned in to me. He's an amazing listener and his eyes are extraordinarily expressive.

Unfortunately, our little slice of heaven is interrupted by a woman's voice. I turn to see a very attractive woman with sleek dark hair and perfect eyebrows.

"Hi Mark!" the woman says extra-cheerfully with Samantha from earlier in tow.

Mark turns and politely greets her, but he doesn't release me from his arms.

"Aren't you going to introduce me to your friend?" she asks, giving me a not-so-subtle once-over.

"Of course," he says. "This is Fin, and Fin, this is Madison. And you already know Samantha."

Samantha and I nod at one another.

"Nice to meet you—Fin is it?" Madison's tone is decidedly patronizing. "Is Fin your actual name or just a little pet name Mark came up with for you?" Her fixed, perfect smile doesn't mask her smugness.

"No, Fin is my *actual* name." *Biatch.*

Mark swiftly intervenes. "Well, it's nice to see you again, Madison. Enjoy the party."

But Madison isn't relenting. "So what do you do, Fin?"

I decide to play. "I just finished my Master's so I'll be job hunting soon."

"Well congratulations!" Madison says with false effusiveness. "From community college?"

I feel my body stiffen.

"Madison, that's enough," Mark rebukes.

He takes my hand to leave, but I've got this. "Actually, Madison, community colleges don't typically offer Master's degrees."

"Oh, well I'm not familiar with the community college curriculum. I went to Stanford and Samantha here went to Bryn Mawr."

I nod and smile confidently, then glance over at Mark who is looking at me with pride. We proceed to have a mutual admiration party with our eyes. It's amazing how that's possible.

"So where did the two of you meet?" Madison asks us.

"At a bar," Mark responds, looking only at me. "We hit it off instantly." He gives me a knowing smile and, as inappropriate as Madison is being, our happiness is unstoppable.

Madison's brow arches. "Well congratulations, Fin. You seem to have captured the heart of this elusive bachelor for more than one night. Quite impressive. Speaking of which, I still have your tie, Mark, if you'd like to drop by some time and pick it up."

Jealousy instantly flares inside of me.

Mark glares at Madison. "Tie? Just donate it."

Madison clearly hasn't gotten the reaction she was looking for and flushes slightly, but just as she's about to leave, I hear someone call out to me. And unfortunately, Madison hears it too.

"Hey Sharon!"

I turn to see one of the regulars from the restaurant.

He's not someone I speak to often and I don't even know his name, but the regulars all know me. I greet him politely.

"I almost didn't recognize you," he says as his eyes migrate down my body. "You look so different outside the bar, hon."

I cringe at the overly familiar tone with which he speaks to me. Mark seems to know the guy and I immediately sense Mark's dislike for him.

"Hi Doug," Matt says curtly. "Did your wife find you? I think she was looking for you."

Doug chuckles. "Oh, well I better not keep the lady waiting if I know what's good for me. See ya later, Sharon." He gives me a not-so-subtle wink goodbye which I don't acknowledge.

Unfortunately, Madison has observed all of this and promptly swoops in.

"Sharon? I thought you said your name was Fin?"

Before I can figure out how to extricate myself, Mark comes to my rescue.

"You were right, Madison. Fin is a nickname I use because on our first date, let's just say we had an 'incident' involving a goldfish. No need to get into the details, right Finny?"

When I meet Mark's eyes, I have to purse my lips to keep from laughing but Mark somehow doesn't crack a smile.

"No, really, do tell," Madison implores.

I now see a mischievous gleam in Mark's eyes and brace myself for what is to follow.

"So Fin really wanted a goldfish because her other one had just died from overfeeding and—"

"Excuse me, I did not overfeed it," I interrupt. "It just

got very fat."

Our eyes meet and this time he's the one who looks like he's going to crack.

"Right, well anyway," he continues, "she got impatient because the clerk was helping someone else with a guinea pig. So she scooped some water into a baggie and fished the goldfish out of the tank, but when she went to put it into the baggie, she missed and it fell to the floor. Somehow it survived and the clerk got the fish back into the tank, but he was pretty ticked off at us. We ended up getting kicked out of the store and we laughed the whole way home, and the rest, as they say, is fish-tory."

I muffle a giggle at Mark's silliness and he responds with a wink in a my direction.

"How sweet." Madison says dryly. Our humor seems to have been lost on her and she and Samantha excuse themselves.

Mark leads me to another area of the dance floor and immediately apologizes for Madison's rudeness. "I'm sorry about that. She can be a little much. I should probably also tell you that she and I went out—just once— but believe me, it was absolutely nothing," he assures me. "It was after last year's gala."

"Well, I think she might still have a thing for you. And not to be crude, but she seems like a real 'see you next Tuesday.'"

He chuckles. "You're not wrong. I'm not sure what I even saw in her, but it didn't take long for me to realize she's definitely not for me."

"That's because I'm for you." I punctuate my statement with a kiss and it's not an innocent one. I'm feeling a little possessive I suppose and if Madison is still observing us, I want her to know with absolute certainty that Mark is *m-i-n-e*.

He takes my cue and unabashedly kisses me back, not seeming to care what anyone in the room might think.

As expected, Mark eventually asks me about the guy we ran into earlier.

"So how do you know Doug?" he asks.

"He comes to the restaurant sometimes but I rarely speak to him. I didn't even know his name."

"Well I don't like the guy. He's kind of a fixture around here and he has a reputation for being a flirt. Was he making you uncomfortable back there? Because I have no problem saying something to him if you want me to."

"No, that's not necessary, but thank you. He's just one of the regulars at the bar. He's harmless."

Mark raises a brow. "I didn't think you were still tending bar."

"Only when we're short-handed. But I've been there a while so the regular customers all know me. Don't worry, I know how to set clear boundaries. That's one reason why I don't use my real name there."

Mark's brows furrow with concern. "I just want to make sure you're safe. I hope you're careful when you leave at night."

"I am, and I've never had an incident. I also carry mace just in case. But nothing's ever happened, don't worry."

"I'm not loving the sound of all this, Fin. I don't mean to sound overprotective but I'd feel much better if someone walked you to your car at night."

I understand his concern. My mom is the same way on this particular subject.

"That's not always possible, but I'll try to time it so I leave with someone whenever I can," I reassure him. "And I do appreciate you looking out for me." I graze my lips along his to distract him and it seems to do the trick. "Anyway, can you point me to the ladies room?"

"Oh, sure, it's just past the foyer on the left." His eyes then catch someone on the other side of the room. "Oh, there's my dad. When you're done, just meet me over there. I can't wait for you to meet him."

"Okay, BRB." I give him a wink and head to the ladies room.

Not to sound too unworldly, but the club's ladies room is by far the nicest one I've ever seen. There are upholstered benches in a sitting room just before entering the ladies room and an assortment of toiletries on the marble counter, including toilet water, hair products, and mints. This, in turn, causes me to wonder why anyone would refer to a type of perfume as "toilet water," but I digress.

While in the bathroom stall, two women enter and their voices are all too familiar to me. It's Madison and Samantha. I really don't feel like going another round with Madison so I'm just going to wait it out in the stall.

"Can you believe he's with that little whore?" Madison asks Samantha.

"What do you mean?"

"What I mean is that she's got to be a hired escort. She's too young for him and did you hear that guy call her by some other name? 'Sharon' I think it was? She probably uses fake names when she's 'working.'"

I can feel my blood start to boil and I'm this close to bursting out of the stall and slapping the undoubtedly smug look off of Madison's face. But that would only embarrass Mark.

"Do you really think she's an escort?" Samantha asks.

"Sam, she's wearing a dress that looks like it came off of a Marshalls rack, and she went to *community* college. Need I say more?" Madison begins giggling and Samantha joins in.

"Yeah, that orange dress is *so* juvenile!" Samantha agrees. "He must be pretty hard up to be using an escort service. That or he's slumming."

"Thank goodness I didn't sleep with him after the gala last year," Madison says. "He's hot and all, but the entire night all he did was blab on about some waitress he was hung up on. Do you know he actually didn't even want oral when I offered? What guy turns down a blow job? I guess I need to be a waitress or a whore to get his attention. I'm not sure which is worse?!"

Their obnoxious cackling trails away as they finally exit.

I step out of the stall to see my flushed expression in the mirror. My eyes now travel down to my "juvenile" dress. Mark said he loved it and I believe him. More importantly, I love the dress. Madison and Samantha's catty insults are nothing I haven't heard before. Growing up, my mom never made a lot of money and my clothes were hardly the most expensive or stylish, but I managed to put myself together pretty well, all things considered. Some women are just so insecure that they need to put other women down to boost themselves up. But my mother has always instilled in me that my self-worth is not measured by what others think of me. So, while I am certainly irritated by Madison and Samantha's insults, what is actually pissing me off more is the disparaging way they spoke about Mark.

I must admit, however, that there is one thing that Madison said that does intrigue me: *Could it be that **I'm** the waitress Mark was talking about with Madison that night?*

The idea that he might have been pining for me is making my heart do a celebratory dance. I'm also very relieved that he never slept with Madison or let her touch him. She doesn't deserve that privilege.

I reapply my lipstick, do a final once-over, and return to the party. I'm certainly not going to share any of what Madison and Samantha said with Mark. He'll just get angry about what they said about me and I honestly don't care what they think.

Standing in the doorway, I scan the room until I see Mark at a table on the other side of the room. He doesn't see me yet and I take this opportunity to observe him from afar. He's so handsome and carries himself with such quiet confidence. As he speaks with a man who I presume to be his dad, he must be telling him a story because he's using his hands and is very animated. It makes me smile just watching him talk. I see what I've always seen in him: a self-assured, joyful, unpretentious man with a sweet, sensitive soul. I don't think he shows his sensitive side to everyone, but he shows it to me every day.

Thoughts of Mark are making my heart swell and, if I'm being completely honest, I think my feelings for him go well beyond anything I've ever felt for a man before. Actually, I'm certain of it. The passion I feel for him is always present inside me and it's not simply lust. It's so much more.

I suddenly feel an unwelcome pang of sadness, followed by the sting of guilt. I've been intermittently battling these feelings all week. With Mark in my life, they were bound to return. But now is not the time to dwell on the past and I immediately drive these feelings away —at least for tonight.

As soon as Mark spots me from across the room, he breaks into a huge smile and waves me over. I can feel every cell in my body smiling back at him. His eyes are fastened on me as I walk towards his table and that alone is making my face flush. *This man...*

"Hey there!" he says with a grin as he pulls out a chair for me. "I was wondering if you got lost on your way back from the ladies room," he teases. "I want to introduce the two of you. Dad, this is Fin."

"Fin, it's so nice to meet you. Please, call me Rick." As we shake hands, Rick places his other hand over mine in a sweet, fatherly way. "So Mark was just telling me that you took your social work exam this week. What a wonderful career choice!"

"Thank you. I do think it's my calling."

Mark squeezes my shoulder affectionately and it makes me tingle all over.

"She put herself through school and has worked really hard to get to where she is," Mark says.

"That's very impressive," Rick says. "It sounds like you're well on your way to doing a lot of good in this world."

We chat a little more and Rick seems very genuine and kind. I like him already.

"Well, I don't want to keep the two of you so I'll let you get back to the party," Rick says. "It was very nice to meet you, Fin, and I hope to see you again very soon." He gives Mark a discrete wink before leaving, but I catch it.

Mark turns to me. "So, we could dance a little more, or we could head back to your place. Whatever you'd prefer."

"The latter sounds nice."

Knowing smiles converge on both of our faces. His hand rests on the small of my back as he ushers me through the room and over to his mom who breaks away from some guests when she sees us.

"Are you two heading out already?" she asks.

"Yes, I need to pick up my car from the shop. I had a flat earlier."

"Oh dear, yes, you better take care of that. Well, thank you for coming, sweetheart." She embraces Mark. "And I'm so glad you could join us, Fin. I hope to see you again very soon."

"I hope so too. And thank you again so much for including me tonight. I had a wonderful time and everything was just beautiful."

"Oh! Well thank you! I'm so glad you had a nice time," she says, giving me a hug goodbye.

Chapter Sixteen

~ Fin ~

Present Day

After stopping to pick up Mark's truck from the repair shop lot, we head back to my place.

While I pour us something to drink, Mark apologizes again for Madison's behavior towards me.

"It's okay," I assure him. "Let's not give it another thought. Although I will say that if she and Samantha are representative of the club's membership, I probably don't really fit in there, which is fine."

"I understand why you'd say that, but there really are nice people there. Matt and his wife Jennifer belong there too and I think you'd really like Jennifer. She's very down-to-earth."

"I met her very briefly when Matt first started dating her and she seemed very nice."

"We'll have to plan to get together with them. They just had a baby."

"Oh! I had no idea. I'll have to send them one of my baby blankets. Matt has always been so kind to me."

"You make baby blankets?" he asks.

"I don't sew them. I just use fleece and cut and tie off the ends. You can pick out a different design for each side of the blanket and there are tons of designs to choose from."

"Cool. Maybe you can show me how to make one and we can make one together for them."

"Sure! Just find out what color scheme they picked so we can get something that compliments it."

"Done." He squeezes my hand affectionately.

While I do enjoy dressing up on occasion, I much prefer comfy clothes and go to change into some soft cotton yoga pants and a simple crop top. When I return to the living room, I find Mark wandering through my bookshelves. His eyes light up when he sees me.

"Now *this* is what I've been thinking about all night." He approaches and draws my body to his. "I think I like you best *au naturel* like this."

I smile. "Noted. How about you go *au naturel* too and we snuggle on the couch?"

He grins. "I don't think I've ever snuggled before." He sits on the couch, bringing me to his lap. "Is it anything like cuddling? Because I absolutely *love* cuddling."

I giggle. "Oh you do, do you? Well, cuddling pales in comparison to snuggling. Just think of that snuggly teddy bear from the commercial. Do you know the one I'm talking about?"

"I remember that commercial! Yeah, that little bear was pretty cute."

"He talked too. He had this cute little voice." I try to imitate the bear, then Mark does, and then we both start giggling like we're twelve.

Mark takes his dress shirt off, revealing his white T-shirt, and I immediately curl up in his arms.

"You're snuggly soft, too," I say, nuzzling into his shirt which smells like a combination of clean laundry and him. "I'd like to climb all over you like a baby goat."

He chuckles and kisses the top of my head. "You're adorable, you know that?"

"Well you're adorable too."

"Oh no. Are we turning into that annoying couple who talks baby talk to one another? Because if we are, we need to knock it off immediately. No one will want to be around us."

"Oh, I agree completely. This stops right now," I say calmly, while inside, my heart is leaping because he just referred to us a "couple."

We sigh contently in each other's arms and as I nuzzle into him, his hands slowly migrate from my arm to my shoulder, to my hair, and then to my face, which his fingers gently explore in silence until he finally speaks.

"So, have you given any more thought to what we were discussing earlier tonight?"

I look up at him knowingly. "You mean mini-golf?"

"A little more than *mini*-golf I think."

"Oh...you mean what we were discussing while I had my hand down your pants."

"Excuse me, your hand was in my pocket."

"Semantics."

"Well, anyway, have you...thought about it?"

I shift to straddle him, bringing my lips close to his. "I have," I whisper into his mouth, "and I want to."

"Want to what?" he replies softly.

"Want to...have my way with you."

"And do I also get to have my way with you?"

"Mm-hmm..." I brush my lips along his and whisper, "You can do whatever you'd like."

His eyes twinkle at me. "Whatever I'd like?"

"Whatever you'd like."

Our lips connect and he lifts me up into his arms and carries me down the hallway to my bedroom. There is a candle on my nightstand which he lights before joining me in bed. I gaze up at him, watching his eyes track his fingers as they gently brush my hair away from my face. He takes his time with me and slowly leans down, pressing his lips to my neck and breathing me in, then pulling back to meet my eyes again. Even in the candlelight, I can see so much emotion in his eyes, and perhaps a little fear too. I lightly caress his cheek as a sacred hush descends upon us.

"Mark, I trust you completely," I say gently. "I want us to be together."

He swallows hard. "Fin, I..."

"You don't need to say anything more. It's okay."

"It's just that I haven't been with anyone in a while." He suddenly looks so vulnerable.

"That's okay, I haven't either." I hesitate but decide to share more. "The truth is, I haven't been with anyone since we were together."

"You haven't?"

"No." The corners of my mouth curve up slightly. "I'm very choosy."

"So then basically I'm in competition with myself?"

"Yup."

His eyes smile down at me. "Well then hopefully I wasn't too good the last time."

"You weren't bad."

He raises his eyebrows. "Oh, as I recall, I was pretty spot on."

I grin. "You were fucking awesome."

He gives such a genuine laugh and any lingering nervousness seems to vanish.

And that's when he says it.

"I love you, Fin."

His words instantly ignite something deep within me. My heart begins accelerating as if ready to launch, making it impossible for me to hold back my own feelings any longer.

"I love you, too, Mark."

He lets out a small exhale and reaches for my hand, gently kissing my palm. "Maybe it's too soon—I don't know—but I couldn't go a second longer without telling you how I felt. I love you."

I tear up as I give him a gentle smile. "There's no magic timetable where love is concerned. I think when it's real love, you know very quickly."

"What I do know is that I've never felt this way about anyone before...ever," he says. "Only you." His eyes study mine, as if seeking a response.

I draw him to me for a gentle kiss. "Neither have I," I whisper against his lips with a soft smile.

He returns my smile. "You know when I first realized I was falling for you?"

"When?"

"It was the very first night we met. When I came back to pick you up, I couldn't find you at first and I panicked. I really did. I thought maybe you blew me off. And that's when I got this feeling that I've never had before. It was more than just disappointment. It was more like fear. I was afraid I was never going to have the chance to know you...That's when I knew."

I smile through fresh tears and reach for his cheek. "I was there, sweetheart. I was just in the ladies room making sure I looked nice. I wanted to look nice for you."

Tears now form in his eyes too. "You looked so beautiful that night, Fin, so beautiful that you ruined me for any other woman."

I smile. "That was the plan."

And with that, he blankets my face with kisses, the likes of which I have never experienced before. When our lips finally meet, we consume each other like we're starving. With each kiss, he moans softly under his breath and I return his moans with my own and whisper over and over again how much I love him. I can tell how much he needs to hear these words. They're fueling him and I can feel the emotion pouring out of him and into me. My heart craves his love the way a flower craves sunshine and water, and it feels like my heart is blooming. It's never bloomed before but it's blooming for him.

I have **never** been made love to the way that he makes love to me tonight. He loves me with every fiber of his being; with his words, his body, and his heart. It's exquisite, nourishing, and debilitating.

I will never be the same again.

Chapter Seventeen

~ Mark ~

Present Day

As the morning sun peeks in through the window, it casts a beautiful glow on Fin who is still sleeping beside me. She's curled up around her pillow looking so damn cute with those little freckles on the bridge of her nose. I want to kiss each one, just like I did last night, but I don't want to wake her. It's the most amazing thing, but even when she's sleeping, her sweetness permeates the room.

I lean back in bed, reflecting on last night. We said *I love you*, both with our words and our lovemaking. I've always found that word—*lovemaking*—to be so cheesy, but today it finally makes sense. My heart is soaring to new heights just thinking about how much I love Fin and how happy she makes me. I really didn't intend to tell her I love her last night, but what I've been feeling for her just couldn't be contained a second longer. I thought it might scare me to say it, but it didn't. Because when I'm with Fin, I'm completely unafraid. I hide nothing. I don't need to. Being with her feels so natural and right, and I know it probably sounds corny, but love has got to be the best feeling in the world.

Fin begins to stir and when she opens her eyes and sees me, the most magnificent smile spreads across her face. I could stare at her smile all day long.

"This is weird," she says, her voice a little raspy from

sleeping.

"Weird?"

"Yeah, usually I wake up and look for your morning text. But here you are."

"Do you want me to go into the other room and text you?"

She giggles and reaches for me. "No, in-person Mark is much better than texting Mark."

I kiss her. "Plus we can't do that in a text."

"Or this," she says with a devilish grin, wrapping her leg around me and squeezing my ass.

"Boy, you wake up wide awake," I tease. "One minute you're snoring and the next minute you're accosting me."

Her eyes grow wide. "I do **not** snore...or accost."

"You absolutely do accost, and I love it. And as for the snoring, I knew you'd deny it so I recorded you." I hold up my phone.

"Seriously? Give me that." She snatches my phone away from me and holds it up to my face to unlock it, then immediately goes to my videos. "I knew it," she declares. "There's no video of me here."

"So then you admit you snore!"

"I admit nothing and you have no evidence...But you're the lawyer here."

I grin, taking the phone back. "Are you sure you don't want to cop a plea?"

"Nope," she says confidently.

So. Damn. Cute.

"So what do I get if I prove my case?" I ask.

"Hmm...You decide."

"That's a big responsibility. But okay, if I prove my case, you need to put on that cute barmaid's outfit of yours and prance around in it for me, then undress for me just like you did the first night we were together."

Her eyes flicker. "That's oddly specific...Almost like you've fantasized about this before."

"So do you want to change your plea or not?"

She shakes her head defiantly.

"Okay, you asked for it..." I go into my deleted videos and begin to play the snoring video for her, at which point she snatches my phone away from me again.

She examines the video. "Well, counselor, I'm not sure about the legality of you recording me without my consent, but no worries." She gives me one of her winning smiles and hits Delete.

"Hey! You just tampered with the evidence!"

"And *that* is how it's done," she declares, handing me back my phone.

I playfully roll on top of her. "You're very sneaky, you know that? But I still proved you snore, so do I get my reward?"

"Oh, you'll get your reward alright, just not right now."

"Okay, good. Because that outfit is definitely one I need to see you in again..." I give her another kiss and we lay back, side by side.

She turns to me. "So I learned something about you last night."

"And what's that?"

"You like candles," she says. "I like that you embrace your feminine side."

"Huh? I really don't care about candles, but I figured you did," I explain. "Did you know that candles are a multi-billion dollar industry?"

"Seriously?"

"Uh-huh. I worked on a merger of two candle companies. It's crazy how much money these candle companies make."

"So did the company give you a lifetime supply of candles?" she asks wishfully.

I chuckle. "No, but I can ask my client to send me some if you want."

"Yes, please!" She wraps her arm around me and snuggles into my chest. "I guess these are the perks of dating a high-powered attorney. Free candles. Cool."

"Well I hope you see other perks to dating me besides scented candles."

"Of course I do. You're very handsome, and you're a great kisser—oh, and you like goats. Those are my main criteria for a boyfriend. The candle thing is a bonus of course."

I can't resist her a moment longer and shift to settle above her, careful not to put my full weight on her.

"You are completely irresistible to me," I say. "We need to have sex again...Now."

"Okay." She grins up at me mischievously, running her fingers through my hair, down my back and to my ass. My hard shaft is now begging for her touch and she knows it.

"I just realized that I forgot to mention one of your most important attributes," she says.

"And what's that?"

"Your..."—she glimpses downward with a shameless grin—"very large...um...putter. It's quite impressive."

My eyes lock with hers. "Well, my putter is only as good as the putting green...and yours...is meticulously groomed." I brush my lips against hers.

"Precisely," she says with a twinkle in her eyes.

"It's very important that the green always be neat and trimmed. That way the balls can glide easily into the hole." She grins.

My girlfriend is perfect. "Talking golf with you is so fucking hot, Fin."

She smiles to herself. "I was just thinking, are you going to yell *fore* to warn me when your ball is coming?" Even she can't suppress a small giggle.

"Oh...so *that's* why they call it foreplay," I quip. "I never understood that."

We laugh and then she playfully rolls me onto my back and straddles me, pinning my arms (and other appendage) down.

"Mark Jansen, you are as silly as me, and I love you for it."

We may never leave this bed again.

Once we're sated (for now anyway), we shower—together of course. We don't have sex again but easily entertain ourselves using the shower gel I got her, and I even shave her legs—because I can.

In the afternoon, we head to a nearby park where we find a quiet spot under a tree and soak in the gentle breezes and the sound of rustling leaves. With Fin's head resting in my lap as if it was made just for her, I play with her silky copper strands and listen to her share a few funny stories about her childhood. I love listening to her. I feel at peace.

I'm not sure I can imagine a more perfect day. Waking up beside her, making her laugh, having sex (and more sex), and just being with her, fills me with overwhelming gratitude and love. Unfortunately, time is almost up again because I need to head back to Boston tonight.

"I wish we lived closer," she says with a sigh, looking up at me.

"Believe me, so do I."

"I should find out the results of my exam this week and I've already started applying for positions. I was thinking of expanding my job search to the Boston area. What do you think?"

I'm pleasantly surprised. "Would you really consider moving away from Shelby Falls?"

"I've been thinking about making a move for a while now," she says, "and things with us just feel so right. And when it's right, it's right, you know?"

I lean down and kiss her soft lips. "Nothing has ever felt more right to me. I honestly don't feel like I deserve to be this happy."

She sits up to face me. "Of course you do! We both do! I want this to work and I do think us living closer to each other makes the most sense. So you like the idea?"

"I love it, and you." I give her another kiss on the lips.

"And I love you." She strokes my forearm affectionately. "So then I'll start checking on line for openings in the Boston area."

"Okay, but will your mom be alright with this? I know how close you two are."

"She'll be fine. Above all else, she wants me to be happy. And you make me exceedingly happy." She smiles. "Once she meets you, I know she'll understand."

"Maybe I can take you both out to dinner next weekend."

"Actually, we usually do Sunday dinners together so how about joining us for dinner tonight before you head back to Boston?"

"Even better."

She immediately calls her mom who is eager to meet me, so dinner is a go. We then head back to Fin's place which inevitably leads to us naked in her bed again. I've never met a woman with this healthy a sex drive before. Most of the women I've dated don't seem to need sex much more than once a week, but if I had my druthers, I'd be having sex with Fin every day. And Fin, well she's right there with me, and for the first time in my life I don't feel like I need to curb my sexual appetite. I've never felt this strongly about a woman before and I want to express my feelings—often.

"This really isn't too much sex for you?" I ask her as we lay in bed together after making love.

"Is it too much for you?"

"Not for me but I just want to make sure you never feel pressured because I know my sex drive can be pretty high at times."

She props herself up on her elbow to look at me. "Do I look like I'm feeling pressured?"

I search her eyes. "You look pretty damn happy to me."

"Good. So you can just settle down and stop over-thinking, okay?"

I nod and then become distracted by her perky breasts, her nipples still hard from sex. I touch them one last time, knowing it'll be a week before I can touch them again.

"Can I ask you something?" she asks more seriously.

"Of course."

She reaches for my horseshoe charm. "Does this charm have a special significance for you?"

I knew this question was coming. "Yes, it was my mother's. She was wearing it the day she died."

Fin's caring eyes rest on mine, waiting for me to continue.

"It's gotten me through a lot over the years. When I was little, wearing it made me feel like my mom was with me somehow, if that makes sense."

"It does." She takes my hand and kisses my palm.

"I wish I had something of my dad's too," I say, "but I know he gave her the charm, so it kind of feels like it belonged to both of them in a way."

"It's lovely." She kisses my chest before resting her head down. I wrap my arms tightly around her and we lay together for a few more minutes, savoring our time together.

Fin is a little anxious about dinner tonight, as she really wants her mom to like me. But parents always seem to like me, so I'm really not worried.

"Just tell her you love her cooking and she'll love you," she says as we walk through the door. "Mom, we're here!"

Her mom comes out of the kitchen wearing an apron and a smile that immediately reminds me of Fin's. It really is amazing how much they resemble one another.

"You must be Mark! Finola has told me so much about you." She extends her hand out to shake mine.

"Hello, Mrs. McAdams. It's so nice to meet you." I present her with wine and flowers.

"Oh, these are beautiful! Thank you! And please, call me Alyssa. Why don't you two come in and sit down. Everything's already on the table."

We make our way to a lovely dining room with a

built in corner china cabinet and oversized upholstered dining chairs. It has a warm, inviting feel.

"Please sit," Alyssa says. "Can I get you both something to drink?"

"I'll have some wine," Fin says, locating a corkscrew for the wine I brought.

"Everything smells incredible," I say.

"I hope you like lasagna," Alyssa says. "It's a family recipe."

"I love lasagna," I say, pouring each of us a glass of wine.

Alyssa serves us and her eyes are fixed on me as I take my first bite.

"This is really delicious," I tell Alyssa. "Now I know where Fin gets her cooking skills from." I give Fin a quick wink.

Fin looks up at me approvingly and squeezes my hand under the table.

"So Finola tells me you're a lawyer in Boston," Alyssa says.

"Yes, but I grew up in Shelby Falls."

"Oh, I don't recognize your last name. Did you graduate together?"

"No, I'm a few years older and I didn't go to East High, I went to West." *And by a few years, I mean ten years, but who's counting.*

"Oh, I see," Alyssa says. "And your parents, what do they do?"

"My mom does a lot of volunteer work and my dad is in insurance."

"And they're still living in Shelby Falls?"

I nod, which seems to please Alyssa.

"Do you have any brothers and sisters?" she asks.

"Mom," Fin interjects, "Dan met Mark last weekend and already grilled him."

"No, it's fine, Fin, I'm happy to answer any questions your mom has. And no, I don't have any siblings."

Alyssa pours herself a glass of wine. "So how was the gala last night? Did the two of you have a nice time?"

"Yes, we had a great time!" Fin eagerly chimes in. "I also got to meet Mark's parents. You would really like them, Mom."

"I'm sure I would. That gala is quite the party I hear."

"It's a lot of fun," I say. "You'll have to come with us next year. My mother is on the planning committee."

Alyssa glances over at Fin, somewhat surprised. Maybe it was too soon for me to speak with such certainty about a future event. I hope I didn't come across as too forward, but Fin seems to read my mind and reassures me with another squeeze to my hand.

"Yes, you'll definitely have to join us next year," Fin tells her mother.

"Sounds very nice," Alyssa says, popping up. "Let me go check on the cheesecake."

As soon as she leaves, Fin looks over at me, her eyes beaming. "She likes you, I can tell."

"I hope so."

"I know so." Just as she leans in for a quick kiss, Alyssa returns and we immediately separate.

Alyssa's tone now turns more serious. "So I'm glad you're here, honey, because there's something I need to speak with you about."

It sounds like this may be personal and I don't want to intrude. "Maybe I should head out so the two of you can talk," I offer.

"No, you don't need to go," Fin insists.

"I just want to do whatever makes you both the most comfortable," I say.

"Then please stay," Fin says.

Alyssa turns to Fin. "Does Mark know about the situation with...your father?"

Fin's eyes squarely meet her mom's. "Yes, Mark knows everything. Whatever you have to say, you can say in front of him."

Alyssa nods hesitantly. "Okay, well then, I received some news yesterday. It seems your father is out on parole. I'm not sure if he'll try to contact you or Danny, but I wanted to warn you. I doubt he will but I still want you to be vigilant."

I see Fin's jaw immediately tense up. "Why would he contact us now? It's been twenty years."

"I don't think he will but I just wanted you to be aware."

"He has no use for us," Fin says dismissively. "I'm sure he'll stay away." But Fin doesn't look entirely convinced.

"You're probably right, sweetheart. I'm sorry I had to bring this up tonight, but it couldn't wait."

"No, you were right to tell me," Fin says, "but can we please change the subject to something more pleasant? Is the cheesecake ready? My mom makes the best cheesecake, Mark."

I nod and try not to react to what Alyssa has just told us but none of this is sitting right with me.

"The cheesecake is just cooling," Alyssa says. "I'll go get it."

Fin then turns to me, acting as if the prior discussion about her father never happened. "So when do you need to head back to Boston?"

"My meeting isn't until ten in the morning so I can stay until about eight."

"Oh, good." She averts her eyes as a small sigh escapes her mouth. She's far too honest to be able to conceal her feelings and I can see the apprehension on her face.

I gently rest my hand on her back. "Are you okay?"

Her eyes lift to meet mine. "Yes. The news about my father just took me by surprise, that's all."

I nod and am about to ask her more about her father when Alyssa returns with the cheesecake. Not another word is uttered about her father and we all try to enjoy the rest of the evening. And Fin is right. Her mother's cheesecake is the best I've ever had.

As we say our goodbyes, Alyssa extends an open invitation to me for Sunday night dinner and gives me a big hug. Other than the worrisome news about Fin's father, it was a very nice evening.

On the ride back to Fin's, she does her best to remain upbeat, assuring me that her mom liked me a lot, but she's uncharacteristically subdued and I understand why. The news about her father has to be a little unnerving.

She doesn't even seem to notice when I park the car and just stares ahead, preoccupied with her thoughts.

"I'm going to stay over with you tonight," I announce.

She turns her head. "But how?"

"I'll leave early in the morning. It's no big deal."

She pauses to consider. "No, I don't want you to do that. You'll be too tired for work, won't you?"

"I wake up early anyway and I keep a spare jacket and tie at the office, so I can just drive directly there. It's no trouble at all."

Her eyes are now clearly saying *Yes*. "You really don't mind?"

"Fin, I want to be here for you. I love you."

She eagerly wraps her arms around me, pressing her head tightly to my chest and breathing out with relief. "Thank you. I want you to stay."

We climb the stairs to her apartment, wash up, and get into bed, where she once again returns to my chest. I'm worried about her.

"Do you want to talk about it?" I finally ask.

"Not really—I mean, I am a little worried, but I'll be fine."

I don't say anything more as I want to give her the space she needs.

She eventually tilts her head up at me. "I *am* a little afraid that my father might try to contact me or, I don't know, even try to find me. Maybe I should privatize all of my information. But if he wanted my address, he probably already has it by now."

I hesitate to ask my next question, but I need to know she's safe. "Did he ever...was he ever...violent?"

She shakes her head. "No, my mom has never said he was violent. I think he was convicted for dealing drugs. I should probably know this but I just don't care. I don't want to have anything to do with him."

Various scenarios now begin to enter my mind, none of them good. But I don't want her to sense my worry. "You know I'm just a phone call away, and if you ever feel at all nervous, I want you to call me immediately, okay?"

"I will." She looks up at me gratefully. "Thank you. I'm so glad you're here tonight."

"Me too." I give her a quick kiss. "Now try to get some rest."

"Okay," she says with a yawn. "I love you." She nuzzles back into me and closes her eyes.

"I love you, too."

I lay awake until I hear her sleeping soundly. She looks deceptively peaceful and I'm relieved for the time being.

Chapter Eighteen

~ Mark ~

Present Day

"I passed!" Fin exclaims from the other end of the phone with such force that I nearly fall out of my desk chair.

"That's fantastic!" I say. "I knew you would!"

She giggles. "I'm officially a social worker! Can you believe it?!"

I laugh. "I'm so happy for you, babe. How do you feel?"

"Relieved, happy, excited, nervous, and happy again." She giggles with joy.

I smile. "We'll celebrate when you come visit tomorrow, okay? What time do you think you'll be here?"

"I'm closing tonight so I should be at your house a little before noon."

My worry antenna instantly goes up but I'm careful to pose my next question as casually as possible. "So will somebody be there to walk you out to your car after work?"

"Yes, I promised I would do that and I've been very careful, don't worry."

"Okay, but promise to text me when you get home tonight. I don't care how late it is."

"I will. Anyway, I better go get ready for work but I can't wait to see you and I'm so excited to hear your band play tomorrow night!"

"Great, see you tomorrow then. Love you, Finny, and I'm so proud of you."

"Love you too."

As soon as we hang up, my concern for Fin's safety takes a firm hold of me. I've been feeling this way all week, ever since last weekend when Alyssa told us about Fin's father being paroled. I'm sure a psychologist would say that my fear of losing someone I care about stems from the sudden loss of my parents. But between guys like that "regular" from the restaurant ogling Fin at the gala and the possibility that her father might show up, I think my concerns are justified. I don't know her father, but from what I do know, he sounds a little unpredictable.

But there's more that concerns me here. I've never shared this with Fin—or with anyone other than my parents really—but when I was younger, I occasionally had panic attacks. The doctors said they weren't uncommon in people who have gone through a trauma like the one I went through. They didn't happen a lot, but when they did, they came on without any warning. My heart would start to race and I'd get very overheated and feel like I couldn't breathe. The last time I remember having one was during a test in middle school and I couldn't bring myself out of it and actually had to go to the nurse's office. After a few minutes, I was able to calm myself down, and I don't think I've had another one since. But, when I think about Fin being at the restaurant late at night, with the possibility of some creep following her to her car or her father showing up, an uncurbed anxiousness begins to brew inside me. Fin has become a huge part of my life and if anything ever happened to her, well, my head starts spinning just thinking about it.

I need to find a way to get myself in check.

* * *

Running helps clear my head and I also do some of my best thinking when I'm running. As I round the corner to head back to my house before Fin arrives today, I suddenly remember that I have a contact at a school district in my area, so I leave her a voice mail. Maybe her district has a social worker opening for Fin or she knows of another school district that might. I'll feel so much better when Fin isn't putting in late nights at the restaurant anymore.

It's not long before noon rolls around and Fin's car is pulling into my driveway. I meet her outside and the moment she puts her car in park, she jumps out and right into my arms.

"I missed you!" she says with that glorious smile of hers as she reaches up to give me a kiss.

"I missed you, too, Finny." I hold her tight, not wanting to release her just yet.

She pulls back for another kiss. "It's been lonely without my guy to snuggle with."

I chuckle. "Tell you what, we can snuggle all night if that's what you want."

"That's what I want." She grins. "Oh, and if we happen to want to do *more* than that, I took care of that issue too, so no need for any other precautions..." She gives me a cute wink.

"I definitely like the sound of that."

We share a longer, more sensual kiss, her tongue lingering on mine. It amazes me that she can arouse me with just one kiss, but she can.

I throw her duffle bag over my shoulder and lead her up the steps and into the house. "Come, I'll show you around."

My house is a traditional Cape with light grey siding, white shutters, and a dark walnut mahogany door that's original to the house. There are two dormers in front for the two upstairs bedrooms, with an additional bedroom on the main floor. The interior has a fairly open floor plan with a large living and dining area that is decorated in a minimalistic style. I spent way too much on a grey sectional from Crate & Barrel, but I really think it makes the room.

Fin voraciously absorbs everything like a sponge and soon hones in on a framed Matisse print that hangs in the living room. "I love the bold colors!"

I grin. "I thought you'd like that one. It's called *The Goldfish*. It kind of reminds me of our fake first date."

She grins and approaches me, wrapping her arms around my neck and pressing her body tightly against mine. "Your house is a beautiful reflection of you and I love everything about it."

A burst of energy surges inside me and I lift her up into my arms. The happiness I feel when I'm with her is like nothing I've ever experienced before.

As she wraps her legs around my waist, I press my lips to hers, moaning lightly under my breath. "So, what would you like to do now?" *I know full well what I want to do.*

She flashes a knowing smile. "How about you show me your bedroom?"

I grin. "Sure, it's upstairs."

She immediately drops down and scurries up the stairs. I try to catch her but she's very fast. Once she finds my bedroom, she hops onto my bed, giggling.

I pause in the doorway, admiring her sass.

"Nice sheets," she says, stroking them seductively with a knowing grin. "Sooo soft."

I approach the bed. "Egyptian cotton. Not as soft as your skin, but nothing is."

"Come here. NOW." She crooks her finger with playful eyes.

I kick off my shoes and then pull off hers, tossing each one over my shoulder where they land with a thud.

"Oooh, the old shoe toss move," she says. "Very smooth."

"You like that? Wait 'til you see what I can do with your bra and a shooting target."

She bursts out laughing. Honestly, she has the most adorable, infectious laugh and the two of us laugh until we wear ourselves out, eventually laying back on the bed together.

She inches her foot towards mine and asks, "Do you remember that first night we met when you gave me a foot massage in your car?"

"It's permanently ingrained in my memory, why?"

"That was a very bold move by you, you know."

"Well, what you did with your feet on my lap that night was just as bold."

Her lips curve upwards. "I don't know what you mean."

"Oh, so you don't remember feeling for my hard-on with your feet?"

She giggles. "Oh *that*..."

"Yes *that*..." My lips graze hers. "You drove me completely wild that night, in the best possible way."

She grins and whispers, "Let's get naked."

I feel myself hardening. "You know you're my soulmate, right? You say everything I'm thinking."

"Well then you are a very naughty boy for thinking what you're thinking right now."

I chuckle and feel the heat rising in my face.

"You're blushing, Mark Andrew Jansen. Which means you are most definitely my soulmate. Because my mom once told me that blushing is a sign of true affection and it can't be faked."

"Well she would be right then because I am completely and madly in love with you." I press my lips to hers for a deeper kiss. "So how'd you know my middle name? I don't remember telling you."

"Alexa told me."

I chuckle. "You are absolutely fantastic."

A gleam now appears in her eyes. I know that look.

"I was just thinking," she says. "How about we pretend we're texting and tell each other all the things we want to do to each other?"

We do sometimes get graphic when we text. It's very hot and usually results in me needing to relieve myself (sexually). But we've never done this in person. Surprisingly, I'm now feeling a little inhibited.

"I don't know, I feel like I might offend you."

"I won't be offended, I promise."

I consider it for a moment. "I want to, but I don't think I can...but I do have another idea."

"I'm listening..."

"How would you feel about me giving you a hickey?"

Her eyes shimmer. "I'm all yours."

But when I look at her beautiful neck, to my utter amazement, I'm suddenly having second thoughts. "Damnit, I don't think I can do it. Your neck is too beautiful to mar."

"Mar?" She giggles. "You're not acting like yourself today. But if you're going to chicken out, then I'll just have to give you one instead."

I'm on board with that and immediately lay back.

"This will only hurt for a second, Mr. Jansen. Just relax." She slowly unbuttons my shirt. "First I need to prepare the area, so don't move."

"Don't worry, I'm an excellent patient."

I watch her as she leans over me and then swirls her tongue on one spot on my neck. I try not to move but she's so fucking sexy and there is an intense throbbing in my shorts.

Gently blowing on the spot, she softly says, "There, we're almost ready."

My heart is now erratically clamoring with desire for her as our eyes lock and she lowers her lips to my neck.

"You're absolutely sure?" she whispers in my ear.

"Yes," I say with a hard swallow. "And can I just say that you are the hottest woman in the entire universe."

"That's what I wanted to hear."

I close my eyes and can feel myself fully hardening as she uses her lips on my neck. It's quick and painless and so fucking arousing. I open my eyes to find her impassioned green eyes above me, hungry for more. I help pull off her clothes, then mine, and then she is beneath me, beckoning me to enter her. When I do, instinct takes over. I go deep and hard, penetrating her with long, determined strokes, over and over. It feels so damn good but I need to pull out for a condom.

"Mark," she says breathlessly, her eyes glazed over. "We don't need one, remember? I took care of everything. Stay inside me...Please."

I obey. Each soft whimper she makes is fueling me and I can hear my own voice growing louder with each rhythmic thrust into her. As I tease her clitoris with my fingers, her walls begin to tighten around me. She's very close and I want to hold myself off until she comes, but without a condom, the pleasure is too intense and my body is already on the precipice. I somehow hold myself back and the second I feel her coming, I give a final deep thrust into her and our bodies become immobilized, giving way to our own unique rhythmic duo. I'm sure our moans have long since traveled through my open window, but I really don't give a fuck at this point because she feels so damn good.

Afterwards, we lay back, sweaty and out of breath, with the last remnants of arousal in our eyes.

I turn to face her. She looks very content and very beautiful, and I bring her hand to my lips. "I love you, Fin, and I love us."

Her serene eyes gaze into mine and then she leans in and kisses me softly, with exquisite tenderness and love. As she finds her place in my arms, I feel a peace I have never known before.

Chapter Nineteen

~ Fin ~

Present Day

Cooley's, the Boston bar where Mark and his band are playing tonight, is quickly filling up and is almost at capacity, and it's only nine o'clock. It's an older bar that is a converted fire station, so there's all sorts of firefighter memorabilia hanging on the walls and the original brass fireman's poll is even still there. The upstairs has a full bar and pub and the downstairs where Mark's band is playing has a smaller bar and an area for live music. Mark is downplaying the crowd size and says the bar is just a popular college hangout and has nothing to do with their band. But I'm not buying it and, in any case, it still feels great to have a large audience to play for.

We've been here for a little over an hour setting up. I had no idea how much work goes into playing live music but it's quite an undertaking to transport the drum set, sound system, and all of the other music equipment. I can definitely understand why Mark would want to have a pickup truck. Unfortunately, there is little I can do to help so I've just been staying out of their way.

Mark's bandmates all seem very cool and down to earth. Mark and the lead singer/guitarist, Josh, have been friends since Harvard and Josh is also an attorney in Boston. He's a very good looking guy and is recently divorced, and since we arrived, I have already noticed a few college women hit on him. The bass player, Bruce, is a professional musician and very well-regarded according to Mark, and the keyboardist, Giselle, is a music student at Berklee and seems nice but very quiet. Mark and Josh seem to think that Bruce and Giselle are secretly dating, but they've never come out and said anything.

Once the band is finished setting up, Mark heads over to my table.

"Can I get you something from the bar?" he offers. "The music might sound better with a drink in you."

"Stop! You're going to be amazing. But actually, do they have mozzarella sticks?"

"Mozzarella sticks?" he says with a laugh. "You're a very cheap date. Let me go grab you some." He heads to the kitchen and soon returns with mozzarella sticks and boneless wings.

"Thanks!" I dive in.

"If you need anything else, just ask Harry behind the bar. I need to go help with the sound check. We go on in a few minutes."

I give him a good luck kiss and can't resist grabbing his perfect, muscular ass. He gives me a squeeze in return and I don't mind one bit. It's gotten to the point where even in public, we have trouble keeping our hands off of one another.

Finally, after several sound checks, and without any announcement, they launch into their first song —"Peace of Mind" by Boston.

Wow.

I am completely blown away. They are absolutely fantastic, and so tight, and there are definitely some people in the crowd who are fans. I always thought it would be pretty cool to date someone in a rock band, but the reality of it is ten times cooler. Mark is up there rocking out with total abandon and it's sexy as hell. He's completely absorbed in the music and looks so at ease performing. Even though I know it's just him, somehow it feels like I'm watching a different person—*and that person is my boyfriend!* As I watch him play, with so much joy and freedom, I can't stop smiling.

The audience is very into them and they play for a little over an hour straight. Once their set is done, Mark starts to head over to me, but a few girls stop him along the way. I spotted them checking him out earlier so I'm not surprised. He's of course friendly and gracious towards them, but the moment I catch his eyes with mine, he gives me a huge smile. Just that one smile makes my heart flutter wildly. I'm so madly in love with him, it's not even funny.

He politely excuses himself from the girls and the moment he reaches me, words fly from my mouth. "You were amazing! I can't believe how talented you are!" I then assault him with a gigantic hug.

He laughs. "Well, I'm glad you liked it."

"I did! And I think those girls liked it a lot too," I tease.

"Oh, them? They're just college girls."

"Well, as a member of the opposite sex, I can tell you that they were definitely into you. But that's okay because I know you belong to me." I graze my body against his and he immediately responds by pulling me tightly to his torso.

"I do belong to you, Finny." He brushes his soft lips to mine, causing arousal to fill my core.

"Yes, you do, and you have the hickey to prove it."

"Yeah, and my bandmates are never going to let me live that down by the way. They've been merciless with me all night."

I shut him up with a kiss, stroking my tongue along his.

"Hey! Can you two stop sucking face long enough to help pack up?" Josh teases Mark.

"Don't be a dick," Mark says as he breaks away from me to finish up.

I offer to help but there's really nothing for me to do. Once they've gotten everything packed up and into Josh's van and Mark's truck, Mark and I head out by ourselves.

As we drive home, Mark reaches for my hand and gently strokes it with his thumb. He's quiet, but I think that must be commonplace after being so pumped while performing. I glance over at his strong profile and the peaceful smile on his face. He's delicious.

"You're very sexy, Mark Jansen, you know that? *Very* sexy."

He glances my way and when I see the sexy simmer in his eyes, my core heats up with desire.

"Not half as sexy as you," he says, stroking my thigh. "I saw you dancing out there tonight and you've got some moves I've never seen before. I'd like to see some of those again when we get home."

I suppress a smile. "Would I be clothed or nude?"

"Both."

And there's that sexy twinkle in his eyes that gets me every time.

"Hmmm..." I say, my eyes drifting to the throbbing

erection in his jeans.

"Yes, hmmm…"

My tongue runs along the seam of my lips and I'm this close to making him pull over so I can go down on him. I need a subject change and fast.

"So…what do drummers usually do after a show?" I ask.

He grins. "In my case, eat."

"Oh, well then let's go grab you a bite out."

"I'd rather do Chinese take-out and eat back at the house, preferably nude in front of the fireplace with you."

"I'm not opposed."

We end up eating at the kitchen table—fully clothed —and I somehow manage to eat yet again. Dumplings are a major weakness of mine.

"I'm stuffed," I announce.

"You know it really is a pleasure watching you eat. You savor every bite."

"So you enjoy watching me eat, do you?"

"I do." He pulls me to his lap with a playful grin. "So how 'bout we go upstairs so you can show me some of those moves from earlier?"

I nod. "But first I have a special request. Will you play something just for me on the drums?"

He chuckles. "Okay, but there's an admission charge."

"Oh?"

"Yeah, I do a little drum solo in exchange for you wearing that cute barmaid's outfit you promised to wear for me again."

"Oh, that's right, I still owe you, don't I."

"Mmhmm…" He runs his finger along my lower lip.

After more shameless flirting, he agrees to play something for me and takes me upstairs to the second bedroom where he keeps a drum set.

I return to his lap and he starts to play a slow, steady beat. "Want to guess what I'm playing?"

I listen for a moment. "I don't know… maybe 'Battle Hymn of the Republic'?"

He chuckles. "Wow, that's a really good guess. But no, it's actually the beat that my heart is making right now. Sometimes when I'm around you, I can feel it beating really strongly in my chest." He reaches for my hand and brings it to his chest.

"I can feel it," I say quietly.

I take the drum stick from his other hand and close my eyes, connecting with my body's natural rhythm. "This is mine," I say, tapping lightly on the same drum he's using.

Slowly, our drumbeats begin to synchronize as our hearts beat as one. We relish the feeling of oneness.

"Kind of relaxing," he says softly.

"Relaxing and exciting at the same time."

He nods, taking my drum stick and putting them both aside. He then delicately lifts my shirt and presses his lips to my stomach, gently lowering me down onto the bass drum. I raise my arms as he removes my shirt and bra in one swift motion. As I lay bare-chested on the drum staring up at him, he slowly forms a trail of kisses from my navel upwards through the valley between my breasts and up to my lips.

"Fin," he softly utters into my mouth, "never in my life have I loved someone the way that I love you."

My pulse races. "Just keep loving me like this forever."

"You know I will." He lifts me up into his arms and carries me to his bedroom.

As we linger in bed the next morning, just relaxing and enjoying each other's company, I can think of nowhere on earth I would rather be. He's so attentive to my needs, but not in an overly sappy way, and he has this playful, loving way about him that brings out my own playfulness. I especially love it when I can get a hearty laugh out of him; he has such a fantastic laugh. But then there is also a more cerebral side to his personality too. We can talk for hours without it feeling like any time has passed. This really is the first time in my life that I've felt this connected to another person and I can feel myself starting to really rely on him emotionally. Yet it doesn't feel like I've lost my independence because he isn't possessive or stifling.

After more sex, followed by lunch, Mark takes me on a tour of his neighborhood which is nearly perfect. It reminds me of one of those idyllic neighborhoods that you see in movies about all-American families in the Midwest. The streets are lined with large, mature trees and sidewalks, and the homes are older but well-maintained. Every house is a different style, from colonials to tudors to capes—not the cookie cutter houses you see in newer developments. There are kids outside playing basketball while dads are mowing the lawn, and it feels very safe. It's the kind of neighborhood I've always wanted to live in.

Afterwards, we stop at this adorable little coffee shop called Mel's that Mark has been raving to me about. We sit at the counter on these round swiveling stools affixed to a black and white tiled floor. Mark orders us a frozen coffee concoction topped with a mound of whipped cream sprinkled with finely chopped almonds. The owner is indeed a guy named Mel whose lifelong dream was to open a coffee shop when he retired. As soon as he spots Mark, he comes over to greet us.

"Hello, my friend! Thanks for stopping in. And who is this lovely lady?" Mel gives Mark a tiny wink.

"This is Fin," Mark says, putting his arm around my waist and giving Mel a knowing smile. "And Fin, this is my favorite coffee connoisseur, Mel."

"It's very nice to meet you," I say.

"It's nice to meet you too, Fin." Mel extends his hand to mine.

"I couldn't let Fin leave town without trying one of your famous frozen coffees," Mark says.

"Which one did you get?" Mel asks me.

"White chocolate, and it's absolutely delicious!" I say.

"That was always my wife's favorite," Mel says. "She's actually the one who came up with that particular flavor. She would have loved knowing that it's a hit."

I nod, surmising that his wife must have passed away.

"Fin, let me get you a vanilla scone, too," Mel insists, walking over to the pastries. "On the house. Any friend of Mark's is a friend of mine." He takes out a scone with white icing and sets it down on a plate for Mark and me.

"Thanks, Mel. Wait 'til you try this," Mark says, lifting the scone to my lips. "Nobody does scones like Mel."

I take a bite, and then another. "Oh my gosh, this is fantastic! I love to bake but I've never been able to master scones. This one is so moist inside."

Mel soaks in the compliment. "Glad you like it. Let me know the next time you're in town and I'll make you a special batch."

Mark and I easily finish off the scone and Mark insists that he send some home with me.

Mel boxes up a few and returns. "You know, my wife was a redhead too. Not a day went by when she didn't remind me of how lucky I was to have fallen in love with a redhead. And she was absolutely right. The best thing that ever happened to me."

"I don't doubt it." Mark gives my hand a gentle squeeze.

I grin. "Well I think I'll keep him around too, Mel."

"A very wise decision," Mel says. "I knew it was going to take someone really special for this one to settle down. Looks like he finally met his match." Mel shoots another wink in Mark's direction as he heads back to the kitchen.

Once Mel is out of earshot, I ask, "Did you tell Mel about me before today?"

Mark smiles. "I might have mentioned you, here and there."

I giggle. "Here and there, huh? Well I'm glad. But you do realize how this works in the movies, don't you? Once you've told the local coffee shop owner about me, there's no turning back."

He grins. "I am well aware."

I slurp up the last of the frozen coffee with a straw and then we say our goodbyes to Mel. But before heading back to Mark's house, we have to make a brief stop at Mark's office downtown so he can quickly take care of something. It's a Sunday so there isn't a lot of traffic and we're able to park just a block away from the building.

The lobby is very modern inside with very tall tropical plants that are planted in raised beds, surrounded by granite tile flooring. The building is twenty-six stories high, so it's not officially a skyscraper, but it's still taller than any building I've ever been in.

As we enter Mark's personal office on the eighteenth floor, I am immediately struck by the floor to ceiling windows and the view of the Charles River. "This is an incredible view!"

"Yeah, I got really lucky with this office. I'm never giving it up if I can help it."

I spot a jacket and tie hanging on the back of his door and immediately envision him in it masterfully negotiating a multimillion dollar deal. Some men look particularly hot in a jacket and tie and Mark definitely falls into that category. My unintended sigh causes him to look up from his laptop.

"Sorry, I'll just be another minute or two," he apologizes. "I have one more file to download."

"It's fine, I was just...admiring everything."

His eyes twinkle in my direction. I watch him as he clicks away and, G-d help me, he's even sexy doing something as mundane as clicking and dragging a mouse. *I wouldn't mind being that mouse right about now.*

"I've never really pictured you at the office," I say. "It's a hot look for you." I walk over to him and trace my finger lightly down his arm.

He glances up from his screen. "Are you coming on to me? Because if you're coming on to me, just say the word and I'll have this desk cleared off in about ten seconds flat—actually, make that five."

"I'd like to see that." I giggle.

He raises his brows and takes the dare, feverishly

clearing his desk of all files.

"Guess it's a good thing your desk isn't very cluttered," I say with amusement.

He leans up against his desk and draws me to him, gathering my hair and putting it to one side. The need filling his eyes lures me even closer.

"You know, counselor, if we defile your desk in this manner, you're going to think of me every time you're working."

"That's okay, I already do think of you when I'm working."

"I see..."

He takes me by my waist to lift me up onto the desk, but instead I lower myself to my knees, eyeing his crotch and slowly unzipping his shorts. He's already filling out his boxers and I surrender to the urge to press my face to his crotch and inhale his scent. I moan into him.

"Fin..." he murmurs. "Let's take it slow so we can savor this."

I look up at him, my chin lightly grazing his crotch, as I run my tongue in between my lips. "But I can't resist you...or this..." I press my lips to his crotch and play with his erection over his boxers. He hardens even more and I can hear his breathing quicken which is making my lower region quiver with anticipation.

I pull down his boxers and run my lips along his smooth, hard shaft. I stop to admire his length and can't decide if I want to blow him or take him inside me. He makes that decision for us, kicking off his boxers and shoes and pulling me onto the desk with him. The late day sun is streaming through the blinds, casting an enticing light on his lean, muscular build. His broad shoulders, defined arms, and flawless abs are a thing of beauty.

He watches me undress down to just my demi-cup bra, which I leave on. I straddle him and lean down to kiss him, inviting him to touch my breasts, but only over my bra. My breasts are my pleasure point and he knows it, so he purposely delays removing my bra, instead taunting me as he strokes them and uses his lips and teeth on my nipples over my bra, coaxing them out until they are begging to be freed. My straps dangle down past my shoulders and my bra slowly begins descending just enough for my hardened buds to show. I want his lips and tongue on them so badly, desperate for him to latch onto them. He teases them with his tongue and once he has me in a state of frustrated ecstasy, he slowly pulls down my bra with his teeth, finally freeing my breasts from their bondage. He unclasps and tosses my bra, leaving my breasts hanging freely over his mouth.

"Beautiful," he says before taking my nipple in his mouth, sucking and swirling his tongue around it and bringing it to a ripe peak. His shaft easily glides back and forth through my folds, the pleasure so intense that I think I might come right now. I guide his shaft inside me and he begins moving in and out of me, slowly and patiently. His eyes are closed and I lean down, pressing my full breasts against his chest and kissing him hard. As our tongues tangle, his shaft expands inside me. He penetrates me slowly and methodically, lightly moaning under his breath. As he lightly pinches my nipples, I raise my torso and arch my back so that he has full access to my breasts which are begging for more. I'm so close and start to ride him hard until I feel his legs stiffen under me. He's resisting coming but I know he won't be able to hold out much longer.

"I love you, Fin," he says breathlessly as we move together. "I...fucking...love...you." Each word is punctuated with a hard, determined thrust inside me.

"Deeper...harder..." I breathlessly plead.

His deepening thrusts combined with the touch of his fingers on me bring me to my tipping point. Obscene language not fit for print begins flying out of my mouth. My panting has now turned wild as I moan for more. He holds me firmly by my waist and takes full control, his thrusts quickening and growing more purposeful.

"You feel so good," I gasp. "So. Fucking. Good..." My voice trails off as he takes us to a stratosphere I've never been to before.

I almost cry, it's so intense, and as we come together, his head slams hard against the desk, as he releases into me over and over again.

Afterwards, I collapse in his arms. The sweat from our bodies seals us together and I soak in his scent, burrowing into his neck and kissing the hickey I gave him yesterday.

We remain still, allowing our weakened bodies to calm.

He finally speaks. "That was fucking incredible. Every time we're together, I think it can't get any better, and then it does."

"And it's going to keep getting better and better," I say. "You'll see."

"I don't know if my body can take it."

"Told you I could keep up with you."

He chuckles and presses his lips to the top of my head. "You know, if the cleaning crew is around and heard us, my law career is over."

I lift my head with concern.

"I'm kidding!" He grins.

I playfully smack him. "Don't scare me like that." I lay my head back down on his chest.

"It's okay, I'll just pay them off and everything should be fine."

I tilt my head up again. "Are you serious?"

His deadpan expression now gives way to unbridled laughter.

I playfully straddle him and hold his arms down. "Now you're really going to pay, mister."

"It'll be worth every penny."

Chapter Twenty

~ Fin ~

Present Day

I returned to Shelby Falls last night following our "afternoon delight" (I've always wanted to be able to work that into a sentence), but now I'm heading back to Boston because last night, Mark's school contact was able to arrange an interview for me with the head of HR for a school district in the Boston area. I'm meeting with her today and was told that they have an opening, so if all goes well, I may be moving to Boston sooner than I thought. I haven't been on a job interview in forever, but I know I'm well qualified, so I'll just try to tap into that inner confidence.

When I arrive to the interview, I'm met by a receptionist who escorts me down the corridor to the last office. There is an attractive, well-dressed woman on the phone and when she sees me in the doorway, she waves me inside and motions for me to take a seat.

"Yes, yes," she says to the person on the other end of the line. "I understand. We're working on that as we speak."

She soon hangs up and stands to greet me. "Hello, Finola! So sorry about that," she apologizes, shaking my hand. "We have a younger student whose mother is very ill and she's going to need some additional support when she returns to school in the fall. I know the family well and it's heartbreaking."

I nod sympathetically.

"Oh, I'm sorry, where are my manners!" she says. "I'm Candace Garcia, but please call me Candy." She smiles warmly and then shifts her eyes to a document on her desk. "So I just received your resume this morning, Finola. Very impressive. I'm very familiar with the program you attended and I'm happy to see that you already have some experience working in a school system. Did you enjoy working there?"

"Yes, very much! I worked in a high school but I'm also very interested in working with younger students."

"Well your timing couldn't be any more perfect because the position we need to fill is at the elementary school level. So why don't I tell you a little bit more about the job."

She goes on to explain the general duties which would consist of individual and group sessions throughout the school year and some additional duties during the summer months.

"What we're looking for right now though is a little bit of a unique situation. The student I was telling you about earlier is going to need to be transitioned to a new social worker because her current social worker, Miranda, is going on maternity leave very shortly. So what we'd like to do is integrate a new social worker such as yourself into their sessions now so that things go as smoothly as possible once the school year begins in the fall."

I nod. "If I can ask, how old is the student?"

"Chloe will be entering second grade. She's very sweet but she's going through a lot and definitely needs extra supports. Right now, she's living with her uncle because her mother is too medically fragile to care for her. It's a very sad situation and unfortunately her mother's prognosis is very poor."

"I'm so sorry to hear that. It sounds like a very delicate situation."

"Yes, and we're looking for someone to start as soon as possible," Candy says. "So let me ask you—is this position something you would be interested in?"

"Yes, I'm very interested."

"Wonderful."

We go on to discuss more details and the job really does sound ideal for me. If selected, I would receive some training from the social worker who is leaving and should be well prepared by the time the school year begins. By the end of the interview, Candy appears eager to offer me the position and says that she is just required to speak with one of my references first, so I provide her with my professor's contact information.

"Assuming everything checks out, which I'm sure it will, I'll be able to make you a formal offer as early as tomorrow, and maybe we can even set up a meeting with Chloe and Miranda, her current social worker, tomorrow if you're available."

"Of course, and thank you so much for meeting with me today, Ms. Garcia—"

"Candy," she says with a smile as she escorts me to the reception area. "I'll be in touch very soon."

As soon as I step outside, I break out into a huge smile and immediately call Mark. I feel like I'm talking a mile a minute.

"That's fantastic!" Mark says. "So when would they want you to start?"

"Candy, the head of HR, said as soon as possible. She just needs to check my reference and I know my professor will give me an excellent reference so I think I have the job!"

"Wow! I'm so happy for you and, selfishly, I'm also glad because we won't have to be apart as much."

"Yes, exactly! Oh, and Candy also said I may even be able to meet Chloe—that's the little girl I'd be working with—as early as tomorrow, so I'm just going to double check that the other manager at work can cover for me tonight. Assuming he can, is it okay if I stay over tonight?"

He laughs. "Can you do me a favor and never ask me that again? Of course you can stay with me. I'd prefer you never leave actually. I'll be home by about six so just head back to my place whenever you want and then I'll take you out for sushi to celebrate. There's a spare key in between the front door and the screen door."

I grin as I hang up the phone. *How did I get so lucky to have another chance with this man?* It feels like a dream come true to have someone in my life who I can really trust and love unconditionally, and who feels the same way about me. And, while the independent side of me would never embrace the concept of being taken care of by *anyone*, would it be so wrong of me to want that just a tiny bit? Because I do...with Mark.

But then the all-too-familiar pang of guilt rears its ugly head again. If I'm not honest with Mark soon, I'm afraid he'll never be able to trust me again. I *can't* let that happen. *But once he learns the truth, will he ever be able to see me the same way?* My mind is telling me that's a chance I'll have to take and to trust that our love will carry us through. But my heart...well...it's doing its very best to protect me, reminding me that revealing the truth means reliving the pain all over again and risking losing Mark forever. I honestly don't know if I'm emotionally capable of going back to that dark place again.

But my heart also knows what the right thing to do is. I need to tell him—and I will—before this lie wrecks everything. Just not today.

On my way back to Mark's, I pick up a few things at the grocery store and then head to his house. I really do love his home. The sophisticated simplicity of the decor, the calming colors, the coziness. It already feels so comfortable to me, like it could be my home too. His kitchen is my dream kitchen, with white shaker-style cabinets, marble counters, and hardwood floors. As I lay out tonight's dinner ingredients on the luxurious white marble island, I smile to myself. I've never cooked in a kitchen this nice before and, while Mark said he would take me out for dinner, I really want to make something special for him to show my appreciation for everything he's done for me.

It's six on the dot when I hear Mark walk in the door, punctual as usual. Barefoot and smiling, I look over my shoulder at him as he enters the kitchen and takes a whiff.

He raises his brows. "You cooked?"

"Yes, when I'm happy, I cook."

"Wait a minute, I know that smell." His eyes grow wide. "Is that my mom's lemon chicken?"

"I told you I'd make it for you one day if you were a very good boy. And you've been particularly good lately." I give him a love tap on his nose.

His eyes roam over my body, lingering on my tan legs which are accentuated by my cutoff white denim shorts.

"Sometimes I think I've died and gone to heaven, or should I say *heav-fin*." His eyes are twinkling at me as he leans in for a kiss.

I giggle. "You and your witticisms."

He lifts me up onto the counter and I wrap my legs around his waist, so content to be in his arms.

"You know you're my good luck charm," he says, pulling me tight against his groin. "Can I wear you all the time just like this?"

I grin. "I'm a size 6."

"Well you fit me like a glove." He presses his lips to mine and whispers, "A nice tight fit too."

Our lips form what can only be described as perfect kisses and they're causing an electrical current to run through my entire body.

"You know," he says, "after you left last night, I was lying in bed—already missing you—and I started thinking back to the night we first met. I was trying to remember the very first moment that we saw each other."

"And what did you remember?"

"You were mixing a drink and when you turned around, our eyes eventually met and you smiled, and I remember it all feeling very familiar to me, almost like we'd met before."

His eyes hold mine and I have goosebumps from his description.

"Do you believe in past lives?" I ask.

"Maybe. Do you?"

"Yes, I actually think that sometimes people who were in love in a past life will try to find each other again in their next life. We may not be recognizable to one another by sight, but I believe that our souls still remember how it feels to be with that person. I think human beings are always searching for that feeling of oneness."

"So did I feel at all familiar to you when you first saw me?" he asks.

"I confess I don't remember the first moment we saw each other as well as you do, but I was probably a little distracted working. But what I *can* tell you is that when you came back to the restaurant later that night to pick me up, this feeling of total exhilaration took over. I don't think anyone had ever had that effect on me before. But you definitely did."

He laces his fingers with mine. "Yes, it was definitely intense. By the end of the night, I was very aware of my feelings for you and just how much I liked you."

I trace my finger along his lower lip and smile. "Mark?"

"Yes?"

"Take me to the bedroom."

He chuckles softly. "Right now? Before dinner?"

"Yes, right now."

He lifts me into his arms and carries me upstairs, our eyes never separating.

Sometimes I feel this urgent need, deep within me, to be with him and he understands it because he feels it too. Whenever we make love, we share this incomparable feeling of gratitude. The emotional gratification can be overwhelming.

Tonight, tears form in our eyes from the intensity of our lovemaking.

I choose to believe that these are the joyful tears of our souls reuniting.

Chapter Twenty-One

~ Fin ~

Present Day

"I got it!" I yell into Mark's bathroom.

He pops his head out of the shower. "You got the job?!"

"Yes! And I accepted!"

He pulls me against his dripping body and gives me a deliciously wet kiss. "Congratulations, babe."

"Thanks, *babe*," I say with a giggle.

"What? You don't like me calling you *babe*, babe?" he teases.

"No one's ever called me that before. I suppose if I were a true feminist, I would object. But somehow it's sweet coming from you." We kiss again. "Now finish up so I can shower next. I said I'd meet Miranda, the social worker, this morning."

"You know, you're very bossy in the morning." He flashes me a cute smile before resuming his shower. Then we swap and I shower while he shaves at the sink. It all feels very natural.

As I slip on a new summer dress, I watch Mark as he expertly ties a Windsor knot. It's funny but I don't think I've ever really watched a man tie a tie before. It's sexy, and not to sound crass, but I just want to jump his bones every time he wears a tie. He must see the lust in my eyes because there's now a familiar twinkle in his.

"Yes...?" he says, clearly reading my mind.

"It's just, well, that tie. You look very enticing in it."

"I do, don't I..." He approaches me all twinkly. "But unfortunately I have a meeting this morning. I told you you should have taken a shower with me."

I groan when the smell of his body soap wafts into my nose. We share one final, delicious kiss before reluctantly separating. This will have to hold us for a while because I'm heading back to Shelby Falls after my school meeting and won't see him again until the weekend.

Unless...

"Want me to drop you off at your office?" I offer. "I have time before my meeting."

"That's sweet of you, but I can take the T."

"It's okay, let me take you," I insist. "Besides, I want to talk to you about something."

We grab some yogurt parfaits that I made yesterday and head to my car. Boston drivers are a unique species, especially during rush hour, and I'm still learning my way around the city, so Mark drives.

While battling traffic, I broach my next subject. "So, I've been thinking about where I'm going to live once I move here..." I catch myself nibbling nervously on my lower lip.

"Okay..."

"Have you thought about it at all?" I cautiously ask. "Just wondering."

He tries to hide the very beginnings of a smile, but it's there. "As a matter of fact I have. I was just waiting for the right time to ask you."

My heart jumps. "Ask me what?"

He glances my way as if assessing the risk before he speaks. "If you'll move in with me."

This is exactly where I was headed, but I don't want

to be presumptuous. "Like move in, move in, or just temporarily stay with you?"

"Whatever you want it to mean." Optimism fills his eyes. "The longer the better as far as I'm concerned."

My lips form a cautious smile. "As long as you're absolutely sure. I don't want to impose."

He chuckles. "I am absolutely, positively sure, but the question is, are *you* absolutely sure? Because there are no take backs."

My smile widens and I slap his arm playfully.

"Is that your way of saying *Yes*?" A huge grin spreads across his face.

I giggle happily. "Yes! That's Y-E-S in all caps followed by three exclamation points, a dance emoji, and a smiley face."

"What—no prayer hands?"

This makes me laugh. "Are you mocking me?"

"Never." We stop at a traffic light and his adoring gaze locks with mine, followed by a quick kiss just as the light turns green.

"Well then I guess it's settled. I'm moving in!"

"Yes you are," he says, reaching for my hand. "And just think, no more need for morning texts because we'll wake up every morning in bed together. And then we can have morning sex. And then shower together. And then have your famous salsa and cream cheese omelets, and then work out at the gym—"

"Whoa, whoa, whoa, who said anything about the gym? I hate the gym."

"You hate the gym? How did I not know that?"

"Have you ever heard me mention the gym before?"

"Well, no, but I figured that was because you were busy studying for your exam."

"Nope, that had nothing to do with it. So is that a deal breaker or can we agree on another form of exercise, like maybe hiking? I like hiking."

"I like hiking." He smiles. "Or, there's always sex."

"Yes, there's always sex. Or ping pong." I grin.

"Ping pong?"

"Yes, my serve is unreturnable."

"Well we'll just have to see about that."

"Plus I'm ambidextrous so I throw everybody off."

Something about that last statement strikes him as particularly funny and he gives me one of his hearty laughs.

We soon reach Mark's building and he pulls over.

"Okay, this is me," he says, leaning over to kiss me goodbye. "Have a great meeting and call me when you're done, okay?"

"I will. And you have a great day too. Oh, and try not to think about us rolling around on your desk." I wink. "Sooo unprofessional."

He cradles my face in his hands and gives me a full-on kiss. "See you in a few days, babe. I love you."

I switch to the driver's seat and as he reaches the entrance of his building, I lean out the window and yell, for everyone to hear, "Love ya, babe!"

He turns with a smile and gives me prayer hands before entering the building.

I'm a few minutes early for my meeting with Miranda, so I wait for her in the school office. The staff are extremely friendly and I have a really good feeling about this position. Even though I'm a little nervous, I know I can do this job and I'm excited to be able to use my skills and hopefully help this little girl, Chloe, through a difficult time.

Miranda meets me in the school lobby and gives me a tour and overview of Chloe's case before Chloe arrives. Chloe's mother is in a facility receiving care for a rare form of cancer and her condition is terminal. Chloe's father's parental rights were terminated shortly after her birth and she's currently staying with her mother's brother, Peter. He travels a lot for his job so Chloe has been spending a fair amount of time in after-school programs and with babysitters. She's entering second grade and isn't fully aware of how serious her mother's condition is, but her mother's absence has caused her to have some social anxiety.

"She's very sweet and bright, but the absence of her mother has been rough on her," Miranda says. "The teachers are finding that she's having trouble focusing and her schoolwork is starting to suffer. She also doesn't have many friends and I think that's partially a result of her being with sitters a lot and not having anyone to arrange play dates for her."

"She sounds like a very sweet little girl who is dealing with a lot of changes," I say.

"She's a great kid. I forgot to mention that she loves reading. She used to participate in a reading program but the woman who worked with her left last year and then Chloe's mother became ill, so Chloe no longer participates. She's definitely lacking a stable adult figure in her life right now."

As I listen, my heart goes out to this little girl.

We're finishing up our discussion when an attractive man arrives with Chloe, who immediately runs over to the toy chest in Miranda's office. The man is dressed in a business suit and his broad shoulders are hard to ignore. Something tells me he used to play football.

Miranda introduces us. "Peter, this is Finola McAdams. She's going to be working with Chloe while I'm on maternity leave."

He extends his hand. "Very nice to meet you. I'm Chloe's uncle. Chloe, come meet Ms. McAdams," he calls to Chloe who has already spread out some toys on the table.

She obediently comes over to us and I introduce myself to her. I'm immediately struck by the close bond that Chloe and her uncle seem to have. That's reassuring to see.

"Chloe, I need to go on an overnight trip for work," Peter tells her, "so Amber is going to pick you up today and stay with you and then she'll take you to go see mommy tomorrow, okay?"

Chloe nods but doesn't say anything.

"Okay, sweetie," he says, giving her a hug and kiss. "You go have fun and I'll see you tomorrow night." He looks over at us appreciatively. "Thanks, Miranda. You have my cell if you need to reach me. Nice to meet you, Finola."

Once Peter leaves, I watch as Miranda and Chloe begin playing together with a dollhouse, carefully arranging furniture and dolls to Chloe's liking. Miranda then invites me to take the lead.

I sit beside Chloe at the table and begin to help her arrange the dollhouse. "I hear you like to read," I say. "I love reading."

Chloe nods, barely looking up from the dolls.

"Maybe we can read together some time," I say.

"Okay," Chloe says, glancing curiously up at me, then adding, "Me and Jennifer read together sometimes, but she had to move away to be with her boyfriend. Now she's married."

"Well, sometimes people need to move away and that can be hard. But I bet she misses you a lot."

Chloe nods again.

"Maybe next time I see you, I'll bring a book for us to read. Would that be okay?"

Miranda chimes in. "You like the *Junie B. Jones* series, don't you Chloe?"

"Jennifer loves Junie B. and so do I. She says we are both like Junie B. because we like being silly." Chloe's face lights up as she speaks about Jennifer and the more she talks, the more I think I'd like to speak with Jennifer to gain some more insight into Chloe.

The rest of our visit seems to go well and Miranda is very pleased with how quickly Chloe warms up to me. As I head back home to Shelby Falls, I'm feeling hopeful that perhaps I can help Chloe and I'm also feeling hopeful about my own future.

Chapter Twenty-Two

~ Fin ~

Present Day

At the blink of an eye (or the turning of a page), it's Friday evening. Between working at the restaurant and starting to pack up my apartment, I haven't had a moment to relax. But it feels so good to be moving ahead with my new career and moving forward in my relationship with Mark. The restaurant has been anticipating my departure for several months now, so they already hired a new manager to replace me and he's ready to assume full duties, so my final shift will be tomorrow night. I've been working at the restaurant for four years and have developed strong friendships with some of the staff, so leaving is definitely bittersweet. But it's time.

Mark should be here any minute and the plan is for us to move my things to his house on Sunday. My brother is still in town and is also going to help out. I'm really glad that he and Mark will have a little more time together before Dan has to return to San Diego next week.

When I hear Mark walking up the outer stairs to my apartment, I quickly meet him at the door and throw my arms around him.

His smiling lips meet mine. "So, you excited for the big move?"

"Of course! But I'm pretty wiped out from packing all day. How I could have accumulated this much stuff is beyond me. I have no idea how everything's going to fit in your house."

"No worries, we'll make room." He checks the time. "I didn't realize it was this late. Maybe we should get to bed a little early and then we can get a fresh start in the morning."

I tug at his waist. "I have an even better idea. How about you join me for a shower?"

"But I thought you were tired?"

"I'm *never* too tired for you. And actually, I've been thinking about something new..." I take his hand and lead him to the shower.

First I put on a little show for him, slowly stripping down to nothing. His eyes track my every move with anticipation. Then I tell him to undress and as he takes off his boxers, I'm very pleased to see that he's more than ready for what I have planned.

Chapter Twenty-Three

~ Fin ~

Present Day

Tonight is my final shift at the restaurant. Dan and Mark had planned to come by the restaurant tonight, but I told them not to. I'm feeling kind of emotional and I just want to treat it like any other night. So they're going to finish packing up my kitchen instead.

I was hoping the evening would be uneventful but of course there was an emergency. One of the cooks set off the smoke alarm so everyone had to evacuate until the fire department did a safety check. All of the dinner orders that were in progress were ruined and many patrons left rather than wait. So it was a bad night for business.

As I wind down my shift, it's feeling oddly anti-climactic; that is until our head manager, Steve, and the rest of the staff surprise me with a cake and gift. Some of the off-duty staff even stopped by to say goodbye, which nearly made me cry. I love the people I work with and I'm going to miss them.

"You can cut out early if you want," Steve offers. "It's been light ever since the fire department left so the bar has stopped serving."

"That's okay. I still need to pack up some things from the office and I want to take care of it tonight because I'm really going to be pressed for time after this. My new boss wants me to start this week."

"It's still hard to believe you're leaving," Steve says. "We're all really going to miss you."

"Don't worry, I'll pop in when I'm in town and see how you guys are surviving without me," I kid.

After a hug goodbye, I head back to the office to finish boxing up my things. Unfortunately, it's taking much longer than I thought it would.

How did I manage to accumulate this much junk? And why did I save about a half dozen sets of cheap wired earbuds that don't even work anymore? Wtf?!

It's after eleven when Steve lets me know everyone has cashed out and left, which is a little early for a Saturday night. I offer to lock up so that he doesn't have to wait around for me and then I text Mark to let him know I'll be home shortly. I don't tell him I'm the only one here because I don't want him to worry. It'll be fine.

When I'm finally done packing, I lock up the office, but before I leave, I take one final turn around the bar. It feels surreal, like I'm in the last scene of the final episode of a television show when the main character is surveying the place where so many memories have been made and then turns off the lights for the very last time to a hushed audience. My hand glides across the worn leather seat of the stool where Mark sat the night we first met. Had I not worked here, I never would have met him. I sigh to myself. What a blessing he is to me.

I dim the lights over the bar one last time and turn to leave.

"Oh my G-d!" I cry out. There's a man standing in front of me.

"Sorry, I didn't mean to scare you, the door was open," the man says apologetically.

I nod. "It's okay, but I'm sorry, we're closed for the

night."

"Actually, I came here to talk to you."

My radar instantly goes up. While he doesn't look dangerous, you can never tell. "I'm sorry," I repeat firmly, "but we're closed. Can you please come back tomorrow when we reopen?"

"Finola," the man says.

The hairs on the back of my neck stand up. I don't know this man but he seems to know me. He doesn't appear to be drunk or high but I'm not entirely sure. I try to remain calm. "Sir, you're going to need to leave or I'll have my manager escort you out."

"Finola, I know you're alone. I waited until the parking lot was empty. But there's no need to be afraid. It's me, your father."

The blood instantly drains from my face and my heart feels like it's stopped. I quickly scan his face for any familiar features. He appears to be about my father's age and does indeed resemble an old photo of him. Fear takes hold of me.

"I don't know who you are but I need you to leave," I repeat firmly.

"I told you, Finola, I'm your father. I got out on parole a few weeks ago."

My mind is scrambling to decide how to respond. "I want you to leave please."

"Okay, but first just let me explain."

"No, please leave."

"Okay, okay, I understand. You don't know me and I'm sure you've heard a lot of bad things about me. But I'm making a fresh start now and I need your help."

"My help?"

"Yes, I need to get an apartment and they'll want

a reference and I really have no one else except your brother, and I'm assuming he won't do it. So you're it."

I do my best to appease him so that he'll leave. "I need to think about it," I lie. "I'll speak with my mother tomorrow."

He immediately reacts, sounding more agitated. "No, please don't say anything to her."

"Well, if you want to give me your phone number," I say calmly, "I'll let you know tomorrow."

He appears somewhat relieved and gives me his number which I pretend to enter into my phone. But instead, I text Mark.

Me: 911 Dad here

I quickly exit my texts. "Okay, I have your number. I'll call you tomorrow." I begin walking to the main entrance to usher him out and am in the process of reaching into my purse for my mace (just in case) when he places his hand on my shoulder to stop me. The scent of beer wafts towards me.

"I need one more favor from you," he says. "I need some cash for a security deposit."

With my heart racing, I calmly turn around to face him. "I promise I'll call you tomorrow, okay?"

"I'm assuming the restaurant keeps some cash on hand here, right?" he says. "I just need a little loan to get by until I get a job."

"That would be stealing. I can't."

"I'll pay back every penny in a few weeks. You're a manager here, right? You can fudge the numbers for a few weeks until I can pay you back, can't you?"

"I'm sorry but if I did that, I'd lose my job. I need this job."

"Listen, I really am sorry to do this to you. If I can just get a little cash to get by, I promise I'll pay you back and then you won't hear from me again."

My mind races through my options. He's got to be a good seven or eight inches taller than me and he's in excellent shape. I don't think I can get around him fast enough to escape. *I need to do something.* I swiftly pull my mace from my purse but, just as swiftly, he takes it from my hand and stands in the way of me leaving. I'm now scared to death. I don't know him or what he's capable of and he definitely smells of alcohol.

"I'm not going to hurt you, Finola. I'd never do that. Just take me to the safe and I'll make it look like a break in. Then I promise you I'll be on my way." He begins steering me towards the back of the restaurant.

I've always been trained not to fight if the restaurant is being robbed, so I slowly walk to the back with him, passing the corridor leading to the side exit door.

And that's when I see Mark.

Chapter Twenty-Four

~ *Mark* ~

Present Day - About Fifteen Minutes Earlier

I open my eyes to the sound of an incoming text from Fin. It's a little after midnight and I must have dozed off.

Fin: **911 Dad here**

I jump out of bed and hastily throw on a T-shirt and jeans. I start to text her back but realize I can't because that may tip off her father. As I run to my truck, I call Dan. Adrenaline is rushing through me like a dam has broken.

"Hello?" Dan's voice is groggy. I probably woke him up.

"Dan—just listen to me, it's Mark." I'm speaking quickly and can hear the shaking in my voice. "Fin just sent me a 911 text that your dad just showed up at the restaurant."

"911? Oh for fuck's sake!"

"I'm going there now so let me get off the phone so I can call the cops and—"

"No—let me call my buddy who's on the force." While he's trying to appear calm, I can hear the worry in his voice. "I'm leaving now," he says. "If you get there before me, just stay in your car until I get there, but I'll probably beat you."

He clearly doesn't know how I drive.

If that asshole lays a hand on her, he's going to wish he

was never fucking born.

I break every traffic law and make it to the restaurant before Dan or the police arrive. Crazy, irrational thoughts are racing through my head. Fin's car is the only one in the lot and my heart is pounding out of my chest. I notice the side door of the restaurant propped open and start to walk over to let myself in but stop myself and decide to stick to Dan's plan. *But damnit, I can't just stand out here.*

Luckily, Dan arrives not a minute later.

"Let's go in," I insist as I begin to open the side door.

"Wait," Dan whispers, grabbing the door. "I spoke to my cop friend and he's on his way. Here's what we're going to do. You're going to go in and get Tim's attention with this cash," he says, holding up a wad of bills, "and then while you're distracting him, I'll take him from behind."

"Tim's your dad, yeah?" I ask, taking the cash.

Dan nods. "Yes. There's a grand in fifties there. Got it?"

I nod as we quietly enter through the side door. I remain hidden in the corridor at first and can see Tim walking Fin towards the back of the restaurant. Nothing good can come of this. I somehow manage to catch Fin's eyes as she walks by. She looks frightened and my protective instinct takes over.

I call out to Tim. "Let her go—NOW."

My words startle them both, causing Tim to release his hold on Fin for a second. But when she tries to run, he blocks her and takes her by the hand.

"I've got what you want," I say, calmly holding up the wad of cash and shaking it like I would a toy at a dog.

Tim turns to Fin. "Do you know this guy?"

Her frightened eyes shift to mine. "No."

"Listen, man, I think you've got the wrong idea here," Tim says. "My daughter and I are just having a little visit."

"No, I think I've got it just right. I've got a thousand in cash for you. All you have to do is let her go."

Tim raises his brows. "Spread the cash out on the table where I can see it."

I lay it out and he examines it but doesn't let go of Fin. Once he confirms it's all there, he collects the money and gives me a look of relief, but also what appears to be gratitude.

"I don't know who you are in relation to my daughter," he says, "but I'm assuming the two of you know one another." Fin and I make eye contact but don't respond. "I want you to know that this is just a loan and I'll pay you back in a few weeks, with interest. You have my word. I'll let Finola know when I'm coming by and you can meet me here."

Tim now turns to Fin, still holding her hand. "I'm so sorry about all of this, Finola, I really am. This is not how I wanted our first meeting to be, but you were the only one I could turn to." He looks over at me and then back at Fin. "But I'm grateful that you have someone in your life who cares about you the way this man clearly does." Tim squeezes Fin's hand before releasing it.

Out of my peripheral view, I see Dan and the next thing I know he's tackling Tim to the floor.

"What the hell!" Tim yells.

"Hi Dad," Dan says sarcastically, pinning Tim down to the floor.

"Danny, you've got the wrong idea! Let me go!"

"You idiot," Dan says through clenched teeth. "All

you needed to fucking do was stay away from us. But you had to fuck it up just like you always do."

"I didn't do anything," Tim pleads. "Finola's friend here was just offering to help me out, right Finola?"

Fin crouches down and looks her father dead in the eyes. At first it looks like she's about to say something to him, but instead she just stares at him, as if trying to glean something.

We all startle as the police enter the restaurant and immediately apprehend Tim. Dan speaks with the police while I whisk Fin away to a private corner. I can feel her shaking and it takes every ounce of self-control not to go over to that asshole of a father and knock him out for what he's put her through.

I take her in my arms and she clings tightly to me.

"Are you okay? Did he hurt you?" My voice is trembling despite my best efforts.

She shakes her head. "No, he didn't hurt me. But I'm so glad you got my text." She looks down and her face contorts slightly, as if ready to cry. "I was so scared." I envelop her again and she buries her face into me.

"It's going to be okay," I say, softly stroking her back. "I'm so sorry you had to go through this, sweetheart." I press my lips to the top of her head and hold her as tightly as I've ever held another person.

She eventually calms and looks up at me, speaking softly. "I looked into my father's eyes and they're green like mine."

My heart is now breaking for her. *How the fuck could he do something like this to her?!* I can see how hurt she is and there's not a damn thing I can do about it.

It's three a.m. before we're finally done giving our statements to the police and Tim is finally taken into custody. We're all exhausted and I'm not about to let Fin drive home. She's very quiet on the drive back and soon tucks her legs underneath her and falls asleep. She doesn't even wake up when I carry her upstairs to her apartment and into bed. I remove her shoes and cover her with a blanket, wondering how she could possibly look so tranquil.

I, on the other hand, am far from peaceful and feel a tension headache coming on. With a moment to now reflect on everything that happened tonight, I honestly don't know what I would have done to Tim if anything had happened to Fin tonight. She means everything to me and even just the idea that she could have been hurt sets off tremendous anxiety.

I quietly get into bed, trying not to disturb her, but the moment I lay back, she stirs and wraps her arm tightly around my waist, nestling into me. I don't let her go all night.

Chapter Twenty-Five

~ Fin ~

Present Day

I am rudely awoken by the morning sun which glares through my bedroom window. I had a very restless night's sleep as thoughts of my father replayed in my head all night long. Every time I woke up, the thoughts returned.

Last night was the first time I've ever seen my father in person—well, except when I was too little to remember. At first, when I realized it was him, I felt a flurry of excitement, as if maybe he actually wanted to get to know me. But any excitement I had quickly turned to fear and anger once I realized he just wanted my money. While there's a small part of me that wonders what he would have done had I not cooperated, my gut tells me that he never would have hurt me. He seemed desperate, but not violent.

I find Mark in the kitchen and glance at the clock on the microwave. It's 11:15 a.m.

"Why did you let me sleep so late?" I ask. "We still have a lot of packing to do."

"You were exhausted. We'll finish in plenty of time, don't worry." He hands me a cup of coffee. "Here."

He pours himself a cup and we sit down on the couch together.

"I'm so sorry about last night," I say. "What a disaster."

"Fin, you don't need to apologize. It wasn't your fault."

"I know that. He showed up just as I was about to leave and I think he'd been drinking too because he smelled of beer. Geez, what a fantastic ending to my job." I roll my eyes with a half-hearted laugh.

"Yeah, you really know how to go out in style, babe." He attempts a smile but worry lingers on his face.

"Well, at least I got cake. That's the most important thing, right?" I put on my best smile for him.

"Very true…But seriously, are you okay?"

"Yeah, I'm just kind of stunned I think…and a little worried. Do you think he'll be able to get out on bail?"

"He violated his parole so I'm assuming he's going back to prison, but I'll speak to my friend who's a prosecutor just to be sure. Don't worry."

But I am worried, I can't help it, and I suddenly have the urge to bite my nails, something I haven't done in years. Mark instinctively takes my coffee and sets it on the table, then brings my hands to his lips.

"I have an idea," he says. "How about we go see some baby goats today?"

A small giggle escapes my lips. "We don't have time for that!"

"Oh, there's always time for goats."

He winks at me and I climb onto his lap, nuzzling into his neck. "Thanks, but I'll be fine," I say, "and besides, we really need to finish loading the van."

"Okay, you just tell me what you need me to do."

"Right now, I just need you right where you are, with me."

"Okay." He lifts my chin and gently kisses me. "And if you want to talk about it, I'm here for that, too."

I remain in his lap and we sit in silence for a few minutes while he draws what feel like circles followed by two taps on my shoulder.

I look up at him curiously. "Are those circles you're drawing?"

"They're smiley faces."

That brings an instant smile to my face.

"Ah...there it is," he says. "That gorgeous smile of yours."

The twinkle in his eyes does wonders for my mood.

"You do know that you're the best boyfriend ever."

"Oh, I know that."

* * *

It's been about two weeks since I moved in with Mark and it already feels like my home. He's gone out of his way to make sure I have everything I need, and with each day that passes, I'm even more blown away by how generous and caring he is. He does so many thoughtful things for me without ever being asked. Just yesterday he warmed my towel so that when I got out of the shower, it was nice and toasty for me (he threw it in the dryer for a minute). He always insists on doing the dishes after dinner and often surprises me with a latte and something sweet from Mel's shop. Perhaps these gestures will diminish once we're out of the "honeymoon" phase, but somehow I don't think so.

My new job is still relatively quiet since school isn't yet in session, but Miranda has been training me and I've been continuing to observe her sessions with Chloe. This morning is my first one-on-one session with Chloe and Miranda isn't attending. I decided to integrate a blanket-making activity into today's session so that, as we work on the blanket, it gives us a chance to talk without any pressure. Once Chloe picks out the fleece fabrics she likes best, we work together to cut and tie off the ends to make a throw.

"So is there someone you'd like to give the blanket to?" I ask.

Chloe nods. "My mommy. She gets cold a lot."

"I'm sure she'll love it. Do you have fun visiting your mommy?"

"Yes, but sometimes she isn't feeling good and I can't see her. Uncle Peter says the medicine makes her tired. She stays in bed a lot."

"Do you miss her sometimes?"

"Not that much. I see her a lot."

"That's wonderful. And I bet it must be fun living with your Uncle Peter, too."

"He's funny and he lets me go to bed at nine. Mommy makes me go to bed at eight thirty."

"Ah, yes, I like to stay up late too." I pick up a book. "So guess what? I brought a Junie B. Jones book if you want to read it together."

"Okay!"

We prop up some comfy pillows to lean on and then take turns reading aloud. I'm very pleased to see that her reading is well above grade level. She's clearly very bright and I suspect her struggles with schoolwork are largely due to the recent changes at home.

Just as we're finishing a chapter, Peter arrives.

"Hi Uncle Peter!" Chloe runs over to him and he lifts her up into his arms.

"Hey there, kiddo! Did you have fun?" he asks.

"Yes! But do I have to leave yet?"

Peter looks over at me for confirmation and I give a

thumbs up. Chloe goes to a dollhouse where she begins happily arranging furniture and dolls.

"So how did things go today?" Peter asks discreetly, glancing over at his niece.

"Good. She's very sweet and she loves reading. I did want to ask you—have you noticed any particular changes in her since her mom went into the facility?"

"Oh, well, she's definitely a little quieter. She was always a silly kid but now she's a little more reserved, less carefree. I guess that's the best way to describe it. More subdued."

"That's understandable," I say. "I'm sure you're all going through a lot. If there's ever anything I can do, you have my cell so please don't hesitate to reach out."

"I appreciate that, Finola. Thank you." He gives a warm smile.

"You're very welcome. And please, call me Fin."

Chloe overhears. "Fin? Is that your name?"

"Yes, it's a nickname."

"It reminds me of a fish," she says with a giggle, sucking in the sides of her face to resemble a fish.

"Well that's because I *am* a fish! A goldfish to be exact. That's why I have red hair."

Chloe now gives a hearty laugh and that's when I realize I've never really heard her laugh until just now. She has a fantastic laugh.

"You're not a goldfish, Fin!" Chloe protests.

"I'm not?! I thought I was!" I grin.

Peter smiles at the two of us. "You two are quite the pair. Okay Chloe, we need to get going so we can see mommy before dinner." He glances my way. "And we'll see *you* next Friday."

"Okee-dokee." I give a thumbs up. "Oh, and Chloe has

a surprise for her mom. She picked out the fabrics all by herself." Chloe beams as I hand her a gift bag with the blanket inside.

To my surprise, Chloe gives me a big hug. It's one of the sweetest hugs I've ever received.

When I get home, I begin preparing something special for dinner: miso glazed salmon. Nobody enjoys my cooking quite like Mark does. As a bachelor, he ate mainly take-out, so he's always extremely appreciative when I make a home-cooked meal and says I prepare his mom's lemon chicken better than even she does. I think he's just saying that, but it's still very sweet of him to say.

As I cut up some vegetables for dinner, those familiar pangs of guilt return. The ones reminding me that I've been lying to Mark. They've been coming more and more frequently now that we're living together. My eyes tear up with fear and I look down at my trembling hand holding the knife. *I need to tell him the truth.* I take a deep breath and strengthen my resolve. This can't wait another day and as much as it will pain me to tell him, this is not about me. It's about respecting him and doing what's right. After dinner, I'll tell him and I just pray nothing will change between us. *Please G-d.*

As I hear the front door open, my worries miraculously disappear because Mark is home. He finds me in the kitchen sautéing vegetables and embraces me from behind.

"Hi, beautiful," he says, pressing his soft lips to my cheek.

Despite the fact that his kisses are no longer new, they still make me blush. He says he loves that about me.

This particular kiss has set my heart on fire. I turn around and wrap my arms around his neck, molding my body tightly to his. We share a sexy, exploratory kiss.

"I missed you," I whisper against his lips.

"I missed you too." His voice is gentle and sweet and he kisses me again.

"So how was your day?" I ask.

"Very good. I brought in a new tech client so the managing partner is very happy."

"Fantastic!"

"So how did it go with Chloe today?" he asks as he loosens his tie.

"Good! She seems to really be starting to warm up to me."

"Well, she's very lucky to have you."

"I know I need to maintain an appropriate distance but it's so hard to do that with her. I want to make sure she's getting enough attention and love. Her mom is deteriorating more rapidly than anticipated and her uncle works a lot, so she's with babysitters a lot."

Mark lets out an exhale. "I hate to even bring this up but has her family made arrangements for Chloe's future?"

"I'm not sure whether her uncle would become her guardian but I think he's her closest relative. Her father's parental rights were terminated several years ago."

Mark looks troubled. "This is more your area of expertise than mine, but I hope her mom has thought ahead and taken the necessary legal steps so Chloe doesn't become a ward of the State. I know it's painful to think about, but she should designate someone as

Chloe's guardian while she's still able to."

"You're right. Miranda and I haven't discussed this yet but I'll speak with her about it. Maybe you know a lawyer we can refer the family to?"

"Yes, I do. I'll get you her contact info. She's excellent."

"This is so upsetting to think about. I hope I'll be able to help Chloe."

"I know you'll do everything you can for her. I wish I'd had someone like you when I lost my parents. I think it would have made a huge difference in my life."

I pause, realizing that this conversation may be bringing back unpleasant memories for him. "I'm so sorry you had to go through so much loss at such a young age." I approach him, gently caressing his cheek.

He takes me securely in his arms, closing the space between our bodies. "Thank you, Finny. I don't tell you nearly enough how special you are to me."

"Yes you do. You say it all the time, with your glances and your smiles and your magical kisses." My lips curve upwards knowingly.

His lips graze mine and then he gives me a slow, tender kiss. "You mean like that?"

"That was a good one." I grin. "I think it was saying that I'm the best thing that's ever happened to you."

He chuckles. "Well that's a given."

I giggle into his mouth. "You're turning me on, Mark with a 'k.'"

"I'd love to rectify that situation but I forgot to mention that Matt and Jennifer are in town and want to stop by."

"Oh! With the baby?"

"Yes."

"Oh good! I'm so glad they reached out to you. So I guess that means everything is smoothed over between you and them?"

"We're getting there. It's a good sign."

It looks like my conversation with Mark is going to have to wait.

Chapter Twenty-Six

~ Fin ~

Present Day

Matt and Jennifer's baby, Olivia, is without a doubt the most adorable baby I've ever seen. She gives the cutest smiles and giggles and she's extremely curious. Mark seemed a little cautious holding her at first, but then the next thing I knew he was carrying her around like a pro and showing her the Matisse goldfish print on the wall which she was completely fascinated by.

"I think Olivia has a crush on you, Uncle Mark," Jennifer says with a grin.

Mark is now dancing with Olivia whose eyes are literally glowing up at him. It's the cutest thing watching them together and it makes me love him even more if that's possible.

"You know, Olivia," Mark says sweetly to her, "you wouldn't even exist if it wasn't for me. I'm the one who got your mommy and daddy together."

Matt laughs in disbelief. "Well I don't know about that."

"Oh, I do. Had I not lured the two of you into the bedroom together all those years ago, there's no way either of you would have had the guts to go for it."

Jennifer smirks in Mark's direction. "Well...you may have helped things along a little."

"See, even Jenn agrees with me," Mark says. "You see what I have to deal with here, Olivia? When you get older, you'll defend me, right?"

Olivia smiles up at him, seemingly mesmerized. I can't help but giggle, wondering if that's how I look when I look at Mark. Probably.

Mark smiles in my direction. "And what's so funny over there, Miss Fin?"

"I'll tell you later," I say with a lingering giggle.

"I'll look forward to that." He gives me a quick wink.

"I'm trying to decide which one of you Olivia looks like," I say to Matt and Jennifer.

"I think she takes after Jenn." Matt looks over at his wife adoringly before giving her a quick peck. "She's sweet to the core."

"Thanks, but I think she gets all her best qualities from you," Jennifer tells her husband.

The two pause to smile at one another and it's clear how much in love they are.

"Well, I think we can all agree on one thing," Mark says. "And that is that Olivia is the cutest baby on the planet. She's the perfect combination of both of you."

"Oh! I almost forgot," I blurt out. "Mark and I made something for Olivia." I hand the gift to Jennifer.

She unwraps the present and finds the homemade fleece baby blanket that we made along with some goat's milk baby products.

"The colors are perfect!" Jennifer exclaims. "And I was actually just reading about goat's milk soap. It's very gentle on babies' skin."

"Oh, I'm so glad you like it!" I say.

Matt interrupts. "Hold on, did I just hear you say that you and Mark made the blanket together?"

"Yes, he was actually the one who picked out the unicorn fabric."

Matt eyes Mark with amusement. "Unicorns, huh?"

"Yes," Mark confirms. "You got a problem with unicorns?"

"No...I've actually grown very fond of them over the past month. They've invaded our home and are apparently magical creatures, aren't they, Olivia." Matt smiles at his little girl.

When Olivia spots her daddy, she immediately reaches her arms out for him.

"Just in the nick of time," Mark says, transferring Olivia back to Matt. "I think something went down in her diaper. I'm here for everything but that."

"Okay, Livvy, let's get you cleaned up," Matt says, grabbing the diaper bag. "Maybe Uncle Mark and I will take you out for a walk around the block while it's still light out."

Olivia kicks up her legs.

"We'll take that as a *Yes*," Matt says.

Jennifer offers to change the baby but Matt says he's all set. Olivia is daddy's little girl for sure.

The guys leave for their walk and I make a pot of tea for Jennifer and me.

"So I hear you started a new job at an elementary school," Jennifer says. "How do you like it so far?"

"I'm really enjoying it, but I still have so much to learn. They hired me to work with one student in particular. Her name is Chloe and her mom is very ill."

Jennifer's eyes instantly widen. "Chloe? Wait, is her mom's name Camille?"

"Yes, why? Do you know them?"

"I used to be Chloe's reading buddy when I lived in Boston!"

I put my cup down. "Seriously? You're *that* Jennifer?!"

"Yes, and actually, now that I think about it, Chloe's uncle did tell me she was getting a new school social worker. So that's you, then?"

"Yes! Oh my gosh, I was actually going to get your number from Peter so I could call you!"

"That's such a coincidence. I speak with Peter every so often but the last time he and I spoke, he said that Camille wasn't doing well at all. It's absolutely heart-breaking."

I nod. "It's terrible. Chloe is so sweet and her mother still hasn't told her just how serious her condition is. I don't think she wants to frighten her. Peter said that ever since Camille went into a facility, Chloe's been a lot quieter and less social."

Jennifer's expression saddens. "She's such a great girl, and so bright, and very funny. She always was a little shy but I wonder if the situation is causing her to withdraw even more."

"It would be completely understandable."

"Is there anything I can do to help? I want to help."

"I think you just being there for her like you've been doing really helps her feel supported. She says she loves it when you read together on your calls."

We agree to arrange another video call for them as soon as possible. Jennifer also offers to visit Chloe, which is extremely kind given that she's a new mother.

Jennifer and I go on to discuss some of her favorite haunts in the Boston area, as she lived here for several years before moving back to Shelby Falls to be with Matt. There are a few bookstores that I'll definitely have to check out. Jennifer is such a sweetheart and I'm so glad she and Matt decided to visit today. I really think it meant a lot to Mark too.

Later that evening in bed, it doesn't take long for Mark to begin waxing poetic about Olivia and all of the cute things she did earlier.

"Did you see how she smiled when I showed her the bright colors in the pictures?" His eyes are beaming with pride. "She's very observant."

"She's absolutely adorable and you were so good with her."

"A lot of my cousins already have kids, so I'm used to being around babies." He then pauses, playing with the edge of the blanket as if contemplating something. "I want to ask you a question but I don't want to upset you."

"You won't," I assure him. "What is it?"

"Well, we've never really talked about this but do you want to have kids?"

I smile with relief. "Yes, I do. Do you?"

"Definitely," he says, equally relieved. "Having a family of my own is something I've wanted my entire life."

"I want that too," I say, holding his eyes with mine. "With you."

As we settle into one another's arms, I am confronted with the painful truth that we *did* almost have a child together. I forcibly drive this thought from my head and instead hold fast to the belief that one day we will have a family together.

And I pray for the second time today.

Chapter Twenty-Seven

~ Mark ~

Present Day

I'm suddenly awoken by the sound of Fin's screams.

I bolt upright. "What's wrong?!"

Fin is still half asleep but looks terrified. "My father was here!"

"Your father?"

"Yes, he was here! He broke into the house!"

"Honey, calm down. No one is here. You just had a bad dream."

"No! He broke into the house and tried to take me and our baby away!"

She's clearly confused. "Honey, it was just a dream. I'm right here and everything's fine." I hold her until she seems to calm down.

"You really didn't hear anything?" she finally asks.

"No, but I'll go check downstairs. You just sit tight." I go downstairs and check the doors and garage, then return to Fin. "Everything is locked," I reassure her. "Can I get you a glass of water?"

"No…I guess it must have been a dream. I'm sorry I woke you. I think I'm just very worried that my father is going to get out of prison and find me again."

"He won't. He's locked up and he's not getting out any time soon. Don't worry." As I put my arms around her, her body begins to slowly relax.

"The dream felt so real," she explains. "We had a little boy and I couldn't find him in his crib, and then my father was holding him and threatening to take him if I didn't come with him. You weren't there and I started screaming for him to give me back our baby but he wouldn't! I woke up before I could see what happened next."

"Shhh, it's okay, it wasn't real," I reassure her. "There's no baby."

I rub her back, but when I try to comfort her more, she pulls away, pulling her legs up to her chest and holding them tightly to her body. She isn't making eye contact and when she finally does turn to look at me, she looks distraught as she fights back tears. She then turns away again.

"There's something I haven't told you," she says quietly into her knees as a single tear descends her cheek. "I don't want to, but I have to. I'm just afraid." She looks over at me again, as if seeking the courage to continue.

She doesn't sound like herself at all and is visibly exhausted. "Honey, it's the middle of the night and you're upset. We can talk about this in the morning."

She wipes away the single tear resolutely. "No, I need to do this now. I need you to know the truth." There is a defiance in her voice and I can see there's no stopping her.

"Okay, then tell me. It'll be fine, I promise." *But I don't feel fine. Something isn't right.*

Her voice stills. "It's about our baby."

Chapter Twenty-Eight

~ *Fin* ~

Two Years Earlier

As I wait in the exam room for my very first prenatal visit, there is still ample time to berate myself again for making such a colossal mess of my life. A life that I've been planning since I was about fifteen. The plan was for me to work my way through college and eventually get my Master's in Social Work because I really want to help kids who are facing similar challenges to the ones I faced growing up. But in one night, I ruined everything.

What were you thinking? Having a one-night stand with a virtual stranger in the back seat of his pickup truck? You know the pill isn't 100% effective, not to mention that you could have gotten an STD.

And now you're pregnant.

The father—Mark—didn't even believe me when I told him about the pregnancy a few days ago. He was distant and cold and said there was no way he could be the father because he "pulled out." I probably shouldn't have been shocked by his reaction but I was. When we were together, he seemed like a genuinely nice guy, someone I felt a connection with. He honestly didn't strike me as a dick at all, but clearly he is. He all but called me a liar when I told him about the baby. I became flustered with him, which isn't like me at all, and I even confessed that I haven't slept with anyone but him in well over a year, but he still clearly thinks I'm lying.

What a fucking asshole. While I could insist on a paternity test, our mutual friend Matt told me that Mark is a womanizer and always has been, so do I even want this jerk in my life or the baby's? After the way he's conducted himself, I don't think I do.

But the reality is that I don't think I can do this alone. I can barely support myself much less a baby. I'd be putting every last dime I earn into day care, leaving nothing left to support us. We could move in with my mom (who I haven't yet told about the pregnancy), but her apartment is too small. She works full-time so I can't lean on her to watch the baby during the day while I work. And then there's the issue of my schooling. Most of my courses are at night. So the only solution I see is to quit school and see if the restaurant will let me work nights. That way I can take care of the baby during the day, my mom can watch the baby at night (hopefully), and I can then earn enough money to support us. I was actually up for a promotion to restaurant manager, but that would require me to work some day shifts, so that would be out. But at least as a manager, I'd have health insurance.

That's right, I don't even have health insurance; just a small major medical policy for emergencies. Does a pregnancy count as an emergency? I doubt it. How will I be able to afford all of the doctor's appointments, the delivery, and the baby's future pediatric appointments? I don't think I can earn enough money at the restaurant to pay for everything. I would need to try find an additional part-time job—hopefully one that offers health insurance. Is that even possible?

This is certainly not how I want to bring a child into the world. I know first hand what it feels like to not have a father in your life. It sucks. I also know what it feels like to live paycheck to paycheck and the stress that that caused my mother throughout my childhood. I don't want that for myself or my baby.

Tears begin to well up in my eyes. *What am I going to do?*

My doctor soon enters the examination room and confirms what my drug store pregnancy test already revealed. "Congratulations, Finola. You're six weeks along," she says with a smile. "Now I see that you didn't provide any information about the father. Is the father going to be involved?"

"No, he's not."

She nods and goes on to explain what type of prenatal vitamins I need to start taking, along with providing an overview of the timeline for appointments. "Since this is your first pregnancy, are there any questions that I can answer for you?"

I don't even know where to begin. "I'm not sure if you would know the answer to this but right now I only have a major medical policy, so do you know if the delivery would qualify for coverage under that type of policy?"

"That's a very good question. I think it might, depending upon your policy, but you would need to discuss that with our insurance biller and your insurance company. Danielle can go over all of this with you. Do you have any other questions before we schedule your next prenatal visit in a few weeks?"

I hesitate before asking my next question. "Since I'm only a few weeks pregnant, I also just wanted to understand all of my options."

She meets my eyes. "Are you asking about termination options?"

I hesitate again before nodding.

"Yes, well, since you're very early on in your pregnancy, there is a medication that you can take orally to terminate the pregnancy. It's extremely safe for you at this stage, but you would need to decide in the next week or so because there's only a short window to do this. Are you considering termination?"

"I'm not sure. I just wanted to understand my options. I'm in school and I work a lot, and the father isn't in the picture, so I'm just not sure I can even afford to have a child." I try not to break down in front of her, but I'm so overwhelmed and scared.

"I understand. It can be overwhelming. For now, I'll give you some information about the medication I was telling you about and you can read it over and think about it. If you do decide to proceed with this medication, I do want to let you know that there will be a lot of bleeding and cramping, similar to a very heavy period, so you will want to plan on being out of work for one to two days."

Since I have no further questions, the doctor leaves me to get dressed in silence, save for the sound of peppy, piped-in music. I think I'm in a state of mild shock. I'm certainly in no condition to discuss insurance with Danielle. I feel overheated and I need to get out of here NOW.

By the time I arrive back at my apartment, I have a splitting headache, more than likely due to the stress of all of this. I can't even tell my mother because it will just upset her and I don't want to burden her. No, I need to figure this out on my own.

A feeling of aloneness overwhelms me. If I'm being

completely honest, I don't know if I can do this all by myself. I feel tremendous shame and guilt for even thinking of terminating the pregnancy. *Am I weak for not feeling ready to have a child by myself? Is it self-centered of me to want to finish my degree and create a stable life for myself **before** having a child?* I do want to have a child, but not like this. I want more for my child. I want him or her to have a father. That's extremely important to me. This is the most difficult decision I've ever had to make and being honest with myself is mandatory.

Not wanting to do anything rash, I won't make any decisions today.

But as the day progresses, I'm growing more and more anxious. I need to decide, and I think I already have.

A feeling of relief washes over me, followed by tremendous guilt for feeling relieved, followed by intense sorrow for what I am about to do.

The next day, I call the doctor's office to obtain a prescription for the medication. I make a silent promise to myself to carry this secret with me to my grave. *I will tell no one.* That's just how it has to be. Because there are those who will never understand or agree with my decision and might judge me. But the fact is that they don't need to understand. This is *my* decision to make and only I know what is best for me.

* * *

I've been sitting at my kitchen table for the last fifteen minutes just staring at the prescription medication. I can still change my mind. It's up to me. Tears gather in my eyes, awaiting my final decision. I look down at my abdomen and gently touch it. I don't know if I can do this. A tear trickles down my cheek.

But my mind hasn't forgotten all the reasons why I decided to do this. Those reasons haven't changed. It's just really hard to actually do this, especially all by myself. I ask myself the question one last time and my answer remains the same.

So I steel myself and swallow the medication. I refuse to cry even though I want to.

I will myself to do something, anything to get my mind off of this nightmare. I try to watch a show but the sadness won't leave me. I finally take a nap to put myself out of my misery. A few hours later I feel the medication start to take effect and, just as the doctor said, there is a lot of cramping and bleeding over the course of several hours and through the night.

And then it's over.

But it will never really be over for me. I will have to live with this decision for the rest of my life and I pray it was the right one.

As I climb into bed Sunday night, I suddenly feel an excruciating emptiness. The baby is gone and a wave of unbearable loneliness consumes me. But the tears won't come.

Chapter Twenty-Nine

~ Mark ~

Present Day

Fin's voice trails off in defeat, her arms still wrapped tightly around her legs, barely able to make eye contact with me.

"The baby would have been about a year and a half by now, just like in my dream," she says despondently.

I nod robotically. I've heard every single word that she said but my mind is still reeling and trying to process everything. I feel numb. We could have had a child in the next room right now fast asleep...had I not been such a ***fucking asshole*** and listened to her when she tried to tell me about the pregnancy. I will ***never*** forgive myself for abandoning her like I did and leaving her all alone to cope with the unthinkable. This is ALL my fault. My heart aches for her and for the loss of our baby. But I cannot and will not let her see how upset I am because I do not want her beating herself up any more than she already has. This isn't about me, it's about Fin and what ***she*** needs.

I swallow back the encroaching army of tears and don't speak until I'm absolutely certain I am in complete control of my emotions.

"Fin, come here." I reach out my arms for her but she doesn't come.

Her tear-filled eyes eventually lift to meet mine. "I'm so sorry," she says softly, barely holding back her tears.

"I should have told you. I understand if you don't want to be around me right now." Her tears finally give way and silently fall.

It's excruciating seeing her cry and all I want to do is make the pain go away—for both of us. I need to hold her.

"Fin, I love you. Please, just come here."

She studies my face and then hesitantly inches towards me. I immediately wrap myself around her like a cocoon and she quietly weeps in my arms. She's held this secret for so long and I can feel the raw anguish in her cries.

"It's okay, babe, everything's going to be okay, I promise." I gently caress the back of her head, desperately trying to fight back my own tears, but to no avail.

So we let go—together—holding on tightly to one another and crying, until our tears are finally spent. Then it's completely silent, save for the sound of our breaths.

I slowly pull back and meet her weary eyes, cupping her cheek. "Honey, listen to me, *none* of this is your fault —it's *mine*. You had to make one of the most excruciating decisions all by yourself and I think you're the bravest person I know."

"No," she protests. "I wasn't brave at all, I was weak. I should have fought harder to make you hear me."

"Fin, you tried your best but I wasn't listening to you. That's all on *me*. You did nothing wrong."

"But knowing you like I do now, I'm positive I could have gotten through to you. I just needed to try harder. And if I had, everything would be different now."

"How so?"

"You would have helped with the medical costs and

we would have worked things out so we could have the baby..."

She's right. We would have found a way. But I can't let her know that. It would break her heart.

I frame her face with my hands. "Sweetheart, listen to me. We really don't know what we would have done back then. You think you know, but you don't—not for sure."

She startles. "Are you saying you might not have wanted to have the baby?"

I know my answer to that question will completely devastate her. Because the truth is that I would have wanted to have the baby and I would have loved him or her with all my heart.

So I lie.

"I don't know what I would have wanted," I say. "I'm just not sure."

She looks directly into my eyes, perplexed by my response, and somehow I keep it together for her sake.

"I...I don't know how you can say that," she stammers. "You said earlier tonight that you wanted to have kids so I just assumed that you would have wanted to have the baby."

I can do this.

"Yes, I do want a family," I say. "But all of this happened over two years ago and we weren't even together. I don't think we should try to speculate about something this important."

She just stares at me, her emerald eyes searching deep inside mine—for the truth. I hold my ground and don't dare look away.

And then she reaches for my face, her gentle, steady eyes holding mine as she caresses my cheek with her thumb. "I know what you're doing. And I love you for it."

"Fin, I—"

"But you can't protect me from the truth. We need to be honest with each other, even if it hurts. It's the only way to move forward."

There's no escaping her eyes, or the truth.

"Fin...I don't know if I can do this." Talking about loss, feeling loss, accepting loss—this all terrifies me ever since my parents were killed.

"Then let me do it for us," she says gently, with a renewed strength and calm in her voice that I didn't expect. "The truth is that we would have had the baby, even if we had to make some major changes in our lives. And I know we would have loved our baby and given him or her the most loving home. I know this in my heart."

I swallow hard, taking her hand in between mine. "That's all true."

She wraps her arms around my middle and we just hold each other, finding solace in one another's arms, neither of us letting go of the other until we're both ready.

When we finally pull back, regret and something resembling fear lingers in her eyes. "I was so afraid to tell you. I thought you were going to hate me and I might lose you."

"Honey, I could never hate you. **Never**. I love you. You're the one who should be hating me. This is all my fault."

She shakes her head. "It's not."

"How can you say that? Our baby would be sleeping in the next room if I hadn't allowed my stupidity or jealousy, or whatever the hell it was, get in the way. I'm so angry with myself and so ashamed of how I treated you."

"No, Mark, you're forgetting one important fact. I was a part of this too. You may want to take responsibility for all of it, but please don't. Because things are rarely all one person's fault and I need to accept responsibility too. Otherwise, I'll never be able to truly forgive myself and heal."

I pause to think. "I don't know."

"Well I *do* know." She starts to get emotional, her face full of remorse and resolve. "I'm asking for your forgiveness."

I shake my head. "Fin, there is nothing to forgive."

But she shakes her head defiantly. "Yes there is. You know there is."

I'm astounded by how strong-willed she can be at times. But her assertiveness and confidence are also qualities that I love about her. She's determined and unbending when she believes in something or someone and I can see this isn't something she's going to budge on. I would do absolutely anything for this woman—anything—and if I have to concede on this, I will.

I exhale in resignation. "You win. I'm going to say these words, but not because I think you've done anything that needs forgiving. Because I don't...But yes, I forgive you."

She lets out a relieved breath and dives headfirst into my chest, hugging me tightly. "Thank you. You have no idea how much I needed to hear that."

I pull back, still holding her securely in my arms. "But now I need to ask you for the same thing. Can you ever forgive me?"

Her warm gaze immediately consoles me. "I already have, a long time ago."

Relief washes over me. This woman has the most incredible way of supporting and lifting me up. It's just how she was made and how she loves.

I feel myself tearing up. "Fin, I love you, so much more than I ever thought possible, and it scares the hell out of me sometimes. Because I don't think I could ever survive losing you."

She looks into my eyes with a calming tranquility and strokes my cheek with the backs of her fingers. "Don't be scared, my love. I'm not going anywhere. I'm yours."

Our lips impatiently collide and I pour every ounce of myself into our kiss, inhaling her love.

I whisper into her ear, "If angels exist, you're mine."

"And you're mine," she whispers back.

We lay back in bed together, face to face, smiling. As I stroke her hair back from her face, I feel my eyes relax into hers as a wave of peace surrounds us. It's her. It's all her.

She finds her place on my chest and we finally close our eyes. But just as I'm on the verge of sleep, she whispers, "One day, we *will* have a family of our own, just like you've always wanted."

Her words trigger my eyes to open and when I do, I find her gazing up at me.

I hold her gaze. "We will, I promise."

She smiles up at me and when I look into her eyes, I see not only love, but trust too. I will safeguard it and her forever.

Chapter Thirty

~ *Fin* ~

Present Day

I don't think I've ever been this happy in a relationship before. Deliriously happy actually. And ever since I told Mark the truth about the baby, I feel even closer to him. Keeping that secret was like keeping a part of myself from him and I was always afraid that when I finally did tell him, it would destroy his trust in me. But it didn't. In fact, it made us stronger. I now realize that it took sharing the truth with him for me to properly grieve, and that's because I needed him beside me to grieve *with*. While we can't change the past, I think we can finally put that part of it behind us and concentrate on our future together.

The summer is coming to an end, and with it, the start of a new school year. Chloe and I have gotten to know each other very well this summer while Miranda has been on maternity leave and I'm hoping she'll feel more comfortable in school this year. Unfortunately, her mother Camille is deteriorating and today her Uncle Peter called to tell me that Camille would like to speak with me in person. We've only spoken by phone so perhaps she just wants to meet me.

After receiving approval from my supervisor, I drive to a facility in a neighboring town where Camille is receiving palliative care. I've never been to a facility like this before and, while it's nicely furnished and the staff seem very friendly, it is eerily quiet. I make my way down the hallway to Camille's room where I find a thin woman sitting in a chair hooked up to oxygen. When she sees me, she takes off her oxygen mask to greet me. Even in her weakened state, she's extremely attractive with a beautiful smile. I smile back, but underneath I feel tremendous sadness for her and Chloe.

"Hello, Finola. It's so nice to finally meet you. I'm Camille." Her voice is quiet and she speaks very methodically, as if regulating her breaths.

"It's very nice to meet you, too," I say. "Chloe has told me so much about you."

"Well she adores you. My brother, Peter, tells me she talks about you all the time."

I smile. "Chloe is a very special little girl. You've raised a wonderful daughter."

"Thank you. She's my only child and she really is my whole world." Camille breaths in some oxygen before continuing. "Thank you for coming today."

"Of course," I say.

"So I asked you here because there's something I need to speak with you about. I don't know how much you know, but my prognosis is very poor, and I need to make plans for Chloe's future." She pauses again for oxygen before resuming.

I nod. "I'm so sorry. I want to help in any way that I can."

"Thank you. I'm hoping you'll be able to. I'm going to need to designate a guardian because her father isn't in the picture. His parental rights were terminated shortly after she was born."

I nod again.

"Peter is Chloe's closest relative and he loves her very

much, but he's single and travels a lot for work. If she lived with him, she would end up being with babysitters half the time and I need to make sure she has stability in her life."

"I understand."

"I realize I don't know you well," Camille says, "but I've always had very good instincts about people and my instincts tell me you are someone I can trust my daughter with." Her eyes begin to mist and I feel my own doing the same.

"I promise I'll be there for her in any way that I can," I assure her.

"I appreciate that, Finola." She pauses for more oxygen. "I don't know quite how to ask you this but would you ever consider sharing guardianship with Peter and having Chloe live with you? Peter would be involved in all of the decisions but I just think Chloe needs a stable home with a caregiver who can really be there for her on a daily basis."

I try to mask the surprise that is probably written all over my face. I'm terrible at hiding my feelings and I certainly wasn't expecting this. I do care about Chloe very much but this would be a huge commitment and there are so many considerations.

I carefully choose my words so as not to offend Camille in any way. "I'm truly honored that you would trust me with your daughter and I want you to know that I absolutely adore Chloe. I just need some time to think about this and I also need to discuss this with my boyfriend since we live together. This would need to be a joint decision."

Her eyes brighten with hope. "Oh, of course, I completely understand and I want you to take as much time as you need. Does your boyfriend know Chloe?"

"Yes, Mark has met her a few times and they get along very well. He has a very playful way about him and definitely keeps her laughing."

Camille smiles. "That's wonderful to hear. I didn't realize you were living with someone, so I would of course want to meet Mark to be absolutely sure this is right for everyone."

"Of course," I say. "I would also need to clear this with the school to be sure this wouldn't violate their policies and also make sure they can reassign Chloe to a different social worker."

"I'll consent to whatever the school wishes to do as far as her sessions are concerned. What's most important to me is that I have the very best guardian in place for her. And I think that's you, Finola. Honestly, you have no idea what a relief this is—the fact that you're even considering this."

As we say our goodbyes, I feel an immense sorrow for what this woman is going through. How horrible to have to prepare for your daughter's life without you.

Over dinner, I explain the situation to Mark and, at first, he's a little surprised, just as I was. He quietly takes everything in and is laser-focused. I'm not quite sure what to make of his silence.

He finally asks me a question. "So how do you feel about all of this?"

I sigh. "I feel very sad for them both and I honestly didn't see this coming at all. But now that Camille's asked me, it does feel right. Still, this would be a huge change—for both of us—and potentially a life-long commitment. So, regardless of how *I* feel, this needs to be a decision we both make." I study his expression but it's hard to read. "So how do you feel about all of this?"

His quick reply startles me. "I'm 100% in favor of it."

"Really? You don't have any reservations?"

"Honestly, no. Chloe's a really special kid and I know how fond you are of her. It's such a sad situation. No kid should have to watch a parent dying. It's cruel. When my parents died, at least it happened in an instant. Sounds crazy to say that, but it's true."

I rest my hand on his. "You would understand more than anyone how this feels."

"I want to do whatever I can to help her," he says. "So yes, if this is something you want to do, I support that."

The more we talk, the more certain we are that this is the right thing to do. As far as the logistics of Chloe living with us, we have an extra bedroom and because I work at her school, my schedule aligns perfectly with hers. So I would be able to spend a lot of quality time with her.

"Let's take the night to think about all of this," I say. "This is too important a decision to rush into."

Mark nods.

"But Mark, I don't think it's an accident that I met Chloe. I think this was meant to be. And you're the one who led me to her."

He holds my hand up to his lips. "I do think things happen for a reason," he says. "The twists and turns of our lives don't always seem to make sense, until they do. Both of us know what it's like to not have a parent in our lives and now we have the chance to really help her."

"Have I told you lately how truly wonderful you are?"

"Well...you certainly have in bed..." His eyes twinkle

playfully.

I climb onto his lap. "Well, yeah, I have been loud and clear about that." I grin knowingly. "You're amazing in that department."

"My ego thanks you."

I give him a sexy kiss, swirling my tongue inside his mouth.

"Fin..." I can hear the quiet longing in his voice and he swallows hard.

Lifting up my shirt and kissing the valley between my breasts, I can feel him hardening beneath me. He carries me upstairs to the bedroom and shows me just how much he loves me, over and over again.

Chapter Thirty-One

~ *Fin* ~

Present Day

It takes no more than a hot second for Mark to completely charm Camille. He definitely has a way of winning people over, and by people I mean women. Not only is he very handsome, but he also has a great sense of humor and is very amiable. If I were another type of person, I might be plagued by jealousy at seeing how women gravitate to him, but I'm not the jealous type. I know he loves me and isn't interested in being with anyone but me. I've never been more sure of anything in my life.

By the end of the week, Camille's lawyer has drawn up the guardianship papers. Peter and I will serve as co-guardians for all decision-making, Chloe will live with Mark and me, and Peter will of course be able to see her as frequently as he can. The school has been very accommodating and is reassigning Chloe to another social worker until Miranda returns from maternity leave. As sad as this is, I think we're all very relieved that there is now a plan in place.

Mark and I have been re-doing the spare bedroom, taking our decorating cues from Chloe so that she feels as connected as possible to the space. She chose a light lavender for the walls with a crisp white trim, and Mark and I have been busily painting. Each time Chloe visits, she brings another one of her stuffed animals and she has taken great care to arrange them on her new bed in a very particular way.

Mark has also been relentlessly spoiling her with toys but this really does need to stop. Today at the toy store, I once again caught him red-handed with an armful of stuffed animals.

"I think we need to impose a moratorium on stuffed animals, babe," I announce, taking a baby elephant out of his hand and returning it to the store shelf.

"But he's really cute," he protests, taking it back off the shelf.

I roll my eyes in defeat. "I give up."

"I have a stuffed elephant that my dad gave me when I was born. When the trunk is raised up like this one, it's good luck."

My gaze softens. "Okay, we'll keep this one. But no more for at least a week."

One hour and five toys later, we drop our packages down on the bench in our foyer just as my cell phone rings. It's Peter.

"Am I catching you at a bad time?" Peter asks.

"No, we just got back from the store. Mark went a little nuts there, but it's all good. What's up?" There is now silence on the other end of the phone. "Peter? Are you still there?"

"Yeah," his voice crackles. "It's just that...well...Camille passed away about an hour ago."

I gasp. While we all knew this was coming, it somehow feels like a complete shock.

"Oh, Peter, I'm so sorry." Mark's eyes dart to mine and I mouth the news to him. He looks as shocked as I feel and we both stare blankly at one another.

"I think I told you that Camille didn't want a service

and asked to be cremated, so I need to finalize the arrangements," Peter says robotically. "I haven't told Chloe yet. She's with a babysitter at my house. Would you be able to pick her up in about an hour and bring her to your house to stay over?"

"Of course," I say. "We'll keep her with us for as long as you need."

He breathes a sigh of relief—and sadness. "Thank you. I'll come over tomorrow and, if it's okay with you, I'd like us to tell Chloe together."

"Okay. Mark and I are so sorry for your loss, Peter."

As I put down my phone, I reach for Mark and we just hold one another. Numbness sets in.

The following day, Peter comes over and we all share the difficult news with Chloe. She looks a little puzzled at first and barely says a word. Because she's been in a state of transition for so many months, perhaps she doesn't fully grasp the finality of the situation.

"Mommy's really gone?" she finally asks Peter.

"Yes, honey, Mommy's in heaven now." Peter's voice cracks as he tries not to break down in front of her. "She told me that she loves you more than anything in this world and she always will."

"Mommy told me that too." She pauses. "But are you sure she's already in heaven?"

"Yes, I think she is," Peter says. "And you know you can talk to her whenever you want. A good time might be when you say your prayers."

Chloe nods as though this all makes perfect sense. "Can I go to my room now?"

We all look at one another. "Sure," I say. "Do you want me to come with you?"

She shakes her head.

"Okay, I'll be up in a few minutes," I say. "And maybe we can play with your dollhouse, okay?"

Chloe nods and quickly scurries upstairs.

Once out of earshot, Peter tears up and buries his face in his hands. He's going to need time to process everything. We sit quietly with him until he's ready to speak.

"I hope she's going to be okay—Chloe I mean," Peter says. "This is just so hard."

Mark nods. "I'm really sorry. If there's anything we can do, we're here for you."

"I feel like I'm losing not only my sister, but my niece too." Peter says.

"I'm so sorry, Peter," I say, struggling with what I can possibly say to help him. "You're welcome in our home any time and we want you to come over as often as you'd like."

"Yes, absolutely," Mark reiterates. "You're always welcome here, any time." Mark leans over and gives Peter a gentle pat on the back.

Peter nods appreciatively. "Thank you. What you guys are doing for Chloe is so incredible. She's so lucky to have you both. Really, thank you." He reluctantly gets up from the couch. "I'll bring over the rest of her things tomorrow. Let me just say goodbye to her."

We lead him upstairs and find Chloe playing on her bed with her dolls.

"Hey, pumpkin," Peter says. "I need to take care of a few things at my house and you're going to be staying here with Fin and Mark just like we talked about, okay?"

Chloe looks over at me and Mark, then back at Peter, and then nods hesitantly.

"Everything's going to be okay, I promise," Peter says, squeezing his eyes shut as he gives Chloe a hug and kisses the top of her head. She looks upset but this little girl manages to hold it together better than the three of us combined. Peter quickly sees himself out, clearly not wanting to break down in front of her.

My eyes now meet Mark's, in search of answers as to how we can best help Chloe right now. He knows all too well how hard this must be for her.

"Do you want to come downstairs and play a video game with me?" Mark asks Chloe.

"Okay, but first I need to finish putting my dolls to sleep," she says.

"Okay, gotcha. Well you just let me know when you're ready to play, okay?"

Mark leans in to kiss my cheek. "I'll be downstairs if you need me," he says into my ear, his concerned eyes latching onto mine. While he's masking it well, I sense that none of this is easy for him given his own experience with loss.

"We'll be down shortly," I reassure him. I then find a spot beside Chloe on her bed. "Mind if I join you?" I ask.

"Okay."

I reach for one of her dolls. "She's so beautiful," I say. "She looks a lot like you with her wavy brown hair and dark brown eyes."

"She's supposed to look like me," Chloe says. "Mommy and me picked her out together."

"What's her name?"

"Joy. It's mommy's middle name."

"Well, she's very pretty, just like you."

The corner of Chloe's mouth turns up into a reserved smile. "I think she's kind of shy," she says. "That's why she doesn't talk a lot."

"That's okay. When she's ready, she'll talk."

She nods. "I told Mommy I'm living with you and Mark now and she said that's a good thing."

"You told her?"

"Yes, when I came upstairs I told her. She says she's glad."

I wind my arm around her. "You know, it's okay if you're feeling sad about Mommy. I'm feeling sad and Mark is too. Maybe you and Mark can talk later because he knows how you're feeling...His mommy and daddy went to heaven too when he was little."

Chloe's eyes grow wide. "They did? Do you think Mommy can be friends with them?"

Such a comforting thought.

"Definitely," I say.

"That's good. I want Mommy to have friends up there. Can I ask Mark if he can ask his mommy and daddy to look for Mommy?"

"Sure, let's go tell him." I reach for Chloe's hand and we head downstairs, finding Mark killing time on his phone. He jumps up from the couch the minute he sees us.

"Everybody doing okay?" He tries to sound upbeat but concern fills his eyes.

My eyes reassure him. "Yes, Chloe actually wants to ask you something about your parents, if that's okay."

His initial surprise is quickly replaced with an eagerness to help and he and Chloe take a seat on the couch.

"So what would you like to know?" His voice is gentle and sweet.

"I was wondering, do you think my mommy can be friends with your mommy and daddy up in heaven?"

He's a little stunned but quickly recovers. "Oh, well, sure! In fact, I wouldn't be surprised if they aren't friends already."

"That's what I was thinking too," Chloe declares. "Mommy is very friendly and if your mommy and daddy are nice, then they can all be friends. She'll need friends up there."

The corners of his mouth curve upwards slightly. "You know, you're very smart to think of that, Chloe. You're right, we all need friends, even in heaven. Good thinking, kiddo." He tousles her hair affectionately and she smiles up at him proudly.

"I can play a video game now if you want," Chloe offers.

"I thought you'd never ask." He hops up to turn on her favorite racing game and my heart warms with affection.

While cheering on Chloe, I lightly massage Mark's shoulders and neck from behind. His smiling eyes briefly dart up to mine and instantly melt my insides.

Chloe's laughter begins to fill the room and she begs Mark to let her win.

"But you always win!" Mark protests while of course letting her win, which leads to Chloe squealing with delight. Given the sadness that ushered in the day, I'm so grateful for the light that Mark always seems to be able to inject into even the most dire situation. That's his way. Perhaps it's what helped him survive his own loss.

"Thanks," I whisper into his ear. "She seems to be doing okay."

"We'll be here for her every step of the way." He reaches up to kiss my lips. "You and I."

After tucking Chloe in for the night, Mark and I collapse in bed early. It's been a very emotional day for all of us. And while Chloe seems to be doing okay at the moment, we know that there will be periods of loneliness and sadness, which is natural. We just need to let her know that it's okay to feel all of these feelings as they arise.

I sense Mark is a little on edge because when he's anxious, he clams up. Maybe the situation with Chloe is bringing back some unpleasant childhood memories. How could it not? He of all people knows what it feels like to lose a parent at such a young age. They're your whole world. While he hasn't talked about any of this, and I don't want to push him, I make him turn over so that I can work the knots out of his back. After a few minutes of massaging his back and head, he drifts off to sleep.

I tiptoe one last time into Chloe's room and find her sleeping soundly, surrounded by her stuffed animals. Then I return to bed and decide to read a little. Reading usually helps me fall asleep but it just so happens that I've hit a major cliffhanger in my book so I'm still reading when I feel Mark begin tossing and turning in his sleep, which is very unlike him. His eyes remain closed but he's mumbling something over and over that I can't quite make out. He almost sounds like he's going to cry and I'm starting to become concerned, but I don't think it's a good idea to wake him in the middle of a dream, so all I can do is watch him helplessly.

After a minute or two, he gets up for some water. When he returns, he asks about Chloe and I assure him that she's sleeping soundly. Relief washes over his face.

"Are you okay?" I ask as he gets back in bed. "You

were talking in your sleep."

"I was?"

"Yeah, and it seemed like you were upset about something."

"Oh...sorry...I think I was just dreaming." He lets out an audible sigh. "It was probably about my parents' accident. I have this recurring dream."

"Do you want to talk about it?"

He pauses and then nods. "In the dream, my parents and I are in the car the night of the accident. We're driving along and then all of a sudden there are these blinding headlights in front of us. My mom screams to get down and then there's this loud crash into the front of our car. Sometimes that's when I wake up, but usually the dream continues and we're all in the car and everything stops and there's this eery silence. I yell for my parents but no one answers. So I just keep yelling and yelling, hoping they'll wake up. But they don't. That's probably what you heard me doing in my sleep."

"Is that when you wake up?"

"Yes."

I caress his arm. "I'm so sorry, honey."

"Sometimes—" He halts, his voice too unsteady to speak, and when he looks up at me, there are tears in his eyes. "Sometimes I can see their faces. They're so still, Fin. Completely motionless. I yell but...you know... they're gone. It's dead silence." There is a vulnerability in his eyes that I've never seen before.

I immediately take him in my arms and squeeze him tight. And that's when I feel him completely surrender, his grief sprinting to the surface, followed by tears.

"I'm so sorry, sweetheart," I say through my own tears as I stroke the back of his head. "Nobody should have to go through what you went through. It's terrible."

As we hold one another in silence, his trembling begins to subside and his body calms.

He slowly pulls back and wipes away his tears before speaking. "The date of their passing is coming up. It's September 26th, so they're probably just on my mind."

I use my thumb to brush away one last tear from his cheek. "Would you like to go and visit their gravesite that day?" I suggest. "I could go with you if you want."

His eyes search mine. "I actually visit the cemetery every September 26th, but how did you know that?"

"I didn't. I just thought you might want to."

His lips now curve up slightly and he leans in, gently pressing his lips to mine. "You are so wonderful. Yes, it would mean a lot if you would come with me. I want you to."

I get him a fresh glass of water and then the two of us settle quietly in bed until my head and hand find their home on his chest. His heart slows to a soothing, steady rhythm.

After a few minutes, he whispers, "Are you still awake?"

I tilt my head upwards. "Yes."

"I was just thinking about something that happened to me one September 26th."

My eyes lock with his. "Tell me."

Chapter Thirty-Two

~ *Mark* ~

Almost Fifteen Years Old

September 26th was, is, and always will be the worst day of my life. It's been eight years since my parents were killed and you'd think I'd be over it by now, but I don't think it's something you ever really get over. It's a loss I feel every single day of my life. And my life is just beginning, so I better learn to deal with this or I'm going to have a miserable life.

The truth is, my aunt and uncle are wonderful parents to me. They love and support me in every way parents should. It's not their fault. I think I just need to work harder at appreciating all that I do have—what some people never have, even with biological parents. But on September 26th, it's hard for me to do that.

I always visit my parents' gravesite on this day. Every year my Uncle Rick (I call him Dad now) and I go to the cemetery and leave flowers, and then he waits for me in the car. He knows I prefer to be alone and this year is no different. I have so much I want to tell them but I'm not sure where to even begin.

I slowly approach their graves.

"Hi. I...um...So today's the day...It's been eight years since, you know, everything happened. It feels a lot longer than that though. I'm turning fifteen soon. I know—it's hard to believe, right?" A taller stalk of grass by the corner of my mom's grave interrupts my thoughts and I yank it out before continuing.

"I've been trying to talk to you every night before I go to sleep. I'm not sure you can hear me, but I feel like maybe you do. But in case you don't, I want you to know that everything is good here. I'm getting good grades at school and I'm actually not a bad golfer, Dad. I know how much you loved golfing. I'm even going to compete in a few tournaments next summer. I really like it. Remember how when I was little you used to take me out on the course with you and let me help the caddie choose your clubs? That really stuck with me for some reason.

"Oh, and Mom, you know that horseshoe charm Dad got you? You remember the one I'm talking about. You were wearing it...well...anyway, I started wearing it. It's right here." I pull it out from under my shirt. "Here, see it? A few guys have ribbed me about it, but I really don't care. I like it. Anyway, not much else is happening really. I'm okay, I mean, well, I do miss you a lot still." I squat down so their graves are at eye level. "Sometimes it's lonely, but don't worry, I'm okay. I am." I stand up to get ready to leave.

"Well I guess I better go because Uncle Rick is waiting for me. But there is one last thing I wanted to tell you." My hands start to get clammy and I feel myself starting to tense up. "I started calling Uncle Rick and Aunt Leslie 'Mom and Dad.' I think they wanted me to and I didn't want to hurt their feelings. They were really happy when I started doing it. I hope you understand. I think you do, right?"

I wait for some sort of sign from them, but there is none.

"Okay, well, I better go. I hope you're doing okay

up in heaven. Hopefully there's cable up there! I know, that's a bad joke. I'll try to come up with a better one next year...Okay, well, I love you and I miss you a lot... Bye."

I give a small wave and when I turn to leave, a crushing loneliness bears down on me. This always happens when I leave. Every time. My tears are a half a second away from falling, but I stop them, just like I always do.

But then the strangest thing happens. From out of nowhere, this cat jumps out in front of me and won't let me pass. First he just stares at me and then he starts meowing loudly. He's orange and I think he's called a Tabby cat. I watch him, and he watches me, and then he casually walks over to my mom's grave, jumps up on top of her gravestone, and continues to stare at me with these intense marble-like green eyes. Something about the way he's looking at me is freaking me out. I stare back at him, willing him to speak.

"What do you want?" I finally ask with exasperation.

He doesn't move. I don't move either. We're like two statues.

"You're standing on my mom's grave," I scold. "Get down."

But the cat won't move. In fact, he makes himself right at home and starts licking his paw. I am so pissed off at this cat right now, it's not even funny.

"Get off!" I yell.

But he ignores me and goes right on licking his paw. Finally, as if sensing my fury, he jumps down, but instead of leaving, he comes over to me, rubbing his body up against my leg. I look for a collar but there isn't one.

When he lets out another loud meow, I can't help but laugh.

"Are you trying to tell me something?" I ask him.

I can't believe I'm talking to this cat, but this is what it's come to.

He meows loudly again.

I crouch down to his eye level to see if I can glean something from his eyes and then, to my surprise, he licks my cheek. I don't know if cats kiss but that's what it seems like he's doing. He then rubs my leg one last time and runs away.

I feel oddly peaceful after seeing the cat.

When I get home, I decide to take out some old family photo albums. I like to look at them once in a while. There are a bunch of pictures of my parents and some of me as a baby. There are also some pictures of my mom and dad when they were younger.

And then I see it.

A photo of my mom...holding an orange cat. I pull the photo out of the album and examine it more closely. It looks *exactly* like the cat I saw earlier at the cemetery. In the photo, the cat is sitting on my mom's lap licking her face and my mom has a huge grin on her face.

Sometimes photographs actually have sound. This one does. She's laughing.

I smile.

Chapter Thirty-Three

~ Fin ~

Present Day

I rest my chin on Mark's chest, contemplating everything he's just told me.

"So do you think the cat was a messenger of some
kind?" I finally ask.

"I'm not sure," he says. "It was strange though, don't
you think?"

"Definitely. Maybe he was sent there by your parents
to comfort you."

"You think?" Hope fills his eyes.

"Yes, I do think it's possible."

"That was my thought too, but then I thought maybe
I was imagining things."

"No, I don't think so."

Mark's eyes search mine and suddenly he looks a little spooked.

"What is it?" I ask.

"I just realized something. Your eyes are very similar
to the cat's green eyes. I never put that together until
now."

I smile. "Well I hope you don't think I'm a reincarnated cat."

"Well, you do purr a lot during sex so..."

I giggle and whisper a *meow* into his mouth as his
lips play with mine. He gives a low, sexy growl and rolls
me onto my back, settling above me. His expression

grows more serious as he brushes my hair away from my face, like he's about to kiss me, but instead he just smiles down at me.

My eyes soften under his gaze. "I love you, Mark with a '*k*.'"

We share a slow, tender kiss.

He pulls back with a tiny twinkle in his eyes. "I just thought of another similarity between you and cats." He glances downward. "Your...you know..."

My grin widens. "Oh, right, my..."

"Yes..." His fingers lightly touch me over my panties, causing me to heat up with anticipation. "But to get back to your original question," he says, "no, I do not think you're a reincarnated cat."

"Well that's good. Especially since my spirit animal is a frog."

"I'm sorry, a frog?"

"Yes, I feel a camaraderie with them."

"You're kidding, right?" But he doesn't look entirely convinced.

I burst out laughing. "Mark! You are such an easy mark sometimes!"

He shakes his head to himself. "Well I never know with you. You can be all over the place."

My brows raise. "Huh? Explain."

"You're just not someone who fits neatly into a box. You can be very pragmatic, but then you'll surprise me with something totally unexpected. You're complex."

"So I'm a complex carbohydrate versus a simple carbohydrate."

He chuckles. "See? That right there—that's why I'm so wild about you."

We share another slow, delicious kiss.

"Thank you for making me laugh, Finny, and for listening to my crazy cat story. I feel a lot better now."

"Thank you for trusting me with it."

"I've never told anyone about that before, but I knew you'd understand. You have this way of making everything better, Fin, you just do."

Still hovering above me, passion fills his eyes as he leans in and kisses my neck and travels down my chest, lifting my T-shirt to unveil my hardening nipples.

"I can't get enough of you," he says as he lightly nibbles on each one. As he swirls his tongue around them, I let out a needy moan.

"Mark..." I say under my breath. "Please....go down on me." My entire body is begging to be touched and I feel a dull ache below.

"Patience," he says, latching firmly onto my ripe points and sucking harder. My ache for him grows more intense.

He eventually slides down my body, parting my legs and expertly tracing his tongue through my folds. No one has *ever* aroused me the way that he does and my body gives an anticipatory shudder.

"Oh my G-d," I breathlessly cry out to warn him.

His lips and tongue consume me like he's starving and I climax so intensely that he has to cover my mouth for fear I'll wake up Chloe.

Now it's his turn. I play with him, running my fingers and palm up and down his length and breathing on him, but withholding my lips for now. As his breathing begins to intensify, I use my tongue on him, licking and sucking every inch of his thickness and running my lips down to his very engorged sacs. I exhale against his scrotum, licking his balls while fondling his shaft, and he spreads his legs wider for me. I know how much he gets off on this and can feel his entire body tensing and resisting as he moans with pleasure. I love how free and uninhibited he is in bed. Not a hint of embarrassment or self-consciousness. My lips return to his smooth, rock hard shaft, slowly bringing him deeper and deeper into my mouth until I reach the base, and when he's ready, his stream shoots hard and fast into my mouth. I relish every warm drop of him, sucking him to completion. I simply can't get enough of this beautiful man—his love, his scent, his taste, his need for me.

We soon fall deeply asleep under the spell of love.

Chapter Thirty-Four

~ Mark ~

Present Day

I return from an early morning round of golf to the sound of *Mamma Mia!* blaring from the living room. Fin and Chloe are singing and dancing and they scream when I sneak up on them from behind. They haven't been able to make it through a single verse without messing up the lyrics—and I love it. They also like to sing at the top of their lungs—also fine with me. I join in at the chorus because, let's face it, "Dancing Queen" is a great tune. I take Chloe in my arms and spin her in circles until we're both dizzy.

It's been a little over a month since Chloe moved in with us and, while she definitely misses her mother, she seems to be adjusting fairly well, all things considered. We've tried to be here for her in every way that we can. When I lost my parents, the first year was by far the worst and I'm determined to do everything in my power to support her. Although I'm not her legal guardian, Fin has made it clear that we are a team in raising Chloe and it means so much to have her trust me like this.

Peter has remained very involved in Chloe's life and therefore, by extension, ours. He visits Chloe frequently and often takes her on weekend outings, and we want him to be as much a part of Chloe's life as he wishes to be. My relationship with my aunt and uncle after losing my parents was critical to my own recovery and the fact is that as much as Fin and I want to be here for Chloe, we are newcomers in her life. There's just something different about the relationship with a blood relative that can't be replicated. Witnessing how close Chloe and Peter are is making me fully appreciate just how lucky I was that my aunt and uncle took me in. I'm not sure I've ever really expressed just how grateful I am to them. I hope they know. I need them to know.

I set the dinner table while Fin takes dinner out of the oven. We invited Peter over for Sunday night dinner, a tradition that Fin wanted to continue in our home. So all afternoon, Chloe has been anxiously awaiting Peter's arrival and the moment she sees his car in the driveway, she yells for me to come to the front door. We find Peter standing on our doorstep loaded to the gills with wine, flowers, and toys.

"Pete, you really didn't have to bring anything, but thank you! Here, let me help you." I take the wine and flowers from his hands.

"Thanks for having me to dinner," Peter says. "Hey there, pumpkin!" Peter lifts Chloe up high in the air and she squeals with delight.

"Uncle Peter, come see the new video game Mark got me!"

He puts her back down and she immediately takes him by the hand and leads him away.

While I'm getting the game connected for them to play, Fin emerges from the kitchen. "Thank you, Peter! The flowers are lovely."

"My pleasure," Peter says. "Thanks for having me. I haven't had a home-cooked meal in weeks. My travel schedule has been horrendous lately."

"Well, just relax and dinner will be ready soon," Fin says, retrieving a crystal vase for the flowers.

"Uncle Peter, play with me!" Chloe clamors. "Nobody can beat me—not even Mark!"

"Not even Mark?" Peter shoots me a grin.

"It's true," I confirm. "She's the champ."

Peter raises a brow. "Well we'll just have to see about that. Bring it on, Chloe!"

I leave them to their game and go help Fin in the kitchen.

"Everything smells delicious, babe," I say, wrapping my arms around her from behind and kissing her neck. She's wearing this cute apron that she knows I find incredibly sexy. I know—it's just an apron—but on her everything looks sexy.

She turns her head for a quick kiss and that's all it takes to trigger movement below. I press my now noticeable erection against her perfect ass.

"Keep it in your pants, darling," she whispers. "We have company."

I groan. "Well then you shouldn't have worn this. It reminds me of that barmaid's outfit you used to wear."

She giggles. "Which reminds me, I promised you I'd wear that again for you and…"

"…do what you do best," I finish.

"And what's that?"

"Look sexy as hell, and very…fuckable…"

She smiles seductively up at me and I whisk her around, my aroused state immediately catching her attention. Her lips curve up into a knowing smile as she lightly touches me over my shorts.

"Honey," I quietly plead, "I need to be able to walk back out there without looking like a sex-starved teenager, so kindly remove your hand from my—"

"Cock?" she slowly whispers into my mouth.

"Fuck...Fin, you need to stop. I could play a drum solo with what's going on inside my boxers."

She giggles quietly. "Well you started it," she says while squeezing my ass.

"Not helping..."

I somehow will my body to calm down and we bring everything to the dinner table.

I can definitely understand why Fin likes having Sunday night dinners. It's a really nice way to mark the end of the weekend and the beginning of the week ahead. I haven't had much of an opportunity to spend time with Peter given our competing work schedules, so I'm really glad he came tonight. He's a great guy, very funny, and Chloe adores him. Having all of us together around the table tonight, it's finally starting to feel like we're melding into a family unit. What is clear is that we all have this little girl's best interests at heart and are committed to making sure she always feels loved and supported.

Fin's chicken pot pie is a huge hit and Chloe is in all her glory—that is until Peter gets ready to leave. Her mood instantly changes from boisterous to sullen.

"It's okay, pumpkin. I'll come visit again very soon." Peter kneels down to Chloe's level. "I have some work meetings this week but I promise we'll get together again soon, okay?"

"But why can't you live here with us?" Chloe asks, suddenly on the verge of tears.

Peter glances over at Fin, then back to Chloe. "Honey, I have my own place, you know that. Don't worry, I'll see you again very soon."

Chloe nods with uncertainty.

"Chloe has lots of fun activities this week, so we're going to be very busy, aren't we, Chloe?" Fin says, trying to keep things light.

But Chloe just stares blankly at Fin.

"Well that sounds like fun," Peter says. "Fin, I'll call you so we can discuss Chloe's schedule. I'm trying to re-arrange a few things so I can start picking her up one or two afternoons a week."

Fin gives the okay sign.

"Thank you both again so much for having me for dinner," Peter says. "Everything was delicious."

We all escort Peter to the door.

As Peter kisses the top of Chloe's head and hugs her goodbye, I sense that he's a little choked up. Chloe's eyes are glued to her uncle as he leaves and once he's gone, she immediately asks if she can be excused to go to her bedroom.

Fin and I spend some time cleaning up and doing the dishes.

"Did you notice that Chloe seemed more upset than usual when Peter left tonight?" I ask.

Fin sighs, passing me a dish to dry. "Yes, I did. I feel so badly that she has to go through these goodbyes every time he visits. And I'm sure this is painful for him too. I wish there was another way but, short of him moving in, I don't see a solution."

"Right." I let out a big exhale. "The whole situation is a lot more complicated than I originally realized. I understand why Camille wanted Chloe to live with us, but I'm not sure that Chloe being separated from Peter is the right thing for either of them. He's her only family."

"But Peter travels so much for work," she says, "and I know Camille felt strongly that Chloe not be with baby-sitters all the time. As important as family is, she also needs stability. I think maybe it's just going to take more time for everyone to adjust."

But neither of us are feeling particularly certain of anything.

Chapter Thirty-Five

~ Fin ~

Present Day

"Hey, where are you guys?" I ask.

"We're driving home now," Mark says. "And we have a surprise."

"Yes, Fin!" I hear Chloe yell from the back seat of the car. "We have a big surprise!"

I giggle. "Okay you two. See you in a few."

I usually bring Chloe home after school, but today Mark picked her up because I had a last minute work meeting with my boss that I couldn't easily reschedule. I feel badly because I know he has a lot going on at work this week, but he insisted it was no trouble at all. He's the type of person who just does what has to be done and never complains.

By the time I've changed into my cotton tee and leggings, Chloe is racing through the front door grinning from ear to ear.

"Look what Mark got me!" She holds up a new smart phone.

"Oh?" I glance over at Mark. "What prompted this?"

"Oh, just kind of a spur of the moment thing," he says with a smile. "Chloe was saying how much she misses Uncle Peter and we thought it would be nice if she had a way to call and text him whenever she wants to."

"Yes, Fin, it was a spur of the moment thing!" Chloe

repeats. "It was my idea and Mark said I was very smart to think of it!"

I meet Mark's eyes, then return to Chloe's. "Okay, well, let's just talk to your Uncle Peter first to make sure he's okay with this too."

Mark looks a little surprised. "Oh, sure."

"Can I *please* text Uncle Peter now?" Chloe begs Mark.

"In a few minutes," Mark says.

"Okay!" Chloe says, skipping away to her bedroom. She adores Mark and rarely disagrees with anything he says.

Once we're alone, I attempt to explain. "I know you were trying to do something nice, and I think the phone's a great idea, but we just need to discuss these things with Peter first. He may not want her to have one yet."

His face colors slightly. "I'm sorry, I guess I should have discussed it with you first, but she was just so excited." He averts his eyes from mine, as if embarrassed, and begins to walk away.

I reach for his arm. "Wait a second."

He turns and I can now clearly see the embarrassment on his face.

"You understand why we need to talk to Peter first, right?" I ask gently.

"Of course. I get it, Fin. It's fine." But he now seems irritated. "Listen, I've got a lot of work back at the office that I didn't get to this afternoon, so I'm going to head back there now to finish up a few things."

My eyes widen. "Now? Before dinner?"

He nods.

"Oh, I didn't realize you were going to need to go back in. I'm really sorry. My meeting came up unexpectedly and I couldn't easily get out of it. I tried Peter but he couldn't get her either. He had a meeting."

Mark's face flushes. "I actually had a meeting too, but I rescheduled it." He breaks eye contact and turns to leave.

My mouth opens but no words come out and my stomach begins to twist into a knot. He never mentioned a meeting when I called him and now I feel incredibly inconsiderate. Come to think of it, I don't think I even thanked him for picking up Chloe. I start to go after him but stop myself. I think I need to give him some space. But as the front door closes and I hear him drive away, I immediately regret letting him leave like that and can feel the knot in my stomach getting bigger.

Chloe and I spend the rest of the evening doing homework and reading and, after many pleas to call Peter on her new phone, I eventually capitulate. As it turns out, Peter isn't upset at all about the phone and, in fact, thinks it's a great idea and tells me to thank Mark for taking care of everything. I'm relieved but now I feel even worse about how I reacted earlier. Here Mark bailed me out this afternoon, missed his own meeting, then bought Chloe the phone, and all I had to say was that we should have consulted Peter first. While that may be true, my delivery really sucked.

After putting Chloe to bed, I straighten up our bedroom to kill time, but I'm now very much on edge. It's getting late and there's still no sign of Mark. When he works late, he usually texts to let me know when he'll be home. By nine o'clock, worry begins to set in. He's either annoyed with me or something is wrong. I check my phone for the hundredth time. It's now 9:04 p.m.

By 9:18 p.m., my imagination has completely run

wild. Something might really be wrong. Maybe he's hurt. Maybe there was an intruder in his building. Maybe he's sick...or worse. Thanks to my particularly enthusiastic imagination this evening, the possibilities are literally endless. I finally call him but it goes to voice mail. So I text him, but he doesn't respond, which is very odd. He always responds very quickly. My heart is now pounding out of my chest and I'm about two seconds away from calling the police when he texts me. He's heading home now and apologizes for not texting earlier, explaining that he accidentally left his phone in the car. I respond with an "ok."

About fifteen minutes later, I hear the front door open.

I scurry downstairs to find him with his head in the refrigerator getting something to drink. My nerves are frayed and I feel the heat rising in my cheeks as I stand in the kitchen doorway. While I'm relieved that he's okay, at the same time, I'm very upset.

He startles when he sees me, but his expression quickly turns to confusion when he sees what I can only assume to be my very red face.

"Hi, you're back," I say as calmly as possible, despite the clamoring in my chest. "Did you finish up everything you needed to?"

"Not completely. But it was getting late so I'll finish up in the morning."

I nod. "When I didn't hear from you, I got worried."

At the sound of my anxious voice, his expression immediately turns to concern and he approaches me. "I'm sorry, I didn't mean to worry you. I just got so caught up in what I was doing that I completely lost track of time. And then when I went to text you, I realized I'd left my phone in the car. I'm really sorry—I should have called you."

"It's okay, I just got a little scared, that's all. You always text." My voice sounds unsteady despite my best efforts to stay calm.

He sets down his water and draws me to his warm body. I settle into his arms and he apologizes again for worrying me, pressing a kiss to the top of my head. I feel calmer already.

I tilt my head up to meet his eyes, my arms still wrapped around his waist. "So you still have a lot more work to do?"

"Not a lot, but I just couldn't wrap my head around this one issue I was working on."

"Did you finally figure it out?"

"Not completely, but it was getting late and I couldn't focus anymore. It's okay—I'll just go in a little early tomorrow morning to finish it up."

"Well you must be starving. I'll make you something."

"No, I'm fine. I ate."

My eyes narrow with doubt. "What did you eat?"

He chuckles softly. "A protein bar, why?"

"That's not a meal. Let me reheat something for you." I start to pull away but he pulls me back into him.

"Fin, I'm fine, really. I'm just tired and I want to go to bed."

I carefully study his expression. I see no hint of annoyance but I'm not comfortable going to bed without making absolutely sure he isn't upset about what happened earlier with the cell phone.

I tread lightly. "Can we talk?"

"I'm pretty beat. Can we talk tomorrow?"

I try to hold back my words but they rush out of me. "Okay, but I just wanted to thank you for picking up Chloe today. I didn't know what else to do, but if I'd realized you were going to have to cancel your own meeting, I never would have imposed on you like that. I could have explained the situation to my boss and she would have understood."

"Fin, it's okay, really. I understand last minute meetings happen sometimes and I wanted to help."

"Well, I just want you to know how much I appreciate it."

He nods with a weary smile.

Although he doesn't seem upset, my instincts tell me we need to talk. Silently, I take his hand and lead him to the living room where we sit.

I can sense his relief and wait for his eyes to settle on mine before speaking. "I want to apologize to you for how I reacted to the whole phone thing earlier. It was very insensitive of me."

He immediately holds his hand up in protest. "Fin, there's nothing to apologize for. You were absolutely right. I should have checked with you first and then you could have run it by Peter."

"Well I still want to apologize. It was very thoughtful of you to get her the phone and it's something that never would have even occurred to me to do. But it occurred to you because you have such a big heart and you're always looking for ways to make her happy. I love you for that."

As I rest my hand on his, a sweet blush of relief creeps over his face.

"This is all just a lot more complicated than I realized," I say with a sigh. "We all want to do what's right for Chloe, but having three adults involved in every decision can be really hard."

He nods. "It is complicated, but that's not your fault." He scrubs his face and closes his eyes briefly before continuing. "I'm sorry too. I never should have left the way that I did earlier, without us talking things through first. The second I walked out the door, I felt horrible. I wasn't upset with you—I was upset with myself, and the situation."

"It's okay," I say, feeling my emotions rising to the surface as our hands squeeze tightly together.

"No, it's not okay. I shouldn't have shut down on you like that. I'm sorry."

As our eyes begin filling with tears, we immediately reach for one another, winding our arms tightly around each other. We decompress into one another's arms, letting our love do the rest.

He gives a tender kiss to the side of my head. "We'll figure this out, don't worry."

I lift my head to meet his eyes. "I know we will. This is new territory for all of us, but I want you to know that I trust you and your judgment completely."

He brushes my hair back and kisses my forehead. "That means a lot. But I also need to remember that I'm not Chloe's guardian—you and Peter are—so I'll just need to figure out how I fit in here."

I pull back, my eyes widening in protest. "How *you* fit in? Please don't think about it that way. I see you and I as a team as far as Chloe is concerned, regardless of the legalities, okay?"

"I appreciate that, but the legalities can't be ignored."

"Listen to me, YOU are the reason we're able to help Chloe. Without you, none of this would be possible. I need you, and Chloe needs you. Your legal status doesn't change that."

He gives me a resigned smile. "Okay, well, we can talk more about this tomorrow. I'm pretty wasted at this point."

I nod, gently stroking the nape of his neck. "Okay, but I'm not changing my mind. Legal status be damned."

By the time I'm done washing up, Mark is already asleep. But I can't sleep. What Mark said about trying to figure out how he fits in is breaking my heart. He has always struggled with the feeling that he didn't truly belong to anyone after his parents died and I *never* want him to feel like he doesn't belong or that he's an outsider. And especially not in the home that he created for himself.

I'm not sure how to fix this but I've got to. Because he means *everything* to me and he deserves better than this.

Chapter Thirty-Six

~ *Fin* ~

Present Day

I sip my coffee, enjoying the cooler fall morning air as it flows in through the French doors. Chloe is out pumpkin picking with Peter for one of their Saturday morning outings and Mark had to meet a client at the office, so the house is unusually still. It's been a crazy week and next week will be even crazier. A school field trip on Tuesday, Chloe's ballet class on Wednesday, her soccer practice on Thursday, and a Planning and Placement Team meeting for one of my students on Friday. The weeks have been jam-packed, but after some initial growing pains, we seem to have settled into a fairly regular routine. I take her to school with me every day and then bring her to her after-school activities, unless Peter is available, in which case he picks her up and then usually takes her out for dinner. Mark has been incredibly supportive through it all, pitching in without hesitation, and he and Chloe have grown very close.

Ever since Mark and I had the disagreement about the phone, I've been careful to be sensitive to Mark's feelings as far as parenting is concerned. I've included him in all decisions concerning Chloe and I think he's starting to realize that we really are a team in every way.

He usually avoids working weekends, but unfortunately this morning's client couldn't be rescheduled. So, with the house all to myself, I am in the enviable position of having to choose between reading a new book or baking chocolate chip cookies. Baking is something my mom and I used to do together and I always find comfort in it. Plus I have a major sweet tooth.

Baking it is.

My mom's chocolate chip cookie recipe has a secret ingredient—caramel chips—and I can't wait for Mark and Chloe to get home and try them. Hopefully they're still warm when they get home.

The doorbell rings just as I'm taking the first batch of cookies out of the oven. It's probably just a package, so I ignore it, but then it rings a second time.

When I open the door, my jaw drops. "Dan!" I hug my big brother tightly. "Why didn't you tell me you were coming?!"

"Surprising you is much more fun." He grins and gives me another big hug.

"I've missed you! How long are you here for?"

"I got in late last night and need to head back to San Diego tomorrow morning. They just sent me here briefly to take care of something."

I groan. Our time together is always too short and I really miss him in between visits.

"Come sit down." I usher him inside. "Would you like anything? I just made cookies."

"I thought I smelled something good. Yeah, cookies would be great."

Dan takes a seat on the couch while I bring us some milk and warm cookies.

He glances around while dunking a cookie into the milk. "Nice place. Where's Mark?"

"He had to meet a client at the office but he'll be home soon, and I know he's going to be really happy to see you again. He really likes you, despite the fact that you grilled the hell out of him when you first met him."

"He's a really good guy. I approve." He takes a big bite of the cookie and hums his approval. "So does he work a lot on weekends?"

"Not really, but sometimes it just can't be avoided. He works really hard."

"And you two are still going strong?"

"Yes." I grin. "I'm crazy about him."

"I'm really happy for you, sis, you deserve it. You know, he's crazy about you too. It was obvious from the second I met him."

"Really?" I say through the huge smile that overtakes my face.

"Absolutely. You should have seen the look on his face when he saw me in your doorway that first day." Dan chuckles to himself. "I think he thought I was your boyfriend or something and he looked so pissed!" He breaks out into laughter.

I groan at my brother. If he only knew that wasn't the first time...

"Seriously though, Mark's a stand-up guy and I know he'd do anything for you. That night with Tim, he wouldn't have thought twice about taking a bullet for you. I had to literally hold him back from storming the restaurant."

My face flushes with pride and love for Mark. None of this surprises me but I love knowing it nonetheless.

Dan finishes off his milk. "So, any chance I'll get to meet the famous Chloe I've been hearing so much about?"

"Definitely. She's out with her uncle right now, but they should be back any minute."

Just as I utter the words, Peter and Chloe walk through the front door. Chloe is chattering away and runs in carrying a box of donuts.

"Fin! We got some cider donuts for you and Mark!" Chloe announces before coming to a screeching halt when she sees a stranger in the room.

"Thank you!" I say. "Guess what? We have a surprise visitor who'd like to meet you."

Peter walks in behind Chloe. "Oh, I'm sorry, we shouldn't have just barged in like this."

"Oh, no worries, this is just my brother, Dan."

"You know, you could sound a *little* more excited," Dan jokes, extending his hand out to Peter, then turning his attention to Chloe. "And you must be the brilliant Chloe I've been hearing so much about."

Chloe has suddenly become mute, which is to be expected given that she tends to be shy around strangers.

Dan reaches for something in his bag and crouches down to Chloe's eye level. "Chloe, I hear you like books, so I brought you one of my favorites, *The Lion, the Witch and the Wardrobe*." He holds up the book to show her.

Chloe's eyes brighten, but her lips remain sealed shut.

"Thank you, Dan," Peter says, taking the book. "I love that book. I can't wait to go home and read it."

"Uncle Peter, he was talking to me, not you!"

"Really?" Peter teases. "My bad."

Chloe now snatches the book from Peter and her eyes light up as she examines the cover. "Fin, can you help me read it?"

"Of course, sweetie. And maybe Uncle Peter can read

it with you too."

"Great! You'll have to let me know how you like it," Dan says. "Fin, I just need to grab something from the car. I'll be right back."

Chloe is insistent that we start the book, so Peter, Chloe, and I take a seat on the couch together.

"Why don't you two read it and I'll listen," Peter says.

"Well, okay then." I begin to read the first chapter aloud with my best *Downton Abbey* imitation. This then leads to Chloe getting the giggles, which then causes Peter to start laughing too. So I literally can't get through a sentence without being interrupted by their laughter. Now I'm laughing too.

"We're not going to make it through the first page if you two don't settle down!" I say, pretending to be annoyed. "So shush so I can read!"

"Geez, Chloe, you're a real troublemaker, aren't you," Peter kids.

Chloe giggles.

"No, Uncle Peter. Chloe is an angel. I think it's *you* who's the troublemaker."

Peter wiggles his eyebrows at me playfully. "Now how would you know that?"

"Oh, just a hunch," I tease.

Peter squeezes my shoulder playfully. It's just a friendly gesture, but unfortunately that's exactly when my brother reappears. He shoots me a warning glance, which I promptly ignore. He's always been very overprotective and he's clearly misread the situation.

"So Fin, when did you say Mark would be back?" Dan asks pointedly.

I check the time. "He said his meeting would only take about an hour, so he should be home any minute."

As if on cue, we hear the front door open, followed by Mark's footsteps walking down the hall towards us. When he appears, Dan pops up from behind the couch and yells "surprise" like it's a surprise birthday party. I wish I'd gotten a picture because Mark's confused expression is absolutely priceless. We all have a good laugh.

"It's not my birthday until next month so I was trying to figure out what was going on!" Mark says. The two of them do this cute guy handshake-hug thing. It warms my heart to see my two favorite guys bonding.

"Fin didn't mention you were coming into town," Mark says.

"I didn't know!" I chime in. "He just showed up at the door! He's such a goof."

"Oh, come on, you know you love it when I surprise you," Dan says. "Besides, it was a last minute thing. I'm just in town until tomorrow."

"We'll take you out for lunch," Mark says, walking over to give me a kiss hello on the cheek.

We have a full house and I certainly shouldn't be thinking dirty thoughts right now but my body has a mind of its own. Between those broad shoulders of his in a dress shirt and that little bit of weekend scruff, I feel the heat rising in my face (and elsewhere) and Mark, as if reading my mind, flashes me a flirty grin. I *know* he knows and I blush even harder.

He chuckles and leans in towards me, whispering in my ear, "Stop being so fucking cute."

He then turns his attention to Chloe. "Hey princess, did you and Uncle Peter have fun picking pumpkins?"

Chloe gives an exaggerated nod. "Yes! We got a humongous pumpkin! And we got a surprise for you too…

Donuts!"

Mark's eyes widen. "Awesome!"

"Chloe picked out a Boston cream one just for you," Peter says. "She said they're your favorite."

"Thanks Chloe!" Mark gives her hair an affectionate tousle. "I'll be right back. I just want to get changed." Mark heads for the stairs.

"Mind if I check out your drum set?" Dan asks as he follows Mark.

"Sure, they're upstairs. Come on up."

Chapter Thirty-Seven

~ Mark ~

Present Day

As soon as Dan and I reach the spare bedroom where I keep my drum set, it's clear that Dan has another agenda.

"So I didn't want to share this in front of Fin, but I need to tell you something." Dan's tone is hushed and it sounds important.

"Sure, what is it?"

"I got a letter from Tim."

My heart halts. "Your dad?"

"Yup. He wrote to me and he also included a letter for Fin."

My jaw clenches with concern because Fin finally seems to have moved past the incident with Tim from over the summer and this is undoubtedly going to trigger her anxiety about him.

"His letter to me was just a bunch of BS about him being sorry and wanting to change. I'm sure his letter to her is more of the same. I just wanted to let you know before I gave it to her since I would hate to see her get sucked back into his shit. But as you know, Fin can be a softie..."

I groan under my breath. "Damnit, this is going to bring back the whole thing from over the summer."

"Tell me about it. Trouble seems to follow Tim wherever he goes. That's why my mom never let him contact us over the years."

I need to ask my next question, as uncomfortable as it is. "Have you ever known Tim to be violent?"

"No, but I always operate under the assumption that he's unpredictable, you know?"

I nod. "Was there a return address on the letter?"

"Yes, he's at a facility in Massachusetts. I already checked and it's about forty-five minutes from here."

Fuck. My pulse begins firing rapidly. This is way too close for my comfort level.

"My guess is that he's probably located in Mass. because this is where he violated his probation," Dan says. "Anyway, I just wanted to give you the heads up."

I'm definitely concerned that Tim might somehow be able to manipulate Fin into visiting him. The thought of Fin being anywhere near this guy again is making my skin crawl.

Dan tries to shift gears but I'm having trouble focusing on anything he's saying at this point. All I can think about is the letter and how Fin is going to react.

Dan waves his hand in front of my face. "Earth to Mark."

"Oh, sorry, what were you saying?"

"I was saying that you've got a great house. Fin always wanted a house growing up, but my mom could never afford one. I have to tell you—I've never seen my sister this happy in a relationship before. She's head over heels for you, man."

That immediately snaps me out of my fog and I smile. "Well, I'm crazy about her too. I just want to make her happy."

"And you guys are adjusting okay to having Chloe living with you?"

"Yeah, it's all good. I mean, there have been a few bumps along the way, but that's to be expected."

Dan eyes me. "Peter seems pretty involved in everything. Is he here a lot?"

"Yeah, he's very close with Chloe and he shares guardianship with Fin, so he's a big part of Chloe's life."

"I can see that…Do you mind if I give you a piece of advice?"

"Shoot."

"I think what you guys are doing for Chloe is incredible and she's very lucky to have you. But from where I'm standing, Peter seems a little too involved in your household. It kind of seems like he's become part of your family, and even though that sounds great in theory, my concern is that he's going to cause problems for you and Fin."

I honestly don't know what to say. "I appreciate your perspective, but this really is what's best for Chloe. And Peter is always very respectful and happens to be a really good guy."

"I'm sure he is, but over time, you may start to resent his presence. I just think you guys need to establish clear boundaries from the start because otherwise it's going to be hard to later on. That's all I'm saying."

He has a point. Boundaries wouldn't necessarily be a bad thing here and, the truth is, the current revolving door arrangement with Peter has been a little intrusive at times. But I just don't want to do anything that would negatively impact on Chloe. She needs to come first.

"I'm not trying to stir up trouble here, I'm really not," Dan says. "I just want to see you guys make it, that's all. Don't get me wrong, Peter seems like a nice enough guy. But he looked a little too comfortable around Fin and I wouldn't want him developing feelings for her. It wouldn't be the first time."

That gets my undivided attention. "What do you mean?"

"Just that Fin has always had a lot of male friends because she's so easy to talk to, and I'm usually pretty good about telling when a guy likes her. Nothing against my sister but she can be completely clueless when it comes to that. I could be completely wrong about Peter but I don't think I am. Just be careful."

I pause, trying to remember if I've ever noticed Peter exhibit any romantic feelings for Fin, but I come up empty. I'm not sure what Dan observed exactly but our guardianship situation is definitely a little unique and, to an outside observer, Peter's friendliness could be misinterpreted as more than just platonic. But Fin, Peter, and I are just trying to create a nurturing environment for Chloe, that's all. I know Dan's heart is in the right place, but Fin and I are very committed to one another and I'm not concerned.

Dan and I return downstairs to find Chloe, Peter, and Fin on the couch together with Chloe wedged in between them. Fin is reading a chapter aloud in this crazy British accent that has Chloe and Peter cracking up. It really is one of the cutest things I've ever heard and Dan and I both have to stifle a laugh. We don't want to interrupt and hang back until they're done with the chapter.

It may be that I'm just more tuned in after what Dan said about Peter, but something a little odd catches my eye. As the three of them are reading together, I notice Peter's hand, which is draped loosely along the back of the couch, inadvertently touch Fin's shoulder. This doesn't go unnoticed by Fin and I see her body stiffen slightly. I can't explain why, but something about her reaction causes me to flinch. And then this unexpected wave of panic follows.

Is it possible Peter does have feelings for Fin? Have I missed the signs?

My heart is now pounding out of my chest and I suddenly have this all-consuming need to claim Fin and fireman carry her out of here. I know how crazy this sounds, but I love this woman so deeply, to my core, that even just the possibility that I could lose her to another man—however unfounded—is suddenly suffocating me. I can't lose her. I won't.

She must have a sixth sense where I'm concerned because all of a sudden she turns around and smiles at me.

And that's all it takes. Just one look from her chases away all of my fear and anxiety. Her steady, reassuring gaze immediately calms me and I know I have absolutely *nothing* to worry about.

"Chloe, let's take a break and we can read more later, okay honey?" Fin says, closing the book. She then comes over to me and subtly runs her fingers down my back to my waistband, hooking her finger in my belt loop. She doesn't let go.

I meet her eyes and silently thank her because, somehow, she knew just what I needed. She answers with a comforting smile which wraps around my heart like one of those fleece blankets she makes.

"How about I make some sandwiches for lunch?" she offers.

"Absolutely not. We're going out, my treat," Dan says.

"I've got to get going, too," Peter says. "Dan, it was very nice meeting you." Peter then takes Chloe in his arms. "Sweetie, how about I come over one night this week and we carve our pumpkin?"

"Yay!" Chloe raises her fist in the air. "And bring some Halloween candy too, Uncle Peter!

"I think I can handle that." He gives his niece a kiss before putting her back down. "Oh, and Fin, we still need to talk about Chloe's schedule this week so I'll call you tomorrow. There's also something else I need to discuss with you."

Chapter Thirty-Eight

~ Mark ~

Present Day

Dan has us all rolling with laughter at lunch, and the more Chloe laughs, the more Dan steps up his game. When he literally licks his plate clean to get a laugh out of her, Chloe declares him to be the funniest person she's ever met. She's not wrong. He's a natural comedian, not to mention a really good guy. I can definitely see why Fin is so close with him.

After lunch, Dan reluctantly lets Fin know about their father's letter. He cautions that if she does choose to read it, not to be fooled by Tim's apologies and declarations of remorse. Fin takes the letter but, to my surprise, not only does she not open it, but her reaction isn't at all what I expected. I thought she'd at least be a little upset, but she dismisses the whole thing as "no big deal." Even after Dan leaves, she doesn't mention the letter and we spend a quiet afternoon with Chloe without another word about it.

After dinner, Chloe ends up falling asleep in Fin's arms while reading, so we carry her up to bed early, leaving Fin and me with the rest of the evening to ourselves.

It's been a long day and I'm more than happy to just relax in bed with Fin. As she snuggles into me and we wrap ourselves around one another, I realize that this is what I've been craving all day: time alone with her. I can feel her soft breaths against my chest and that's when I start to completely unwind.

"I've got to be honest," I say. "You in my bed with your arms and legs wrapped around me like this is just about the best thing in the whole world."

"*Your* bed? Excuse me, this is *our* bed." Her eyes shine brightly up at me.

"Right, *our* bed." I repeat it a few more times for good measure. "I think I'm going to call whatever this thing is that we're doing right now *octopussing*. It feels like you've got eight appendages wrapped around me."

She giggles. "*Octopussing*, huh? Well, in your case there are nine appendages, if you count...you know..." She eyes my boxers.

I chuckle. "That ninth appendage only comes out for you, babe."

This prompts her to give me a slow, sexy kiss. When our lips separate, however, there is a look of concern on her face.

"I noticed you were a little quiet at lunch today," she finally says. "Is everything okay?"

Her question doesn't surprise me. Fin can read me better than anyone, and she's right, I wasn't completely myself at lunch. But I'm not sure I want to share with her why that was. Any insecurity I was feeling in relation to Peter seems completely ridiculous in hindsight. However, I do think Dan was right about one thing: we do need to establish clearer boundaries with Peter.

"Everything's fine," I say. "I was just a little preoccupied thinking about something Dan said to me."

Her brows raise. "What did he say?"

"He was just pointing out that maybe we should set better boundaries with"—I pause—"Peter."

"Peter?"

"Yeah, just better boundaries so things don't get awkward down the road. Like maybe we have a more regular schedule for his visits with Chloe, you know?"

"Oh, well sure, we can absolutely do that. His travel schedule is a little unpredictable but we should be able to come up with a schedule." She rests her chin on my chest, studying me. "So was that it?"

She knows me too well. I hesitate to say more, but I also don't want to keep things from her.

"Well, Dan did also say something else."

"What did he say?"

I take a deep breath. "He thinks Peter might have feelings for you."

She gasps and immediately sits up. "He said what?"

"He meant well. He was just trying to help."

"Well, he's wrong!" Fin lets out a frustrated grrr sound. "Sometimes my brother can be such a trouble-maker. I absolutely do *not* think Peter has any romantic feelings for me. None whatsoever. Geez, I hope he didn't worry you."

I think back with embarrassment at how I over-reacted when I saw Peter's hand graze Fin's shoulder. Dan's words definitely got to me.

"I really wasn't worried," I say as convincingly as possible. "And I trust you completely, you know that."

"I know you do. I just think Dan needs to mind his own business. He thinks he knows best about every-thing where I'm concerned." She rolls her eyes and lets out an exhale as she lays her head back down on my chest. "I don't need him making trouble for us where there is none."

"I completely agree. Which is why I wasn't even

going to tell you, but I should know by now that you can read me like a book."

She smiles up at me. "I know that when you're quiet, it's usually because something's bothering you."

We relax back into one another's arms, each of us with our own wandering thoughts. Inevitably, my mind turns to the more pressing matter of Fin's father's letter.

"So, have you thought anymore about whether you want to read your father's letter?"

Fin sighs with resignation. "I don't know. I feel like it's going to set me back if I read it. What do you think I should do?"

"I just don't want it to make you anxious about him again, but if you want to read it, I support that and we'll work through it together."

"I feel like not knowing what's in the letter is going to worry me as much as knowing." She rests her chin on my chest. "I think I have to read it."

"Okay, it's your call. Do you want to read it now?"

She nods and retrieves the letter from the dresser. As she opens the envelope, I see her wince at the Massachusetts return address. Her hands are shaking slightly as she unfolds the letter and I watch as her eyes track the first few sentences in silence before she stops. "I'd like to read it with you," she says.

She rejoins me in bed.

Dear Finola,

I don't know exactly how to begin this letter but I want to try to explain my actions from over the summer. If you're reading this, I want you to know how much I appreciate you hearing me out.

When I got out of prison last summer, I was determined to make a fresh start. But I soon realized that was easier said than done. I have no savings but I did manage to get a job as a janitor briefly in California. But that was just a temporary job. I have no ties to California so it seemed to make more sense to move back East. I didn't plan on trying to find you or Danny. I assumed you wouldn't want to have anything to do with me and I understand. But I didn't realize how hard it would be to get back on my feet after being away for so many years. No one wants to hire a felon and I couldn't even qualify for a credit card. I figured if I could just get enough money for a deposit for an apartment then maybe I could begin to rebuild a life for myself. Your brother is too angry with me to ever lend me money so you were my only hope.

I remember you as an infant, Finola. You were such a happy child, always smiling. You were so good natured. Crazy as it sounds, I had this feeling that you might be open to helping me out, so I decided to track you down in Shelby Falls. But I swear to you, I never intended to threaten or hurt you. I just thought maybe you could lend me some money and I had every intention of paying you back. But then when I got to the restaurant and realized you had access to so much cash, I made a huge mistake. I never should have asked you to steal from the restaurant. I know I put you in a terrible spot and I'm <u>really</u> sorry. I was just so desperate to make a fresh start and I wasn't thinking clearly. I'm so sorry if I frightened you. You have to know that I would <u>never</u> hurt you. I'm not trying to excuse what I did that night, just trying to explain my mindset.

I'm sorry for making such a mess of things. Like so many things in my life, I wish I would have done things differently that night. I also want you to know how proud I am of you. You are such a bright, kind person and my biggest regret is that I've been absent from you and your brother's lives all these years. I feel that loss every day. I never wanted to complicate your lives so I resisted contacting you. Maybe that was a mistake, I don't know. But I never forgot you. I have so many regrets and wish things could have been different.

I hope maybe one day we'll have the chance to get to know each other. I'd like that. I care about you and Danny and I promise that if you ever have it in your heart to give me another chance, I'll do everything in my power not to disappoint you. That's a promise.

There is one last thing I want to share with you. It's an old Irish poem that I memorized as a kid and if you remember nothing else about me, please remember this poem because it's how I feel about you. I only want the best for you, sweetheart.

> *May the road rise up to meet you.*
> *May the wind be always at your back.*
> *May the sun shine warm upon your face,*
> *The rain fall soft upon your fields,*
> *and until we meet again,*
> *may God hold you in the palm of his hand.*

> *With love, your father,*
> *Tim*

By the time Fin finishes reading her father's name,

she's in tears. I cradle her in my arms as she weeps. "I don't know what to do," she says through her tears. "What should I do?"

Her vulnerable eyes look up at me for answers. I lightly stroke the back of her head, pressing my lips to her forehead and trying to find the right words. "I can't tell you what to do, but maybe if you tell me how you're feeling, things will become clearer."

She nods, sitting up and brushing away her tears. "I'm feeling confused. I believe him when he says he's sorry, but I don't know if I can ever really trust him, and I don't know if I have the strength to get to know him and risk him disappointing me."

"When you say 'disappointing you,' in what way would he disappoint you?"

"By not caring about me the way he claims to. I want to know my father but what if he isn't capable of being a real father to me?"

I nod. "The thing is, there's no way of knowing unless you try, but I do understand not wanting to be vulnerable with him." I take a deep breath. "My instinct is always going to be to want to protect you, but if I look at this as someone who lost my own parents, I would probably give anything for the chance to get to know my father…But it's an emotional gamble, like you said."

She nods, sniffling away the last of her tears. "I think I need to sleep on it. I'm too emotional right now."

As we lean back in bed, her head burrows into my chest, feeling for its home. I hold her close until her breathing slows and then allow myself to drift off to sleep.

Chapter Thirty-Nine

~ *Fin* ~

Present Day

"Chloe, it's time to leave! We're going to be late for school!" I yell upstairs.

Chloe hurries downstairs, backpack in hand.

"Mark, we're leaving! Don't forget, I'm taking Chloe to ballet after school!"

Mark appears at the top of the stairs. "Okay, have a good day you two." He flashes us that winning smile of his and Chloe and I each blow him a kiss, which he pretends to catch.

Chloe's ballet class is an hour long and, while there is a viewing room where parents can hang out and watch, I could really use some down time and decide to return to my car and close my eyes for a cat nap.

Unfortunately, about five minutes in, there is a tapping on my car window. To my surprise, it's Peter.

I roll down the window. "Hi!" I say. "I thought we agreed I'd pick up Chloe from ballet today. Did I mix up the dates?"

"No, I just had some time and thought I'd come see her because she's always asking me to come watch her dance. Then I saw you in your car. Are you okay?"

"Yes, I'm just taking a little break."

"Well, I'm actually glad I ran into you because there's something I really need to discuss with you."

"Sure, we can talk now if you want."

He walks around to the passenger side and gets in. His demeanor suddenly grows more serious. "So, it's about Chloe...and me," he begins. "I've been doing a lot of thinking these past few weeks and I've decided to take a job that doesn't require any travel and has a more regular schedule. That way I can really be there for Chloe every day."

"Oh, that's wonderful!"

"It was a difficult decision but I think it's the right one for Chloe—and for me."

I nod, a little more cautiously, as I sense there's more.

"The reason Camille didn't make me the sole guardian was because of my heavy travel schedule. I completely understood. She didn't want Chloe with babysitters all the time."

"Yes," I say. "She explained her reasoning to me when she first asked me if I would share guardianship with you."

"Oh, good, I'm glad she explained that piece." Peter takes a deep breath before continuing. "Fin, you and Mark have been absolutely amazing and you've really been there for Chloe in every way. She's so lucky to have you both in her life. But over the past several weeks, I've realized that her home is with me."

He waits for me to respond but I'm honestly speechless and can only nod.

"She's my only niece and I want to be the one to raise her and be as close to a parent to her as I can be. I'm sure you can understand why this is best for Chloe."

As I try to process what he's just said, my head is now reeling. I somehow summon the strength to put my own feelings aside and be as supportive of Peter's decision as I can be.

"I understand completely," I say with a composure that even surprises me. "You don't need to justify anything to me. You're her family and I'm happy for you, and for Chloe. Of course Mark and I will miss her terribly, but we only want the best for her."

Peter lets out a relieved exhale. "Thank you so much, Fin. I'm so glad you understand. I knew you would."

I'm still in shock, and very upset, but I don't want Peter feeling at all guilty about his decision, so I conceal my emotions as best as I can.

"There's no need to thank me," I say. "You just let me know what needs to be done as far as any guardianship changes are concerned."

Suddenly, there is another knock on my car window and it scares the shit out of me, until I see who it is.

Chapter Forty

~ Mark ~

Present Day

As I enter the parking lot of the dance studio, I pull alongside Fin's car and notice that her tire looks a little low. I get out to take a look and that's when I realize that Fin is actually inside the car.

I knock on her window and she startles and immediately opens the door and jumps out. "You scared me," she says nervously. "Is everything okay?"

"Yes, I texted you but you didn't respond. I had some free time this afternoon and Chloe's always asking me to come watch her ballet class so—"

But my words come to a screeching halt when I see Peter emerging from Fin's car. I look at Peter, then at Fin, then back at Peter who looks apologetic. I have no idea what's going on here but Fin looks upset. I try like hell to make sense of what I'm seeing.

Why were they alone in her car in the middle of the afternoon?

I'm unable to fend off my jealousy and the same panicky feeling I got when I saw Peter's hand graze Fin's shoulder has now returned—only worse. There is a tightening in my chest and I feel like I did a few years ago when I saw Fin running into the arms of someone I thought was her boyfriend. I lost her that day.

But before I can form a coherent sentence, Fin rushes to explain. "What a coincidence! Peter came by for the exact same reason as you did!" She turns to Peter. "Chloe's class is finishing up soon so maybe you should head inside and we'll be in shortly."

Peter nods. "Sure, unless you'd like me to stay and tell Mark what we discussed?"

What we discussed? My jaw instantly tenses and it feels like my shirt collar is choking me like a noose. I scan Fin's face for answers that I'm not sure I want to hear, but her face is unreadable.

"No, that's okay," she tells Peter. "You go ahead."

The moment Peter is beyond earshot, Fin's calm demeanor vanishes. She starts to speak but abruptly stops and I can hear the trembling in her voice. Something is wrong. ***Very wrong.***

Her sad eyes draw me to her and when I reach for her, she collapses in my arms.

"What's wrong?" I ask.

She chokes out, "I need to tell you something."

"Okay, just take a deep breath and tell me. Whatever it is, it'll be okay." My pulse is firing rapidly, but not out of fear for myself—out of worry for her.

She looks up at me with a resigned pain in her eyes. "It's about Chloe."

"Chloe?" Fear for Chloe's well-being now takes over. "Is she okay?!"

"Yes, she's fine." She swallows hard. "But Peter just told me that he wants her to live with him and he wants to assume full guardianship."

My mouth flys open. I can't believe what I'm hearing. "What?"

"Yes, that's what he wanted to talk to me about. He's changing jobs so that he won't have to travel anymore; that way Chloe can come live with him." Fin's voice is quivering as she fights back tears. "I can't believe this is happening."

I'm speechless and draw her back to my chest. I sensed Peter was feeling conflicted but, quite honestly, I didn't see this coming at all. My mind tries to process all of this, but it's a lot.

I spot Peter and Chloe walking out of the building together. "Hold on, Peter and Chloe are headed this way. I'll take care of it."

I swiftly head them off and suggest Peter take Chloe to dinner, which he's more than happy to do. Then I quickly return to Fin.

"They're going to dinner," I say, drawing Fin back to me in a tight embrace.

Fin suddenly pulls back with tears in her eyes. "I hope it isn't something I did."

My eyes meet hers head on. "Absolutely not. You've been wonderful with Chloe. And I can see how much she loves you. Peter knows that."

She nods, her eyes still sad and deflated.

By the time we get home, the initial shock has worn off and we're already much calmer. Fin heats up some leftovers but neither of us have an appetite.

"I know in my heart that this is the best thing for Chloe," Fin says as she pushes some peas around on her plate. "And I know this is what Camille would have wanted too. But I'm still very sad."

I reach across the table and hold her hand. "I'm sad too. But like you said, it really is best for her to be with her family. After seeing her with Peter these past few weeks, I think we both know that she belongs with him."

She nods with tears in her eyes. "I know she does."

I squeeze her hand, doing my best to keep my emotions in check for her sake. As upset as I am, she doesn't need me falling apart. My main concern right now is Fin and helping her through this.

"It'll take some time, but we'll all adjust," I say. "Better that it happened now rather than down the road."

She lets out a resigned breath. "True."

The minutes until Chloe returns from dinner seem to drag on endlessly. When Peter finally drops her off, we agree to tell Chloe the news tomorrow. So tonight may be Chloe's last night with us.

It's a particularly hard night for Fin and me. We find ourselves praising Chloe for every little thing that she does, as if trying to fill her up with as much of our love as possible. At bedtime, I watch as Fin carefully tucks Chloe in, making sure the blanket is just so and giving Chloe her favorite stuffed animal to sleep with. Fin manages to hide her sadness from Chloe, but I can feel it.

"Good night. Sweetest dreams," Fin says, stroking Chloe's hair away from her face before kissing her forehead.

"G'night," Chloe says with a yawn.

Fin backs away and then I lean down to give Chloe a kiss on the cheek. "Good night, Princess. We love you."

"Me too." Chloe then reaches her hands up to me and, as if sensing my sadness, she pulls my head down and kisses me on the cheek.

As I turn to leave, a single tear trickles down the same cheek she just kissed.

Chapter Forty-One

~ *Mark* ~

Present Day

Since Chloe moved out two weeks ago, we've only spent one day with her, but that's been by choice, as we wanted to give Peter and her time to adjust to their new living arrangement. Luckily, Fin still gets to see Chloe every day at school, so I don't think it's been quite as big of an adjustment for Fin as it has been for me. I miss Chloe very much but I'm trying to see the positives here. We were able to help her through a very difficult period following her mother's passing and I'm extremely grateful for the time that we did have with her. We can't, and shouldn't, take Peter's decision personally. The truth is that, up until last summer, we were complete strangers to Chloe and there really is no substitute for a family bond. Fin and I know Chloe belongs with Peter, so while it does hurt sometimes, ultimately we just want her to be happy. That's what counts most.

Fin's and my relationship has definitely been put to the test these past few months, but in truth, each challenge has only strengthened our love and trust in one another. I've never been in a relationship for this long and it feels like we're in a really healthy place. Fin is the first person I've ever wanted to share my life with, have kids with, and wake up every morning with, and I know she feels the same way.

With all of the recent changes involving Chloe, Fin

has yet to revisit the subject of her father. I admit I'm a little relieved because I *am* concerned that interacting with her father may lead to disappointment and hurt feelings. And yet, in my heart, I know that if I were her, I would want to get to know my father, no matter the risk. The choice is hers and I will support her in whatever she decides.

This morning, she finally broaches the subject.

As she sips her coffee, her eyes meet mine over the rim of her mug. "So I've been thinking about it and I've finally decided what I want to do about my father."

I brace myself. "Okay…so what did you decide?"

"I think I want to contact him. Even if it may not be the exact relationship I'm hoping for, I still want the chance to get to know him…What do you think?"

I place my hand on hers. "I think you should do whatever you feel is best for you. If you want to try with him, I support that—and you."

She exhales with relief. "Will you come with me?"

"You mean to visit him?"

"Yes, I want you there with me."

"Of course." I definitely want to be with her in case things go south.

"Okay, then I'll call the correctional facility today to find out when I can visit him."

I nod. "Are you going to let Dan know?"

"I haven't decided. It's different for him because he was older when my father left and he actually remembers it. So I'm sure he's going to be pissed at me. I think it's probably best if I don't tell him until after the visit, and only if there's actually something to tell."

She's right. Dan is going to be very upset and I can't say that I blame him after what Tim put her through this summer. I can still remember the look of fear in her eyes as he was leading her to the back of the restaurant. I don't think I can ever forgive him for frightening her like that.

I just have to keep reminding myself that I need to be supportive and that I'll be with her the entire time she visits him. If he tries to pull *anything* at all, I'll intervene.

* * *

As we head up to the correctional facility, which is about forty-five minutes north of us, I occasionally glance over at Fin who has been extremely quiet for most of the car ride. She hasn't let go of my hand since we began driving and has spent most of the way there staring out the window in silence. But just as we reach the tall gates of the facility, her body tenses up and she squeezes my hand tighter. I do the talking at the armed checkpoint, never letting go of her hand as we're escorted into the facility.

Despite what Fin was told on the phone, the officer now says that only one visitor is permitted in the room with Tim.

"But the officer I spoke with said I could bring a friend with me," she insists.

"I'm sorry, ma'am. I don't know who you spoke with but the rules have always been one visitor only."

Fin's face flushes and I can see she's on the verge of turning around and leaving. I intervene and, after explaining my concern for Fin's safety during the visit, the officer eventually compromises by allowing me to sit in a waiting area immediately outside of the private visiting room. I can't go in with her, but at least I'll be right outside the door. Fin isn't happy but we have no choice.

For the next twenty-six minutes—the longest twenty-six minutes of my life by the way—I wait on the other side of the closed door to the visitation room.

Chapter Forty-Two

~ Fin ~

Present Day

As I wait in the small visitation room for my father to arrive, I notice that it's eerily quiet, save for the sound of heavy steel doors occasionally slamming shut. The slams grow louder and closer, and then the visitation room door suddenly opens and a guard escorts my father in. He looks different than I remember. Thinner, more worn.

There are no physical dividers, just a table with a chair on either side, and he sits down across from me. The guard remains standing by the door.

My heart begins to race. Not out of fear. Rather, in anticipation of what is to follow.

When my father's eyes meet mine, he gives me a smile, which makes him look more youthful.

"I didn't know you were coming until about fifteen minutes ago," he says. "If I'd known, I would have made sure to shave and wear a nicer jumpsuit." He gives a weary smile but I don't react.

"Well, it was kind of a last minute decision."

He nods cautiously. "I see. Well, I'm glad you decided to come. Did you get my letter?"

"Yes, I did."

"I'm glad your brother gave it to you. I wasn't sure he would."

His words immediately tick me off and I feel the

heat climbing up my face. Dan can be overprotective at times, but he would never have kept my father's letter from me and I won't tolerate him being disparaged like this.

"Tim, Dan would *never* do something like that. You don't know him—he's not like that."

There is instant regret in my father's eyes. "I'm sorry, I only meant that he might have wanted to protect you. Anyway, I'm glad you got it." He shifts nervously in his seat. "So, how are you?"

"Good." I pause. "How are you?"

"Okay, all things considered. I've been doing a lot of reading. They have an excellent library here. Not much else to do." He gives a weary chuckle.

I nod. I think I better just dive in. There isn't much time. "So, if you wouldn't mind, I was wondering if I could ask you a few questions. I just know so little about you."

His eyes brighten. "Of course, anything."

"Thanks, and I apologize for my directness but we have very little time."

He puts up his hand. "No apology needed."

I forge ahead. "So why were you originally incarcerated?"

"Didn't your mother tell you?"

"Not specifically, no."

He looks a little surprised. "Oh, I assumed she would have...Well, I'm embarrassed to have to say this, but I was dealing drugs—for a guy who was a much bigger fish than me. He was the one they really wanted but I got swept up in the net. Then I got saddled with some racketeering charges which lengthened my sentence."

"And before that you were in the military?"

"That's right, the Army. I was deployed overseas."

"I didn't know that. So when you returned to the States, did you live with us again?"

"Yes, I was discharged and rejoined your mom, you, and your brother. But unfortunately I just wasn't in a good place mentally. I know that now. I tried to keep a steady job but my mind just couldn't focus. Things were really rough and I couldn't support myself, much less my family. Your mother had to work two jobs and I felt like a complete failure." He runs his hands through his hair and sighs, as if trying to decide how much more to reveal. "So when the opportunity to make some easy cash presented itself, I took it. Selling drugs was easy money. But I'm not proud of any of this."

"I'm not here to judge, I just want to understand."

He lets out a relieved exhale. "Somehow I knew you would keep an open mind." His familiar green eyes lock with my own. "You were always such a sweet baby. You know, when I was deployed, I used to carry around a baby picture of you and you had this big smile on your face. Like your whole face was lit up. I kept it with me all the time and whenever I felt down, I'd look at that smile and it would instantly cheer me up. I missed you very much."

Emotions stir in my heart but all I can bring myself to do is nod. "What about mom and Dan? You must have missed them too?"

"Of course I did. Your mom was my first love and she's the only woman I've ever loved. I missed her terribly while I was deployed. And your brother, well, he was very upset when I left. He was old enough to understand that I was leaving for a long time when I was deployed. I felt very guilty. He needed his dad and I couldn't be there for him. I don't think he ever forgave me for leaving him."

I don't think he ever did either.

"Why did you decide to join the Army?"

"You ask a lot of questions." He smiles. "I'm glad. So let's see, first I need to back up a little. Your mother and I began dating in high school and it really was love at first sight—for both of us. So the summer after we graduated, we saw no point in waiting and decided to get married. We started college that same year but my family didn't have a lot of money and they couldn't afford to send me for much more than a year. Your mother's family actually offered to help us out so I could continue with college, but I wouldn't let them. It didn't sit well with me to have her family helping to support us. So that's when I decided to join the Army. It seemed like a good opportunity at the time. At first I remained local, which worked out great, but eventually I was deployed overseas. You obviously don't get to choose where you go."

As my father shares, each missing piece of the puzzle falls into place. I never knew they'd been married right out of high school, or why my mother never finished college.

"So you said that when you returned to the States, you had trouble focusing on work. Do you think that was related to your time in the military?"

"Hard to say. Maybe. It was a long time ago."

"I'm not sure what programs were available to you back then," I say, "but I wish you'd been connected with people who could have helped you."

"Honey, there *were* people who tried to help me, but I wasn't really capable of following through. Instead, I looked for easy money. That's on me and I regret what I did. I should have tried harder to make an honest living. If not for me, then for my family. I'm so sorry I failed all of you."

The problem-solving optimist in me takes over. "Maybe when you're eligible for parole again, we can connect you with some programs that can help you. I could research some assistance programs for you."

"That's very sweet of you, but I'm not sure there's any program that can help me at this stage of my life. I'm a fifty-year-old convict with no skills."

"You have skills. You just need to tap into them and there are people who can help you get on the right path. There are vocational rehabilitation programs and reintegration programs, and counseling too if you need it."

He gives me a weary smile. "Well, I appreciate your optimism, Finola. I actually did ask for parole reconsideration and they've agreed to review my case, so we'll see."

The guard interrupts us, signaling that our time is up, and my father obediently stands.

"Can we have just one more minute to say goodbye?" he asks the guard, who nods. My father's eyes return to mine. "Thank you so much for coming to see me. You have no idea how much this means to me. If it's okay, can I write you once in a while?"

I hesitate before responding, but my heart is certain. "Sure."

"Thank you," he says softly. "Can you leave your home address for me?"

Fear suddenly kicks in. "I'll leave you my email address."

"Okay, sure. They'll get it to me."

"Okay, well, thank you for answering all my questions, and take care of yourself." I give a small wave.

He smiles before being escorted out.

I find Mark waiting for me just outside the room. He immediately jumps up from his chair and checks to make sure I'm okay, but we don't speak yet, as there is a guard waiting to escort us back to the main entrance.

After leaving my email address with the front desk and getting on the road, I share everything with Mark. His eyes remain on the road while he listens intently to everything I'm saying.

"So I think it went well," I sum up, "for a first visit anyway."

"Yes, it sounds like it." He threads his fingers through mine but remains quiet, as if concentrating on something.

I need to know what's going on in his head. "Do you think it was a mistake for me to visit him?" My question causes him to break away from his thoughts.

He shakes his head in response. "No, I don't think it was a mistake. It sounds like the visit went really well. I'm just being extra cautious. It sounds like he has good intentions, but please, just be careful."

"Don't worry, I will be." I squeeze his hand. "I know I need to get to know him better before making any judgments."

He nods as he lifts my hand up to his lips and gives me a soft smile.

As much as I'm dreading it, I decide to fill Dan in while we're heading home. If I wait too much longer to tell him, he'll never forgive me.

Dan's reaction is just as I expected—actually, it's worse. He's furious and can't believe I visited Tim in prison. He doesn't pull any punches in telling me he thinks Tim is up to something and not to trust him. I hear him out and manage to smooth things over—for now—but it's not easy.

By the time we get home, I'm completely drained and go upstairs, kick off my shoes and collapse into bed. Mark joins me.

"Dan managed to give me a splitting headache." I groan. "The visit with my father went fine, everything was fine, but Dan was being impossible. That's my brother for you."

"He's just worried about you," Mark says.

"I know that, but he's so damn overprotective," I grumble. "It can get really annoying at times."

"It's the price of being loved." He leans over and gives me a kiss on the cheek.

I smile, nuzzling into his chest. "Everything's going to be okay," I say confidently. "I can handle this."

"I know you can."

Chapter Forty-Three

~ Mark ~

Present Day

"Come on in! It's freezing out there!" Fin's mom quickly ushers Fin and me inside.

This year is the coldest Thanksgiving on record in Shelby Falls. But I don't mind it. Other than the fact that I can't golf, I like the chillier weather. Maybe it's because I associate it with my birthday, which happens to fall the day after Thanksgiving this year. No matter how old I am, my parents still insist on celebrating it with me. So, the plan is to have Thanksgiving lunch with Alyssa, dinner with my parents, and then stay overnight there and celebrate my birthday with them tomorrow. Our visit will also give Fin a chance to tell her mom about her visit with her father. She held off telling her until she could do it in person because she doesn't think her mom is going to take it well.

As we enter Alyssa's kitchen, the smell of turkey and stuffing invades our senses. I hand Alyssa a bottle of her favorite wine and we set down the side dishes Fin made on the counter. Fin's eyes wander to something simmering on the stove. She dips in a spoon for a taste.

"Yum...your turkey gravy is the best..." Fin licks the spoon clean.

Alyssa smiles. "Thank you for making the corn casserole and cinnamon rolls! They smell delicious! Please, let me take your jackets and come sit down." She leads us into the living room where we all take a seat.

"So how are you both?" Alyssa asks.

"Good!" Fin says.

"And you, Mark?"

"Oh, can't complain. Other than Fin's snoring, all is good." Alyssa laughs and I give Fin a wink and a grin.

She hates it when I kid her about her snoring and glares playfully at me. "I do not snore! I just breathe deeply when I sleep."

"Call it what you want," I tease and then turn to Alyssa. "This is the only thing we ever fight about by the way."

Alyssa smiles. "Well it warms my heart to see you both so happy. And how are your parents, Mark?"

"Very good. We'll head over to their house later today."

"Wonderful," Alyssa says. "Excuse me for a moment, I just need to check on the turkey. Help yourselves to wine if you'd like." She points to the cabinet as she steps away.

Fin pours us each a glass and rejoins me on the couch. "I really hate to spoil the day by telling her about my father. She's going to be very upset, I just know it. Maybe I shouldn't tell her today."

"Fin, I think you have to. She'll be more upset if you don't tell her. I can go over to my parents' house for a little while after lunch if you want to speak with her alone."

She ponders my offer as she swirls around the wine in her glass. "That might be best."

Alyssa calls for us to come to the dining room where there is an elaborate meal waiting. She takes great pride in her cooking and everything is fantastic. I'm glad we're here to celebrate with her; I would never want her to be alone on a holiday. Our hope is that next year both of our families can spend the holiday together. The only reason we didn't do it this year is because Fin wanted time alone with her mom to tell her about her father and she didn't think her mom would be up for socializing after that.

After dessert, Fin signals to me and I make up an excuse about needing to help my parents with something, leaving Fin and her mom to talk.

Chapter Forty-Three, Continued

~ *Fin* ~

Present Day

"Mom, the dishes can wait. Let's go sit down. There's something I need to talk to you about."

But first she insists on making us some tea. Then we take a seat in the living room.

"So, is this about you and Mark?" She looks at me expectantly. "You two seem to be very happy together."

"Yes, we're very happy. The Chloe situation did put a little strain on us, but we worked through it and I think we're actually stronger because of it."

"I'm so glad. It's obvious how much he adores you, which is how it should be."

"Yes." I take a deep breath and slowly let it out in preparation. "But that's not what I want to talk to you about. I need to talk to you about dad."

My mom's eyes instantly dart to mine. "Tim?

"Yes."

"Has he done something?" Alarm fills her once calm voice.

"No, I mean, well, not exactly."

She puts down her tea. "What does that mean?"

"Well, he wrote me a letter apologizing for what happened last summer and—"

"He damn well better have apologized after what he put you through. He's lucky I wasn't there or I would have—well, I would have made sure he never came near you again."

"Mom, it's okay, he just wanted to explain and he seems very sorry."

"That's fine, but please promise me you won't respond. He can't be trusted."

Ugh, I *know* how much this is going to upset her. "He actually sounded very sincere," I explain, "so I decided to contact him…and then I went to see him."

"In prison?! Finola!" She shoots up from the couch.

"Mom, sit down, please. This was a really hard decision for me to make but I need to do this—for me. He's my father and I want to get to know him, and then I'll decide where to go from there."

She initially just stares at me in disbelief, but her face soon softens and she sits back down beside me. "Honey, I understand why you would want that, and he's not a bad person. I wouldn't have married him if he was. But he's made some bad decisions and trouble seems to follow him. I just don't want you getting caught up in his problems."

I gently place my hand on hers. "I won't. I'm being very careful. And believe me, Mark is not going to let anything happen to me."

"Does Mark agree with your decision?"

"He's supporting me in whatever I decide. He knows this is important to me."

She takes a drink of her tea and nods, then treads lightly. "So then you saw your father?"

I nod.

"Did the visit go okay?"

"Yes, I think so. I asked him a lot of questions and he answered every one. He didn't ask anything of me, other than wanting to know if he could write me again."

"Was he…Did he seem okay? I mean, of course he's not okay—he's in prison. But did he look to be in good health?"

"I don't really have a good frame of reference, but he looked well to me…As well as can be expected."

She takes a slow, deep breath. "Please just promise me that you'll be careful."

I give her a hug and kiss. "Always."

As we drive up to Mark's parents' house, a white colonial with forest green shutters, my eyes are immediately drawn to the slate roof and perfectly pruned evergreen shrubs that adorn the exterior. This is the first time I've been to his parents' house and I can't believe how stately it is. I hop out of Mark's truck and spot a basketball hoop mounted above the three car garage, along with a cute flagstone patio with Adirondack chairs and a fire pit by the side entrance. It's a beautiful home, and I have to admit, I'm a little shocked at how large it is. I knew Mark had a comfortable upbringing, but this house is much grander than I imagined it to be.

And *this* is why I love this man so much. Because he has never allowed money or material things to define him. If you didn't know he came from money, you'd never know it because he's so unassuming and humble, and I have never once seen him show even a hint of superiority over others. I glance over at him and smile, and he smiles back.

Since Mark's parents already saw him earlier today while I was speaking with my mother, their attention is singularly focused on me and they greet me warmly, as they always do. Rick helps with our bags and Leslie immediately shows us into the living room where she has hors d'oeuvres waiting. Shrimp cocktail and baked brie topped with pomegranates. I think I've died and gone to heaven. Leslie gleefully reports that she recently got a new sofa and chair for the living room and I'm immediately struck by what impeccable taste she has. The room is elegantly decorated, yet without being pretentious, and she has chosen a combination of traditional pieces mixed with some very unusual modern art. I can see where Mark got his love of art from. I absolutely love her style.

As the four of us chat over cocktails and Mark entertains us with a few stories, a feeling of overwhelming gratitude comes over me. Leslie and Rick are always very kind to me, but it's more than that. They have this way of making me feel so welcome, like family. They also seem genuinely happy that Mark and I are together and, as Leslie fusses over me, I'm starting to realize that Mark hasn't brought many women home to meet them. Leslie wastes no time giving me the grand tour of the house, complete with showing me several pictures of Mark when he was little. She even brings me up to his bedroom and proudly shows off his academic awards, including the fact that he was valedictorian of his high school class! Mark has never mentioned any of this to me and it fills me with so much pride.

Leslie and I have been gone for several minutes and when Mark calls upstairs and realizes we're in his bedroom, he comes bounding up the steps, interrupting his mom mid-sentence as she's telling me about the time he fell off of a ropes course and broke his leg. I purse my lips together to keep from laughing at his annoyed expression.

"Mom, Fin doesn't need to hear about every bug bite

I got! You're boring her to death."

"No she's not," I protest. "I love hearing these stories. Please continue, Leslie."

He groans and shakes his head.

Leslie smiles. "That's Mark. He's never been one to brag. But he's someone who happens to excel at whatever he puts his mind to. He's also not afraid to go after the things he wants in life."

I notice a slight blush creep up on Mark's face. It's adorable.

"Anyway, I'll let you two settle in," Leslie says. "Dinner should be ready in about half an hour so you two just relax and I'll let you know when it's ready."

Mark embraces her. "Okay, we'll be down in a little bit." Once she's safely downstairs, he closes the door. "Sorry about that. She probably talked your ear off."

"Are you kidding? I loved hearing about your childhood. You haven't shared much about it, so I was happy to hear the stories."

He sighs and comes over to me, reaching his hands out for mine. "Oh Fin, what am I going to do with you?"

"I love you, what do you expect?"

"I expect you to get sick of me, but for some reason you haven't yet."

"And I've got news for you, I never will."

He pulls me flush against him, both of us smiling like two lovestruck teenagers.

I giggle at my next thought. "So are we going to make out on your bed now?"

"Absolutely. You'll be the first."

My brows raise. "I thought you were a heartbreaker in high school. You never brought a girl up to your bedroom?"

"Nope."

I glance over at his double bed with its farm style wood headboard and red and black flannel comforter. "Well then we definitely need to christen this baby tonight with lots and lots of hot sex."

He laughs. "G-d, Finny, I do love you."

"I know you do. And later you're going to *really* love me." I reach up to give him a peck on the lips.

"I can hardly wait." As he aligns his body with mine, I can feel his hardness pressing against me and am immediately turned on.

"I don't know if I can wait until later," I say with an unintended breathlessness. "Your bulge is dangerously close to where I need it to be."

He lowers himself to target my most sensitive area. "Is this the spot?"

I sigh. "You know it is."

He lays me back on his bed and the next thing I know our bodies are a tangled mess and we're rolling around French kissing and dry humping like teenagers.

I gasp for air. "How can we be this turned on with our clothes still on?"

He moans as we continue kissing. "I have no idea but if we don't stop soon, I'm going to need to change my boxers."

"This feels way too good," I say between kisses, "and the idea of us both coming with our clothes on sounds incredible."

He hops up to lock the door and then returns to me with a sexy grin. "You think you can come this way?"

My mouth curves upwards as I eye the huge bulge in his pants. "Well we'll have fun trying."

Chapter Forty-Four

~ Fin ~

Present Day

Luckily, Leslie has prepared chateaubriand for dinner, as I'm a little "turkey-ed" out from lunch. The entire dinner, Mark and I try our best to carry on a meaningful conversation with his parents, but we're so enamored with one another that it's next to impossible. His parents are going to think I'm a complete ditz fawning over their son the way that I am. But Mark isn't concerned in the slightest and boldly coaxes me to sit on his lap after dinner. Despite my protests, he's having none of it and draws me onto him.

"Mark," I whisper in his ear, "your parents are going to think I'm very inappropriate."

But Rick puts my mind at ease.

"I love how openly affectionate you two are with each other. It tells me that you're the real deal."

"Rick took the words right out of my mouth," Leslie says, getting her phone. "Let me get a picture of you." With me still on Mark's lap, Leslie takes a pic. "Do you mind if I post it on my page?"

"Sure," Mark says, "as long as it's okay with Fin."

I nod. "It's fine with me."

After dessert, we all decide on a movie to watch together in the family room. Mark and I get cozy under an afghan on the chaise of the couch but we're much more engrossed in each other than in the movie. From the way we're acting, you'd think we'd either a) never had sex before, or b) are having it way too often. Eventually, Mark capitulates to my wandering hands and announces that we're tired and are going to call it a night. We then head up to Mark's bedroom, far too energetically, and he immediately locks the door.

"You're very subtle," I say, reaching my arms around his neck and pressing my body flush against his.

"Exceedingly." He palms my ass.

"So what would you like to do tomorrow for your birthday?" I ask.

"I think my mom is planning something during the day, but otherwise, we can do whatever you want."

"It's your day so you pick."

"Right now, all I want to do is get into bed and continue what we were doing earlier."

I grin. "Okey dokey."

Mark changes out of his clothes and I put on an oversized sleep shirt with the entire *Peanuts* gang on it.

He smirks. "Very sexy."

"Well I don't want to wear anything too revealing in case your parents see me walking to the bathroom and think we're having sex in here."

"Good thinking. This nightshirt will definitely throw them off course."

I playfully lunge towards him but he somehow evades me and the two of us land in bed together, play wrestling until we've exhausted ourselves.

With both of us flat on our backs, I turn to him with a flirtatious gleam. "You!"

"Me? *You*! You're the one who lunged at *me*!"

I giggle. "Next time I won't miss."

He leans over and plants an unexpectedly tender

kiss on my lips, then pulls back with an adoring smile.

I softly stroke the stubble on his face, meeting his kind eyes. "You," I say softly.

Never leaving my eyes, he takes my palm and kisses the center before laying back. As I nestle into his chest, an odd thought suddenly pops into my head. "So is this the bed you slept in as a kid?"

"From the time I was about thirteen, why?"

"I don't know. It just feels kind of forbidden for us to be sleeping together in the bed you slept in as a kid."

"Nah, it's fine."

I turn my head upwards. "So what were you like as a teenager?"

"Not that different from how I am now." He chuckles to himself. "Boy, you're very curious tonight. What did my mom tell you anyway?"

"It's not that, I just want to know what you were like when you were younger." My mind begins to stray further off course as I trace my fingers up his chest. "I have another question for you."

"Okay, shoot. I'm here all night."

I pause to think about how to ask this. "I can't believe I'm going to ask you this but...did you ever...oh my gosh, forget it. I can't even ask this."

He immediately rotates his body to face me. "Did I ever what?"

I suddenly feel embarrassed, but not too embarrassed to ask. "I'm not sure why this even entered my head...but did you ever...you know...masturbate in this bed?"

He chokes out a laugh. "*That's* what you wanted to ask me? Fuck, yeah! All the time!"

I giggle. "All the time?!"

"I mean, not every day, but yeah, a fair amount. Why?"

"I don't know, just curious." I run my leg up his and wrap it securely around him.

"Just curious, huh?" He runs his finger along my lower lip. "You do realize that just talking about this is getting me all worked up."

The corners of my mouth curve upwards. "So what are you going to do about it?"

"What did you have in mind?"

I know exactly what I have in mind and give a shy grin. "I don't know...maybe I could...watch you touch yourself? Is that too weird?"

He looks a little surprised, but in no way deterred. "Fin, what we do together is for us and us alone, and the idea of you watching me sounds, well, extremely hot."

"Yeah?" I squirm with anticipation.

"Yes...You know, I've thought about you pleasuring yourself."

"Really? Was this recently?"

"Not recently. It was before we started living together. I used to get pretty turned on after some of our texting sessions and a few times you said you needed to take a shower after we got off the phone, so my mind of course went there."

I grin knowingly. "I understand."

He pulls me tight against his hardening shaft and asks in a low voice, "So...you want to watch me?"

I swallow hard. "Yes."

He gives a sexy moan in my ear and whispers, "Okay then."

Chapter Forty-Five

~ Mark ~

Present Day

I don't know why people make such a big deal about birthdays. It's just a day. Yet even at my age, my parents still insist on spending my birthday with me. I really can't blame them this year though, because it's a big one —my fortieth.

I sleep in a little longer than usual and when I wake up, Fin isn't beside me. I throw on some flannel bottoms and a shirt and go downstairs to find Fin and my mom chatting in the kitchen over coffee.

"Oh, good morning, honey," my mom greets me.

"Morning," I say with a yawn and a stretch. "You guys are up awfully early."

"The smell of pumpkin spice coffee lured me downstairs," Fin says, tapping her coffee cup before taking a sip.

"We've been having a lovely chat," my mom says, "and Fin was just telling me about how the two of you met."

My eyes meet Fin's. "Oh?"

"Yes," my mom says, "she said that you came into the restaurant where she worked and immediately won her over with your charm and good looks."

"Well, that's definitely true." I squeeze Fin's shoulders from behind.

"I told her how you asked me out that same night

and we hit it off instantly." Fin looks up at me with a knowing smile.

"That we did." I kiss the top of her head.

"Well that's how it should be," my mom says. "When it's right, everything just feels effortless, like the most natural thing in the world."

I nod. "I agree 100 percent."

"Oh! I nearly forgot to wish you a happy birthday!" My mom jumps up. "Happy birthday, sweetheart!" She gives me a big hug and kiss. "So, I hope you don't mind, but I took the liberty of inviting the Conroys over for lunch and cake today." The Conroys are Matt's parents, and Matt's and my parents go way back to when Matt and I first became friends. "Matt and Jennifer are also going to join us and they're bringing baby Olivia too!" my mom adds.

"That sounds great. Thanks for planning it." I give my mom a kiss on the cheek. "I think I'll grab a shower then." My eyes dart to Fin's. "Maybe you want to get ready too and then we can run out and get something for the baby?"

That's just an excuse. I just want Fin all to myself...in the shower preferably.

Fin hops up from her chair without hesitation, clearly reading my mind. "Sure, that sounds like an excellent idea."

"Okay, you two go get ready." My mom purses her lips as if to hide a smile and I swear she knows what we're up to.

Once upstairs and safely in my bedroom, I pull Fin in for a kiss.

"Much better," I say. "It didn't feel right without our

morning kiss."

We have this thing where each morning, before we say anything to each other, we kiss. But this morning Fin left before I woke up.

She kisses me again and smiles. "So I guess this is what it feels like to kiss an old man, eh?"

"Oh, sorry, should I take out my dentures first?"

She crinkles her nose. "Ewww."

I chuckle. "So when do I get that birthday present you promised me last night?" I close the distance between our bodies.

"Oh...you mean the one involving the pole dance?"

"That's the one."

"That'll have to wait until we get home, but I do have some other presents for you. Want to open them now, birthday boy?"

"You didn't have to get me anything."

"Of course I did!"

She retrieves two gifts and anxiously waits for me to open the larger one first. When I see what's inside, my jaw drops.

"Fin, this is fantastic!" I carefully take out a drumhead that's been autographed by one of my favorite drummers of all time, Stewart Copeland. I glance up at her incredulously, then back down at the drumhead. I can't believe she found this.

"So you like it?!" she asks.

"I love it! Where did you find it?"

"A music memorabilia site on line. It also comes with a certificate of authenticity. I'm so glad you like it!"

I'm so moved by the gesture and feel my throat tightening with emotion. I wrap my arms around her, but a hug feels so inadequate in comparison to how I'm feeling right now. I pull back, trying to find the right words.

I must look freaked out or something, because her brows furrow with concern. "What is it? Is something wrong?"

I shake my head. "No, nothing's wrong. I'm just very touched by the gift, that's all." I meet her loving eyes. "I can't believe you remembered that I like him."

"Of course I remembered! You talked about him for like a solid hour one night!" She giggles. "It was cute."

I chuckle with embarrassment. "Well I don't know about that. But seriously, thank you. This is one of the most thoughtful gifts I think I've ever received. It means a lot." I lean in to kiss her. All I want to do is show her how much I love her.

She smiles up at me. "There's still one more gift. Think you can handle it?" She presents me with the second box.

"I hope so," I say as I open the box to find a very soft pale blue scarf. Not that it's not nice, but I'm assuming there's a deeper meaning behind it and look to her for the explanation I know is coming.

"It's made from mohair," she explains with a gleam in her eyes. "And I bet you can't guess where mohair comes from."

I smile. "I'm going to take a wild guess and say *goats*?"

Her mouth drops open. "Seriously?! How did you know that?"

"No idea. I just did."

"Smarty-pants." She shakes her head, pretending to be annoyed, as she carefully places the scarf around my neck and ties it. "There. I wanted you to have something to remember our first date by."

"Oh, I could never forget that day. Best first date ever."

"Best *any* date ever." Her tender gaze roams my face before she gets on her tiptoes and kisses me. "Happy Birthday, my love."

We spend the next half hour in bed just kissing and appreciating one another.

It's great to see Matt and Jennifer again, along with Matt's parents, but the undisputed star of the hour is Olivia. She's crawling around everywhere in this little fleece sleeper with bunnies on it, so someone always needs to keep a close eye on her so she doesn't get into trouble. I think she may be frustrated by the sleeper, as she's been occasionally kicking her feet like she's trying to escape from it. And her little belly laugh when Matt tickles her—well, it's just about the best laugh I've ever heard.

"Your daughter is without a doubt the cutest human being on earth," I tell Matt.

Matt beams. "She really is."

"Did you ever think we'd be sitting here, so happy with how our lives have turned out?"

"It kind of feels surreal sometimes," Matt says. "Almost like I'm looking down at my life from above. But I knew we'd get here eventually."

"Even me, huh?" I grin.

"Yes, even you. In spite of yourself, you found an incredible woman who clearly adores you. I'm really happy for you and Fin."

"Thanks. She's the best thing that's ever happened to me, Matt." I glance over at Fin who is bouncing Olivia on her knee, and when our eyes find one another, I can feel

WHAT LOVE CAN BE

her love from across the room. "The crazy thing is that if I hadn't been such a jerk to Jenn that night at the wedding, I don't think we would have ever gotten together," I say. "It took you calling me out on my behavior for me to find out how wrong I was about her. So in a way, I really have you to thank for leading me back to her."

Matt chuckles. "Well, however it happened, I'm really happy for you both. Fin definitely brings out the best in you...So are you thinking about a future with her?"

My heart speeds up at just the thought. "I think I need your advice about that. We've only been dating for six months, but I know I want to spend my life with her, and I think she feels the same way. I just don't want to freak her out by proposing too soon, you know?"

Matt smiles. "I wouldn't worry about that. I see the way she looks at you and something tells me she'd marry you in a heartbeat."

I let out a relieved exhale. "Okay, well, thanks for the vote of confidence."

Matt pats me on the back. "Just trust your heart and you'll be fine."

Olivia suddenly begins crying without warning, bringing our visit to an abrupt end. We've apparently hit the bewitching hour and Olivia's beginning to have a meltdown. Jenn says she just needs to go down for a nap and Matt insists that she'll be out like a light once they get her in the car, so they quickly pack up, and Matt's parents soon follow in tow. Once everyone has left and we've helped my parents clean up, it's five o'clock and Fin and I decide that we too need to pack up.

Not long into the car ride back to Boston, Fin falls asleep, leaving me to agonize for the rest of the drive home about one thing and one thing only: how and when to propose.

Chapter Forty-Six

~ Fin ~

Present Day

My phone vibrates with a new email, but it's not an email address I recognize. I soon realize why. It's from my father's prison.

> From: Westgate Prison
> Date: December 15
> Subject: Inmate McAdams, T.
> To: Finola McAdams
>
> Dear Ms. McAdams:
>
> Inmate Timothy McAdams is scheduled for parole reconsideration before the Parole Board on December 21 at 10:00 a.m., Westgate Prison, Room 401.
>
> If you wish to attend and/or provide a statement, please respond to the above email address no later than December 18.
>
> Thank you.
> Westgate Parole Board

I recall my father saying he was seeking parole reconsideration but I'm not sure why I'm receiving this notification. Perhaps because I was involved in his parole violation, or maybe he listed me as an interested party. I suppose my input might be helpful to the Board in making their decision, but I'll need to think about whether I'm comfortable giving a statement.

Since visiting him a few weeks ago, my impression of him has definitely improved. We've emailed a few times and he's always extremely apologetic and seems to be making an effort to get to know me. I must admit that being able to communicate with him and get to know him has actually been really nice. While I don't condone his past criminal behavior or the way he conducted himself last summer, I'm absolutely certain that he would never harm me. My main concern about him being paroled is that if he doesn't have the right supports in place, it'll just be another setup for failure. I do think that my input at the parole hearing may carry some weight if I can convince the Board that I will be able to help with his transition this time around.

"The prison contacted me today about my father's parole reconsideration hearing," I tell Mark as we sit down for dinner.

"Oh?"

"Yes, I was invited to attend the hearing and give a statement if I want to, and I'm thinking about doing it."

Mark's brows furrow with concern. "Will your mom be okay with that?"

"I'm not sure, but I think my father is trying really hard and he deserves the chance to be happy. He's done his time and I think he's sorry for what he's done in the past."

Mark tentatively nods. "I obviously haven't met him other than last summer so it's hard for me to judge one way or the other. I just don't want you to get your hopes up too much. It's going to be a hard road for him."

"I realize that and I'd like to be as supportive as I can."

"I know you do. It's one of the things I love most about you—your generous heart and your ability to see the goodness in people."

I smile. "I do think that with love and encouragement, most people will rise to their full potential."

"You just tell me how I can help you."

"Can you help me write a statement in support of his parole? I want to be sure I hit all of the key points."

"Sure, we can work on it tonight if you'd like."

I go over and sit on his lap. "You're amazing, you know that?"

"I am, aren't I?" He grins.

"You are..." I give him a kiss, running my tongue along his.

* * *

Instead of merely sending a written statement to the Parole Board, I've decided to attend the hearing in person because I think reading my statement aloud will make more of an impact. Mark took the day off from work so that he could come with me for moral support and I'm extremely grateful because I'm a little anxious.

As we wait for the Board to convene, my nerves set in. I hope I'm doing the right thing. I think I am. I just want the opportunity to get to know my father and perhaps even develop a healthy relationship with him. A chance is all I'm asking for. Even Dan has been supportive of my decision, which is a little surprising frankly.

Once the Board is ready to proceed, my father is escorted into the room. When he sees me, his lips curve into a soft smile, causing my heart to stir. *I know I'm doing the right thing.*

After the Board makes a few introductory remarks, I'm given the opportunity to speak. I'm not normally nervous speaking in front of others, but this feels different—very personal. Statement in hand, I go to a small podium and begin to read it aloud.

"Good morning. My name is Finola McAdams and I am Timothy McAdams' daughter. I'm here to speak in support of my father's request for parole reconsideration. I've only recently been in communication with my father, as he's been incarcerated for most of my life. He's told me about the circumstances of his incarceration as well as his prior military service. While he was never officially diagnosed with a service-connected disability, it is my belief that when he returned from his deployment overseas, he may have been suffering from some degree of trauma, so it likely would have been very difficult for him to hold down steady employment. He needed to find a suitable job that paid enough to support my mother, my brother, and me. So I can understand my father feeling tremendous pressure to succeed for the sake of his family, and I believe this unfortunately led to his trouble with the law.

"I am a social worker and firmly believe that counseling and vocational rehabilitation can make all of the difference for someone who is returning to the workforce after a lengthy incarceration. My father has served his sentence and I believe that with the right supports in place, he can be a highly productive member of society. I am willing to work closely with vocational programs to help ensure his success and I can also assist in getting him into group therapy and having him evaluated for any veterans benefits to which he may be entitled. I acknowledge that this is going to be a challenging time for him but I am prepared to give him the support that he needs. Thank you for your consideration."

As I return to my seat, my father slowly turns his body to look at me and I can see the emotion and gratitude in his expression. I send him back a reserved but hopeful smile.

My father is then given the opportunity to speak and he reads a short statement expressing regret for his actions and reaffirming his commitment to following the terms of his release if granted parole. After the Board enters a final report into the record, they huddle for a moment before asking Mark and I to wait in the hallway.

I'm extremely anxious for my father and can't sit, so we take a walk to the other end of the hallway.

"So do you think it went okay?" I ask Mark.

"I think your statement definitely made an impression on the Board. They were listening very closely and I think you did everything you possibly could." He gives my hand a squeeze.

"Did you see my father look over at me after I was done speaking? He seemed pleased."

Mark nods. "Yes, he looked very appreciative—as he should be. You went out on a huge limb for him today and he's very lucky to have you in his corner."

"I just didn't want to regret not having done everything I could to help him."

Mark lightly strokes my back. "You know, it's also okay if you wanted to do this for you, too."

I smile up at him, so grateful that he understands my desire to have a relationship with my father.

We're soon interrupted by the clerk's voice calling us back into the room. The Board didn't deliberate for very long and I'm hoping that's a good sign. However, once everyone is seated, the Chairperson informs us that they aren't rendering a decision today but expect to do so in the next few days. It's disappointing but at least it's not a denial. As soon as the hearing concludes, I try to approach my father, but before I can even say good-bye to him, he's escorted away—but not before he turns to look at me one last time. He gives me a small wink and mouths the words "thank you." It makes my entire heart warm.

* * *

The next few days are tense as we wait for the Board's decision. I check my email incessantly but there's no word yet.

But then, on my drive to work this morning, I receive a call from the correctional facility.

"Ms. McAdams, my name is Carl Johnson and I'm one of Westgate's community liaisons. I'm calling because I understand that you spoke at Timothy McAdams' parole hearing."

My heart instantly begins pounding out of my chest. "Yes, I did. I'm his daughter."

"Well I just wanted to reach out and discuss a few matters with you if you have a moment," he says.

"Of course." My heart continues to race with hope, but also with fear of a disappointing outcome.

"So even though a decision hasn't been made yet about your father's parole, it's best to be prepared because we'll have a very short window after that. It's very important that the appropriate supports are in place in the community before an inmate is released. We of course want our parolees to succeed with their reintegration."

"Yes, I understand."

"So, in the event that your father is granted parole, would you be willing to let him reside with you temporarily if necessary? Sometimes there can be a delay in securing suitable housing."

I pause to think. This certainly isn't something I can commit to without speaking with Mark. "My boyfriend and I live together so can I get back to you tomorrow about that?"

"Of course, no problem. In the meantime. we also need to think about a work program for your father. These programs are designed to help build skills to make individuals more marketable, but unfortunately the pay is pretty low so it may be that he'll need additional financial support initially. Is that something you would be willing to help out with if necessary? If not, that's okay. We just need to know so that we can allocate some additional funds for him."

"I just started a new job and I don't have a lot of disposable income, but I'll certainly do whatever I can to help him out. Any additional funds you can obtain for him would be a huge help though."

"Very good then. I think that about covers it for now. As soon as I hear something, I'll be back in touch. Just let me know what you decide as far as having your father live with you, and if you have any questions, you can reach me at this number."

Once we hang up, I begin mulling things over but I really need to speak with Mark first since this needs to be a joint decision. Knowing him, he'll say it's all fine, but this is his home and having a virtual stranger living with us is a huge ask, so it's important that he really be okay with this and not feel pressured to agree.

The rest of my work day drags on like watching the last drops of maple syrup drip from the bottle. I can't easily speak to Mark while I'm working, and besides, our conversation should be in person.

As soon as the school bell rings, I rush out the door and head home, immediately calling Mark to find out when he'll be home. He texts that he can't talk because he's in a meeting, but then texts a short while later to say that he's leaving the office now.

The moment I see his truck pulling into the driveway, I run to the front door, startling him as he enters.

He laughs. "What's going on?"

"Nothing, I just need to discuss something with you, that's all."

His brow arches. "Can I get changed first?"

"Oh, sorry, of course."

He looks at me with curious amusement as I follow him to the bedroom, trying my best to be patient as he gets changed and tells me about his day. Once he's finished, I immediately lead him downstairs to the couch and then proceed to bombard him with the details of my morning call with the community liaison. He calmly listens to me without interruption.

"I'm sorry, I didn't mean to throw all of this at you at once," I say. "I'm just a little anxious."

He strokes my upper arm. "It's okay. Take a breath."

I inhale and let out a slow deep breath. "I know having my father move in with us isn't what you bargained for and I don't want you to feel pressured, so you just need to be honest with me."

Mark pauses to consider everything I've told him. While he always likes to carefully think things through, he's not one to overthink and is very decisive once he makes up his mind.

He finally speaks. "It should be fine," he says. "I just want to be sure this is what you really want and you're not just doing this because you feel obligated. Because they can make other living arrangements for him that don't involve you, so you should only do this if it's something you want to do."

I immediately nod. "I want to do it—as long as you're okay with it."

"I'm good if you're good."

"You sure?"

"I'm sure." He gives me a warm smile, and with it, my peace of mind is restored.

I seriously don't know what I did to deserve this man —I really don't—and it's impossible for me to ever adequately express how much I appreciate him, but I'm sure as hell going to try.

* * *

The next day, I receive the good news that my father's parole has been granted. The community liaison, Carl, said he believes my statement definitely influenced the Board's decision, reinforcing my belief that I did the right thing. He says my father's housing won't be available for two weeks and that he will be meeting with my father shortly about work programs. I'm very optimistic that things are going to go a lot more smoothly for him than they did last summer. And of course this time around I'll be here as an added safety net just in case he needs my help. He won't have to go through this alone.

With my father's release date in sight, I bite the bullet and call Dan.

While he seems neutral about our father being granted parole, he's furious when he learns that he'll be staying with us for a few weeks. He says Tim has a "target on his back," which is a gross exaggeration. But Dan knows me well enough to know that he's not going to change my mind, so he ultimately gives up and just cautions me to be very careful.

The call to my mother is much more difficult. To say that she is displeased would be an understatement. It's not that she doesn't think my father deserves to be paroled; she just doesn't want him living with us and is extremely worried about our safety. I think she's also afraid that he's going to disappoint me, just as he disappointed her in the past. I've tried to reassure her that I'm going to take things very slowly with him, but she also needs to understand how important this is to me. He's the only father I have and I finally have the chance to have a real relationship with him for the first time in my life. I need to do this. For me.

Chapter Forty-Seven

~ *Fin* ~

Present Day

Ever since we received the call that my father will be discharged today, I've been a nervous wreck and am seriously wondering whether I was crazy to think this was a good idea. But Mark and I are on our way to go pick him up, so I guess we'll find out soon enough.

I would have thought it would have taken much longer to discharge him, but the process is actually surprisingly quick. My father only has a few personal belongings so, after loading them into Mark's truck, the three of us begin the drive back home in relative silence. It's hard to know what to say and I'm honestly stunned that my father is actually sitting here in the car with us. It feels almost surreal. Yes, he's my father, but he's also basically a stranger to me. I don't even know what to call him. Dad? Tim?

I try my best to distract from the awkwardness of the moment, grasping for anything to say. "We have a spare bedroom downstairs and you'll also have your own bathroom," I explain.

"I can't thank you enough for helping me out like this," my father says. "I really appreciate you putting me up in your home, Mark."

"It's no trouble at all, really," Mark says.

"Well, I'm hoping I won't need to impose on you for too long. They're lining me up with a work program and an apartment so I should be out of your hair in no time."

"No worries," I reassure him. "The room is yours for as long as you need it." I absolutely don't want him feeling any unnecessary stress. Just reacclimating to the real world is stressful enough. "So is there anything you'd like me to pick up for you, like a particular shampoo or any other toiletries? Or maybe you'd rather we stop on the way home and that way you can pick up whatever you'd like?"

My father's expression goes blank. "I...I'm not sure. It's been a long time since I've bought shampoo. Maybe you can just pick out whatever you think is best."

I am such an idiot. Of course he doesn't know what brand he likes. He's been in prison for twenty years, you moron!

"Okay, I'll pick you up a few essentials," I say. "And maybe tomorrow we can go and get some clothing for you."

"I don't want to burden you," he says. "I can take a taxi to the store."

I shake my head. "No, really, it's no trouble at all."

"Fin's right, we're glad to help," Mark adds.

"Okay, then yes, that sounds good," my father says. "Thank you."

I breathe a sigh of relief. So far so good.

As I make up my father's bed and get him situated, it strikes me that as strange as it feels to have him in our home, it must feel even stranger for him to be here. Even just having a private room is probably a big adjustment for him. And he seems to notice even the smallest things, like the fragrance of the hand soap in his bathroom or the lamp by his bedside—as if each thing is a luxury. Seeing our life through my father's eyes, I am beginning to realize just how much we take for granted.

Once my father is comfortably settled in his room, I start to close the door behind me, but he insists I leave it open. At first this surprises me, as I assumed he would want his privacy. But I wonder if maybe he doesn't like the feeling of being confined to a room. As I turn to leave, I can't help but notice how alone he looks sitting at the edge of his bed. It hurts my heart.

* * *

Other than what my father was wearing yesterday when he was discharged, and a few random shirts and pants they sent him off with, he has no clothing to speak of. So today we're taking him shopping at one of Mark's favorite stores. We don't know whether he'll be working outdoors or not, but I want to be sure he's prepared for the cold weather and select a warm, ultra-lightweight down jacket for him, as well as waterproof gloves and hiking boots. We also buy him a few flannel shirts that he seemed to like. He's insistent on paying us back with the small stipend he has, but I have no expectation of that, nor do I want him to. But he seems hell-bent on paying his own way and I certainly respect that.

By the time we're through, it's lunchtime and I'm starving.

"We've been wanting to try this new burger place," Mark tells my father. "Maybe we'll go grab lunch there?"

"That sounds good to me," I say, looking over at my father. "Are you up for that?"

"Actually, if it's okay with you, I think I'd like to just head back to your place and rest. I have chronic insomnia so I'm a little tired."

"Oh, sure, whatever you'd like," I say. "We'll head back." I resist the urge to offer him solutions like melatonin or classical music. I sense that he's feeling a little overwhelmed and I don't want to add to it.

Once we're home, I offer to make him something hot to eat, but he says he'd like to make himself a turkey sandwich, which he quickly eats, and then he goes to his bedroom to rest. Mark and I are a little tired too from the past few days, so we decide to unwind in bed as well.

I snuggle into Mark's chest as he plays with a few strands of my hair. "I hope he's doing okay," I say. "I obviously don't know him well but does he seem a little withdrawn to you?"

"I think maybe it's just a lot for him," Mark says. "If you think about it, he hasn't had this kind of freedom in years, except briefly last summer. And given how badly that went, he's probably anxious. It's got to be frightening to realize you're totally on your own after everything has pretty much been decided for you for the past twenty years."

"You're right." I tip my head upwards. "You know, you have this remarkable ability to put yourself in someone else's shoes and really understand how that person is feeling, and yet at the same time, still be able to pull back and be objective."

He kisses my forehead. "Well, I don't know about that."

"Stop being so humble." I reach up for a kiss. "Thank you."

"Not sure why you're thanking me."

"Because you've been so flexible and supportive through this whole situation with my father. It means the world to me. I still can't quite believe my father is downstairs and I'm actually going to get the chance to know him after all these years."

Mark nods. "That's big. I'm really happy for you, Finny." He presses his lips to mine and I hum with satisfaction.

"So...how about we use this time to have a little fun?" I suggest, trying to hide a mischievous smile.

There's a glint in his eyes. "I'm right there with you, babe."

Chapter Forty-Eight

~ Mark ~

Present Day

It's been about a week since Tim moved in with us and things seem to be going pretty smoothly so far. He's already met with his job coach and is supposed to start his work program this week. His housing isn't finalized yet, but we've assured him that he can stay with us for as long as he needs to.

I'm up early for a Saturday morning, but that's only because I want to get some work done before the day gets underway. I really try not to let my work interfere with our weekends. As I enter the kitchen to make some coffee, I'm surprised to find Tim already brewing a fresh pot.

"Good morning," I say. "You're up early."

"Yeah, I'm used to getting up early. I'm not sure I'll ever be able to undo my years of being woken up at the crack of dawn." He gives a small laugh.

I nod. "I actually like the early morning hours. I find I'm able to get a lot of work done at this time of day."

"Well please, don't let me interfere with your work. I'll just take my coffee and be out of your hair."

I hold up my hand. "No rush." I pour us both a cup and sit down, taking a sip. "You make a mean cup of coffee, Tim."

He laughs. "Not too strong for you?"

"Nope, just the way I like it."

He grins. "So Fin tells me you're a corporate lawyer."

"Yes, I am."

"How do you like it?"

"I enjoy it."

"Well you seem to have done very well for yourself."

"I can't complain. I do work hard, but I've been able to keep a pretty healthy balance between my work and my personal life, which is very important to me."

"Well, I can see that you're very good to my daughter and that's all I care about."

I nod and wait for him to continue, as I sense he's gearing up to say something else.

"We haven't really had a chance to talk much, you and I," he says, "and I just want to thank you for being there for Fin last summer at the restaurant when I went a little out of my mind. I wasn't myself that night and I'm glad you were there for her. Truly, I can't thank you enough."

My eyes lock with his. "I would do anything for Fin. *Anything.*"

"I can see that. Believe it or not, you and Fin remind me a lot of Alyssa and me when we were first married."

My brows raise. "Yeah?"

"Yes. Alyssa is an incredible woman. So much strength and so supportive. I never should have joined the Army. It changed everything for us." He lets out a deep breath.

"Being away must have been very hard on all of you."

"It was much harder than I expected. Had I known I'd be deployed overseas so quickly, and for so long, I don't think I would have joined. When I returned, I wasn't the same person and Alyssa and I were never the same. We fought a lot, mostly about me finding work.

My family needed me and I never felt like I could be the man they deserved." He sighs with regret. "I made some bad choices."

"I'm sorry" is all that I can think of to say.

"Well, that's just how it goes sometimes," he says. "Life is one big, complicated riddle and just when you think you've got it figured out, something new pops up." He gets up to refill our cups.

"Well, if it's any consolation, I think you're on the right track and we'll do whatever we can to help you out."

"I appreciate that, Mark, I really do. You're a good man and I'm glad Fin has you in her life." He pauses. "If I can ask, how is Alyssa doing?"

I'm not sure how open to be on the subject of Alyssa and am purposely vague. "Oh, she's great."

He nods tentatively. "Is she married?"

I hope this isn't confidential and shake my head *No.*

This seems to be a big relief to him. "I don't mean to seem like a jerk, because I really do want her to be happy, but I'd be lying if I said that didn't make me a little hopeful."

"Oh?"

"I just, well, I never stopped loving her and, who knows, maybe if I can get my act together this time, I might have a chance to prove myself to her again."

I'm not exactly sure how to respond and simply nod.

"So is she still an incredible cook?" he asks.

I grin. "Absolutely."

Tim grins back. "She always was an amazing cook. What I wouldn't give for her roasted chicken. It was the best chicken I've ever had in my life."

I chuckle. "Fin definitely inherited Alyssa's cooking

skills. You'll have to ask Fin to make you one of her special omelets. She'll be thrilled."

"I'll have to do that."

Fin suddenly appears in the doorway. "Do what?

"Ask you to make me one of your famous omelets," Tim says.

Fin's eyes instantly brighten. "Of course!"

I go over to give Fin a morning kiss. "I have a little work to get done this morning, okay?"

"Oh, do you need to go to the office?"

"That's probably best." I steal one more kiss from her. "I'll be back by noon."

Chapter Forty-Nine

~ Fin ~

Present Day

After Mark leaves for the office, I whip my father up an omelet filled with cream cheese because I've noticed that he likes a lot of cream cheese on his bagel. Sure enough, he absolutely loves it and cleans his plate. *Day made.*

Afterwards, he decides to get a haircut as he wants to make a good impression for his first day of work on Monday. I'm so proud of him. He has a very positive attitude and I really think things are looking up for him—finally.

With time to myself, I decide to do some baking. Oatmeal chocolate chip cookies to be exact. Kind of the best of both worlds in my opinion, although some purists might balk at the combination. Once the first batch is done, the whole house smells heavenly. Just as I put the second batch in the oven, the doorbell rings.

"I told you you don't need to ring the bell," I say as I open the door, assuming it's my father. Except it's not my father. Instead, I see a slickly dressed, husky man holding a briefcase. "Oh! Sorry, I thought you were someone else," I explain. "Can I help you?"

"Yes, good morning, Ms. McAdams. I'm here to see Tim McAdams and I understand he's staying with you."

"I'm sorry, you are...?"

"Oh, I'm sorry, ma'am. I'm Tim's parole officer, Larry

Carmichael. Please call me Larry." He shakes my hand. "May I come in?"

"Actually, he's not here right now. Did you schedule a visit with him?"

"No, this is an unannounced visit to see how everything is going."

"Oh, well since he's out, is it possible for you to come back another time?"

"If it's okay, I'd prefer to wait for him. I can wait outside if you'd like."

I certainly want to be cooperative, so I invite the man inside and he takes a seat in the living room. While he waits, I offer him some cookies, still warm from the oven and he sits quietly, scrolling on his phone while I putter around for what feels like an eternity. Finally, after an excruciating twenty minutes, my father returns and I immediately meet him at the front door to warn him about the visit. I don't want him to feel blindsided. But when my father sees Larry, his calm expression immediately changes to one of dread.

"Hello, Tim." I notice that Larry gives him an almost too familiar smile.

My father's eyes immediately dart to mine. "I'm sure you have things to do, so I'll take it from here." There is a sharpness to my father's tone that I've never heard before.

I slowly nod. "Okay...sure."

While something about this doesn't quite feel right, I give them their privacy and return to the kitchen to clean up. It's not my intention to eavesdrop, but it's impossible not to hear my father and Larry's voices getting louder.

"Listen, you've got one week to get Benny the 10k

and he wants 1k today," I hear Larry demand.

"Lower your voice, Larry. My daughter's in the next room," my father says in a hushed tone. "You know I can't get my hands on that kind of cash that fast. I haven't even started my job, man. C'mon, can't you just let Benny know I'm good for it and that I just need a little more time? He knows I won't screw with him."

"You know that's not how this works, Tim. I need a grand today and the rest by this Friday. Got it?" Larry's voice turns more snide and intimidating.

It's clear that this man is no parole officer and he's certainly no friend of my father's. But my instinct tells me not to call the police; that could just put my father in danger. My heart is accelerating as I quickly think this through.

"I told you, I don't have that kind of money," my father insists. "I can get you five hundred today."

That's my father's entire stipend.

"What do you take me for? An idiot?!" Larry barks. "I said I need 1k *today!*"

There is a pause, followed by a scuffle, and I run out to find my father in a choke hold. A surge of fear rushes through me. *I need to do something NOW.*

"Fin, leave NOW," my father struggles to vocalize, pointing to the front door.

"She's not going anywhere until *I* say so!" Larry yells. "Your dad here needs a little favor from you. One thousand dollars in cash. Can you be a good girl and go get that for him?"

I immediately nod. "I just need to go to the bank." My voice is noticeably shaking.

"You go *directly* there and back, and don't you get smart with me and try to call anyone, unless you never want to see your dad again! Understand?"

"Yes, I'll be quick. You'll get your money, I promise." My pulse is firing on all cylinders..

"You better not be playin' with me or your dad's going to suffer the consequences." He points to his pocket and I can see the outline of a pistol.

My heart pounds with fear as I grab my purse to leave. But just as I'm about to open the front door, Mark walks in.

"Hey, babe," Mark says. "Where are you going?"

I whisper in his ear, "Shhh, just come with me." I grab his arm.

But as we turn to leave, Larry appears in the foyer with my father still in a choke hold. Mark's eyes quickly dart to mine and then back to the two of them. Mark's jaw tightens with resolve.

"Fin, go outside," Mark orders.

"Now *that* ain't happening," Larry tells Mark as he gives him the once-over. "You look like the kind of guy who keeps a wad of spare cash in the house, am I right?"

Mark's eyes travel to mine before answering *Yes*. But I know for a fact that he doesn't keep that much cash in the house.

"Great," Larry says smugly. "Then I need you to go get me a grand right now."

"I'm happy to do that...*after* you let her go," Mark says.

Larry chuckles. "This isn't a negotiation, man. Go get me the cash...NOW."

Mark's jaw remains clenched as he calmly tells Larry that the cash is upstairs.

"Okay, but hand over your phone first," Larry says.

Mark hands it over and then slowly walks past us

towards the living room, with Larry following close behind. But once in the living room, I notice Mark pause slightly. That's when I see him suddenly grab the glass platter of cookies from the coffee table and turn and smash it on Larry's head. Larry looks dazed and releases my father for a moment, but then recovers enough to lunge at Mark, knocking him to the floor. A feeling of sheer terror overtakes me when I hear the sound of Mark's head hitting the corner of the coffee table.

"You son of a bitch!" Larry shouts, pinning Mark down with his full body weight.

I frantically scan the room for a heavy object and my eyes land on a bottle of scotch we received as a holiday gift. I'm about to hit Larry with it when my father pulls Larry off of Mark and wrestles him to the floor. Together, my father and Mark pin Larry face down. My father tells Mark to go get some rope which he quickly retrieves from the garage.

"I'll take it from here," my father tells Mark. "You get Fin out of here and call the cops."

"You're so fucked, Tim," Larry mutters under his breath. "Benny won't put up with this shit."

My father doesn't respond as he ties Larry's hands behind his back.

Mark rushes to my side. "Are you okay? Did he hurt you?"

My hands are noticeably shaking. "I'm fine, but are you hurt? You hit your head so hard on the table!" I'm very worried that he could have a concussion and I really think he needs to be checked at the hospital.

"I'm fine," he insists. "I just want to make sure that creep didn't lay a hand on you." He glares in Larry's direction.

I shake my head. "No, he didn't.'

"Why don't you sit down and I'll call the police," Mark says.

I reluctantly sit as he paces about the room while speaking with the 911 operator, the only sign of his agitation.

Once the police arrive, they immediately arrest Larry because apparently they already have an arrest warrant for prior assault charges. My father is understandably nervous as he gives his statement to the police because this could jeopardize his parole. But the officer doesn't appear concerned about my father's actions and just asks that we all be available for further questioning if necessary. Once the police leave, we try to make sense of what happened.

"I'm so sorry," my father says, scrubbing his face in frustration. "I had no idea about any of this. Larry was apparently trying to collect on a debt from over twenty years ago for Christ's sake. Had I known, I never would have stayed here and risked putting the two of you in danger." He gets up. "I'm going to collect my things and go and stay in a hotel until my housing comes through. It's not safe for you."

I jump up. "Absolutely not. You're staying right here." I take my father's hand and make him sit back down. "Dad, I know you didn't know about any of this and I don't blame you at all. I'm just glad everyone's okay."

My dad now looks me straight in the eyes, stunned, and I know why. This is the first time I've called him *dad.*

He places his hand on mine, his face full of emotion. "Thanks for being so understanding, sweetheart. You don't know how much that means to me."

I meet his eyes again, sensing a subtle but meaningful shift in our relationship, and my heart surges. "I'm still worried about your safety," I say. "Do you think someone else will try to collect the debt?"

He lets out a deep breath. "I have a feeling they'll lay low for a little while, but eventually they'll be back. I must have had some product in my apartment when I went to prison. I'm assuming the police confiscated it before Benny could get it. He was my supplier and probably lost a lot of revenue." He exhales again with frustration. "I'm going to need to pay him back within the week."

"This is crazy," I say. "Maybe you should see if your parole officer can help?"

My dad immediately objects. "No, I owe him the money so I just need to square away the debt."

"But—"

"Fin, let your father handle this." Mark's voice is stern. "You need to stay out of it, for your own safety."

"Mark's absolutely right. I'll find a way to pay back Benny, don't worry. I just hope my place is ready soon because I don't want either of you getting caught up in this again."

"It's okay," I reassure him. "Your safety is my main concern. Will you please let me loan you the money?"

"No, I don't feel right about taking money from you, but thank you."

"It's not a gift," I explain. "I know you're good for it."

"Honey, thank you, but I'll find a way to resolve this on my own."

"Tim, Fin has a point," Mark says. "Let us lend you the money. They'll leave you alone as long as you pay it off, right?"

"I think so, but—"

"No buts, it's done," Mark says, getting up from the couch. "We'll get you the cash when the banks reopen on Monday." Mark's caring eyes meet mine.

"I don't know what to say." My father stands to shake Mark's hand. "Nobody's ever done anything even close to this for me. I *will* pay you back, every penny of it."

"We know you will," Mark says.

My dad looks exhausted and takes my suggestion to go lay down in his bedroom. As I glance around the living room, there are cookies scattered all over the place but Mark and I are too drained to clean up and decide to head upstairs to unwind as well.

Despite Mark's protests, I insist he sit down so that I can examine his head more carefully for any injuries. That's when I find a minor laceration.

"Okay, there's a small cut on the back of your head from when you fell," I say. "Does your head hurt?"

"No, is it bleeding?"

"No, the bleeding stopped. Don't move." I run to the bathroom and return with some antiseptic to clean the cut. "If your head starts to hurt even a little bit, you need to promise that you'll tell me, okay?"

He nods. "I will, but I swear, I feel fine."

I search his face and don't see any sign of pain— thank goodness.

"I really wish you hadn't gone after him like that." I put aside the antiseptic. "It was too dangerous. He had a gun and he could have killed you!"

Mark takes my hand and I sit beside him on the bed. "Listen, there was no way in hell I was going to leave you downstairs with him like that. I didn't know what he might do and I had to try to take him down."

I sigh and then the corners of my mouth curve upwards. "With my cookies?"

He chuckles. "Yes, with your cookies."

As I gaze into the eyes of this beautiful, heroic, loving man, my emotions finally start to catch up with me and tears begin to form in my eyes. I was so frightened when I saw him get knocked down and this feeling of sheer terror overtook me. I don't know what I would have done if anything had happened to him.

He instinctively draws me to his chest, enveloping me with his strong arms. His even breathing helps to calm me.

"It's okay to be upset," he says softly, pressing his lips to my temple.

I tilt my head upwards to meet his eyes. "I *am* upset, but not just about what happened downstairs. I'm upset because of what I've put you through."

"What you've put me through? You haven't done anything."

"Yes, I have," I insist. "Ever since we started dating, you've had to put up with so much because of me. First you had to deal with my father last summer at the restaurant, then I moved into your house and had Chloe move in with us, then I insisted on my dad moving in, and now this happens. I don't even want to think about what could have happened to you today." My voice trails off as I fight back my tears.

Surprise and concern fills his eyes. "Listen to me," he says, gently stroking my hair away from my forehead. "That's not how I see it at all. Quite the opposite. It's because of you that I wake up every single morning with a smile on my face. And it's because of you that I can't wait to come home every night. Sweetheart, you make me feel whole—for the first time in my life." His eyes search mine until he finds what he's looking for in them. "Don't you see," he says softly, "you've shown me what love can be."

My eyes well up with tears. "But your life was so much less complicated before you met me. I feel like a tornado that touched down on your life and torched everything in its path."

He gives a soft laugh. "Well then maybe a tornado is just what I needed."

Even I have to giggle.

I reach for his cheek and stroke it with my thumb. "Thank you."

He draws me to his chest and my arms wind around his middle and up his back. My entire body surrenders to his cleansing embrace and any guilt I was feeling from earlier washes away. I love this man so much.

He suddenly pulls back, as if he's had an epiphany, and gets up to get something from the dresser. Then, without explanation, he asks me to close my eyes, and I, without question, squeeze them shut.

"Now hold out your hand," he says. I do as I'm told and soon feel him place something small in my palm.

My heart comes to a screeching halt. *Could it be...?* I impatiently hold my breath, waiting for him to say something.

"Okay, you can open your eyes now," he announces.

When I open my eyes, my jaw drops at the sight of the most stunning engagement ring I think I've ever seen. It's an emerald cut aquamarine stone surrounded by sparkling pavé diamonds with a diamond studded band. It's magnificent. I look up at him to be sure it's what I think it is and he gives me a shy nod.

I giggle with glee. "It's absolutely gorgeous!" My heart is ready to burst as he sits down beside me and takes my hand in his. But it's the words that follow that will forever be engrained in my mind.

"I've been thinking about something you once said — about how sometimes people from a past life will try to find each other again in their next life. I wasn't sure if I believed it, but the idea kept running through my head and the more I thought about it, the more I think it might be true for us. Because what I've come to realize is that I've been searching for you my entire life. I used to think that the reason I never found love was because I was closed off, but that wasn't it at all. It was that I hadn't found *you* yet. I was saving my heart for you, Finny."

I nod, gazing at him through my tears. "And I was saving my heart for you. I'm certain of it."

His eyes begin to mist and he smiles. "I just thank G-d I looked into those beautiful eyes of yours that first night we met because it was your eyes that drew me to you."

"I think our souls recognized each other before we did."

"Yes, our souls knew immediately."

"Thank you for finding me," I whisper, choking back my happy tears.

He smiles softly. "I'm sorry it took me so long."

He presses his lips to mine with exquisite gentleness and love. My mouth parts for him and we share a deep, lingering kiss. When our lips finally part, he asks me for the ring and then, to my delight, he drops down on one knee.

"So Finola Sharon McAdams with the unforgettable green eyes and mesmerizing smile, will you marry me?"

I smile at my soulmate as a single tear trickles down my cheek. "You know I will."

He lets out a relieved exhale before carefully sliding the ring on my finger.

We hug and laugh and kiss and hug some more. This moment is so much better than I could have ever imagined. *Because it's real.*

I extend my hand to admire my engagement ring, in particular the shimmering aquamarine stone. It's a beauty.

"So you really like it?" he asks, beaming with pride.

"I *love* it! It's so elegant—and very unusual. I think Princess Diana had an aquamarine ring, come to think of it."

"I know it's not as traditional as a diamond, but there's a reason I picked this ring."

"Oh?"

"Yes, it turns out that when you combine green and blue—our eye colors—it makes aquamarine." He beams at me.

"Oh! So the stone represents our union...I *love* that!"

"Me too."

He draws me to his chest and we embrace in silent serenity, just breathing together and allowing our souls to soak in the joy of the present moment. As our gazes fix on one another and our eyes merge, their crystalline blue and green waters flow seamlessly together to form our own aquamarine sea. Our bodies soon follow.

Chapter Fifty

~ Fin ~

Present Day

It's been two weeks since my father started his work program and I'm incredibly proud of him. He's been working very hard and his job coach is optimistic that he'll find steady work very soon. Things fell through with his original housing, but that's okay. Selfishly, I like having him live with us because it gives me an opportunity to get to know him better. And Mark has been so amazingly supportive throughout all of this.

The Benny situation thankfully seems to have resolved itself. My father paid off the debt the same day we lent him the money and Benny seemed to be willing to let bygones be bygones. He even offered my dad a "sales" job but my dad wisely declined. He says he wants to do things differently this time and I believe in him.

Not surprisingly, my mother remains skeptical when it comes to my father. I know she's just looking out for me, but what she doesn't understand is that while I do hope that he and I can build a real relationship, I don't have unrealistic expectations of him. I'm just letting things play out organically and am trying to appreciate every moment with him. I really think if my mother would just keep an open mind, she would see that he's changed.

Since it's just a matter of time before my parents come face to face with one another, I've decided that tonight is as good a time as any, so I've invited my mother over for dinner. My father will be there too, of course, and much to my delight, my mother didn't make a fuss about it. She even insisted on bringing a main course and dessert.

When I told my dad she was coming, I could swear I saw a gleam in his eyes.

Hmmm...

Just as my mom arrives, I coincidentally make myself scarce.

"Dad, can you please get the door?" I yell from the kitchen. "My hands are full." I look over at Mark and give a sly grin.

"Oh, you're not nice," Mark says with a smirk. "They're going to kill you."

"They'll get over it."

I try to eavesdrop from the kitchen but can't make out what they're saying. As I hear them approaching, I quickly take my position at the stove. Moments later they enter the kitchen, my mom carrying a roasted chicken in a baking dish and my father holding a cheesecake.

"It's so good to see you both!" My mom greets us with a big hug and kiss. "I've missed you! But first things first. Let me see the engagement ring!"

I proudly hold out my hand with a wide grin.

"Oh my, it's stunning!" she says. "Mark, you have excellent taste! I'm so happy for you both." She hugs us both again.

"Dinner's almost ready so why don't you all sit down in the dining room and I'll be right in," I say.

But my mom insists on carving the chicken she brought.

"Do you need any help carving?" my father asks.

"Thanks, but I'm all set," she says.

We bring everything out to the table and my mom soon appears with the chicken, beautifully plated.

"Oh Mom, it smells delicious! I can't remember the last time you made roasted chicken. Yours is my favorite."

"Mine too," my dad chimes in. "Your mother's chicken is out of this world. She puts whole garlic cloves into the bird as I recall."

My mother blushes slightly. "I can't believe you remembered that. It was so long ago."

"I suppose it was, but I have a lot of fond memories from those years." The two of them just stare at one another for a moment, speechless.

"Well, everybody dig in!" I say, trying to temper my excitement at having all four of us together for the very first time.

My dad can't compliment my mom enough about the chicken, and her cooking in general, and my mom is having trouble concealing how happy she is that my dad is enjoying the meal. Something tells me her meal choice was no accident. Inch by inch, I watch her slowly let her guard down with him. She even laughs at his corny jokes. Mark and I glance at one another in utter disbelief. This is going so much better than I could have ever imagined.

After dinner, we all relax in the living room and my dad shares more about his work program. I pepper him with questions, hoping my mom will see how hard he's working to make a new life for himself.

"I really enjoy working with my hands," he says. "I especially like doing kitchen renovations. You know, cabinetry, counters, and backsplashes."

"I'd really like to replace the floors in the kitchen," Mark says. "I've watched some tiling videos but maybe you can give me some tips, Tim."

"Of course, I'd be glad to," my dad says. "Or, I can do it for you if you pick out the tile you like."

"I'd actually like to learn how to do it, so maybe we can work on it together," Mark says.

I give Mark's thigh an appreciative squeeze. I know he's not particularly fond of manual labor and is just doing this to build my dad's confidence and get to know him better. And I love him for it.

I notice that my mom seems to be hanging on my dad's every word, particularly since she's a fan of television renovation shows.

"Maybe you can take some before and after pictures of your projects," she suggests. "I'd love to see them!"

My dad's face lights up. "Sure, I'll take some pictures next time and text them to you. Here, just enter your phone number so I have it."

He starts to hand her his phone but she just stares at him blankly.

"Or not," he hastily adds, pulling it back with embarrassment.

"No, it's okay," she says, a little flustered. She enters her number and returns the phone to him. I notice their hands briefly touch during the exchange. "I really do hope things work out for you, Tim."

His eyes fill with hope. "Thanks. I've been working really hard to build a new life for myself, one that I can be proud of." It's clear how much my mom's opinion means to him and it warms my heart. I believe in him.

"You'll do great." My mom reassures him with a

smile.

"So what kind of work do *you* do?" he asks her.

"I'm an insurance adjuster."

"She's being modest," I say. "She actually supervises a whole team of adjusters."

"That's wonderful, Alyssa! Congratulations!"

"Thank you." My mom's cheeks redden and she suddenly checks her watch. "Oh my, I didn't realize how late it is. Let me help you clean up, honey, because then I need to head home."

"Why don't you just stay over?" I say. "I already made up the bed for you in the upstairs bedroom."

"It's okay, I can make the trip back to Shelby Falls tonight. But I should head out soon or I won't get home until after midnight."

My dad pipes up. "Alyssa, it's late. Are you sure you're not too tired?"

She gives him a familiar smile. "Tim, it's not that late. I'll be fine."

"I'm sure you will be, but why push yourself? Fin already has the room ready for you."

She looks over at me hesitantly. "Well, I suppose I could stay if it's not any trouble."

"Great!" I say. "I'll lend you some pajamas."

"Actually, I wasn't sure how late it would get, so I brought some essentials. My overnight bag is in my car. I'll go get it."

As my mom starts to get up, my dad immediately pops up too. "I can get your bag for you. It's chilly out there."

"You don't have to do that," my mom protests.

"It's okay, I want to."

Their eyes meet and the two seem to be in their own

little world for a moment. My mom then hands my dad her car keys.

"Actually, I'll walk out with you, Tim," Mark says. "I need to run to the pharmacy before it closes so I'll be back in a few minutes." Mark gives me a quick peck before leaving.

Mom and I head for the kitchen to do the dishes.

"Honey, aren't you going to take off your engagement ring first?" she asks.

"Oh, right, I keep forgetting."

"It's such a beautiful ring." She stops to embrace me again. "I'm so thrilled for you and Mark. You two are a match made in heaven. Have you decided on a wedding date yet?"

"Not yet. Believe it or not, we've talked about eloping."

"Really? But why?"

"We really don't feel the need to have a big wedding. We're also toying with the idea of a small destination wedding with just immediate family."

"That sounds very nice. Whatever you decide, it should be what's best for the two of you."

I nod. "Anyway, enough about me. What I really want to know is how you think dad is doing. He seems to be doing well, don't you think?"

She lets out a breath. "He does, but time will tell."

"You know, he speaks very highly of you," I say. "He talks about what an amazing mother and wife you were and he knows he made a lot of mistakes with you—with all of us."

"I really would like to believe he's changed."

"Just keep an open mind, mom, that's all I ask."

"I can do that."

She gives a warm smile just as my dad pops his head into the kitchen. "Where would you like me to put your bag, Alyssa?"

"Oh, you can just leave it here. Thank you so much."

"Of course. Can I help with clean up?" he asks me.

"No, we're all set, but thank you," I say.

"Oh, okay then." He pauses as if trying to decide how to proceed—with my mother. "I guess I'll say good night then. Thank you both again for dinner. Everything was delicious." He comes over to give me a kiss goodnight on the cheek.

"Good night, dad." I smile up at him.

"Good night, sweetheart," he says.

His gaze then travels to my mother but he doesn't say anything further. He gives us both a final, cute salute goodbye, which elicits a shy smile from my mother.

My mom and I finish cleaning up and once Mark returns, we head to bed for the night.

At around midnight, I go downstairs to the kitchen to get a cold glass of water. My father's bedroom is near the kitchen and I notice that the door is ajar and the light is still on. That's odd; he's usually asleep by now.

"Shhh, Tim, keep your voice down," I hear my mom say in a hushed tone. "I don't want them hearing us."

I freeze in my tracks.

"So shut the door then," my dad says with a laugh.

"*That's* not happening," my mom replies.

"C'mon, Lyssa, we're just talking."

Lyssa? I've never heard anyone call my mom *that* before.

"Right now we're just talking, but you know as well as I do that closing that door is a very bad idea," she says.

He chuckles. "Just stay a little longer and talk. I promise, I'll be the perfect gentleman."

There's a pause. "I'll hold you to that," she finally says, closing the bedroom door.

My jaw drops another notch as I hear my mom's giddy laughter through the bedroom door and I sneak away like a cat burglar.

Chapter Fifty-One

~ Mark ~

Present Day

"Oh good, I'm glad you're both awake," I say as I enter the kitchen the morning after our dinner with Fin's parents.

Alyssa and Tim look up from their coffee cups in unison.

"Fin's still asleep and there's something I really need to discuss with you both privately. It's about our wedding."

"Oh!" Alyssa perks up. "Fin said you two were mulling over a few ideas."

"Yes, but I want to do something a little different from what we've discussed. It's going to take some coordination and I need your help."

Alyssa's grin widens. "Of course!"

"Yes, whatever you need," Tim says. "You name it."

I go on to explain my plan and when I'm finished, Alyssa jumps up to give me a big hug.

"Oh Mark, she is going to love this! Our lips are sealed."

She glances over at Tim who pretends to zip his mouth and throw away the key, eliciting a giggle from Alyssa. I'm not sure what's going on here but they seem to be getting along extremely well.

The three of us immediately clam up as Fin appears in the doorway. "Why are you all up so early? Haven't you ever heard of sleeping in on the weekend?"

"You know I'm an early riser," Alyssa says. "Plus, I need to start heading back home."

Tim's eyes dart to Alyssa. "Really, so soon?"

"Yes, I have some things to take care of."

Tim looks so deflated and I feel for the guy. I think Alyssa senses his disappointment too.

"But," Alyssa pauses, "I suppose I could stay until about noon."

Tim's face instantly brightens. "Well in that case, would you mind if I stole you away for about an hour? There's a kitchen renovation I'm working on and the contractor asked me to pick out a few tiles to show the homeowner. I could really use your help."

Alyssa grins. "Oh, well sure. I'd love to."

Fin and I glance at one another, a little dumbfounded by how well her parents seem to be getting along.

"I'll go get my jacket," Alyssa says, humming as she leaves the kitchen.

As Tim follows her out, he turns and gives us both a wink.

Chapter Fifty-Two

~ Fin ~

Present Day

A familiar pair of lips graze my neck, startling me as I wash dishes at the kitchen sink.

"You scared me! I didn't hear you come in."

He moves on to my earlobe. "Well I'm in—but I wouldn't mind being even further in a little later," he says in a low, sexy voice.

I turn to face him, biting my lower lip. "You know you and your significant other are always welcome."

He presses his lips to mine with a soft moan. "That's one of the many reasons I love you. You never turn me down."

I smile. "So how was your day?"

"Good. How was yours?"

"Good. I'm working with a new student so I planned a lunch for her today with a few classmates and I think it went really well."

"Nice...So before I forget, my mom called today in a panic. She wanted to know if my band could play this Saturday night at a Valentine's Day party at the golf club. The band they originally booked fell through so they really need a fill-in."

"That's only two days away though. Are you sure Josh and everyone else is available?"

He nods. "Yeah, I texted everyone and they're all up for it. But it's our first Valentine's Day together so I wanted to make sure it was okay with you first."

I certainly don't want him to miss out on the opportunity to perform, and besides, we can celebrate Valentine's Day on Sunday instead.

"Totally fine with me," I assure him. "You know how much I love watching you perform and I'm sure it'll be a fun night!"

"I thought we could have our own Valentine's Day celebration on Sunday, just the two of us," he adds. "I read about this new restaurant that overlooks the river and they even have a Sunday brunch."

"Ooh, brunch, huh?" I give him a wink. "You're on."

He looks relieved as his grin widens. "Thanks, babe! I'll let everyone know." He gives me a sweet peck. "Oh, and by the way, my mom said the theme is black and white so the guys are wearing black and the women are wearing cream or something light-colored. My mom mentioned that she has a dress she's never worn before that she thinks would be perfect for you. Do you want to take a look at it and see if you like it?"

"Sure! I do have one dress that could work but your mom's taste is impeccable and I'm sure her dress is much nicer than mine." Leslie always dresses very tastefully, but with a touch of flare, and I have no doubt that I'll love the dress she has in mind.

"Great, I know she'll be thrilled," he says. "She also wanted to invite your mom and dad, if that's okay with you. It should be a fun time so maybe they'd like to come too."

"Hmm...like together? I'm not sure how they'd feel about that."

"They wouldn't have to come together. They're just both invited—together, separate, whatever they want."

"Okay, I'll let them know," I say. "I'm sure they'd love to see your band play and my mom could definitely use a night out. I think my dad would have fun too—except he doesn't have a suit."

"That's not a problem. I have a black tux from when I was a groomsman at my friend's wedding and I think your dad and I are about the same size, so it should work."

"Okay!" I grin. "I'll call my mom now."

Within a few minutes, it's all settled and everyone is on board. Mark is excited about the band performing and he's grinning from ear to ear. It's the little things in life that bring him joy and I don't think there's anything in this life I would deny this man.

He draws me tight against him and it's clear we have unfinished business.

Lust simmers in his eyes. "So...how about we take this upstairs?"

My lips curve upwards. "You're full of good ideas today."

* * *

Even though the party doesn't start until six and Valentine's Day isn't usually a busy travel day, we decided to get an early start to Shelby Falls since the Massachusetts interstate is notorious for having heavy traffic, even on weekends. Mark's band will need to arrive early to set up and I also need extra time because Leslie is having her hair and makeup done and invited me along. I've never had someone do my makeup before, except once at the makeup counter in high school, and it seems a little over the top, but it's a good opportunity to spend quality time with Leslie.

My father is traveling separately and has apparently made afternoon plans with my mom. I'm not all that surprised given what I observed between them when my mom came for dinner. They seemed to be getting along very well and I suspect they may still have feelings for one another. But regardless, I'm just glad to see that they are making peace with the past.

When we arrive at Mark's parents' house in the late morning, Leslie has these tiny little triangular sandwiches waiting for us. She's prepared two kinds— smoked salmon and cream cheese, and ham and brie —and they're carefully arranged on a tiered porcelain china stand. I try not to eat too many but they're very small and so delicious, and I end up eating half a dozen! I can't help that I appreciate food and have a healthy appetite. Mark finds this all very amusing and Leslie is thrilled that I'm enjoying the food, so I suppose there's no need to be embarrassed.

After lunch, Leslie and I spend a lovely afternoon together at her favorite day spa. I've actually never been to a spa before. It's not that I don't enjoy being pampered—I absolutely do. Spas are just a luxury I've never been able to afford. The waiting room is stocked with vitamin water, coffee, tea, and these amazing dark chocolate-dipped biscotti. There are candles for ambiance and small pillows perfectly arranged on settees. After changing into a luxurious robe and furry flip-flops (who knew flip-flops could be furry), we're ushered into a private room for our mani-pedis. Then a stylist arrives to do our hair and makeup. I don't usually wear a lot of makeup but I'm blown away by what a beautiful job she does. She convinces me to do a loose, low chignon bun. Apparently it's popular with the royals. It looks very elegant and the loose tendrils framing my face give a soft, sexy look. By the time we leave, I'm feeling very glamorous and can't wait for Mark to see me.

The dress Leslie is lending (correction: giving) me is absolutely gorgeous. It's an off-white, mid-length, fitted dress with a twist halter neckline and an open back. It's somewhat revealing while at the same time remaining very elegant. Mark loves it when I wear anything with exposed shoulders so I know he's going to adore this dress. But unfortunately, by the time we return from the spa, he's already left for the club to set up, so I won't be able to model it for him until I get there.

"Fin, you look absolutely radiant!" Leslie is beaming. "Do you like the dress?"

"Are you kidding? I love it! I can't wait to show Mark."

"Oh I'm so glad you like it, darling." She embraces me warmly. "And thank you again for joining me today. I wanted to do something nice for you to celebrate your wedding engagement, just the two of us."

"I had such a nice time! Thank you so much for planning it."

She rubs my back affectionately. "We're just so happy you came into Mark's life. I can see how happy you make him."

"He makes me very happy too." My eyes suddenly begin to mist as my emotions rise to the surface. "I feel so blessed to have him in my life. You've raised an amazing son."

Leslie takes my hand, her own eyes now tearing up with emotion. "I'd like to think so. He may not be my biological son, but he's my son in every other way. And I've always told him that it can take time to find the person who is meant for you. Not everyone has the patience to wait for the right love to come along and I'm so glad the two of you did."

She squeezes my hand and I squeeze back.

Leslie and Rick needed to go to the party a little early because Leslie is one of the event chairs, so my parents are picking me up and are expected any minute.

But that was twenty minutes ago. My dad finally texts that they're running a little late. By six o'clock, I'm starting to crawl out of my skin. It's not like my mom to be late and I really wanted to see Mark before the band went on at seven o'clock. My phone soon buzzes with yet another text, this time saying that they needed to stop for gas and will be here in a few minutes. *Ugh.*

By the time they pick me up and we arrive at the party, it's already after seven and I can't help but be a little annoyed because now it's too late for me to even say hello to Mark. It feels like hours since I've seen him —because it has been. I hate to sound like a spoiled brat but it *is* Valentine's Day and I've barely seen him.

We weave our way through the tables to our assigned table which is luckily situated in front, right near the band. The band has already started playing but as soon as I sit down, Mark spots me and gives me a flirty wink, which immediately washes away any aggravation I was feeling, producing that toasty feeling in my core. I give him a smile and a tiny wave hello and he grins back, looking drop-dead gorgeous in his black tux. I sigh inwardly.

Leslie and Rick are seated at our table, along with Matt and Jennifer, and I make the introductions. Mark's and my parents soon begin happily chatting away as if they're long lost friends. I had a feeling they would get along, but seeing it certainly puts my mind at ease and I can completely relax knowing my parents are comfortable.

It's so good to see Matt and Jennifer again. Leslie wasn't sure if they were going to be able to find a babysitter on Valentine's Day, but luckily they did. We exchange warm greetings and they congratulate me on Mark's and my engagement.

"I'd like to think I played a small role in getting the two of you together," Matt jokes.

I grin knowingly. "Well you *were* the one who introduced us, but as I understand it, Mark was the one who had to drag *you* out of the house that night, so..."

Matt chuckles. "Yeah, but if I hadn't needing dragging, we never would have gone to the restaurant that night and the two of you never would have met, so..."

"Well then thank goodness Mark was his usual persistent self!" Jennifer grins.

We all laugh and my attention once again returns to the band—and Mark. They sound great and a lot of people are dancing which is a good sign. Mark's eyes are closed and he seems to be very immersed in drumming. Sexy doesn't even begin to describe him. *Sigh.* Within a second or two of me looking at him, our eyes meet and he wiggles his brows at me, which makes me giggle. Even after all of these months, I still get a rush whenever he flirts with me.

I force myself to tear my eyes away from him long enough for Matt and Jennifer to share Olivia's latest milestones with me. I can see how much joy Livvy brings to their lives, and even though this is their night out, they've already spoken with the babysitter at least once to check on Livvy. Something tells me it's going to be an early night for them.

I offer to get some drinks for the table and, as I wait my turn at the bar, I find myself so engrossed in watching Mark and the band that I don't even hear the woman beside me saying hello. When I finally turn to her, I find myself face-to-face with Madison, the woman who was so rude to me the night of the gala last summer. She looks flawless in a a full length navy blue dress with spaghetti straps and a slit up the side to accentuate her long legs. Her dark hair is sleek and long and the only jewelry she has on are diamond studs, a tennis bracelet, and a sapphire ring. Simple yet very elegant.

"Hello. It's Fin, right?" Madison is all politeness.

My back stiffens. I still remember how she poked fun at my name at the gala. I put on my best fake smile and proceed with caution. "Hello Madison, how are you?"

Her face brightens. "Good, thanks!" She glances over at the band. "I never knew Mark was in a band. They're fantastic!"

All I can bring myself to do is smile and nod.

"So are you two still dating?" she asks.

It's odd. There isn't even a trace of insincerity in her tone. I'm not sure what's changed but if she's going to try to be nice, the least I can do is try as well.

"Yes, we're engaged," I reply.

She seems a little thrown but recalibrates quickly. "Oh! Congratulations!"

"Thanks." I finally reach the head of the line and place my drink order, but Madison continues to engage me.

"I've got to hand it to you," she continues. "Mark is quite the catch. I couldn't get anywhere with him...and believe me I tried," she jokes, blushing slightly and then quickly backpedaling. "I'm sorry, that was completely inappropriate of me. I just meant that you're a lucky girl and, well, I'm happy for you both."

"Thank you. I do feel very lucky." My eyes return to watching the band.

Madison remains alongside me but now seems pre-occupied. As we stare ahead at the band, I notice her glance backwards a few times, as if looking for some-one. When something (or someone) catches her eye, I see her body straighten, as if bracing herself. She anx-iously spins her sapphire ring around her finger.

"That's a beautiful ring," I say.

She looks down as if surprised to see her fingers playing with it. "Oh, thank you. It was my grand-mother's. She gave it to me for my sweet sixteen." She glances backwards again.

"I hope I'm not overstepping, but is everything okay?" I finally ask.

I see a hint of caution in her eyes. "Yes," she hesi-tates, "I—" But she abruptly stops speaking as a couple passes by us. She immediately averts her eyes, but once the couple passes, she resumes watching them as they exit the room.

"I'm sorry, what were we discussing?" she asks, still distracted.

"I just wanted to make sure you're okay."

Her eyes study mine and she seems to conclude that I can be trusted because she lets out a deep breath. "Is it that obvious?"

"No, not at all," I reassure her. "I'm a social worker so I think sometimes I'm just a little more tuned in, that's all."

"Oh, well thanks for asking. I'm just a little on edge because my ex-boyfriend is here with his fiancée and I don't want to run into them."

I nod. "I get it. Is that the couple that just walked by?"

"Yes, that was them. They definitely saw me and I think they—or I should say, she—actually made a point of walking by me. She's very territorial."

I simply nod, not wanting to pry further.

"Jared and I were dating for six months when she came along. He cheated with her and then broke up with me right before the holidays...Merry Christmas. I'm not sure who was more heartbroken, me or my mother."

"Your mother?"

"Yes, she loved Jared. He's a Yalie and an investment banker at his father's firm in town, so he ticks all of my mom's boxes. Needless to say, when we broke up, my mother was devastated. She was married at twenty-two so for me to still be single at thirty is unimaginable." She rolls her eyes.

"Well, it sounds like you're much better off without him."

"Probably, but I really liked him and thought we might have a future together."

While I know very little about Madison, I sense that there's more to her than meets the eye and I can definitely sympathize with her circumstances. It's not easy to find "Mr. Right" and the societal pressure to marry can be suffocating at times.

"Anyway," Madison sighs, "this is all probably TMI but I appreciate you letting me vent." She gives a genuine smile.

"Of course," I say. "And for what it's worth, I think

him breaking up with you was a blessing in disguise. Now you can go out and find the person you were *really* meant to be with."

She stares at me intently. It's as if a lightbulb just went off in her head. "I never thought about it quite like that before—thank you. You've been such a big help." She spontaneously hugs me and I go with it.

Madison's mother, a very attractive, well-dressed woman, beckons her daughter over to her, and with that, Madison thanks me again and dutifully joins her mother and her mother's circle of friends.

Dinner slowly begins to wind down and the band finally takes a break. I eagerly wait for Mark to come over to our table, but instead, he disappears into a back room with the rest of the band. That's so odd. Usually at gigs, he comes right over to see me between sets. A few minutes pass but still no sign of Mark. *Maybe they're eating?* I sigh to myself.

My mother likely senses my disappointment and insists I keep her company while she freshens up in the ladies room.

"Mark is a great drummer," my mom says while powdering her nose.

"Yes, he's very talented," I say, reapplying my lipstick and trying not to sound too grumpy.

I could swear my mom chuckles to herself before catching my eyes in the mirror and smiling. "Cheer up, honey! You'll get to see him soon enough. And just wait 'til he sees you! The dress, the hair, the makeup. My little girl looks so glamorous!"

I giggle. "I do, don't I...Like Cinderella at the ball."

She nods and checks her watch. "Let's go back inside. Maybe you can see him before the next set."

We quickly exit.

Just as we return to our table, the band returns too. Mark gives me a little wave before taking his seat and I contemplate sneaking over to him before they start playing, but I don't want to disturb them. *No, I need to sit tight.*

But before they begin to play, Mark suddenly gets up and walks over to Josh who hands him the microphone. Mark only does backup vocals so I'm assuming his mom asked him to make a few announcements. I glance over at Leslie who is nodding at him, so that explains that.

He taps the mic a few times, waiting for everyone to quiet down. Clearing his throat finally does the trick.

"So, as you know, today is Valentine's Day," he begins. "But tonight is also special to me for another reason." He pauses and meets my eyes head on. "Because this beautiful woman sitting right here in front has agreed to be my wife, and tonight, if she'll have me, I'd like to make it official."

I let out a gasp as blood sprints to my cheeks and I throw my hands to my face. I immediately glance around the table and am greeted with knowing smiles. My eyes dart back up to Mark who is grinning at me.

"As you can see, she had no idea I was going to do this tonight." He chuckles at my astonishment. "So—no pressure or anything—but what do you say? Will you marry me, right here, right now?"

I smile and tear up simultaneously. I feel like I'm going to cry in front of everyone, but then he gives me prayer hands, which makes me giggle.

"So that's a *Yes*?" he asks, eyes twinkling with love.

I nod and say "Yes" as a huge smile spreads across both of our faces, causing the entire room to erupt into cheers.

He walks towards me, reaching his hand out for mine. "Tonight's the night, babe, so get ready." I'm still in complete shock as I place my hand in his and he leads me to the area in front of the band.

Holding the mic away from us, he leans in to my ear. "You look absolutely breathtaking, Finny. I've been wanting to tell you that all night. But before we do this, I just want to make absolutely sure you're okay with this."

I meet his blue eyes and say *Yes* with mine. "It's perfect."

He presses his lips to my cheek. "I love you so much," he whispers, causing my whole body to ignite.

He brings the mic to his mouth again. "This is Fin, by the way," he says, eliciting the crowd's laughter. "Okay, so before we do this," he continues, "I want you and everyone here to know just how much you mean to me." His hand finds mine. "Not only are you the most beautiful woman I have ever laid eyes on, but you're also the kindest, sweetest, most loving person I've ever known and you truly are the person I've been searching for my entire life. But I think you already know that."

I smile, squeezing his hand.

"But words really aren't enough, so I thought, how can I fully express just how much I love you? And then it came to me. I'm going to sing you a song."

My eyes widen in disbelief.

"She's looking at me that way because I'm not much of a singer," he tells the crowd.

I giggle softly through my tears.

"So you'll all just have to bear with me. I chose this particular song because it's one of Fin's favorites and we danced to it in this very room at last summer's gala."

I scan my brain, trying to recall what song he's talking about. We danced to so many songs that night.

His amused eyes meet mine as he signals to the band's keyboardist. "Hit it, Giselle."

The moment I hear the alternating rhythm of the piano keys, I break into a huge grin. He gives me the most adoring look and my heart is melting. Because my soon-to-be husband is standing before me singing "I Feel the Earth Move" and it's one of the sweetest, most wonderful things anyone has ever done for me. Tears of happiness and gratitude flood my eyes. I love this man with every fiber of my being.

Mid-song, he shifts over to the drums and delivers a passionate drum solo and—honest to G-d—I can't believe he's really mine.

But he is.

The moment the song ends, my self-control meter expires and I throw my arms around him so tightly that I'm surprised he can still breathe. He gives me one of his hearty laughs and then we kiss and sway, laugh and kiss some more, and I don't care that complete strangers are watching. I love him so.

After one final kiss, he motions to someone at the bar who I assume to be a Justice of the Peace. Matt joins us too.

"All set?" Matt asks, clapping Mark on his back.

"All set." Mark gives his friend a hug. "Thanks for being my best man. It means a lot."

"It's an honor," Matt says with a smile before turning to give me a congratulatory hug.

Mark scans the room until his eyes land on someone in the way back. He crooks his finger and, to my surprise, I see Peter leading Chloe towards us. She's wearing a lovely peach dress and a crown made of tiny peach roses and the sight of her beaming smile as she walks towards us, bouquet in hand, nearly brings me to tears.

Mark kneels down. "Are you ready, kiddo?"

Chloe nods and timidly hands me the bouquet. Orange ranunculus of course.

I give her a big hug. "Thank you, sweetheart! They're my favorite!" Her eyes glow up at me with pride.

"Before we begin," the Justice of the Peace says, "I just received a text asking me to wait one more minute because there's someone else joining us."

I look at Mark who seems just as surprised as me. Then I turn to look at my mom who is grinning and that's when I hear a familiar booming voice coming from the back of the room.

"You guys didn't really think you were going to do this thing without me, did you?"

My lips curve at the sound of my brother's voice and I turn to find Dan standing in the rear of the room with a huge grin on his face. His timing is impeccable for once.

Mark and I laugh in unison as he weaves through the maze of tables to reach us.

"Hey, sis! Sorry I'm late." He greets me with a wink and kiss on the cheek and then gives Mark a big hug. "Congrats, bud."

He turns to go sit down but Mark insists he remain with us for the ceremony as my "Man of Honor." The term couldn't be more fitting.

The wedding ceremony is a bit of a blur. As I stand beside Mark, our hands threaded together in a tight squeeze, it feels...well...I really can't fully describe how it feels. I'm marrying the one and only love of my life

—my soulmate—and the joy I'm feeling is like nothing I've ever experienced. The moment the JP pronounces us married and we kiss, the outside world fades away and it's like we're in our own little world. I hardly hear the room cheering and whistling in celebration.

Mark soon whisks me away to a private room that is overflowing with ranunculuses and lit candles. He takes me in his arms and we share a slow, deep, emotional kiss that I will never ever forget for as long as I live. The combination of our love and passion is dizzying and when our lips finally part for air, I lose myself in my husband's gorgeous, joy-filled, blue eyes.

"We're married, babe," he whispers, brushing his soft lips against mine.

A huge smile spreads across my face. "Yes, we are." My lips play with his. "And it feels magical."

He kisses me again, humming with longing. "I love you, Finny."

"And I love you—more and more every day."

He pulls back to admire me. "You look so beautiful. I want you to know I had to physically restrain myself from going over to your table tonight."

"When you didn't come over between sets, I couldn't figure out what was going on!"

He chuckles. "Yeah, you definitely looked annoyed. It was really cute. But now you understand—I needed to make sure everything was all set."

I walk my fingers up his chest. "Very, very sneaky, and so romantic." I pull him in for another kiss, our mouths widening as our tongues tangle with desire until we're breathless.

"We better stop," I say reluctantly.

He groans with disappointment.

"Don't worry, I'll make it up to you later, I promise," I say with one final, lingering kiss.

Something in the corner of the room catches my eye. In addition to the ranunculus plants and candles, there are a few bales of hay, an oversized sweatshirt, and a stuffed animal of a goat.

I grin. "I see what you're doing here. A tribute to our first date, sans the livestock of course."

"They wouldn't let me bring in a baby goat. I did try though. Something about the health code…"

"Well aren't you just full of surprises today, Mark with a 'k.'"

"This is what happens when you let me be the navigator," he says. "We end up married."

I giggle and give him a peck. "Married is good. Very *very* good." I stroke his hair back, no longer able to contain a secret of my own. "You know…you're not the only one with a surprise tonight."

He meets my eyes. "Oh?"

"Uh-huh."

His eyes twinkle with curiosity as he looks behind me. "So where are you hiding this mysterious surprise of yours, under your dress?"

"In a manner of speaking." I give him a wink as my heart begins beating more emphatically.

"Okay, well then lay it on me, babe."

"First you need to close your eyes." He does as he's told and I pause to savor his adorable smile and the anticipation on his face. Then I get on my tiptoes and whisper in his ear, "We're having a baby."

His eyes fly open. I memorize his expression because I never want to forget that look of pure, untamed joy. He sweeps me up in his arms and our laughter fills the room. I think he's going to cry, and I know I am. While we've talked about starting a family, we haven't been trying to conceive a child just yet; it just happened.

Our eyes lock in a tight gaze. We say nothing but understand everything. Words would only get in the way. As the blues and greens of our eyes swirl together in a sparkling sea of aquamarine, our souls begin to rejoice, and it is then that we realize that this was the plan all along.

Thank You!

I hope you enjoyed *What Love Can Be,* the second book in the Shelby Falls series. The audiobook, which is narrated by Nelson Hobbs and Amelie Griffin, is available on Amazon and Audible. The first book in the Shelby Falls series, *What Love Can Do*, is also available on Amazon. Each book in this series may be read as an interconnected standalone.

If you enjoyed Mark and Fin's story, please help spread the word by leaving a review on Amazon and social media. Your reviews make a huge difference and are greatly appreciated!

Thank you so much!

xo Katharine

P.S. If you would like to read the Bonus Epilogue and a deleted shower scene that immediately follows Chapter 22, just email me at katharinehopelevy@gmail.com and I will happily share them with you!

SHELBY FALLS SERIES

~A second chance, steamy, small town romance series~

WHAT LOVE CAN DO is the second chance, friends to lovers story of Matt and Jennifer who experience first love and find their way back to one another twenty years later.

WHAT LOVE CAN BE is a dual POV, dual timeline contemporary romance which explores Mark and Fin's rocky beginnings and second chance at love.

Each novel may be read as an interconnected standalone.

What Love Can Do

Jennifer Bantam had a lot to be grateful for and certainly wasn't one to complain. She had a successful editing business and good friends and family. But her love life was far from perfect. By now, she thought she'd be happily married with a family, but fate just isn't cooperating.

But everything changes when, while visiting her hometown of Shelby Falls, she receives a message from someone in her past--the sweet, handsome, and sexy Matt Conroy. While Matt is intent on apologizing for something that happened between them twenty years earlier, Jennifer has no idea what he's talking about and has successfully blocked out these memories.

Matt has never forgotten his first love and is determined to win Jennifer back, but will she be able to trust him again and let down her defenses to be with the man she fell in love with twenty years ago?

Told through dual timelines, this is the story of second chances, never giving up, and the power of true love to make anything and everything possible, if only we have the courage to take that leap.